PRAISE FOR *DANGEROUS WOMEN*

"The fury of a woman scorned is just one of the perils encountered in *Dangerous Women,* a splendid cross-genre anthology featuring original stories by a number of writers, male and female.... An impressive assembly of work by mostly well-known authors, with a few relative newcomers who make a strong impression."

—*Los Angeles Times*

"Venerable editors Martin and Dozois have invited writers from many different genres of fiction to showcase the supposedly weaker sex's capacity for magic, violence, and mayhem....Delivers something for nearly every reader's taste as it explores the heights that brave women can reach and the depths that depraved ones can plumb."

—*Publishers Weekly* (starred review)

"After reading this exceptional compilation—which includes an absolute treasure of a novella from Martin that examines the origins of the Targaryen civil war—I realized that, yes, indeed, fantasy fiction is filled with some seriously badass women."

—Paul Goat Allen, *Barnes and Noble Book Blog*

DANGEROUS WOMEN

{2}

EDITED BY

GEORGE R. R. MARTIN

—AND—

GARDNER DOZOIS

TOR®
fantasy

A TOM DOHERTY ASSOCIATES BOOK / NEW YORK

This is a work of fiction. All of the characters, organizations, and events portrayed in these stories are either products of the authors' imaginations or are used fictitiously.

DANGEROUS WOMEN 2

Copyright © 2013 by George R. R. Martin and Gardner Dozois

Dangerous Women 1, 2, and *3* were previously published together, in a single hardcover edition, as *Dangerous Women.*

A Tor Book
Published by Tom Doherty Associates, LLC
175 Fifth Avenue
New York, NY 10010

www.tor-forge.com

Tor® is a registered trademark of Tom Doherty Associates, LLC.

ISBN 978-0-7653-6882-9

Tor books may be purchased for educational, business, or promotional use. For information on bulk purchases, please contact Macmillan Corporate and Premium Sales Department at 1-800-221-7945, extension 5442, or write specialmarkets@macmillan.com.

First Edition: November 2014

Printed in the United States of America

0 9 8 7 6 5 4 3 2 1

Copyright Acknowledgments

To Jo Playford, my dangerous minion.

—George R. R. Martin

Contents

DANGEROUS WOMEN 2

Introduction by Gardner Dozois

Genre fiction has always been divided over the question of just *how* dangerous women are.

In the real world, of course, the question has long been settled. Even if the Amazons are mythological (and almost certainly wouldn't have cut their right breasts off to make it easier to draw a bow if they *weren't*), their legend was inspired by memory of the ferocious warrior women of the Scythians, who were very much *not* mythological. Gladiatrix, women gladiators, fought other women—and sometimes men—to the death in the arenas of Ancient Rome. There were female pirates like Anne Bonny and Mary Read, and even female samurai. Women served as frontline combat troops, feared for their ferocity, in the Russian army during World War II, and serve so in Israel today. Until 2013, women in the U.S. forces were technically restricted to "noncombat" roles, but many brave women gave their lives in Iraq and Afghanistan anyway, since bullets and land mines have never cared whether you're a noncombatant or not. Women who served as Women Airforce Service Pilots for the United States during World War II were also limited to noncombat roles (where many of them were nevertheless killed in the performance of their duties), but Russian women took to the skies as fighter pilots, and sometimes became aces. A Russian female sniper during World War II was credited with more than fifty kills. Queen Boudicca of the Iceni tribe led one of the most fearsome revolts ever against Roman authority, one that was almost successful in driving the Roman invaders from Britain, and a young French peasant girl inspired and led the troops against the enemy so successfully that she became famous forever afterwards as Joan of Arc.

On the dark side, there have been female "highwaymen" like Mary Frith and Lady Katherine Ferrers and Pearl Hart (the last person to ever rob a stagecoach); notorious poisoners like Agrippina and Catherine de Medici, modern female outlaws like Ma Barker and Bonnie Parker, even female serial killers like Aileen Wuornos. Elizabeth Báthory was said to have bathed in the blood of virgins, and even though that has been called into question, there is no doubt that she tortured and killed dozens, perhaps hundreds, of children during her life. Queen Mary I of England had hundreds of Protestants burnt at the stake; Queen Elizabeth of England later responded by executing large numbers of Catholics. Mad Queen Ranavalona of Madagascar had so many people put to death that she wiped out one-third of the entire population of Madagascar during her reign; she would even have you executed if you appeared in her dreams.

Popular fiction, though, has always had a schizophrenic view of the dangerousness of women. In the science fiction of the 1930s, '40s, and '50s, women, if they appeared at all, were largely regulated to the role of the scientist's beautiful daughter, who might scream during the fight scenes but otherwise had little to do except hang adoringly on the arm of the hero afterwards. Legions of women swooned help-lessly while waiting to be rescued by the intrepid jut-jawed hero from everything from dragons to the bug-eyed monsters who were always carrying them off for improbable purposes either dietary or roman-tic on the covers of pulp SF magazines. Hopelessly struggling women were tied to railroad tracks, with nothing to do but squeak in protest and hope that the Good Guy arrived in time to save them.

And yet, at the same time, warrior women like Ed-gar Rice Burroughs's Dejah Thoris and Thuvia, Maid of Mars, were every bit as good with the blade and every bit as deadly in battle as John Carter and their other male comrades, female adventuresses like C. L. Moore's Jirel of Joiry swashbuckled their way through the pages of *Weird Tales* magazine (and blazed a trail for later female swashbucklers like Joanna Russ's Alyx); James H. Schmitz sent Agents of Vega like Granny Wannatel and fearless teenagers like Telzey Amberdon and Trigger Argee out to battle the sinister menaces and monsters of the spaceways; and Robert A. Heinlein's dangerous women were capable of be-ing the captain of a spaceship or killing enemies in hand-to-hand combat. Arthur Conan Doyle's sly, shady Irene Adler was one of the only people ever to outwit his Sherlock Holmes, and probably one of the inspirations for the legions of tricky, dangerous, seductive, and treacherous "femmes fatale" who

featured in the works of Dashiell Hammett and James
M. Cain and later went on to appear in dozens of
films noir, and who still turn up in the movies and on
television to this day. Later television heroines such as
Buffy the Vampire Slayer and Xena, Warrior Princess,
firmly established women as being formidable and
deadly enough to battle hordes of fearsome supernat-
ural menaces, and helped to inspire the whole sub-
genre of paranormal romance, which is sometimes
unofficially known as the "kick-ass heroine" genre.

Like our anthology *Warriors, Dangerous Women*
was conceived of as a cross-genre anthology, one
that would mingle every kind of fiction, so we asked
writers from every genre—science fiction, fantasy,
mystery, historical, horror, paranormal romance, men
and women alike—to tackle the theme of "dangerous
women," and that call was answered by some of the
best writers in the business, including both new writers and giants of their fields like Diana Gabaldon, Jim
Butcher, Sharon Kay Penman, Joe Abercrombie, Car-
rie Vaughn, Joe R. Lansdale, Lawrence Block, Cecelia
Holland, Brandon Sanderson, Sherrilyn Kenyon,
S. M. Stirling, Nancy Kress, and George R. R. Martin.

Here you'll find no hapless victims who stand by
whimpering in dread while the male hero fights the
monster or clashes swords with the villain, and if you
want to tie *these* women to the railroad tracks, you'll
find you have a real fight on your hands. Instead, you
will find sword-wielding women warriors; intrepid
women fighter pilots and far-ranging spacewomen;
deadly female serial killers; formidable female superheroes; sly and seductive femmes fatale; female wizards; hard-living bad girls; female bandits and rebels;

embattled survivors in postapocalyptic futures; female private investigators; stern female hanging judges; haughty queens who rule nations and whose jealousies and ambitions send thousands to grisly deaths; daring dragonriders; and many more.

Enjoy!

Lev Grossman

A novelist and journalist, Lev Grossman is a senior writer and book critic for *Time* and coauthor of the TIME.com blog TechLand. His quirky 2009 fantasy novel *The Magicians* was a phenomenal international sensation, and landed on the *New York Times* Best Seller list as well as being named a *New Yorker* Best Book of 2009, and its sequel, *The Magician King*, published in 2011, has enjoyed similar acclaim. Grossman's other books include the novels *Warp* and *Codex*. He lives in Brooklyn, New York, and maintains a website at levgrossman.com.

Here he takes us to an ancient, venerable school for wizards, one haunted by a thousand age-old traditions as well as spirits of a different kind, to show us that even the most innocent of pranks can end up having dangerous and even deadly consequences.

THE GIRL IN THE MIRROR

You could say it all started out as an innocent prank, but that wouldn't strictly be true. It wasn't *that* innocent. It was just that Wharton was behaving badly, and in the judgment of the League he had to be punished for it. Then maybe he would cut it out, or behave a little less badly, or at the very least the League would have the satisfaction of having caused Wharton to suffer, and that counted for something. A lot really.

You couldn't call it innocent. But you had to admit it was pretty understandable. And anyway, is there really any such thing as an innocent prank?

Plum was president of the League—unelected but undisputed—and also its founder. In enlisting the others she had presented the League as a glorious old Brakebills tradition, which it actually wasn't, probably, though since the college had been around for something like four hundred years it seemed very likely to Plum that there must have been, at some point in the past, another League or at any rate something along the same lines, which you could count as a historical precedent. You couldn't rule out the possibility. Though in fact she'd gotten the idea from a P. G. Wodehouse story.

They met after hours in a funny little trapezoidal study off the West Tower that as far as they could tell had fallen off the faculty's magical security grid, so it was safe to break curfew there. Plum was lying full length on the floor, which was the position from which she usually conducted League business. The rest of the girls were scattered limply around the room on couches and chairs, like confetti from a successful but rather exhausting party that was thankfully now all but over.

Plum made the room go silent—it was a little spell that ate sound in about a ten-yard radius—and all the attention immediately focused on her. When Plum did a magic trick, everybody noticed.

"Let's put it to a vote," she said solemnly. "All those in favor of pranking Wharton, say aye."

The ayes came back in a range of tones from righteous zeal to ironic detachment to sleepy acquiescence. This business of clandestine after-hours scheming could certainly take a whack at your sleep schedule, Plum had to admit. It was a little unfair on the others, because Plum was a quick study who went through homework like a hot knife through butter, and she knew it wasn't that easy for all of them. From her vantage point on the floor, with her eyes closed, her long brown hair splayed out in a fan on the carpet, which had once been soft and woolly but which had been trodden down into a shiny, hard-packed grey, the vote sounded more or less unanimous.

Anyway, there was fairly evidently a plurality in the room. She dispensed with a show of nays.

"It's maddening," Emma said in the silence that followed, by way of spiking the football. "Absolutely *maddening*."

That was an exaggeration, but the room let it go. It's not like Wharton's crime was a matter of life and death. But a stop would be put to it. This the League swore.

Darcy sat on the couch opposite the long mirror with the scarred white frame that leaned against one wall. She toyed with her reflection—with both of her long, elegant hands she was working a spell that stretched it and then squished it, stretched, then squished. The technicalities were beyond Plum, but then, mirror-magic was Darcy's specialty. It was a bit show-offy of her, but you couldn't blame her. Darcy didn't have a lot of opportunities to use it.

The facts of the Wharton case were as follows. At Brakebills, most serving duties at dinner were carried out by First Years, who then ate separately afterwards. But, by tradition, one favored Fourth Year was chosen every year to serve as wine steward, in charge of pairings and pourings and whatnot. Wharton had had this honor bestowed upon him, and not for no reason. He did know a lot about wine, or at any rate he seemed to be able to remember the names of a whole lot of different regions and appellations and whatever else. (In fact, another Fourth Year with the unintentionally hilarious name of Claire Bear had been tipped for wine steward this year. Wharton showed her up, coolly and publicly, by distinguishing between a Gigondas and a Vacqueyras in a blind tasting.)

But in the judgment of the League, Wharton had sinned against the honor of his office, sinned most grievously, by systematically short-pouring the wine, especially for the Fifth Years, who were allowed two glasses with dinner. Seriously, these were like three-quarter pours. Everybody agreed. For such a crime, there could be no forgiveness.

"What do you suppose he does with it all?" Emma said.

"Does with what?"

"The extra wine. He must be saving it. I bet he ends up with an extra bottle every night."

There were eight girls in the League, of whom six were present, and Emma was the youngest and the only Second Year, but she wasn't cowed by her elders. In fact, she was, in Plum's opinion, even a bit too keen on the League and her role in same. She could have made just a little show of being intimidated once in a while. Plum was just saying.

"I dunno," Plum said. "I guess he drinks it."

"He couldn't get through a bottle a night," Darcy said. She had a big poofy 1970s Afro; it even had an Afro pick sticking out of it.

"He and his boyfriend, then. What's his name. It's Greek."

"Epifanio." Darcy and Chelsea said it together.

Chelsea lay on the couch at the opposite end from Darcy, her honey-blond head on the armrest, knees drawn up, lazily trying to mess up Darcy's mirror tricks. Darcy's spells were marvels of intricacy and precision, but it was much easier to screw up some-body else's spell than it was to cast one yourself. That was one of the many small unfairnesses of magic.

Darcy frowned and concentrated harder, pushing back. The interference caused an audible buzz, and, under the stress, Darcy's reflection in the mirror twisted and spiraled in on itself in weird ways.

"Stop," she said. "You're going to break it."

"He's probably got some set spell running that eats it up," Emma said. "Has to feed it wine once a day. Like a virility thing."

"Of course that's where your mind would go," Plum said.

"Well," Emma said, flushing mauve—gotcha!— "you know. He's so buff."

Chelsea saw her moment and caused Darcy's reflection to collapse in on itself, creepily, like it had gotten sucked into a black hole, and then vanish altogether. In the mirror it looked like she wasn't even there—her end of the couch was empty, though the cushion was slightly depressed.

"Ha," said Chelsea.

"Buff does *not* mean virile."

That was Lucy, an intensely earnest, philosophical Fifth Year; her tone betrayed a touch of what might have been the bitterness of personal experience. Plump and wan and Korean, Lucy floated crosslegged in one of the room's irregular upper corners. Her dark straight hair was loose and so long that it hung down past her bum.

"I bet he gives it to the ghost," Lucy went on.

"There is no ghost," Darcy said.

Somebody was always saying that Brakebills had a ghost. It was like Plum saying there was a League: you could never prove it either way.

"Come to that," said Chelsea, who had consolidated her victory over Darcy in the mirror game by plopping her feet in Darcy's lap, "what *does* 'virile' mean?"

"Means he's got spunk in his junk," Darcy said.

"Girls, please," Plum said, by way of getting things back on track. "Neither Wharton's spunk nor his junk are germane here. The question is, what to do about the missing wine? Who's got a plan?"

"*You've* got a plan," Darcy and Chelsea said at the same time, again. The two of them were like stage twins.

"I do have plan."

"*Plum has a plan,*" intoned tiny, cheery Holly from the one good armchair.

Plum always had a plan; she couldn't help it. Her brain seemed to secrete them naturally. Plum's plan was to take advantage of what she perceived to be Wharton's Achilles' heel, which was his pencils. He didn't use the school-issued ones, which as far as Plum was concerned were entirely functional and sufficient unto the day: deep Brakebills blue in color, with "Brakebills" in gold letters down the side. But Wharton didn't like them—he said they were too fat, he didn't like their "hand-feel," and the lead was soft and mushy. Wharton brought his own from home instead.

In truth, Wharton's pencils were remarkable pencils: olive green in color and made from some oily, aromatic wood that released a waxy aroma reminiscent of distant exotic rain forest trees. God knows where he got them from. The erasers were bound in rings of a dull grey brushed steel that looked too industrial and high-carbon for the task of merely containing the erasers, which were, instead of the usual fleshy pink, a light-devouring black. Wharton kept his pencils in a flat silver case, which also contained (in its own crushed-velvet nest) a sharp little knife that he used to keep them sharpened to wicked points.

Moreover, whatever life Wharton had led before becoming a magician-in-training at Brakebills, it must have included academic decathlon or debating or something, because he had a whole arsenal of spinning-pencil tricks of the kind that people commonly used to intimidate rival mathletes. He performed them constantly and unconsciously and seemingly involuntarily. It was annoying, even over and above the wine thing.

Plum planned to steal the pencils and hold them for ransom, the ransom being an explanation of what the hell Wharton did with all that wine, along with a pledge to stop doing same. By 11:30 p.m. that night, the League was yawning, and Darcy and Chelsea had restored Darcy's reflection and then begun wrangling with it all over again, but Plum's plan had been fully explained, fleshed out, approved, improved, and then made needlessly complex. Cruel, curly little barbs had been added to it, and all roles had been assigned.

It was rough justice, but someone had to enforce order at Brakebills, and if the faculty didn't, then the League's many hands were forced. The faculty might turn a blind eye, if it chose, but the League's many eyes were sharp and unblinking.

Darcy's image in the mirror shivered and blurred.

"Stop it!" Darcy said, really annoyed now. "I told you—"

She had told her, and now it did. The mirror broke: there was a loud sharp *tick*, and a white star appeared in the glass in the lower right-hand corner, with thin cracks branching out from it, as if some tiny invisible projectile had struck it there. Plum thought of Tennyson: *The mirror cracked from side to side . . .*

"Oh, shit!" Chelsea said. Her hands flew to her mouth. "I hope that wasn't, like, super expensive."

The instant it happened, the mirror's face went dark, and it stopped reflecting anything in the room at all. It must not have been a real mirror at all but a magical device designed to behave like one. At first Plum thought it had gone completely black, but then she saw that there were soft shadowy shapes there: a sofa and chairs. The mirror, or whatever it was, was showing them the same room they were in, but empty, and in darkness. Was it the past? The future? There was something uncanny about it—it was as if someone had been there moments ago and had only just left, turning out the lights on their way out.

Plum got up at 8:00 the next morning, late by her standards, but instead of rejuvenating her brain, the extra sleep had just made it all muzzy. She'd counted on feeling all sparkly with excitement and anticipation at the prospect of the impending prank, but instead she just drifted vaguely into the shower and then out of it and into her clothes and downstairs in the direction of her first class. Her mind, she had often noticed, was a lens that alternated between states of lethally sharp focus and useless, strengthless blurriness, apparently without her having any say in the matter. Her mind had a mind of its own. This morning it was in its strengthless blur mode.

As a Fifth Year who'd finished all her required coursework, Plum was taking all seminars that semester, and her first class was a small colloquium on period magic, fifteenth-century German, to be specific—lots of elemental stuff and weird divination techniques and Johannes Hartlieb. Tiny Holly sat opposite her across the table, and such was Plum's strengthless, blurry state that Holly had touched her sharp little nose meaningfully, twice, before Plum remembered that that was the signal that Stages One and Two of the plan had already been completed successfully. She snapped into focused mode.

Stage One: "Crude but Effective." A few hours earlier Chelsea's boyfriend would have smuggled her into the Boys' Tower under pretense of a predawn snog, not out of character for either of them. Nature having taken its course, Chelsea would have torn herself from the arms of her beloved and gone and stood outside of Wharton's door, her back pressed against it, smoothed back her honeyed locks from her forehead in an automatic gesture, rolled her eyes back into her head, and entered his room in a wispy, silvery, astral state. She tossed his room for the pencil case, found it, and grasped it with both of her barely substantial hands. She couldn't get the pencil case out of the room that way, but she didn't have to. All she had to do was lift it up against the window.

Wharton himself might or might not have observed this, depending on whether or not he was asleep in his blameless couch, but it mattered not. *Let him see*.

Once Chelsea got the case over by the window, earnest Lucy would have line of sight from a window in an empty lecture hall opposite Wharton's room, which meant she could teleport the pencil case in that direction, from inside Wharton's room to midair outside it. Three feet was about as far as she could jump it, but that was plenty.

The pencil case would then fall forty feet to where keen Emma waited shivering in the bushes in the cold February predawn to catch it in a blanket. No magic required.

Effective? Undeniably. Needlessly complex? Perhaps. But needless complexity was the signature of the League. That was how the League rolled.

All this accomplished, it was on to Stage Two: "Breakfast of Champions." Wharton would descend late, having spent the morning searching his room frantically for his pencils and not finding them. Through a fog of anxiety, he would barely notice that his morning oatmeal had been plunked down in front of him not by some anonymous First Year but by tiny Holly in guise of same. The first mouthful would not sit right with him. He would stop and examine his morning oatmeal more closely.

It would be garnished, not with the usual generous pinch of brown sugar, but with a light dusting of aromatic, olive-green pencil shavings. Compliments of the League.

———

As the day wore on, Plum got into the spirit of the prank. She knew she would. It was mostly just her mornings that were bad.

Her schedule ground forward, ingesting the day in gulps like an anaconda swallowing a wildebeest. Accelerated Advanced Kinetics; Quantum Gramarye; Joined-Hands Tandem Magicks; Cellular-Level Plant Manipulation. All good clean American fun. Plum's course load would have been daunting for a doctoral candidate, possibly several doctoral candidates, but Plum had arrived at Brakebills with a head full of more magical theory and practice than most people left with. She wasn't one of these standing starters, the cold openers, who reeled through their first year with aching hands and eyes full of stars. Plum had come prepared.

Brakebills was an extremely secret and highly exclusive institution—as the only accredited college for magic on the North American continent, it had a very large applicant pool to draw from, and it drank that pool dry. Though, technically, nobody actually applied there: Fogg simply skimmed the cream of eligible high school seniors, the cream of the cream really—the outliers, the extreme cases of precocious genius and obsessive motivation, who had the brains and the high pain tolerance necessary to cope with the intellectual and physical rigors that the study of magic would demand from them.

Needless to say, that meant that the Brakebills student body was quite the psychological menagerie. Carrying that much onboard cognitive processing power had a way of distorting your personality.

Moreover, in order to actually want to work that hard, you had to be at least a little bit fucked up.

Plum was a little bit fucked up, but not the kind of fucked up that *looked* fucked up on the outside. She presented as funny and self-assured. When she got to Brakebills, she rolled up her sleeves and cracked her knuckles and did other appropriately confident body language, then she waded right in. Until they saw her in class, a lot of the First Years mistook her for an upperclasswoman.

But Plum made sure not to do so well that, for example, she was graduated early. She was in no hurry. She liked Brakebills. Loved it, really. Needed it, even. She felt safe here. She wasn't so funny and self-assured that she never soothed herself to sleep by imagining she was Padma Patil (because sorry, Hermione, but Ravenclaw FTW). Plum was a closet Romantic, as were most of the students, and Brakebills was a Romantic's dream. Because what were magicians if not Romantics—dreamers who dreamed so passionately and urgently and brokenheartedly that reality itself couldn't take it, and cracked under the strain like an old mirror?

Plum had arrived at Brakebills cocked, locked, sound checked, and ready to rock. When people asked her what the hell kind of an adolescence she'd had that she arrived here in such a cocked, locked, and rock-ready state, she told them the truth, which is that she'd grown up in Seattle, the only daughter of a mixed couple—one magician, one Nintendo lifer who was fully briefed on the existence of magic but had never shown much talent at it himself. They'd homeschooled her, and given her her head, and quite

a head it was. Basically, she knew a lot of magic because she'd had an early start and she was really good
at it and nobody got in her way.

That was the truth. But when she got to the end
of the true part, she told them lies in order to skip
over the part she didn't like to talk about, or even
think about. Plum was a woman of mystery, and she
liked it that way. She felt safe. No one was ever going to know the whole truth about Plum. Preferably
not even Plum.

But not-thinking about the truth required a certain amount of distraction. Hence the Accelerated
Advanced Kinetics and Quantum Gramarye and all
her other hard-core magical academics. And hence
the League.

Plum wound up having a pretty good day; at any
rate, it was a lot better than Wharton's day. In his
first-period class, he found more pencil shavings on
the seat of his chair. Walking to lunch, he found his
pockets stuffed full of jet-black pencil eraser rubbings.
It was like a horror movie—his precious pencils were
slowly dying, minute by minute, and he was power-
less to save them! He would rue his short-pouring
ways, so he would.

Passing Wharton by chance in a courtyard, Plum
let her eyes slide past his with a slow, satisfied smile.
He looked like a haunted man—a ghost of his former self. The thought balloon over his head said, per
Milton: What fresh hell is this?

Finally—and this was Plum's touch, and she privately thought it was the deftest one—in his fourth-
period class, a practicum on diagramming magical
energies, Wharton found that the Brakebills pencil

he was using, on top of its bad hand feel and whatever else, wouldn't draw what he wanted it to. Whatever spell he tried to diagram, whatever points and rays and vectors he tried to sketch, they inevitably formed a series of letters.

The letters spelled out: *COMPLIMENTS OF THE LEAGUE.*

Plum wasn't a bad person, and she supposed that at heart Wharton probably wasn't a bad person either. Truth be told, the sight of him in the courtyard gave her a pang. She'd actually had a bit of a crush on buff, clever, presumably virile Wharton in her Second Year, before he came out; in fact, in all psychoanalytic fairness, she couldn't rule out the possibility that this whole prank was in part a passive-aggressive expression of said former crush. Either way, she was relieved that the final stage—Stage Nine (too many?)—was tonight at dinner, and that the whole thing wouldn't be drawn out any further. They'd only had to destroy two of Wharton's precious special pencils. And really, the second one wasn't all the way destroyed.

Dinners at Brakebills had a nice formal pomp about them; when one was cornered at alumni functions by sad, nostalgic Brakebills graduates who peaked in college, sooner or later they always got around to reminiscing about evenings in the ol' dining hall. The hall was long and dark and narrow and paneled in dark wood and lined with murky oil paintings of past deans in various states of period dress (though Plum thought that the mid-twentieth-century portraits, aggressively Cubist and then Pop, rather subtracted from the gravitas of the overall effect). Light came from hideous, lumpy, lopsided old silver candelabras placed along the table every ten feet, and the candle flames were always flaring up or snuffing out or changing color under the influence of some stray spell or other. Everybody wore identical Brakebills uniforms. Students' names were inscribed on the table at their assigned places, which changed nightly according to, apparently, the whim of the table. Talk was kept to a low murmur. A few people—never Plum—always showed up late, whereupon their chairs were taken away and they had to eat standing up.

Plum ate her first course as usual, two rather uninspired crab cakes, but then excused herself to go to the ladies'. As Plum passed behind her, Darcy discreetly held out the silver pencil case behind her back, and Plum pocketed it. She wasn't going to the ladies', of course. Well, she was, but only because she had to. She wasn't going back after.

Plum walked briskly down the hall toward the Senior Common Room, which the faculty rarely bothered to lock, so confident were they that no student would dare to cross its threshold. But Plum dared.

She closed the door quietly behind her. All was as she had envisioned it. The Senior Common Room was a cavernous, silent, L-shaped chamber with high ceilings, lined with bookcases and littered with shiny red-leather couches and sturdy reclaimed-wood worktables that looked like their wood had been reclaimed from the True Cross. It was empty, or almost. The only person there was Professor Coldwater, and he hardly counted.

She figured he might be there; most of the faculty were at dinner right now, but according to the roster, it was Professor Coldwater's turn to eat late, with the First Years. But that was all right, because Professor Coldwater was notoriously, shall we say, out of it.

Or not exactly out of it, but he was preoccupied. His attention, except when he was teaching, always seemed to be somewhere else. He was always walking around frowning and running his fingers through his weird shock of white hair and executing little fizz-poppy spells with one hand, and muttering and mumbling to himself like he was doing math problems in his head, which he probably was, because when he wasn't doing them in his head he was doing them on blackboards and whiteboards and napkins and in the air in front of his face with his fingers.

The students could never quite decide whether he was romantic and mysterious or just unintentionally hilarious. His actual students, the ones in his Physical Magic seminar, had a kind of cultish reverence for him, but the other faculty seemed to look down on him. He was young for a professor, thirty maybe—it was hard to tell with the hair—and technically he was the most junior faculty at the school, so he was constantly getting handed the jobs nobody else wanted, such as eating with the First Years. He didn't seem to mind. Or maybe it was just that he didn't notice.

Right now, Professor Coldwater was standing at the far end of the room with his back to her. He was tall and skinny and stood bolt upright, staring at the bookcase in front of him but not actually taking down a book. Plum breathed a silent prayer to whatever saint it was who watched over absent-minded professors and made sure their minds stayed absent. She glided noiselessly across the thick over-lapping oriental carpets, cutting swiftly through the right angle of the L into its shorter arm where Professor Coldwater couldn't see her. Even if he did see her, she doubted he would bother to report her; worst case, he would just kick her out of the Senior Common Room. Either way, it was totally worth it.

Because it was time for the grand reveal. Wharton would open the wine closet, which was actually a whole room the size of a studio apartment, to find Plum already in position, having entered it on the sly through a secret back passage. Then she would present the League's demands, and she would learn the truth of the matter.

It was the chanciest bit of the plan, because the existence of this secret back passage was a matter of speculation, but whatever, if it didn't work, she'd just make her entrance the normal, less dramatic way. And it was reasonably confident speculation. Plum was almost positive that the passage was there. It ran, or it once had run, between the Senior Common Room and the wine closet, so the faculty could cherry-pick the best bottles for their private use. Its location had been divulged to her by the elderly Professor Desante, her erstwhile undergraduate advisor, when she was in her cups, which was usually— Professor Desante was a woman who liked a drink, and she preferred harder stuff than wine. Plum had filed the information away for just such an eventuality.

Professor Desante had also said that nobody used the passage much anymore, though why nobody would use such an obviously useful passage was not obvious to Plum. But Plum figured that even if it had been sealed up, she could and would unseal it. She was on League business, and the League stopped at nothing.

Plum looked quickly over her shoulder—Coldwater still out of view and/or otherwise engaged—then knelt down by the wainscoting. Third panel from the left. Hm—the one on the end was half a panel, not sure whether she should count it. Well, she'd try it both ways. She traced a word with her finger, spelling it out in a runic alphabet—the Elder Futhark—and meanwhile clearing her mind of everything but the taste of a really oaky chardonnay paired with a hot buttered toast point.

Lemon squeezy. She felt the locking spell release even before the panel swung outward on a set of previously invisible hinges. It was a door, albeit a humble, hobbitlike door, about two-thirds height. Any professors who used it would have to stoop and duck their august heads. But presumably such an indignity was worth it for some good free wine.

Annoyingly, though, the passage *had* been sealed. It had been bricked up, only about three feet in, and the bricks had been bricked in such a way as to form a design that Plum recognized as an absolutely brutal hardening charm—just a charm, yes, but a massively powerful one. Not undergraduate stuff. Some professor had bothered to put this here, and they'd spent some time on it too. Plum pursed her lips and snorted out through her nose.

She stared at the pattern for five minutes, in the dimness of the little passageway, lost to the world. In her mind, the pattern in the bricks floated free of the wall and hung before her all on its own, pure and abstract and shining. Her world shrank and focused. Mentally, she entered the pattern, inhabited it, pushed at it from the inside, feeling for any sloppy joins or subtle imbalances.

There must be something. Come on, Plum: it's easier to screw magic up than it is to make it. You know this. Chaos is easier than order. Whoever drew this seal was smart. But was she smarter than Plum?

There was something odd about the angles. The essence of a glyph like this wasn't the angles, it was the topology—you could deform it a good deal and not lose the power as long as its essential geometric properties were intact. The angles of the joins were, up to a point, arbitrary. But the funny thing about the angles of these joins was that they were funny. They were sharper than they needed to be. They were nonarbitrary. There was a pattern to them, a pattern within the pattern.

17 degrees. 3 degrees. 17 and 3. Two of them here, two of them there, the only angles that appeared twice. She snorted again when she saw it. A simple alphabetical code. A moronically simple alphabetical code. 17 and 3. Q and C. Quentin Coldwater.

It was a signature of sorts. A watermark. A Coldwatermark. Professor Coldwater had set this seal. And when she saw that, she saw it all. Maybe it was on purpose—maybe he'd wanted a weak spot, a key, in case he needed to undo it later. Either way, his little vanity signature was the flaw in the pattern.

She extracted the little knife from Wharton's pencil case and worked it into the crumbly mortar around one specific brick. She ran it all the way around the edge, then she stressed the pattern—she couldn't un-pick it, but she could push at it, pluck its taught strings, so that it resonated. It resonated so hard that that one brick vibrated itself clean out of the wall, on the other side. Clunk.

Deprived of that one brick, and hence the integrity of its pattern, the rest of the wall gave up the ghost and fell apart. Funny that it should have been him—everybody knew Coldwater was a wine lush. Plum ducked her head, stepped over the threshold, and drew the panel closed behind her. It was dark in the passageway, and chilly, much chillier than in the cozy Senior Common Room. The walls were old, unfin-ished boards over stone.

Dead reckoning, it was about one hundred yards from the Senior Common Room to the back of the wine closet, but she'd only gone twenty before she got to a door, this one unlocked and unsealed. She closed it behind her. More passage, then another door. Odd. You could never tell what you were going to find in this place, even after living here for four and a half years. Brakebills was old, really old. It had been built and rebuilt a lot of times by a lot of different people.

More doors, until the fourth or fifth one opened onto open air—a little square courtyard she'd never seen before. Mostly grass, with one tree, a fruit tree of some kind, espaliered against a high stone wall. She'd always found espaliers a little creepy. It was like somebody had crucified the poor thing.

Also, not that it mattered, but there shouldn't

have been a moon out; not tonight. She hurried across the courtyard to the next door, but it was locked.

She fingered the doorknob gently, inquiringly. She checked it for magical seals, and wow. Somebody smarter than her and Professor Coldwater put together had shut it up tight.

"Well, blow me down," she said.

Her internal GPS told her that she ought to be going straight ahead, but there was another door off the courtyard, a heavy wooden one on a different wall. She went for door number two, which was heavy but which opened easily.

She had suspected before, but now she was sure, that she was traversing some magically noncontiguous spaces here, because this door opened directly onto one of the upper floors of the library. It wasn't impossible—or it was, obviously, but it was one of the possible impossibles, as Donald Rumsfeld would have said if he'd secretly been a magician. (Which fat chance. Now there was an impossible impossible.) It was preposterous, and a bit creepy, but it wasn't magically impossible.

The Brakebills library was arranged around the interior walls of a tower that narrowed toward the top, and this must have been one of the teensy tiny uppermost floors, which Plum had only ever glimpsed from far below, and which, to be honest, she'd always assumed were just there for show. She never thought there were any actual books in them. What the hell would they shelve up here?

It looked tiny from below, and it was tiny—in fact, now she realized that these upper floors must be built to false perspective, to make the tower look

taller than it was, because it was very tiny indeed,
barely a balcony, like one of those medieval folly
houses that mad kings built for their royal dwarfs.
She had to navigate it on her hands and knees. The
books looked real, though, their brown leather spines
flaking like pastry, with letters stamped on them in
gold—some interminable many-volume reference
work about ghosts.

And like a few of the books in the Brakebills library, they weren't quiet or inanimate. They poked
themselves out at her from the shelves as she crawled
past, as if they were inviting her to open them and
read, or daring her to, or begging her. A couple of
them actually jabbed her in the ribs. They must not
get a lot of visitors, she thought. Probably this was
like when you visit the puppies at the shelter and
they all jump up and want to be petted.

No, thank you. She liked her books to wait, deco-
rously and patiently, until she chose to read them
herself. It was a relief to crawl through the miniature
door at the end of the balcony—it was practically a
cat door—and back into a normal corridor. This was
taking a long time, but it wasn't too late. The main
course would be half over, but there was still dessert,
and she thought there was cheese tonight too. She
could still make it if she hurried.

This corridor was tight, almost a crawl space. In
fact, it was one—as near as she could tell, she was
actually inside one of the walls of Brakebills. It was a
wall of the dining hall: she could hear the warm hum
of talk and the clatter of silverware, and she could
actually look out through a couple of the paintings—
there were peepholes in the eyes, like in old movies

about haunted houses. They were just serving the main, a nice rare lamb spiked with spears of rosemary. The sight of it made her hungry. She felt a million miles away, even though she was standing right there. She almost felt nostalgic, like one of those teary alums, for the time when she was sitting at the table with her bland crab cakes, half an hour ago, back when she knew exactly where she was.

And there was Wharton, showily pouring his mingy glasses of red, totally unrepentant. The sight emboldened her. That was why she was here. For the League.

Though, God, how long was this going to take? The next door opened out onto the roof. The night air was bone cold. She hadn't been up here since the time Professor Sunderland had turned them into geese, and they'd flown down to Antarctica. It was lonely and quiet up here after the dining hall—she was very high up, higher than the leafless tops of all but the tallest trees. She had to stay on her hands and knees because the roof was so sharply raked, and the shingles were gritty under her palms. She could see the Hudson River, a long, sinuous silver squiggle. She shivered just looking at it.

Which way to go? There was no obvious path. She was losing the thread. Finally Plum just jimmied the lock on the nearest dormer window and let herself in.

She was in a student's room. Actually, if she had to guess, she'd guess it was Wharton's room, though obviously she'd never seen it, because her crush had remained in a theoretical state. What were the odds? These spaces were beyond noncontiguous. She began to suspect that somebody at Brakebills, possibly Brakebills itself, was fucking with her.

"OMG," she said out loud. "The irony."

Well, fuck away, she thought, and we shall see who fucks last. She half suspected that she had stumbled into a magical duel with Wharton himself, except no way could he pull off something like this. Maybe he had help—maybe he was part of a shadowy Anti-League, committed to frustrating the goals of the League! Actually, that would be kind of cool.

The room was messy as hell, which was somehow endearing, since she thought of Wharton as a control freak. And it had a nice smell. She decided that she wasn't going to fight against the dream logic of what was happening; she was going to play it out. Steer into the skid. To leave by the front door would have been to break the dream spell, so instead she opened Wharton's closet door, somehow confident that—yes, look, there was a little door at the back of it.

She couldn't help but notice, by the by, that his closet was full, practically packed solid, with boxes of those pencils. Why, exactly, had they thought he was going to freak out at the loss of two pencils? There were like 5,000 of them in here. The aroma of tropical wood oil was suffocating. She opened the door and stooped through.

From here on out, her travels ran entirely on dream rails. The door in the back of Wharton's closet took her into another courtyard, but now it was daytime. They were losing temporal, uh, contiguousness—contiguity?—as well as spatial. It was earlier today, because there she was, Plum herself, crossing the lightly frosted grass, and passing Wharton, and there was the eye sliding. It was a strange sight. But Plum's tolerance for strange had been on the rise, lo this past half hour.

She watched herself leave the courtyard. That was her in a nutshell, Plum thought: standing there and watching her own life go by. She wondered whether, if she shouted and waved her arms, she would hear herself, or if this was more of a two-way-mirror deal. She frowned. The causality of it became tangled. This much at least was clear: if that's what her ass looked like from behind, well, not bad. She would take it.

The next door was even more temporally noncontiguous, because it put her in a different Brakebills entirely, a curiously reduced Brakebills. It was a smaller and darker and somehow denser Brakebills. The ceilings were lower, the corridors were narrower, and the air smelled like wood smoke. She passed an open doorway and saw a group of girls huddled together on a huge bed. They wore white nightgowns and had long, straight hair and bad teeth.

Plum understood what she was seeing. This was Brakebills of long ago. The Ghost of Brakebills Past. The girls looked up only momentarily, incuriously, as she passed. No question what they were up to.

"Another League," she said to herself. "I *knew* there must have been one."

Then the next door opened on a room that she thought she knew—no, she *knew* she knew it, she just didn't want to think about it. She had been here before, a long time ago. The room was empty now, but something was coming, it was on its way, and when it got here, all hell was going to break loose. It was the thing: the thing that she could not and would not think about. She had seen this all happen before, and she hadn't been able to stop it. Now she knew it was coming, and it was going to happen anyway.

She had to get out, get out now, before the horror started all over again.

"No!" Plum said. "No, no, no, no, *no*."

She ran. She tried to go back, the first time she'd tried that, but the door was locked behind her, so she ran ahead blindly and crashed through the next door. When she opened her eyes again she was in the little trapezoidal lounge where the League held its meetings.

Oh. Oh, thank God. She was breathing hard, and she sobbed once. It wasn't real. It wasn't real. Or it was real, but it was over. She didn't care, either way she was safe. This whole fucked-up magical mystery tour was over. She wasn't going back, and she wasn't going to go forward either. She was safe right here. She wasn't going to think about it. Nobody had to know.

Plum sank down on the ragged couch, boneless. It was so saggy it almost swallowed her up. She felt like she could fall asleep right here. She almost wondered if she had when she opened her eyes again and looked at the reflection in the long mirror that Darcy and Chelsea had cracked earlier. Of course she wasn't in it: magic mirror. Right. Plum was relieved not to have to look at her own face right now. Then her relief went away.

Another girl stood there in the mirror instead of

her. Or at least it was shaped like a girl. It was blue and naked, and its skin gave off an unearthly light. Even its teeth were blue. Its eyes were utterly mad.

This was horror of a different kind. New horror.

"You," the ghost whispered to Plum.

It was her: the ghost of Brakebills. She was real. Jesus Christ, that's who was fucking with her. She was the spider at the center of the web.

Plum stood up, but after that, she didn't move; all moving was over with. If she moved, she wouldn't live long. She'd spent enough time around magic to know instinctively that she was in the presence of something so raw and powerful that if she touched it, it would snuff her out in a second. That blue girl was like a downed power line. The insulation had come off the world, and pure naked magical current was arcing in front of her.

It was beyond horror: Plum felt calm, detached. She was caught in the gears of something much bigger than her, and they would grind her up if they wanted to. They were already in motion. There was nothing she could do. Part of her wanted them to. She had been waiting so long for her doom to catch up to her.

But then: bump. The sound came from the wall to her left—it sounded like something had run into it from the other side. A little plaster fell. The bump was followed by a man's voice saying something like "Oof." Plum looked.

The ghost in the mirror didn't.

"I know," it whispered. "I saw."

The wall exploded, throwing plaster in all directions, and a man crashed through it covered with white dust. It was Professor Coldwater. He shook himself like a wet dog to get some of the dust off. White witchery sparked around both his hands like Roman candles, so bright it made purple flares in her vision.

Always keeping one hand pointed at the blue ghost, he walked toward Plum till he stood between her and the mirror.

"Careful," he said over his shoulder, relatively calmly given the circumstances.

He reared back one of his long legs and kicked in the mirror. It took him three kicks—the first two times the glass just starred and sagged, but the third time his foot went right through it. It got a little stuck when he tried to pull it out.

It was a measure of how shocked she was that Plum's first reaction was: *I must tell Chelsea that she doesn't have to worry about paying for it.*

Breaking the mirror didn't dispel the ghost—it was still watching them, though it had to peer around the edge of the hole. Professor Coldwater turned around to face the wall behind Plum and joined his hands together.

"Get down," he said.

The air shimmered and rippled around them. Then she had to throw her forearm over her eyes, and her hair crackled with so much static electricity, it made her scalp hurt. The entire world was shot through with light. She didn't see but she heard and felt the door behind her explode out of its frame.

"Run," Professor Coldwater said. "Go on, I'm right behind you."

She did. She hurdled the couch like a champion

and felt a shock wave as Professor Coldwater threw some final spell at the ghost. It lifted Plum off her feet and made her stagger, but she kept on running.

Going back was faster than going forward had been. She seemed to be bounding ahead seven-league-boots-style, which at first she thought was adrenaline till she realized, no, it was just magic. One stride took her through the hell room, another and she was in colonial Brakebills, then she was in Wharton's room, on the roof, in the crawl space, the library, the creepy-pear-tree courtyard, the passage. The sound of doors slamming behind her was like a string of firecrackers going off.

They stopped just short of the Senior Common Room, breathing hard. He was right behind her, just as he'd said. She wondered if he'd just saved her life; at any rate, she definitely felt bad about having made fun of him behind his back. He resealed the passageway behind him. She watched him work, dazed but fascinated: moving in fast-motion, his arms flying crazily, like a time-lapse movie, he assembled an entire intricately patterned brick wall in about five seconds.

She couldn't help but notice that this time he caught the resonance pattern, the one she'd used to break the last seal, and corrected it.

Then they were alone in the Senior Common Room. It could all have been a dream except for the plaster dust on the shoulders of Professor Coldwater's blazer.

"What did she say to you?" he said.

"She?" Plum said. "Oh, the ghost. Nothing. She said 'You,' and then she didn't say anything else."

"'You,'" he repeated. He was staring over her

shoulder—he'd already gone absentminded again. One of his fingers was still crackling with a bit of white fire; he shook it and it went out. "Hm. Do you still want to go to the wine closet? That's what you were looking for, wasn't it?"

Plum laughed in spite of herself. The wine closet. She'd completely forgotten about it. She still had Wharton's stupid pencil case in her stupid pocket. It seemed too pointless to go through with it. Everything was too sad and too strange now.

But somehow, she thought, it would be even sadder not to go through with it.

"Sure," she said, aiming for jaunty and almost getting there. "Why not. So there really is a secret passage?"

"Of course. I steal bottles all the time."

He drew the rune word on the next panel over from the one she'd used.

"You don't count the half panel," he said.

Aha. The door opened. It was just what she thought: a doddle, not even one hundred yards, more like seventy-five.

She squared her shoulders and checked her look in a pier glass. The hair was a little wild, but she supposed that would be part of the effect. She was surprised, and almost a tiny bit disappointed, to see her own face looking back at her. She wondered whose ghost the ghost was, and how she died, and why she was still here. Probably she wasn't here for the fun of it. Probably she wasn't a nostalgic alumna haunting Brakebills out of school spirit. Probably she needed something. Hopefully, that thing wasn't, you know, to kill Plum.

But if it was, she would have done it—wouldn't she?—and she hadn't. Plum wasn't a ghost. It was actually worth telling herself that: Having seen a real one—and she hadn't even thought they were real, but live and learn—she knew the difference now, really knew it. I didn't die just then, she thought, and I didn't die in that room. It felt like I did, I wanted to die, but I didn't, because if I had died then, I would have *died*. And I don't want to be a ghost. I don't want to haunt my own life.

She'd just closed the secret door to the wine closet behind her—it was concealed behind a trick wine rack—when Wharton came bustling through the front door with the rumble and glow of the cheese course subsiding behind him. Her timing was perfect. It was all very "League."

Wharton froze, with a freshly recorked bottle in one hand and two inverted wineglasses dangling from the fingers of the other. Plum regarded him calmly.

"You've been short-pouring the Fifth Years," she said.

"Yes," he said. "You have my pencils."

She watched him. Part of the charm of Wharton's face was its asymmetry. He'd had a harelip corrected at some point, and the surgery had gone well, so that all that was left was a tiny tough-guy scar, as if he'd taken one straight in the face at some point but just kept on trucking.

Also, he had an incredibly precious widow's peak. Some guys had all the luck.

"It's not the pencils I mind," he said, "so much as the case. And the knife. They're vintage silver, Smith and Sharp. You can't find those anywhere anymore."

She took the case out of her pocket.

"Why have you been short-pouring the Fifth Years?"

"Because I need the extra wine."

"Okay, but what do you need it *for*?" Plum said. "I'll give you back the pencils and all that. I just want to know."

"What do you think I need it for?" Wharton said. "I give it to that fucking ghost. That thing scares the shit out of me."

"You're an idiot," Plum said. "The ghost doesn't care about wine." For some reason, she now felt like an authority on the subject of what the ghost did or did not care about. "The ghost doesn't care about *you*. And if it did, there'd be nothing you could do about it. Certainly not placate it by giving it wine."

She handed him the case.

"The pencils are inside. Knife, too."

"Thank you."

He dropped it in the pocket of his apron and set the two empty wineglasses down on a shelf.

"Wine?" he said.

"Thank you," Plum said. "I'd love some."

Sharon Kay Penman

New York Times bestseller Sharon Kay Penman has been acclaimed by *Publishers Weekly* as "an historical novelist of the first water." Her debut novel, *The Sunne in Splendour,* about Richard III, was a worldwide hit, and her acclaimed Welsh Princes trilogy—*Here Be Dragons, Falls the Shadow,* and *The Reckoning*—was similarly successful. Her other books include a sequence about Eleanor of Aquitaine—*When Christ and His Saints Slept, Time and Chance,* and *Devil's Brood*—and the Justin de Quincy series of historical mysteries, which include *The Queen's Man, Cruel as the Grave, Dragon's Lair,* and *Prince of Darkness.* Her most recent book is a novel about Richard, Coeur de Lion, *Lionheart.* She lives in Mays Landing, New Jersey, and maintains a website at sharonkaypenman.com.

Here she takes us back to twelfth-century Sicily to show us that a queen in exile is still a queen—and a very dangerous woman indeed.

A QUEEN IN EXILE

Constance de Hauteville was shivering although she was standing as close to the hearth as she could get without scorching her skirts. Her fourth wedding anniversary was a month away, but she was still not acclimated to German winters. She did not often let herself dwell upon memories of her Sicilian homeland; why salt unhealed wounds? But on nights when sleet and ice-edged winds chilled her to the very marrow of her bones, she could not deny her yearning for the palm trees, olive groves, and sun-splashed warmth of Palermo, for the royal palaces that ringed the city like a necklace of gleaming pearls, with their marble floors, vivid mosaics, cascading fountains, lush gardens, and silver reflecting pools.

"My lady?" One of her women was holding out a cup of hot mulled wine and Constance accepted it with a smile. But her unruly mind insisted upon slipping back in time, calling up the lavish entertainments of Christmas courts past, presided over by her nephew, William, and Joanna, his young English queen. Royal marriages were not love matches, of course, but dictated by matters of state. If a couple were lucky, though, they might develop a genuine respect and fondness for each other. William and Joanna's marriage had seemed an affectionate one to Constance, and when she'd been wed to Heinrich von Hohenstaufen, King of Germany and heir to the Holy Roman Empire, she'd hoped to find some contentment in their union. It was true that he'd already earned a reputation at twenty-one for ruthlessness and inflexibility. But he was also an accomplished poet, fluent in several languages, and she'd sought to convince herself that he had a softer side he showed only to family. Instead, she'd found a man as cold and unyielding as the lands he ruled, a man utterly lacking in the passion and exuberance and joie de vivre that made Sicily such an earthly paradise.

Finishing the wine, she turned reluctantly away from the fire. "I am ready for bed," she said, shivering again when they unlaced her gown, exposing her skin to the cool chamber air. She sat on a stool, still in her chemise, a robe draped across her shoulders as they removed her wimple and veil and unpinned her hair. It reached to her waist, the moonlit pale gold so prized by troubadours. She'd been proud of it once, proud of her de Hauteville good looks and fair coloring. But as she gazed into an ivory hand mirror, the woman looking back at her was a wary stranger, too thin and too tired, showing every one of her thirty-five years.

After brushing out her hair, one of her women began to braid it into a night plait. It was then that the door slammed open and Constance's husband strode into the chamber. As her ladies sank down in submissive curtseys, Constance rose hastily. She'd not been expecting him, for he'd paid a visit to her bedchamber just two nights ago, for what he referred to as the "marital debt," one of his rare jests, for if he had a sense of humor, he'd kept it well hidden so far. When they were first married, she'd been touched that he always came to her, rather than summoning her to his bedchamber, thinking it showed an unexpected sensitivity. Now she knew better. If they lay together in her bed, he could then return to his own chamber afterward, as he always did; she could count on one hand the times they'd awakened in the same bed.

Heinrich did not even glance at her ladies. "Leave us," he said, and they hastened to obey, so swiftly that their withdrawal seemed almost like flight.

"My lord husband," Constance murmured as the door closed behind the last of her attendants. She could read nothing in his face; he'd long ago mastered the royal skill of concealing his inner thoughts behind an impassive court mask. As she studied him more closely, though, she saw subtle indicators of mood— the faintest curve at the corner of his mouth, his usual pallor warmed by a faint flush. He had the oddest eye color she'd ever seen, as grey and pale as a frigid winter sky, but they seemed to catch the candlelight now, shining with unusual brightness.

"There has been word from Sicily. Their king is dead."

Constance stared at him, suddenly doubting her command of German. Surely she could not have heard correctly? "William?" she whispered, her voice husky with disbelief.

Heinrich arched a brow. "Is there another King of Sicily that I do not know about? Of course I mean William."

"What . . . what happened? How . . . ?"

His shoulders twitched in a half shrug. "Some vile Sicilian pestilence, I suppose. God knows, the island is rife with enough fevers, plagues, and maladies to strike down half of Christendom. I know only that he died in November, a week after Martinmas, so his crown is ours for the taking."

Constance's knees threatened to give way and she stumbled toward the bed. How could William be dead? There was just a year between them; they'd been more like brother and sister than nephew and aunt. Theirs had been an idyllic childhood, and later she'd taken his little bride under her wing, a homesick eleven-year-old not yet old enough to be a wife. Now Joanna was a widow at twenty-four. What would happen to her? What would happen to Sicily without William?

Becoming aware of Heinrich's presence, she looked up to find him standing by the bed, staring down at her. She drew a bracing breath and got to her feet; she was tall for a woman, as tall as Heinrich, and drew confidence from the fact that she could look directly into his eyes. His appearance was not regal. His blond hair was thin, his beard scanty, and his physique slight; in an unkind moment, she'd once decided he put her in mind of a mushroom that had never seen the light of day. He could not have been more unlike his charismatic, expansive, robust father, the emperor Frederick Barbarossa, who swaggered through the imperial court like a colossus. And yet it was Heinrich who inspired fear in their subjects, not Frederick; those ice-color eyes could impale men as surely as any sword thrust. Even Constance was not immune to their piercing power, although she'd have moved heaven and earth to keep him from finding that out.

"You do realize what this means, Constance? William's queen was barren, so that makes you the legitimate and only heir to the Sicilian throne. Yet there you sit as if I'd brought you news of some calamity."

Constance flinched, for she knew that was what people whispered of her behind her back. To Heinrich's credit, he'd never called her "barren," at least not yet. He must think it, though, for they'd been wed nigh on four years and she'd not conceived. So far she'd failed in a queen's paramount duty. She wondered sometimes what Heinrich had thought of the marriage his father had arranged for him—a foreign wife eleven years his elder. Had he been as reluctant to make the match as she'd been? Or had he been willing to gamble that his flawed new wife might one day bring him Sicily, the richest kingdom in Christendom?

"Joanna was not barren," she said tautly. "She gave birth to a son."

"Who did not live. And she never got with child again. Why do you think William made his lords swear to recognize your right to the crown if he died without an heir of his body? He wanted to assure the succession."

Constance knew better. William had never doubted that he and Joanna would one day have another child; they were young and he was an optimist by nature. And because he was so confident of this, he'd been unfazed by the uproar her marriage had stirred. What did it matter that his subjects were horrified at the prospect of a German ruling over them when it would never come to pass? But now he was dead at thirty-six and the fears of his people were suddenly very real, indeed.

"It may not be as easy as you think, Heinrich," she said, choosing her words with care. "Our marriage was very unpopular. The Sicilians will not welcome a German king."

He showed himself to be as indifferent to the wishes of the Sicilian people as William had been, saying coolly, "They do not have a choice."

"I am not so sure of that. They might well turn to William's cousin Tancred." She was about to identify Tancred further, but there was no need. Heinrich never forgot anything that involved his self-interest.

"The Count of Lecce? He is baseborn!"

She opened her mouth, shut it again. It would not do to argue that the Sicilians would even prefer a man born out of wedlock to Heinrich. She knew it was true, though. They'd embrace her bastard cousin before they'd accept her German husband.

Heinrich was regarding her thoughtfully. "You do want the crown, Constance?" he said at last. She felt a flare of indignation that it had not even occurred to him she might mourn William, the last of her family, and she merely nodded. But he seemed satisfied by that muted response. "I'll send your women back in," he said. "Sleep well, for you'll soon have another crown to add to your collection."

As soon as the door closed, Constance sank down on the bed, and after a moment she kicked off her shoes and burrowed under the covers. She was shivering again. Cherishing this rare moment of privacy before her attendants returned, she closed her eyes and said a prayer for William's immortal soul. She would have Masses said for him on the morrow, she decided, and that gave her a small measure of comfort. She would pray for Joanna, too, in her time of need. Propping herself up with feather-filled pillows, then, she sought to make sense of the conflicting, confused emotions unleashed by William's untimely death.

She'd not expected this, had thought William would have a long, prosperous reign and would indeed have a son to succeed him. They'd been arrogant, she and William, assuming they knew the Will of the Almighty. They ought to have remembered their Scriptures: *A man's heart deviseth his way, but the Lord directeth his steps.* But Heinrich was right. She was the lawful heir to the Sicilian throne. Not Tancred. And she did want it. It was her birthright. Sicily was hers by blood, the land she loved. So why did she feel such ambivalence? As she shifted against the pillows, her gaze fell upon the only jewelry she wore, a band of beaten gold encrusted with emeralds—her wedding ring. As much as she wanted Sicily, she did not want to turn it over to Heinrich. She did not want to be the one to let the snake loose in Eden.

Constance's forebodings about Tancred of Lecce would prove to be justified. The Sicilians rallied around him and he was crowned King of Sicily in January of 1190. Constance dutifully echoed Heinrich's outrage, although she'd seen this coming. She was not even surprised to learn that Tancred had seized Joanna's dower lands, for they had strategic importance, and Tancred well knew that a German army would be contesting his claim to the crown. But she was utterly taken aback when Tancred took Joanna prisoner, holding her captive in Palermo, apparently fearing Joanna would use her personal popularity on Constance's behalf. Heinrich wanted to strike hard and fast at the man who'd usurped his wife's throne. Vengeance would have to wait, though, for his father had taken the cross and was planning to join the crusade to free Jerusalem from the Sultan of Egypt, the Saracen Salah al-Din, known to the crusaders as Saladin, and he needed Heinrich to govern Germany in his absence.

Frederick Barbarossa departed for the Holy Land that spring. The German force dispatched by Heinrich was routed by Tancred, who continued to consolidate his power and had some success at the papal court, for the Pope considered the Holy Roman Empire to be a greater threat than Tancred's illegitimacy. In September, Joanna's captivity was ended by the arrival in Sicily of the new English king, her brother Richard, known to friends and foes alike as Lionheart. Like Frederick, he was on his way to the Holy Land, and was accompanied by a large army. He was enraged to learn of his sister's plight and demanded she be set free at once, her dower lands restored. Tancred wisely agreed, for Richard knew war the way a priest knew his Paternoster. For

Constance, that was the only flare of light in a dark, drear year. And then in December they learned that Heinrich's father was dead. Never reaching the Holy Land, Frederick had drowned fording a river in Armenia. Heinrich wasted no time. Daring a January crossing of the Alps, he and Constance led an army into Italy. They halted in Rome to be crowned by the Pope, and then rode south. The war for the Sicilian crown had begun.

Salerno sweltered in the August sun. Usually sea breezes made the heat tolerable, but this has been one of the hottest, driest summers in recent memory. The sky was barren of clouds, a faded, bleached blue that seemed bone white by midday. Courtyards and gardens offered little shade and the normal city noise was muted, the streets all but deserted. Standing on the balcony of the royal palace, Constance wished she could believe that the citizens had been driven indoors by the heat. But she knew a more potent force was at work—fear.

The Kingdom of Sicily encompassed the mainland south of Rome as well as the island itself, and as the German army swept down the peninsula, town after town opened their gates to Heinrich. The citizens of Salerno even sought him out. Although their archbishop was firmly in Tancred's camp, the Salernitans pledged their loyalty to Heinrich and invited Constance to stay in their city while he laid siege to Naples.

At first Constance had enjoyed her sojourn in Salerno. It was wonderful to be back on her native soil. She was delighted with her luxurious residence—the royal palace that had been built by her father, the great King Roger. She savored the delicious meals that graced her table, delicacies rarely available beyond the Alps—melons, pomegranates, oranges, sugar-coated almonds, rice, shrimp, oysters, fish that were swimming in the blue Mediterranean that morning and sizzling in the palace kitchen pans that afternoon. Best of all, she was able to consult with some of the best doctors in Christendom about her failure to conceive. She could never have discussed so intimate a matter with a male physician. But women were allowed to attend Salerno's famed medical school and licensed to practice medicine. She'd soon found Dame Martina, whose consultation was a revelation.

Constance had taken all the blame upon herself for her barren marriage; common wisdom held that it was always the woman's fault. That was not so, Martina said briskly. Just as a woman may have a defect of her womb, so might a man have a defect in his seed. Moreover, there were ways to find out which one had the problem. A small pot should be filled with the woman's urine and another with her husband's. Wheat bran was then added to both pots, which were to be left alone for nine days. If worms appeared in the urine of the man, he was the one at fault, and the same was true for the woman.

"I doubt that my lord husband would agree to such a test," Constance had said wryly, imagining Heinrich's incredulous, outraged reaction should she even hint that the fault might be his. But she took the test herself, and when her urine was found to be worm-free on the ninth day, her spirits had soared. Even if no one else knew it, she knew now that she did not have a defective womb; she was not doomed to be that saddest of all creatures, a barren queen.

Martina offered hope, too, explaining that sometimes neither husband nor wife was at fault and yet his seed would not take root in her womb. But this could be remedied, she assured Constance. She must dry the male parts of a boar and then make a powder of them, which she was then to drink with a good wine. And to assure the birth of a male child, Constance and Heinrich must dry and powder the womb of a hare, then drink it in wine. Constance grimaced at that, glad she'd be spared such an unappetizing concoction until she and Heinrich were reunited. How would she get him to cooperate, though? She'd have to find a way to mix the powder into his wine undetected on one of his nocturnal visits to her bedchamber. She was so grateful to Martina that she offered the older woman a vast sum to become her personal physician, and Martina gladly accepted, tempted as much by the prestige of serving an empress as by the material benefits.

But then reports began to reach Salerno from the siege of Naples. For the first time, Heinrich was encountering fierce resistance, led by Tancred's brother-in-law, the Count of Acerra, and Salerno's own archbishop. Heinrich had hired ships from Pisa, but they were not numerous enough to blockade the harbor, and so he would be unable to starve the Neapolitans into surrender. Tancred had chosen to make his stand on the island of Sicily knowing that his most dangerous weapon was the hot, humid,

Italian summer. Heinrich's German troops were unaccustomed to such stifling heat and they soon began to sicken. Army camps were particularly vulnerable to deadly contagions like the bloody flux; Constance had been told that more crusaders died from disease than from Saracen swords in the Holy Land.

She'd hoped that the Salernitans would remain in ignorance of the setbacks Heinrich was experiencing, but that was an unrealistic hope, for Naples was less than thirty miles to the north of Salerno. She could tell as soon as word began to trickle into the city, for the people she encountered in the piazza were subdued or sullen, and the palace servants could not hide their dismay. Even Martina had anxiously asked her if she was sure Heinrich would prevail and did not seem completely convinced by Constance's assurances. Salerno had assumed that Tancred would be no match for the large German army and self-preservation had won out over loyalty to the Sicilian king. Now they began to fear that they'd wagered on the wrong horse.

When almost a fortnight passed without any word from Heinrich, Constance dispatched Sir Baldwin, the head of her household knights, to Naples to find out how bad things really were. Standing now on the palace balcony, she shaded her eyes against the glare of the noonday sun and wondered if this would be the day Baldwin would return. She would never admit it aloud, but she wanted him to stay away as long as possible, so sure was she that he would be bringing bad news.

"Madame?" Hildegund was standing by the door.

Most of Constance's attendants were Sicilians, including Dame Adela, who'd been with her since childhood, and Michael, the Saracen eunuch who attracted so much attention at Heinrich's court; the Germans were shocked that Saracens were allowed to live freely in a Christian country and horrified that William had relied upon the men called "the palace eunuchs" in the governance of his kingdom. Constance had taken care not to reveal that William had spoken Arabic or that it was one of the official languages of Sicily, and she'd insisted that Michael had embraced the True Faith, even though she knew that many eunuchs' conversion to Christianity was often pretense. How could she ever make Heinrich or his subjects understand the complex mosaic that was Sicilian society? Hildegund was one of her few German ladies-in-waiting, a self-possessed, sedate widow who'd been a great asset in Constance's struggles to learn German, and Constance gave her a fond smile, nodding when the other woman reminded her it was time for the day's main meal.

Dinners were very different now than they'd been at the outset of her stay in Salerno. Then the local lords and their ladies had competed eagerly for an invitation from the empress, and the great hall had usually been crowded with finely garbed guests showing off their silks and jewels as they sought to curry favor with Constance. For over a week, though, her invitations to dine had been declined with transparent excuses, and on this Sunday noon, the only ones sharing her table were the members of her own household.

The palace cooks had prepared a variety of tasty

dishes, but Constance merely picked at the roast ca-
pon on her trencher. Glancing around, she saw that
few of the others had much appetite, either. Reminding herself that she should be setting an example for
her household, she began an animated conversation
with Martina and her chaplain just as shouting drifted
through the open windows. Riders were coming in.
Constance set her wine cup down and got slowly to
her feet as Baldwin was admitted to the hall. One
look at his face told her all she needed or wanted to
know, but she made herself reach out and take the
proffered letter as he knelt before her.

Gesturing for him to rise, she broke her husband's
seal and quickly scanned the contents. It was not
written in Heinrich's hand, of course; he always dictated his letters to a scribe, for he never sent her a
message that was not meant for other eyes. A low
murmur swept the hall as those watching saw her
color fade, leaving her skin so pale it seemed almost
translucent. When she glanced up, though, her voice
was even, revealing none of her inner distress. "I will
not mislead you," she said. "The news is not good.
Many have died of the bloody flux and the emperor
himself has been stricken with this vile malady. He
has decided that it would be best to end the siege and
yesterday his army began a retreat from Naples."

There were gasps, smothered cries, a few muttered
obscenities from some of her knights. "What of us,
my lady?" a young girl blurted out. "What will become of us?"

"The emperor wants us to remain in Salerno. He
says that my presence here will be proof that he in-
tends to return and the war is not over."

There was an appalled silence. Taking advantage of it, she beckoned to Baldwin and led the way out into the courtyard. The sun was blinding, and when she sank down on the edge of the marble fountain, she could feel the heat through the silk of her gown. "How ill is he, Baldwin?" she asked, so softly that she felt the need to repeat herself, swallowing until she had enough saliva for speech.

He knelt beside her, gazing up intently into her face. "Very ill, my lady. His doctors said he was sure to die if he stayed. I fear that his wits have been addled by his fever, for he did not seem to realize the danger you are in now that he is gone."

Constance did not think it was the fever, but rather Heinrich's supreme self-confidence. He did not understand that the Salernitans' fear of him was dependent upon his presence. When word got out that his army was retreating, the people would see it as a defeat, and they'd begin to fear Tancred more than Heinrich, for they'd betrayed him by inviting her into their city. She could feel a headache coming on, and rubbed her temples in a vain attempt to head it off. The wrath of a king was indeed to be feared. Heinrich's father had razed Milan to the ground as punishment for past treachery, and her brother, William's father, had destroyed the town of Bari as a brutal warning to would-be rebels. Was Tancred capable of such ruthless vengeance? She did not think so, but how were the frightened citizens of Salerno to know that?

"My lady . . . I think we ought to leave this place today. A healthy army travels less than ten miles a day and this army is battered and bleeding. If we make haste, we can overtake them."

Constance bit her lip. She agreed with Baldwin; she was not safe here, not now. But her pride rebelled at the thought of fleeing like a thief in the night. How would the Sicilians consider her worthy to rule over them if she gave in to her fears like a foolish, timid woman? Her father would not have run away. And Heinrich would never forgive her if she disobeyed him and fled Salerno, for his letter had clearly stated that her presence was important as a pledge to his supporters, a warning to his enemies—proof that he would be back. She'd not wanted Heinrich as her husband; still less did she want him as her enemy. How could she live with a man who hated her . . . and he would, for her flight would make it impossible for him to pretend he'd not suffered a humiliating defeat.

"I cannot, Baldwin," she said. "It is my husband's wish that I await him here in Salerno. Even if the worst happens and Tancred comes to lay siege to the city, Heinrich will send troops to defend it . . . and us."

"Of course, madame," Baldwin said, mustering up all the certainty he could. "All will be well." But he did not believe it and he doubted that Constance did, either.

It took only two days for word to reach Salerno of the German army's retreat. The streets were soon crowded with frantic men and women trying to convince themselves that they'd not made a fatal mistake. Constance sent out public criers to assure them that Heinrich would soon return. But as dusk descended, a new and terrifying rumor swept the city—that the German emperor had died of the bloody flux. And that was the spark thrown into a hayrick, setting off a conflagration.

Constance and her household had just finished their evening meal when they heard a strange noise, almost like the roaring of the sea, a distant, dull rumble that grew ever louder. She sent several of her knights to investigate and they soon returned with alarming news. A huge mob was gathering outside the gates of the palace, many of them drunk, all of them scared witless by what they'd brought upon themselves.

Baldwin and her knights assured Constance and the women that the mob would not be able to force an entry into the palace grounds, and departed then to join the men guarding the walls. But soon afterward, they came running back into the great hall. "We've been betrayed," Baldwin gasped. "Those cowardly whoresons opened the gates to them!" Bolting the thick oaken doors, they hastened to latch the shutters as Baldwin dispatched men to make sure all of the other entrances to the palace were secure. Constance's women gathered around her, in the way she'd seen chicks flock to the mother hen when a hawk's shadow darkened the sun. The awareness that they were all looking to her for answers stiffened her spine, giving her the courage she needed to face this unexpected crisis. She'd feared that Salerno would soon be under siege by the army Tancred had sent to defend Naples. She'd not realized that the greatest danger would come from within.

She reassured them as best she could, insisting that

the townspeople would disperse once they realized that they could not gain entry to the palace itself. Her words rang hollow even to herself, for the fury of the mob showed no signs of abating. Theirs had been a spontaneous act of panic, and they'd been ill prepared for an assault. But now those in the hall could hear cries for axes, for a battering ram. When Constance heard men also shouting for kindling and torches, she knew they dared not wait for cooler heads to prevail or for the craven city officials to intervene.

Calling to Baldwin, she drew him toward the dais. "I must talk to them," she said softly. "Mayhap I can make them see reason."

He was horrified. "My lady, they are mad with fear. There is no reasoning with them."

She suspected that he was right, but what else could she do? "Nevertheless, I have to try," she said, with a steadfastness she was far from feeling. "Come with me to the solar above the hall. I can speak to them from the balcony."

He continued to argue halfheartedly, for he did not know what else to do, either, and when she turned toward the stairwell, he trailed at her heels. The solar was dark, for no oil lamps had been lit, and the heat was suffocating. Constance waited while Baldwin unlatched the door leading out onto the small balcony; she could feel perspiration trickling along her ribs and her heart was beating so rapidly that she felt light-headed.

The scene below her was an eerie one. The darkness was stabbed with flaring torches, illuminating faces contorted with anger and fear. She saw women

in the surging throng and, incredibly, even a few
children darting about on the edges of the crowd as
if this were a holy day festival. Some were passing
wineskins back and forth, but most drew their courage from their desperation. They were still calling
for firewood, urging those closest to the street to find
anything that would burn. It took a few moments
for them to notice the woman standing motionless
above them, gripping the balcony railing as if it were
her only lifeline.

"Good people of Salerno!" Constance swallowed
with difficulty, worried that they'd not hear her. Before she could continue, they began to point and
shout. She heard her name, heard cries of "Bitch!"
and "Sorceress!" and then "German slut!"

"I am not German!" There was no worry of being
heard now; her voice resonated across the courtyard, infused with anger. "I am Sicilian born and
bred, as you all are. I am the daughter of King Roger
of blessed memory. This is my homeland as much as
it is yours."

She wasn't sure if it was the mention of her re-
vered father's name, but the crowd quieted for the
moment. "I know you are confused and fearful. But
you've heeded false rumors. The Emperor Heinrich
is not dead! Indeed, he is already on the mend. I had
a letter from him just this morn, saying he expects
to return very soon."

She paused for breath. "You know my lord husband. He remembers those who do him a good service. When he leads his army back to Salerno, he
will be grateful to you for keeping his wife safe. You
will be rewarded for your loyalty." Another pause,

this one deliberate. "But this you must know, too. The Emperor Heinrich never forgets a wrong done him. If you betray his faith, if you do harm to me or mine, he will not forgive. He will leave a smoldering ruin where your city once stood. Dare any of you deny it? You know in your hearts that I speak true. You have far more to fear from the emperor if you bring his wrath down upon you than ever you do from that usurper in Palermo."

She thought she had them, could see some heads nodding, see men lowering clubs and bows as she spoke. But her mention of Tancred was a tactical error, reminding them that his supporters were just thirty miles away at Naples, while Heinrich's army was decimated by the bloody flux, fleeing with their tales tucked between their legs. The spell broken, the crowd began to mutter among themselves, and then one well-dressed youth with a sword at his hip shouted out, "She lies! That German swine breathed his last the day after he fled the siege camp! Send her to join him in Hell!"

The words were no sooner out of his mouth than one of his allies brought up his bow, aimed, and sent an arrow winging through the dark toward the balcony. His aim was true, but Baldwin had been watching those with weapons, and as soon as the bowman moved, he dove from the shadows, shoving Constance to the ground. There was a shocked silence and then a woman cried, "Holy Mother Mary, you killed her!" Someone else retorted that they had nothing left to lose then and more arrows were loosed. Crawling on their hands and knees, Constance and Baldwin scrambled back into the solar and she sat on the floor, gasping for breath as he fumbled with the door. Several thuds told them that arrows had found their mark.

Once she could draw enough air into her lungs again, Constance held out her hand, let him help her to her feet. "Thank you," she said, and tears stung her eyes when he swore that he'd defend her as long as he had breath in his body, for that was no empty boast. He would die here in the palace at Salerno. They all would die unless the Almighty worked a miracle expressly on their behalf. She insisted that he escort her back to the hall, for at least she could do that much for her household. She would stand with them to the last.

She expected hysteria, but her women seemed stunned. Constance ordered wine to be brought out, for what else was there to do? They could hear the sounds of the assault, knew it was only a matter of time until the mob would break down the doors. As the noise intensified, Martina drew Constance aside, surreptitiously showing her a handful of herbs clutched in the palm of her hand. "They work quickly," she murmured, and would have dropped them into Constance's wine cup had she not recoiled.

"Jesu, Martina! Self-slaughter is a mortal sin!"

"It is a better fate than what awaits us, my lady. They are sore crazed and there are none in command. What do you think they will do to you once they get inside? On the morrow, they'll be horrified by what they did this night. But their remorse and guilt will change nothing."

Constance could not repress a shudder, but she continued to shake her head. "I cannot," she whispered, "nor can you, Martina. We'd burn for aye in Hell if we did."

Martina said nothing, merely slipped the herbs back into a pouch swinging from her belt. She stayed by Constance's side, occasionally giving the younger woman a significant look, as if reminding her there was still time to change her mind. Constance mounted the steps of the dais, holding up her hand for silence. "We must pray to Almighty God that His will be done," she said, surprised that her voice sounded so steady. There were a few stifled sobs from her women, but when she knelt, they knelt, too. So did the men, after carefully placing their weapons within reach. Those who'd not been shriven of their sins sought out Constance's chaplain, following him behind the decorated wooden screen that he was using as a makeshift confessional.

Michael had not joined the others to confess, confirming Constance's suspicions that his Christian faith was camouflage. He was a good man, though, and she hoped the Almighty would be merciful with him. The eunuch had stayed in a window recess, monitoring the progress of the assault by the sounds filtering into the hall. "My lady!" he called out suddenly. "Something is happening!" Before anyone could stop him, he unlatched the shutters, peering out into the dark. And then he flung the shutters wide.

By now they all could hear the screams. Baldwin hastened to the window. "The mob is being dispersed by men on horseback, madame! God has heard our prayers!"

The crowd scattered as knights rode into their

midst. The courtyard was soon cleared of all but the riders and the crumpled bodies of those who'd been too slow or too stubborn. Having come so close to death, Constance was hesitant to believe deliverance was at hand, not until she saw for herself. Kneeling on the window seat, she watched as the last of the rioters fled. But she had no time to savor her reprieve, for it was then that she recognized the man in command of the knights. As if feeling her eyes upon him, he glanced her way, and at once acknowledged her with a gallant gesture only slightly spoiled by the bloodied sword in his hand.

"Dear God," Constance whispered, sitting back in the window seat. Martina was beside her now and when she asked who he was, Constance managed a faint, mirthless smile. "His name is Elias of Gesualdo, and he is both my salvation and my downfall. He arrived just in time to spare our lives, but on the morrow, he will deliver me into the hands of his uncle—Tancred of Lecce."

The following four months were difficult ones for Constance. She knew Tancred well enough to be sure she'd be treated kindly, and she was. Tancred and his queen, Sybilla, acted as if she were an honored guest rather than a prisoner, albeit one under constant discreet surveillance. But she found it humiliating to be utterly dependent upon the mercy of the man who'd usurped her throne, and she could not help contrasting her barrenness with Sybilla's fecundity, mother to two sons and three daughters. She was even more mortified when Heinrich adamantly refused to make any concessions in order to gain her freedom. It was not to be her husband who eventually pried open the door of her gilded prison. Pope Celestine agreed to give Tancred what he most wanted—papal recognition of his kingship—but in return he wanted Constance transferred to his custody. Tancred reluctantly agreed, and on a January day in 1192, Constance found herself riding toward Rome in the company of three cardinals and an armed escort.

She'd not find freedom in Rome, for the Pope saw her as a valuable hostage in his dealings with Heinrich, but at least she'd not be living in the same palace with Tancred and his queen. And a prolonged stay in Rome was not entirely unwelcome, for she was not eager to be reunited with the man who'd put her in such peril and then done nothing to rescue her from a predicament of his own making.

The cardinals seemed uncomfortable with their role as gaolers and set a pace that would be easy for Constance and her ladies. There were only three now, Adela, Hildegund, and Dame Martina, for her Sicilian attendants had chosen to remain in their homeland, and after the horror of Salerno, Constance could not blame them. They'd been on the road for several hours when Constance saw their scout galloping back toward their party, his expression grim. Nudging her mare forward, she joined the cardinals as they conferred with him. As she reined in beside them, they forced smiles, explaining that there was a band of suspicious-looking men up ahead who might well be bandits. They thought it best to turn aside and avoid a confrontation.

Constance agreed blandly that it was indeed best, her face giving away nothing. They had forgotten that Latin was one of the official languages of Sicily, and while she was not as fluent as Heinrich, she'd caught two words in the conversation that had ended abruptly as she came within earshot—*praesidium imperatoris*. It was not bandits they feared. The men up ahead were members of Heinrich's elite imperial guard.

Constance did not know how they happened to be here, but it did not matter. Dropping back beside her women, she told them softly to be ready to act when she did. She could see the riders for herself now in the distance. When the cardinals and their men veered off the main road onto a dirt lane that led away from the Liri River, Constance followed. Waiting until the guard riding at her side moved ahead of her mare, she suddenly brought her whip down upon the horse's haunches. The startled animal shot forward as if launched by a crossbow, and she was already yards away before the cardinals and their escort realized what had happened. She heard shouting and glanced back to see that several of the cardinals' men were in pursuit, their stallions swift enough to outrun her mare. But by then the imperial guards were riding toward her. Pulling back the hood of her mantle so there'd be no doubt, she cried out, "I am your empress. I put myself under your protection."

The cardinals did their best, angrily warning the Germans that they'd bring the wrath of the Holy Father down upon their heads if they interfered, insisting that the empress was in the custody of the

Pope. The imperial guards merely laughed at them. Constance and her ladies were soon riding away with their new protectors, the knights thrilled to have recovered such a prize, knowing that their fortunes were made. Constance's women were elated, too. But while Constance felt a grim sense of satisfaction, she did not share their jubilation. She was still a hostage. Even an imperial crown did not change that.

Two years after Constance's fortuitous encounter with Heinrich's imperial guards, Tancred was dying in his palace at Palermo. His was a bitter end, for his nineteen-year-old son had died suddenly in December, leaving a four-year-old boy as his heir, and he knew fear of the Holy Roman emperor would prevail over loyalty to a child. Upon learning of Tancred's death, Heinrich led an army across the Alps into Italy once again.

Upon their May arrival in Milan, Constance had gone to bed, saying she must rest before the evening's feast given in their honor by the Bishop of Milan. Adela had been concerned about her mistress for some weeks, but this open acknowledgment of fatigue, so unlike Constance, sent her searching for Dame Martina. Once they'd found a private corner safe from eavesdroppers, she confessed that she feared the empress was ailing. Martina was not surprised, for she, too, had noticed Constance's flagging appetite, exhaustion, and pallor.

"I've spoken to her," she admitted, "but she insists she is well. I fear that her downcast spirits are affecting her health. . . ." She let her words trail off, sure that Adela would understand. They both knew Constance was troubled by what the future held for Sicily and its people. She'd not said as much, but there was no need to put her unspoken fears into words, for they knew the man she'd married. "I will speak with her again after the revelries tonight," she promised, and Adela had to be content with that.

When Adela returned to Constance's chamber, she was relieved to find the empress up and dressing, for that made it easier to believe she was not ill, merely tired. Once she was ready to descend to the great hall where Heinrich and the Bishop of Milan awaited her, her ladies exclaimed over the beauty of her gown, brocaded silk the color of a Sicilian sunrise, and the jewelry that was worth a king's ransom, but Constance felt like a richly wrapped gift that was empty inside.

Heinrich was waiting impatiently. "You're late," he murmured as she slipped her arm through his. They'd had one of the worst quarrels of their marriage a fortnight ago and the strain still showed. They'd patched up a peace, were civil both in public and private, but nothing had changed. They were still at odds over Salerno. Constance agreed that the Salernitans deserved punishment. She'd have been satisfied with razing the town walls and imposing a heavy fine upon its inhabitants, for they'd acted out of terror, not treachery. Heinrich saw it differently, saying they owed him a blood debt and he meant to collect it. Constance thought that his implacable

hatred toward the men and women of Salerno was a
fire fed by his awareness that he'd made a great mistake, a mistake he would never acknowledge. But
despite her anger, she'd not reached for that weapon,
knowing it would rebound back upon her. Glancing at
him now from the corner of her eye, she felt a flicker
of weary resentment, and then summoned up a smile
for the man approaching them.

She'd met Bishop Milo two years ago at Lodi and
it was easy enough to draw upon those memories
for polite conversation. She was accustomed to making such social small talk. This time it would be different, though. She'd barely had a chance to acknowledge
his flowery greeting when the ground seemed to shift
under her feet, as if she were suddenly on the deck of
a ship. She started to say she needed to sit, but it
was too late. She was already spiraling down into the
dark.

Constance settled back against the pillows, watching
as Martina inspected a glass vial of her urine. She'd
asked no questions during the doctor's examination,
not sure she wanted the answers, for she'd suspected
for some time that she might be seriously ill. She was
about to ask for wine when the door opened and her
husband entered, followed by a second man whose appearance, uninvited, in the empress's quarters shocked
her ladies.

"I want my physician to examine you," Heinrich
announced without preamble. "You are obviously ill
and need care that this woman cannot provide."

Constance sat up in bed. "'This woman' is a li-

censed physician, Heinrich. I want her to attend me."
Unable to resist a small jab, she added, "She studied in
Salerno and was with me during the assault upon the
palace, where she showed both courage and loyalty.
I trust her judgment."

He mustered up a smile that never reached his
eyes. "I am sure she is competent for womanly ail-
ments. Nonetheless, I want Master Conrad to take
over your treatment. I must insist, my dear, for your
health is very important to me."

That, Constance did not doubt; it would be awkward for him if she were to die before he could be
crowned King of Sicily, for then he'd have no claim
to the throne other than right of conquest. "No," she
said flatly, and saw a muscle twitch in his cheek as
his eyes narrowed. But Martina chose that moment
to intervene.

"Whilst I am gratified by the empress's faith in my
abilities," she said smoothly, "I am sure Master Conrad is a physician of renown. But there is no need for
another opinion. I already know what caused the empress to faint."

Heinrich did not bother to mask his skepticism.
"Do you, indeed?"

Martina regarded him calmly. "I do. The empress
is with child."

Constance gasped, her eyes widening. Heinrich was
no less stunned. Reaching out, he grasped Martina's
arm. "Are you sure? God save you if you lie!"

"Heinrich!" Constance's protest went unheeded.
Martina met Heinrich's eyes without flinching, and
after a moment he released his hold.

"I am very sure," Martina said confidently, and

this time she directed her words at Constance. "By my reckoning, you will be a mother ere the year is out."

Constance lay back, closing her eyes. When she opened them again, Heinrich was leaning over the bed. "You must rest now," he said. "You can do nothing that might put the baby at risk."

"You will have to continue on without me, Heinrich, for I must travel very slowly." He agreed so readily that she realized that she had leverage now, for the first time in their marriage. He leaned over still farther, his lips brushing her cheek, and when he straightened, he told Martina that his wife was to have whatever she wanted and her commands were to be obeyed straightaway, as if they came from his own mouth. Beckoning to Master Conrad, who'd been shifting awkwardly from foot to foot, he started toward the door. There he paused and, looking back at Constance, he laughed, a sound so rare that the women all started, as if hearing thunder in a clear, cloudless sky.

"God has indeed blessed me," he said exultantly. "Who can doubt now that my victory in Sicily is ordained?"

As soon as the door closed behind him, Constance reached out her hand to Martina, their fingers entwining. "Are you sure?" She was echoing Heinrich's words, but his had been a threat; hers were both a plea and a prayer.

"I am indeed sure, my lady. You told me your last flux was in March. Did you never think . . . ?"

"No . . . my fluxes have been irregular the last year or two. I thought . . . I feared I might be reaching that age when a woman could no longer conceive." It was more than that, though. She'd not thought she might be pregnant because she no longer had hope.

Adela was weeping, calling her "my lamb" as if she were back in the nursery. Hildegund had dropped to her knees, giving thanks to the Almighty, and Katerina, the youngest of her ladies, was dancing around the chamber, as light on her feet as a windblown leaf. Constance wanted to weep and pray and dance, too. Instead, she laughed, the laughter of the carefree girl she'd once been, back in the days of her youth when her world had been filled with tropical sunlight and she'd never imagined the fate that was to be hers—exile in a frigid foreign land and a marriage that was as barren as her womb.

Dismissing the others to return to the festivities, for she wanted only Adela and Martina with her now, she placed her hand upon her belly, trying to envision the tiny entity that now shared her body. So great was her joy that she could at last speak the truth. "I'd not celebrated Tancred's death," she confided. "I could not, for I knew what it meant for Sicily. It would become merely another appendage of the Holy Roman Empire, its riches plundered, its independence gone, and its very identity lost. But now . . . now it will pass to my son. He will rule Sicily as my father and nephew did. He will be more than its king. He will be its savior."

At that, Adela began to weep in earnest and Martina found herself smiling through tears. "You ought to at least consider, madame, that you may have a daughter."

Constance laughed again. "And I would have welcomed one, Martina. But this child will be a boy. The Almighty has blessed us with a miracle. How else could I become pregnant in my forty-first year after a marriage of eight barren years? It is God's Will that I give birth to a son."

Despite her euphoria, Constance was well aware that the odds were not in her favor; at her age, having a first child posed considerable risks, with miscarriage and stillbirth very real dangers. She chose to pass the most perilous months of her pregnancy at a Benedictine nunnery in Meda, north of Milan, and when she did resume her travels, it was done in easy stages. She had selected the Italian town of Jesi for her lying-in. Located on the crest of a hill overlooking the Esino River, it had fortified walls and was friendly to the Holy Roman Empire; Heinrich had provided her with his imperial guards, but Constance was taking no chances of another Salerno.

Although she'd been spared much of the early morning nausea that so many women endured, her pregnancy was not an easy one. Her ankles and feet were badly swollen, her breasts very sore and tender, and she was exhausted all the time, suffering backaches, heartburn, breathlessness, and sudden mood swings. But some of her anxiety eased upon her arrival in Jesi, for Martina assured her she was less likely to miscarry in the last months. She was heartened, too, by the friendliness of Jesi's citizens, who seemed genuinely pleased that she'd chosen to have her baby in their town, and as November slid into December, she was calmer than at any time in her pregnancy.

Heinrich's army had encountered little resistance, and the surrender of Naples in August caused a widespread defection from Tancred's embattled queen and young son. Constance was troubled to learn of the bloody vengeance Heinrich had wreaked upon Salerno in September, but she heeded Martina's admonition that too much distress might harm her baby and tried to put from her mind images of burning houses, bodies, grieving widows, and terrified children. In November, she was delighted by the arrival of Baldwin, Michael, and several of her household knights. When Heinrich took Salerno, they'd been freed from captivity and he sent them on to Jesi. Constance joked to Martina that her marriage would have been much happier had she only been pregnant the entire time; by now they were far more than physician and patient, sharing the rigors of her pregnancy as they'd shared the dangers in Salerno.

In December, Constance learned that Heinrich had been admitted into Palermo and Sybilla had yielded upon his promise that her family would be safe and her son allowed to inherit Tancred's lands in Lecce. Constance could not help feeling some sympathy for Sybilla and she was gladdened by the surprising leniency of Heinrich's terms. She was staying in the Bishop of Jesi's palace, and they celebrated Heinrich's upcoming coronation with as lavish a feast as Advent allowed. Later that day, she was tempted by the mild weather to venture out into the gardens.

Accompanied by Hildegund and Katerina, she was seated in a trellised arbor when there was a commotion at the end of the garden and several young men trooped in, tossing a pig's-bladder ball back and forth. Constance recognized them—one of the bishop's clerks and two of Heinrich's household knights, who'd been entrusted to bring her word of his triumph. Setting down her embroidery, she smiled at their tomfoolery, thinking that one day it would be her son playing camp ball with his friends.

"The emperor has been truly blessed by God this year." Constance could no longer see them, but she knew their voices. This speaker was Pietro, the clerk, who went on to ask rhetorically how many men gained a crown and an heir in one year. "God grant," he added piously, "that the empress will birth a son." There was a burst of laughter from Heinrich's knights, and when Pietro spoke again, he sounded puzzled. "Why do you laugh? It is in the Almighty's Hands, after all."

"You truly are an innocent." This voice was Johann's, the older of the knights. "Do you really think that the emperor would go to so much trouble to secure an heir and then present the world with a girl? When pigs fly!"

Constance's head came up sharply, and she raised a hand for silence when Katerina would have spoken. "I do not understand your meaning," Pietro said, and now there was a note of wariness in his voice.

"Yes, you do. You are just loath to say it aloud. After eight years, Lord Heinrich well knew he was accursed with a barren wife. Then, lo and behold, this miraculous pregnancy. Why do you think the empress chose this godforsaken town, truly at the back of beyond, for her lying-in? It would have been much harder in Naples or Palermo, too many suspicious eyes. Here it will be easy. Word will spread that her labor pangs have begun, and under cover of night the babe will be smuggled in—mayhap one of Heinrich's by-blows—and then the church bells will peal out joyfully the news that the emperor has a robust, healthy son."

Constance caught her breath, her hand clenching around the embroidery; she never even felt the needle jabbing into her palm. Katerina half rose, but subsided when Hildegund put a restraining hand on her arm.

"Clearly you had too much wine at dinner," Pietro said coldly, which set off more laughter from the young knights. By now Constance was on her feet. As she emerged from the arbor, Pietro saw her first and made a deep obeisance. "Madame!"

The blood drained from Johann's face, leaving him whiter than a corpse candle. "Ma-madame," he stuttered, "I—I am so very sorry! It was but a jest. As—as Pietro said, I'd quaffed too much wine." His words were slurring in his haste to get them said, his voice high-pitched and tremulous. "Truly, I had to be in my cups to make such a vile joke. . . ."

Constance's own voice was like ice, if ice could burn. "I wonder if my lord husband will find your jest as amusing as you do."

Johann made a strangled sound, then fell to his knees. "Madame . . . please," he entreated, "please . . . I beg of you, do not tell him. . . ."

Constance stared down at him until he began to sob, and then turned and walked away. Johann crumpled to the ground, Pietro and the other knight still frozen where they stood. Hildegund glared at the weeping knight, then hurried after Constance, with Katerina right behind her. "Will she tell the emperor?" she whispered, feeling a twinge of unwelcome pity for Johann's stark terror.

Hildegund shook her head. "I think not," she said, very low, and then spat, "Damn that misbegotten, callow lackwit to eternal damnation for this! Of all things for our lady to hear as her time grows nigh . . ."

"My lamb, what does it matter what a fool like that thinks?"

Constance paid no heed. She'd been pacing back and forth, seething, showing a command of curses that her women did not know she'd possessed. But when she lost color and began to pant, Martina put an arm around her shoulders and steered her toward a chair. Coming back a few moments later with a wine cup, she put it in Constance's hand. "Drink this, my lady. It will calm your nerves. Adela is right: you are upsetting yourself for naught. Surely you knew there would be mean-spirited talk like this, men eager to believe the worst of the emperor?"

Constance set the cup down so abruptly that wine splashed onto her sleeve. "Of course I knew that, Martina! Heinrich has more enemies than Rome has priests. But do you not see? These were his own knights, men sworn to die for him if need be. If even *they* doubt my pregnancy . . ."

Adela knelt by the chair, wincing as her old bones protested. "It does not matter," she repeated stoutly. "The chattering of magpies, no more than that."

Constance's outrage had given way now to despair. "It does matter! My son will come into this world under a shadow, under suspicion. People will not believe he is truly the flesh of my flesh, the rightful heir to the Sicilian crown. He will have to fight his entire life against calumnies and slander. Rebels can claim it as a pretext for rising up against him. A hostile Pope might well declare him illegitimate. He will never be free of the whispers, the doubts . . ." She closed her eyes, tears beginning to seep through her lashes. "What if he comes to believe it himself. . . ?"

Adela began to weep, too. Martina reached for Constance's arm and gently but firmly propelled her to her feet. "As I said, this serves for naught. Even if you are right and your fears are justified, there is nothing you can do to disprove the gossip. Now I want you to lie down and get some rest. You must think of your baby's welfare whilst he is in your womb, not what he might face in years to come."

Constance did not argue; let them put her to bed. But she did not sleep, lying awake as the sky darkened and then slowly began to streak with light again, hearing Johann's voice as he mocked the very idea that Heinrich's aging, barren wife could conceive.

Baldwin was uneasy, for it was not fitting that he be summoned to his lady's private chamber; he was sure Heinrich would not approve. "You sent for me, Madame?" he asked, trying to conceal his dismay at his empress's haggard, ashen appearance.

"I have a task for you, Sir Baldwin." Constance was sitting in a chair, her hands so tightly clasped that her ring was digging into her flesh. "I want you to set up a pavilion in the piazza. And then I want you to send men into the streets, telling the people that I shall have my lying-in there, in that tent, and the matrons and maidens of Jesi are invited to attend the birth of my child."

Baldwin's jaw dropped; for the life of him, he could think of nothing to say. But Constance's women were not speechless and they burst into scandalized protest. She heard them out and then told Baldwin to see that her command was obeyed. He'd seen this expression on her face once before, as she was about to step out onto that Salerno balcony, and he knelt, kissing her hand. "It will be done, madame."

Adela, Hildegund, and Katerina had subsided, staring at her in shocked silence. Martina leaned over the chair, murmuring, "Are you sure you want to do this?"

Constance's breath hissed through her teeth. "Christ on the Cross, Martina! Of course I do not want to do this!" Raising her head then, she said, "But I *will* do it! I will do it for my son."

On the day after Christmas, the piazza was as crowded as if it were a market day. There was a festive atmosphere, for the townsmen knew they were witnessing something extraordinary—at least their wives were. Occasionally one of them would emerge from the tent to report that all was going as it ought and then disappear back inside. The men joked and gossiped and wagered upon the sex of the child struggling to be born. Within the tent, the mood was quite different. At first, the women of Jesi had been excited, whispering among themselves, feeling like spectators at a Christmas play. But almost all of them had their own experiences in the birthing chamber, had endured what Constance was suffering now, and as they watched her writhe on the birthing stool, her skin damp with perspiration, her face contorted with pain, they began to identify with her, to forget that she was an empress, highborn and wealthy and privileged beyond their wildest dreams. They'd been honored to bear witness to such a historic event. Now they found themselves cheering her on as if she were one of them, for they were all daughters of Eve and, when it came to childbirth, sisters under the skin.

Martina was consulting with two of the town's midwives, their voices low, their faces intent. Adela was coaxing Constance to swallow a spoonful of honey, saying it would give her strength, and she forced herself to take it upon her tongue. She knew why they were so concerned. When her waters had broken, they told her it meant the birth was nigh, yet her pains continued, growing more severe, and it did not seem to her that any progress was being made. "I want Martina," she mumbled, and when the physician hastened back to her side, she caught the other woman's wrist. "Remember . . . if you cannot save us both, save the child. . . ." Her words were faint and fading, but her eyes blazed so fiercely that Martina could not look away. "Promise . . ." she insisted,

"... promise," and the other woman nodded, not trusting her voice.

Time had no meaning anymore for Constance; there was no world beyond the stifling confines of this tent. They gave her wine mixed with bark of cassia fistula, lifted her stained chemise to massage her belly, anointed her female parts with hot thyme oil, and when she continued to struggle, some of the women slipped away to pray for her in the church close by the piazza. But Martina kept insisting that it would be soon now, that her womb was dilating, holding out hope like a candle to banish the dark, and after an eternity Constance heard her cry out that she could see the baby's head. She bore down one more time and her child's shoulders were free. "Again," Martina urged, and then a little body, skin red and puckered, slid out in a gush of blood and mucus, into the midwife's waiting hands.

Constance sagged back, holding her breath until she heard it, the soft mewing sound that proved her baby lived. Martina's smile was as radiant as a sunrise. "A man-child, Madame! You have a son!"

"Let me have him . . ." Constance said feebly. There was so much still to be done. The naval cord must be tied and cut. The baby must be cleaned and rubbed with salt before being swaddled. The afterbirth must be expelled and then buried so as not to attract demons. But Martina knew that all could wait. Taking the baby, she placed him in his mother's arms, and as they watched Constance hold her son for the first time, few of the women had dry eyes.

———

When word spread six days later that the empress would be displaying her son in public, the piazza was thronged hours before she was to make her appearance. The men had heard their women's stories of the birth and were eager to see the miracle infant for themselves; he was a native of Jesi, after all, they joked, one of their own. The crowd parted as Constance's litter entered the square, and they applauded politely as she was assisted to the ground, moved slowly toward the waiting chair. Once she was seated, she signaled and Martina handed her a small, bundled form. Constance drew back the blanket, revealing a head of feathery, reddish hair. As the infant waved his tiny fists, she held him up for all to see. "My son, Frederick," she said, loudly and clearly, "who will one day be King of Sicily."

They applauded again and smiled when Frederick let out a sudden, lusty cry. Constance smiled, too. "I think he is hungry," she said, and the mothers in the crowd nodded knowingly, looking around for the wet nurse; highborn ladies like Constance did not suckle their own babies. They were taken aback by what happened next. The empress's ladies came forward, temporarily blocking the crowd's view. When they stepped aside, a gasp swept the crowd, for Constance had opened her mantle, adjusted her bodice, and begun to nurse her son. When the townspeople realized what she was doing—offering final, indisputable, public proof that this was a child of her body, her flesh and blood—they began to cheer loudly. Even those who were hostile to Constance's German husband joined in, for courage deserved to be acknowledged, to be honored, and they all knew they were watching an act of defiant bravery, the ultimate expression of a mother's love.

Author's Note:

Constance was obviously a courageous woman, but was she also a dangerous one? The events following Frederick's birth give us our answer. Heinrich's generous peace terms had been bait for a trap. He'd shown his hand during his Christmas coronation by having the bodies of Tancred and his son dragged from their royal tombs. Four days later, he claimed to discover a plot against him and ordered that Sybilla, her children, and the leading Sicilian lords be arrested and taken to Germany. Sybilla and her daughters eventually escaped, but her five-year-old son died soon after being sent to a monastery, said to have been blinded and castrated before his death. Heinrich's heavy-handed rule provoked a genuine rebellion in 1197, and there is some evidence that Constance was involved in the conspiracy. Heinrich certainly thought so, for he forced her to watch as he executed the ringleader by having a red-hot crown nailed to his head. But in September 1197, Heinrich died unexpectedly at Messina. Constance at once took control of the government, surrounded herself with Sicilian advisers, and expelled all the Germans. But she would survive Heinrich by barely a year, in which she worked feverishly to protect her son. She had him crowned and then formed an alliance with the new Pope, Innocent III, naming him as Frederick's guardian before her death in November 1198 at age forty-four. Frederick would prove to be one of the most brilliant, controversial, and remarkable rulers of the Middle Ages—King of Sicily, Holy Roman Emperor, even King of Jerusalem. And Constance? Dante placed her in Paradise.

S. M. Stirling

When all that's left between you and the total collapse of civilization is the law, you need somebody tough enough to enforce it—no matter what the cost.

Considered by many to be the natural heir to Harry Turtledove's title of King of the Alternate History Novel, fast-rising science fiction star S. M. Stirling is the bestselling author of the Island in the Sea of Time series (*Island in the Sea of Time, Against the Tide of Years, On the Oceans of Eternity*), in which Nantucket comes unstuck in time and is cast back to the year 1250 B.C., and the Draka series (including *Marching Through Georgia, Under the Yoke, The Stone Dogs,* and *Drakon,* plus an anthology of Draka stories by other hands edited by Stirling, *Drakas!*), in which Tories fleeing the American Revolution set up a militant society in South Africa and eventually end up conquering most of the Earth. He's also produced the Dies the Fire series (*Dies the Fire, The Protector's War, A Meeting at Corvallis*), plus the five-volume Fifth Millennium series, and the seven-volume series The General (with David Drake), as well as stand-alone novels such as *Conquistador* and *The Peshawar Lancers*. Stirling has also written novels in collaboration with Raymond E. Feist, Jerry Pournelle, Holly Lisle, Shirley Meier, Karen Wehrstein, and *Star Trek* actor James Doohan, as well as contributed to the Babylon 5, T2, Brainship, War World, and the Man-Kzin Wars series. His short fiction has been collected in *Ice, Iron and Gold*. Stirling's newest series include the Change series, consisting of *The Sunrise Lands, The Scourge of God, The Sword of the Lady, The High King of Montival,* and *The Tears of the Sun,* and the Lords of Creation series, consisting of *The Sky People* and *In the Courts of the Crimson Kings*. Most recently, he started a new series, Shadowspawn, which consists so far of *A Taint in the Blood* and *The Council of Shadows*. His most recent novel is a new volume in the Change series, *Lord of Mountains*. Born in France and raised in Europe, Africa, and Canada, he now lives with his family in Santa Fe, New Mexico.

PRONOUNCING DOOM

DUN CARSON
(EAST-CENTRAL WILLAMETTE VALLEY)
DÙTHCHAS OF THE CLAN MACKENZIE
(FORMERLY WESTERN OREGON)
5TH AUGUST, CHANGE YEAR 1/1999 AD

I am riding to pass sentence on an evildoer, Juniper Mackenzie thought. *It's part of being Chief, but I liked being a folk musician a lot better! The old tales were less stressful as songs than real life.*

"Water soon, Riona," she said to her horse, and the mare twitched her ears backward.

The smell of horse sweat from the dozen mounts of her party was strong, though she'd been used to that even before the Change; a horse-drawn Traveler wagon had been part of her persona, as well as fun. It was a hot day after a dry week, perfect harvest weather, which was more important than comfort. It didn't *usually* rain in summertime here, but that didn't mean it absolutely couldn't happen.

In the old world before the machines stopped, rain would have been a nuisance. Now, in the new world—where food came from within walking distance or didn't come at all—it would be a disaster. So the heat and the sun that threatened her freckled redhead's skin was a good thing, and the sweat and prickling be damned. At least there was less smoke in the air than there had been last summer, in the first Change Year.

Her mouth thinned a little at the memory; it had been burning cities then, and forest fires raging through woods where deadwood had accumulated through generations of humans trying to suppress the burn cycle. The pall had lain like smog all over the Willamette country, caught in the great valley between the Cascades and the Coast Range until the autumn rains washed it out.

Always a little bitter on the lips, the taste of a world going down in flame and horror. Always reminding you of what was happening away from your refuge.

With a practiced effort of will she started to force herself back into the moment, to the slow clop of hooves on the asphalt, the moving creak of leather between her thighs and the sleeping face of her son in the light carrying-cradle across the saddlebow before her. Strips of shadow from the roadside trees fell across her face, like a slow flicker as the horses walked.

You had to learn to do that, or the memories would drive you mad. Many *had* gone mad with what they'd seen and done and endured after the machines stopped, in screaming fits or rocking and weeping or just an apathy that killed as certainly as knife or rope or *Yersinia pestis* in the lungs. Many of them people who might have lived, otherwise. Even now there was still very little to spare for those not functional enough to pull their weight, though the definition of *sane* had gotten much more elastic.

What surplus there was had to go to the children; they'd rescued as many orphans as they could. When a youngster learned to laugh again, it gave you heart that the world would go on.

So you're not smelling fire all the time this year. Enjoy that. Think about the children growing up in a world you have to make worth it; your children, and all the others. Don't think of the rest. Especially don't think of what those mass graves in the refugee camps around Salem smelled like, where the Black Death hit. She hadn't gotten very close, on that scouting trip. But close enough—

No.

Scents of dust, the subtly varied baked-green smells of grass and trees and crops, the slight musty sweetness of cut stems. The lands around Dun Carson were mostly harvested now, flat squares of dun stubble alternating with pasture, clumps of lushly green Douglas fir and Garry oak at intervals or along creeks running low and slow with summer.

A reaper pulled by two of those priceless quarter horses traded from the ranching country east of the Cascades was finishing its work as they passed. The crude wire-and-wood machine had been built over the winter from a model salvaged from a museum. Its revolving creel pushed through the last of a rippling yellow-blond field and the rattling belt behind the cutting bar left a swath of cut grain in its wake. The driver looked up long enough to wave, then went back to her work.

Last year they'd used scythes from garden-supply stores and from walls where they'd been souvenirs for lifetimes, and improvised sickles and bread-knives and the bare hands of desperately unskilled refugees working until they dropped. Farming like this was grinding hard work even if you knew what you were doing, and so few did. Fortunately they had a few to direct and teach the rest, some real farmers, some hobbyists, and a few utterly priceless Amish fled from settlements overrun by the waves of starving refugees or the kidnap squads of Norman Arminger, the northern warlord.

We've mostly harvested what we planted last year; now we need to get on to the volunteer fields.

Much—most—of the land planted to grain before the Change had just stood until the kernels fell out of the ear. Chaos and fighting as people spilled out of cities instantly uninhabitable when electricity and engines failed, plague and bandits and sheer lack of tools and skill. A field left like that self-seeded enough to produce a second crop, thin and patchy and weedy but a thousand times more valuable than gold.

Sunlight flashed off the spears of the binders following along behind the reaper. They moved the weapons up each time they advanced to tie a new double armful of cut wheat into sheaves and stand them in neat tripods. She blinked at the way the honed metal cast the light back, remembering . . .

. . . the little girl the Eaters used as decoy giggling and bringing out the knife and cutting for her throat, and the smell so much like roast pork from the shuttered buildings behind her . . .

"Focus," Judy Barstow Mackenzie said from her other side.

And we help each other to . . . not exactly forget . . . put it aside. Are any of us still completely sane? Are there any of us who aren't suffering from ... post-traumatic stress disorder, wasn't it called? Certainly it's the ones who were least anchored in the world-as-it-was who've done best since the Change. The rest cling to us.

"Thanks," Juniper said.

"What's a Maiden for?" Judy said stoutly. "If not to keep her High Priestess on track?"

The tone was light, but Juniper leaned over and touched her shoulder.

"And friends," she said. "Friends do that."

They'd known each other since their early teens—a decade and a half ago, now, and they'd discovered the Craft together. They were very unlike: Juniper short and slight and with eyes of willow-leaf green, Judy bold-featured, big-boned, and olive-skinned, raven-haired and inclined to be a little stout in the old days.

"That too, sure and it is, arra!" Judy said in a mock-Irish accent plastered over her usual strong trace of New York, and winked. "I wouldn't be thinkin' otherwise."

Juniper winced slightly at the brogue. *She* could talk that way and sound like the real thing. Her mother had been genuine-article Irish when she met a young American airman on leave in the London pub where she was working. From Achill Island in the west of County Mayo at that, where she'd grown up speaking Gaelic. That burbling lilt had only tinged Juniper's General American, except when she let it out deliberately during performances—she'd been a singer before the Change, working the Renaissance Faires and pagan festivals and conventions.

Nowadays she used it more and more, especially on public occasions. If people were going to put it on anyway, at least she could give them something more to imitate than fading memories of bad movies on late-night TV.

"It's going to be unpleasant, but straightforward," Judy said seriously. "I did the examination and there's no doubt about it. He's guilty and he deserves it."

"I know." Juniper took a deep breath. "I don't know why I'm feeling so . . . out of control," she said. "And that's a fact. It's . . ."

She looked upward, into a sky with only a few high white wisps of cloud.

"It's as if there were a thunderstorm coming, and there isn't."

The Dun Juniper procession came around the bend and Juniper sighed to herself at the sight of the tarps strung by the crossroads between the roadside firs and oaks and Lombardy poplars. Partly that was sheer desire for shade. Partly it was . . .

Her daughter's fingers flew; Eilir had been deaf since birth:

Why the frustrated sighing, Great Mother? she asked. *They've done what you asked.*

Juniper sent her a quick, irritated glance. Eilir looked as tired as her mother felt, despite being fourteen and very fit. She was tall, already a few inches taller than her mother, strong and graceful as a deer; the splendid body was a legacy of her father, who'd been an athlete and football player.

And a thoughtless selfish bastard who got a teen-

*ager pregnant on her first time and in the backseat
of his car at that. But then Eilir's wit and heart come
from the Mackenzie side, I think!*

Juniper filled her lungs and let the flash of temper
out with the breath, a technique mastered long ago.

She signed: *Do you feel it? There's an* anger *in the
air. In the ground, in the feel of things, like a louring
threat.*

Eilir's pale blue eyes narrowed, then went a little
distant.

I think so, Spooky-Mom, she replied after a moment. *Yes, a bit.*

They both looked at Judy, who shook her head
and shrugged.

"Not me. You're the mystical one. I just made
sure we had clean robes and plenty of candles for
the Sabbats."

The Earth is the Mother's, Eilir signed, her face
utterly stark for once. *Maybe it's Her anger we're
feeling.*

They halted in the center where the roads met. Juniper handed down her nine-month-old son, Rudi,
to Melissa Aylward Mackenzie, swelling with her
own pregnancy.

"I feel it too," the younger woman said seriously.

She was new-come to the Old Religion, like so
many others, but already High Priestess of Dun Fairfax, and here to help with organizing the rite.

"Let's hope we're doing the right thing in Her eyes,
then," Juniper said. "Get the littles in order, would
you, Mellie? This is going to be hard on them."

She nodded soberly, then smiled a little as she

hefted Rudi expertly. Juniper shook her head and stretched in a creak of saddle leather; riding made your back ache. Some distant part of her noticed how casual people had already become about standing in the middle of roads, now that cars and trucks were a fading memory.

We've better things to do than this, she went on to her daughter. Her fingers and hands danced, as fluent as speaking aloud: *It's the harvest and nobody has time to spare. Spending most of yesterday and last night hammering out the ritual and the guidelines for this was hard, even with ten minds pooled together. I hate having to do things on the fly, especially when it's setting a precedent . . . but what else can we do?*

Eilir shrugged. *Lock him up like they used to, until it's convenient?*

Juniper didn't bother to dignify that with an answer; it wasn't meant to be taken seriously. Nor could they spare anyone to supervise a criminal's labor, even if they were willing to go down that road, which they weren't.

Sam Aylward, her chief armsman, held her stirrup as she dismounted. She stretched again as her boots touched the asphalt, settling the plaid pinned across her shoulder with a twitch. The Dun Juniper contingent were all wearing the same Highland costume, one that had started as half a joke and spread because it was so convenient. All in a sort of dark green–light brown–dull orange tartan that owed everything to a warehouse full of salvaged blankets and nothing whatsoever to Scotland.

About a third of the Dun Fairfax folk wore the

kilt too, and the clothing of the rest showed in tears and patches and tatters why the pre-Change clothes were running out so shockingly fast. They just weren't designed to stand up under the sort of daily grind of hard outdoor labor that nearly everyone did these days. And salvaging more from the unburned parts of the cities was getting to be impossibly dangerous and labor-intensive now that the nearby towns had been stripped. Only big well-armed parties could do it at all, what with bandits and pint-sized warlords popping up everywhere and the crawling terror of the Eater bands lurking in the ruins amid their hideous game of stalking and feasting.

A note popped up from the vast sprawling mental file cabinet she had to lug around these days:

Check on the flax and wool and spinning-wheel projects after we've got the harvest out of the way. We don't need to make our own cloth yet, but we have to have the seeds and tools and skills built up for when we do.

She'd been a skilled amateur weaver herself before the Change, and they'd organized classes in it over the winter. Fortunately it was something you could put down and pick up later.

Melissa left her group and walked over to the stretched tarp shelter to the southwest of the crossroads where the children and nursing mothers sat. Rudi gurgled and waved chubby arms, his eyes and delighted toothless smile fixed on her face.

Thank the Lord and Lady he's a good baby. Eilir was a lot more trouble. Of course, I had less knowledge then, and a great deal less help. It really does take a village, or at least that makes it a lot easier.

"They're doing flags for all the Duns," Juniper observed to Chuck Barstow. "It's a good idea, sure. People need symbols."

"Dennie had it right when he insisted on the green flag, though," Chuck said. "We need a symbol for the whole Clan as well. Where do you want it?"

Juniper pursed her lips. She'd made the old sigil of the Singing Moon Coven into a flag: dark antlers and crescent silver moon on green silk. Embroidery was another skill that had turned from hobby to cherished lifeline. The still air of the late summer made it and all the others planted around the tarp shelters hang limp, as if waiting with indrawn breath. Fortunately hers was suspended from a crossbar on the staff, which meant you could see what was on it.

"Next to Dun Carson's, please."

Dun Carson's silver labrys on blood red was planted right in front of the northwest tarp, where the crossroads made a vaguely north–south, east–west cross. Chuck planted the point on the bottom of the Clan's into the earth with a shove and twist. Brian Carson stood with his brother's widow and his orphaned niece and nephew, next to the two tables she'd requested at the center. His wife, Rebekah, stood on his other side, looking a little stiff.

Melissa and her helpers took over the job of looking after the littles. The southeast quadrant held representatives from other duns within a fifteen-mile radius; volunteers came forward to take the horses, unsaddling and hobbling and watering them before turning them loose in a pasture.

How the Change has limited us, thought Juniper. *Fifteen miles is a long way again! This will be re-*

corded and sent out in the Sun Circle. *Some witnessing is a good idea, but turning it into a circus is not.*

There were better than fifty adults under the judgment tarp, probably ten or fifteen teenagers—

—*eòghann*, thought Juniper. *We'll call them* eòghann.

That meant *youth* or *helper* in her mother's language.

We need a name for the teenagers who are ready to begin to learn the adult needs and responsibilities, but not yet given a vote. Eòghann will do, since everyone seems determined to play at being Celts.

Juniper shook herself slightly. The profound silence was broken only by the occasional wail from one of the babies, the hoof-clop of a horse shifting its weight or a cough coming through clearly. No trace of the whine and murmur of machine noise in the background anymore, and that still startled her sometimes with a quietness unlike anything she'd ever experienced unless on a hiking trip in wilderness. It made familiar places unfamiliar.

She stood behind the large folding table. There was a tall chair for her . . .

A bar stool! she thought. *That's funny on more levels than I can cope with today.*

Most people were sitting on sturdy boxes and baskets in neat rows, very unlike the Clan's usual laissez-faire order. Front and center sat the man who was the focus of this day's process, set apart from them by the white tarp under him and a clear circle of aversion.

On either side of him stood men from the Dun. They had knives in their belts, but that was simply the tool everyone carried now. One also had a pickax handle in his hand, though, and the other a baseball bat.

And they're needed, Juniper thought as she took him in with a grimace. *Yes, with this one.*

He was a strong man, of medium height and well muscled, with striking chiseled features and curly black hair he wore fairly short. The sort who quivered with suppressed anger at the world, to whom everything that thwarted his will was an elemental affront.

He's not afraid, really, she thought; she'd always been good at reading people. *Which means he's not only wicked, he's very arrogant, very stupid, or both.*

As she watched, he shot a sudden glance over his shoulder, a flicker of something triumphant on his face, which he schooled at once as he looked forward again.

"Armsmen, take custody of the prisoner," she said coolly, and saw a moment's doubt on his face.

The men of the Dun moved aside for Sam and Chuck and went to sit with the rest. From their expressions, they were thankful to turn the task over to a uniformed authority, and they weren't the only ones.

Besides their kilts, the two men wore what had been chosen as the Mackenzie war kit, though there hadn't been time to craft enough for everyone yet: a brigandine of two layers of green leather (salvaged from upholstery) with little steel plates riveted between, quivers and yew longbows slung across their backs, shortswords and long dirks and soup-plate bucklers at their belts, a small wicked *sgian dub* knife tucked into one boot-top. The plain bowl helmets with the spray of raven feathers at the brow made them somehow seem less human and more like walking symbols.

Chuck Barstow had a spear as well as the war-harness. The prisoner would have been less surly if he knew what it portended, or that Chuck was High Priest of the Singing Moon Coven as well as second-in-command of their militia. The spear's polished six-foot shaft was *rudha-an,* the same sacred rowan wood used for wands. The head was a foot-long section cut from a car's leaf spring, ground down to a murderous double-edged blade and socketed onto the wood white-hot before it was plunged into a bath of brine and blood and certain herbs.

It had also been graven with ogham runes, the ones that had come again and again when she tossed the yew sticks of divination on the symbol-marked cloth of the *Bríatharogam.* Just two:

Úath, terror.

Whose kenning was *bánad gnúise,* the blanching of faces. For horror and fear and the Hounds of An-wyn.

Gétal, death.

Whose meaning was *tosach n-échto,* called the beginning of slaying. For the taking of life and for sacrifice.

Juniper took a deep breath, and closed her eyes for an instant to make herself believe she was truly here and not imagining it. The dull heat she had felt before came back, manyfold, as if the soil beneath her feet was throbbing with rage.

"Bring him before me."

Her own voice startled her, though casting her trained soprano to carry was second nature for a professional singer. Now it was somehow like the metal on the edge of a knife.

"You heard Lady Juniper, gobshite," Sam said, just barely loud enough for her to catch.

The hand he rested on the man's shoulder to move him forward might have looked friendly, from any distance. Juniper could see the wrist and scarred, corded forearm flex, and the prisoner's eyes went wide for an instant as it clamped with crushing precision. Sam had been born and raised on a small English farm; his trade had been a peculiar type of soldiering for half his forty-two years, before chance or the Weavers left him trapped and injured in the woods near her home just after the Change.

His hobby had been making and using the longbow of his ancestors. He was stocky and of middle height, but those thick spade-shaped hands could crack walnuts between thumb and two fingers. And she happened to know that he hated men like this with a pure and deadly passion.

Chuck Barstow looked grimmer; he'd been a Society fighter and a gardener besides a member of the Singing Moon, not a real warrior by trade, though everyone had seen death and battle in the last eighteen months. But he was equally determined as he paced forward to keep the prisoner bracketed. From the way his eyes were fixed and showed white around the blue, he was *feeling* something too, besides the gravity of the moment, and not enjoying it.

Judy Barstow was at the far right of the table next to a woman who sat tensely upright; her white face frightened and her eyes carefully not focused.

Our prime exhibit, thought Juniper. *Even if I just*

*nursed Rudy, my breasts ache. But why is it so hard
to breathe?*

Eilir had moved to sit at the smaller, shorter table,
set in an L to the larger one. She turned and her fingers flew. *Shall I find some cold tea for you?*

Yes, thanks.

She drank the lukewarm chamomile thirstily as her
daughter pulled a fresh book out of her saddlebags.
Ice in summer was a memory, and a possibility some-
day when they had time for icehouses, but you could
get a little coolness by using coarse porcelain.

The book was covered in black leather, carefully
tooled with the words:

*The Legal Proceedings of Clan Mackenzie, Second
Year of the Change.*

And below that:

Capital Crimes.

Eilir opened it to a fresh page, pulled out an ink
bottle and a steel-nibbed pen that had come out of
retirement in an antiques store in Sutterdown. Nobody thought it odd that a fourteen-year-old was
acting as court clerk. Standards had changed.

The first pages of the book contained the rituals
they had come up with last night, after they had
hashed out the legal and moral basis for judging the
case. The first pages of the book covered all that,
written in Eilir's neat print.

Juniper looked over to the Dun Carson witnesses
sitting in the south-east quadrant. Everybody was
still, the sensation of their focused attention like and
unlike a performance.

"I have been called here to listen to the Dun's
judgment against Billy Peers Mackenzie . . ."

"Hey!" the man yelled. "I ain't never said nothing about Mackenzie. That was you-all. I'm William Robert Peers."

Juniper hesitated and then turned her head.

"I will only say this once, Mr. Peers. You will keep your mouth closed until I give you leave to speak. If you speak out of turn again, your guards will gag you. Gags are very uncomfortable. I advise you to be quiet."

"But you can't do that! It isn't legal!"

Sam's hand moved once, and the man stopped with his mouth gaping open. He reached into his sporran, pulled out the gag and shoved it into the man's mouth with matter-of-fact competence, checking carefully to make sure that his tongue lay flat and that it wasn't so large as to stop him from swallowing. The rags wrapped around the wooden core had been steeped in chamomile and fennel seed tea and dried so that it wouldn't taste too foul. Straps around the head held it in place without cutting at the corners of his mouth. He struggled, though it was as ineffectual as a puppy in a man's hands.

"I said I would speak only once. All of you, take heed. If I state a consequence will follow, it will follow. Second chances belong to the times before the Change, when we were rich enough to waste time arguing. You have one minute to stand quiet."

A glance at her watch.

She gazed dispassionately at the struggling man trying to spit the carefully constructed gag out of his mouth. Then she began to count the measured seconds out loud. After the tenth second passed, it caught Peers' attention. At the twentieth second, he stopped struggling.

"Better. If you cause any further disruption, you will be knocked unconscious. I have no time to waste now, in the midst of harvest."

Peers jerked, started to struggle again, saw a sudden movement out of the corner of his eye as Sam raised a hand stiffened into a blade, flinched and subsided. Juniper waited and then turned again to the north leg of the crossroads. She lifted her arms, and Judy placed her staff in her hands; it had the Triple Moon—waxing and full and waning—above two raven heads of silver, and the shaft was also of mountain rowan.

"I have been called here by the Óenach of Dun Carson and by the Ollam of Dun Carson; Sharon Carson, Hearthmistress, Cynthia Carson, Priestess and First Armsman of Dun Carson, Ray Carson, Second Armsman and Herd Lord in Training, and Brian Carson, Herd and Harvest Lord, pro-tem, and his wife, Rebekah Carson, the tanner.

"I am Juniper Mackenzie, Chief of the Clan Mackenzie. I am Ollam Brithem, high judge over our people."

Juniper winced at the power she was claiming. *But I am needed as chief, and so I must take this burden on. Threes; everything in threes. Continue, woman, get this over.*

"I am called here, by Óenach, Ollam, and the Gods to hear, to judge, and to speak. Does any deny my right, my obligation, or my calling? Speak now or hold your tongue thereafter, for this place and time is consecrated by our gathering. All we do here is holy—and legal."

Distantly, she was aware that Peers tried to struggle again and quickly subsided as Sam gripped the back of his neck.

A long silence and she continued, face raised to the sun, eyes closed against its burning light:

"Let us be blessed!"

"*Manawyddan*—Restless Sea, wash over me."

A green branch sprinkled salt water over her. She tasted the salt on her lips like tears. Four Priestesses came with green branches, each trailed by a child holding a bowl of salt water. Each cleansed the people in one of the quarters; the last pair assiduously cleansed the empty northeastern quarter.

"*Manawyddan*—Restless Sea! Cleanse and purify me! I make myself a vessel; to listen and to *hear*."

"*Rhiannon*—White Mare, stand by me, run with me, carry me! That the land and I can be one, with Earth's wisdom."

She bent and took a pinch of the dry dust from the road and sprinkled it in front of her. There was a long ripple as the Dun Carson people did the same, and the witnesses.

"*Rhiannon—White Mare, ground me.*"

"*Arianrhod—Star-tressed Lady;* dance through our hearts, our minds, and through our eyes, bring Your light to us."

She took a torch from Eilir and lit it; the resinous wood flared up. Eilir took it to the four corners of the crossroads and lit each torch.

"*Arianrhod—Star-tressed Lady;* Bring Your light to me, to us, to the world.

"Sea and Land and Sky, I call on you:

"Hear and hold and witness thus,

"All that we say

"All that we agree

"All that we together do.

"Honor to our Gods! May they hold

"Our oaths

"Our truths."

Then she spoke formally: "Let all here act with truth, with honor and with duty, that justice, safety and protection all be served for this our Clan, and may Ogma of the Honey Tongue lend us His eloquence in pursuit of Truth."

"This Dun's Óenach is begun! By what we decide, we are bound, each soul and our people together."

She turned in place, looking at all the people assembled, and rapped the butt of her staff on the ground.

"I am here, we are here, the Gods are here. So mote it be!"

"So mote it be!" the massed voices replied.

She noticed that Rebekah said the words and was glad. They weren't actually religious and it meant she was participating in the Clan's work, rather than standing back, claiming religious exemption. She moved over to the chair and hoisted herself up on it. She could feel Chuck move into place behind her, still holding the spear upright as a symbol of her justice.

The morning sun was pouring down on the tarps and she could feel the heat and sweat that started to trickle down her back and breasts. The kilt had been comfortable while riding down to the crossroads through the forest . . . now the soft wool was sticking to her legs and her kneesocks made her legs itch.

Well, I'm not the only one uncomfortable on all the levels possible.

Juniper tapped her fingers on the table and took up the gavel that Sam had crafted her yesterday evening as they hashed out procedure. She banged it once on the block of wood and spoke formally:

"We are gathered here to make a decision with regards to the matter of the sexual assault visited upon Debbie Meijer yesterday by William Robert Peers, know to us as Billy Peers Mackenzie, who denies that he has accepted the name or Clan of Mackenzie."

She frowned and moved her hand to stop another blow to the struggling Billy. "You will be given your time to talk at its proper place."

He shook his head, his eyes angry and desperate, and she pursed her lips and shook her head in her turn, pointing to the poised hand. He subsided, but his black scowl remained.

"First I am going to address the greater issue. What right have we to judge and sentence and carry out these sentences upon the members of our community and those who dwell upon our land? For more than a year, we have been hurrying from incident to incident, making it up as we go along . . ."

A crack of laughter interrupted her. That was a charge often leveled at pre-Change wiccans: *They just make up the ritual as they go along.*

"But all just law is based on need and precedents and the will of the people. Not much of it is from the legal system that covered the needs of a highly urban, complex society that numbered hundreds of millions and was rich enough to spare the time for slow careful perusals of accusations and defenses.

"We no longer live in the old world of cities and bureaucracies. We live in small, closed villages where the question of guilt is frequently easily established and we have no real need of the elaborate forensic apparatus used previously to establish the *beyond doubt* criteria used before."

She met Billy's angry eyes: "This is how we have been operating and how we will continue to operate in future, until we see a need for something different. Our methods and their success or failure were discussed and reviewed by myself and my advisors. We have reviewed the past seventeen months of work and dispute in the duns and codified the results."

She gestured to the book beneath Eilir's hand: "Clan Mackenzie is a conglomeration of independent settlements that have asked for and received membership in the Clan, that we may support each other and defend each other in a world where nobody can survive alone and no single family can survive alone. These are the means we have found to live together, and live decently. *And it has worked.* We are alive, where millions . . . hundreds of millions . . . almost certainly *billions* . . . have died."

A low murmur went through the group as she looked around, meeting their eyes. That was why so many had joined the group she'd started with a few friends and coven-members meeting at her country retreat, and taken up all its ways. It was what she'd meant that first day, when she'd told them . . .

"It's a Clan we will have to be, as it was in the old days, if we're to live at all."

A low approving rumble at that; the words were already folklore. Perhaps the trappings that had come along with that thought weren't necessary, were just the by-product of that group's obsessions and pastimes from before the Change . . . but the whole thing *worked,* and nobody was going to argue with that. Herself least of all.

Then she went on: "*Salus populi suprema lex*: The good of the people is the highest law. If a person lives in a Dun of the Clan, they are a member of that Dun and subject to the rules, benefits, and obligations of the group. No one compels them to remain, but if they do, it is on the group's chosen terms. This includes the reality of work, of mutual defense, and the obligation to respect others. The Ollam and Óenach of a Dun have every right to judge wrongdoing in their territories and by their people or towards their people.

"Who chooses the Ollam? The people of the Dun. Dun Carson was led by John and Sharon Carson Mackenzie until his death fighting the Protector's men when they tried to take Sutterdown last year. Dun Carson is led by an Ollam of five at this time. They have collectively requested that the Chief Ollam of the Clan deliver the doom in this matter, and that it be witnessed by as many sober and credible members of the other Duns as is possible. We are here today for this purpose."

Two more people were taking down her words in shorthand. Juniper paced her speech to make it easier on her own scribe-daughter to read her lips.

"I will hear first from Debbie Meijer, who also resides in Dun Carson, but has not accepted the name of Mackenzie."

She watched as the injured woman's eyes focused on her, as if she'd been jarred out of some inward prison that was protection as well. Everyone looked lean and fit these days, as well as weathered, but there was gentleness to her face, as well as pain; she had blue-green eyes, and brown hair caught beneath a kerchief. She shrank back for a minute and then rose at Judy's quiet urging and walked forward. Juniper watched her swallow and clench her teeth. She made a slight gesture and Debbie's face contracted. She shook for an instant and then faced the Dun's members.

"I am Debbie Meijer. I've lived with you at Dun Carson since . . . since the Protector's men stole us from Lebanon, and I, uh, escaped. I've not taken the Clan or the name; I've been waiting for my husband, Mark, to come back. Those of you here all know that the 'tinerants have been seeking news of the people stolen from Lebanon, but not much has been heard.

"I . . . I've done my best to fit in and be useful. It's been hard. I've learned and learned and learned for more than a year. I went from an independent, competent citizen to a dependent, stupid member of a farming community."

A wave of motion shook the Carson and Rebekah stepped forward, holding out a green branch.

"I recognize Rebekah Carson." Juniper smiled at Debbie and raised a hand with a gentle gesture to stay her words for a moment:

"Debbie is a good, hard worker who has struggled with the grief she feels for the loss of her husband and her family, who were all on the east coast. We have all liked and supported her."

Juniper hesitated, suppressing a stab of anger; that support had been sadly lacking in some respects. She'd said they were to be as a Clan, and that meant that each protected the other.

No, that needs to be said; but later. Now Debbie needs to finish.

She looked up. Peers was slouched, managing to look as insolent as a man could while gagged and standing under Sam Aylward's hand. He turned his head, caught Debbie's eyes, and moved his hips, slightly but unmistakably.

Juniper's finger pointed. Sam Aylward carefully did *not* smile.

Crack.

Sam's hand slapped across his face, with a sound like leather hitting a board and a speed that was deceptive because of the brisk unhurried casualness of the motion. The man's head whipped around and he staggered. Blood showed around his lips and nose, and his eyes widened with shock.

"You will be respectful," Juniper said flatly. Then: "Please continue, Debbie. Tell us what happened."

Debbie bit her lip and met Juniper's eyes. Her defensive posture straightened and her voice firmed up.

"Yesterday wasn't where it started. Yesterday was where it ended. I've been here since August, last year. Billy Bob came in March or April . . ."

"April!" somebody called from the assembly.

Debbie nodded. "It started right away. He stood in line next to me at suppertime and rubbed himself on me. Cynthia saw him do it and reamed him out in front of everybody. He said that he was only trying to be friendly, and I was a cold bitch and Cynthia a buttinsky kid."

Juniper felt her lips thin out; her eyes went to the Carson girl. Cynthia nodded, but didn't speak.

"After that," continued Debbie, "he was more careful about who'd see him. He followed me when he could, grabbed me, and would touch me every time he could. That hip thing he just did . . . he'd do it every time he could when we were all together. Ray caught him at it a couple of times and told him to stop and Brian backed him up . . . but it just made him a bit more careful.

"He tried to . . . He knocked on my door . . . I guess it was late April, late at night. I didn't even think about the danger; I just opened it and he shoved it open and tried to get in. It hit me in the face and breast and hurt and I screamed and everybody poured out. He tried to say that I had invited him in, but nobody believed him.

"After that, I had to keep my door locked. In May, he tried to climb in the window and I slammed it on his fingers . . . After *that* I had to keep my window closed and just put up with the heat. Ray and Brian were pissed because he said I had slammed his fingers in a door, not the window, and he hadn't done anything. But Tammy saw him fall that day and then they believed me. They kept him away from me by making sure he worked away from the house and I worked close. Sharon and Rebekah told me to be careful to not do anything more to excite him or provoke him. But I *wasn't* doing anything. It was all him.

"Yesterday, we were harvesting and after dinner I

went up to my room to change my shirt. I'm glad for the kilt. Pants would be brutal in this heat and I don't like shorts, but I needed a lighter shirt; I was sweltering.

"He was hiding behind the door of my room and he punched me in the back and I stumbled—turned to scream and he punched me in the stomach, threw me on the floor, ripped off my panties . . ."

Juniper caught Judy's eyes and she moved closer to the woman, who'd gone rigid, her voice flat, her face expressionless.

". . . raped me . . . I couldn't breath from the punch. Then he flipped me over and half on the bed and did it from behind and through the behind. He gagged me with my shirt and bit my breasts all over and then punched me again and left me there. Cynthia found me later."

"Not much later," said Cynthia. "When she didn't come back down, I went upstairs. At most ten or fifteen minutes."

Juniper nodded and pointed at Brian. "How did he evade your watchfulness?"

The man looked chagrined. "Well, he didn't. He's just such a slacker, I never thought of it. I just thought he'd gone off somewhere to have a nap. Ray wanted to go look for him, but I told him we were too busy. I shouldn't have ignored him."

"Some nap!" exclaimed Debbie, tears suddenly rolling down her flaming cheeks.

Judy led her away, a careful arm around her shoulders.

Juniper nodded, feeling the anger on her face and knowing it scared Brian Carson.

"Judy?" she asked.

Judy Barstow came forward again: everyone knew she'd been a registered nurse and midwife before the Change, and in overall charge of the Clan's health care since. She wasn't as popular as Juniper— her brisk, no-nonsense personality was a little more abrasive—but nobody doubted her competence.

"I conducted the examination yesterday evening. Debbie has been hit. There is a bruise on her back, between the shoulder blades. There is a wound, made by a ring from the placement. She was, indeed, struck in her solar plexus. Soft belly tissue doesn't show bruises as easily, but there are two marks similar to the ring mark on her back. By tomorrow, I believe she'll have serious bruising on her front. I also believe there is internal damage, probably to her spleen. I hope it will heal, but for now, she's on light duty, mostly off her feet.

"She was clearly raped, vaginally and anally. There is considerable trauma and damage to the surrounding structures as well as rips and tears from fingernails. Sperm was present in both places."

Juniper nodded, her stomach roiling. *I wish Eilir didn't need to hear this! Or any of the Clan's children. Unfortunately they all need to hear it, loud and clear.*

"One last item, then, before I speak as Ollam and Brithem. Brian compiled a set of weregeld statements for Billy Bob and Debbie."

She looked down and made a moue at them.

"Billy Bob's will not surprise many people. He arrived empty-handed except for a belt knife and an ax, but not hungry, on a bicycle in late April of this year, claiming to have come from Hood River where the Portland Protective Association, in the person of one Conrad Renfew . . . now calling himself *Count* Conrad Renfew . . . took over. He was accepted into Dun Carson. His record since then has been that of a slacker and troublemaker. Brian considers that he hasn't actually done enough work day to day to cover his room and board. He also shorted, cheated, or went absent on sentry go twice before being removed from the sentry rolls altogether.

"I am going to send out an advisory to all the Duns. We now have intelligence about Hood River. Though the Portland Protective Association took it over, for once the people of Hood River are actually *grateful* to them for this."

That brought another murmur, this time of surprise. The PPA's Lord Protector was, at the very least, a psychopath, though a very able and surprisingly farsighted one; his followers ranged from extremely hard men to outright thugs. But there were times when people would accept the hardest hand if it meant life and peace enough to sow and reap, and the Association was trying very hard indeed to get agriculture going again in its territories. Nor did they tolerate outlaw raiders . . .

If only because it's competition, she thought mordantly, and went on:

"They had a homegrown bandit problem, a very bad one. Any Dun that took in Hood River people over the period from March through late April will need to look carefully at them. They may be the bandits themselves, the ones Renfrew didn't hang or behead. I suspect that is the case here.

"To continue. Debbie's weregeld sheet states that she arrived with the titles to seventy acres outside of Lebanon and another hundred acres up by Silverton. This she handed over to the Clan in November when the Kyklos asked for free title to the lands they took possession of in September. We received a large consignment of goods in return for that and several other property titles. Debbie is credited with a proportional value of that shipment. Debbie is a hard worker, very community minded, and easy to get along with. She has been learning a number of skills for our Changed world, caring for dairy cattle, butter-making and cheese-making, and sewing and preserving food as well as the standard tasks."

Juniper folded her hands over the papers and looked into the insolent hazel eyes of the gagged man before her.

"Before I say anything about this particular case, I have something to say that will be sent to all the Clan territories. *Dun Carson failed to protect Debbie Meijer.*"

She paused, to allow Eilir to catch up and to control herself. She caught Brian and then Rebekah's eyes. They dropped theirs and flushed with shame.

"Harassment, bullying, tormenting, destructive teasing . . . none of these are acceptable behaviors in a world where everybody depends on everybody else and nobody can move away. Children are taught by admonishment and example because they know no better. But adults are expected to listen and understand and conform. Chronic problems must not be allowed to fester. We of the Clan *must* be able to trust each other; our *lives* depend upon it."

Juniper drummed her fingers on the table and scowled into the sneering face of the gagged man. "Billy Bob brought up the legality of our actions. I will address this point first."

She felt an angry satisfaction to see how he hated that she spoke of him by the nicknames he'd used back when he'd arrived in Clan Mackenzie territory.

"Clan Mackenzie is a sovereign state. We are neither bound by nor follow the legal system of the old United States of America, which is utterly unsuited to this world we find ourselves in. Therefore, Mr. Peers, you are not in Kansas anymore, and we will not allow you to try legal quibbles or time-wasting efforts to negotiate yourself out of your just desserts, no, that we will not!

"Now is the time when you will speak. When I tell you to not speak anymore, you will close your mouth and not speak anymore. When I ask you a question, you will answer it directly. You will not speak other than to answer the questions I put to you until I give you leave to speak freely.

"Do you understand?"

She saw the sly look in his eyes as he nodded and nodded herself in turn.

"Do you agree to only answer the questions put to you and to be silent when ordered?"

The way his teeth showed reassured her that she was reading the situation well. He nodded, slowly, as if he were forcing his head to move against rigid sinews.

"The gag will be used, if necessary. Be warned that attempts to blame your victim will be met with gagging. Rape is an offense against the Goddess

Herself and an insult to the Horned Lord, Her consort and lover. It is a vile mockery of the Great Rite by which They made and maintain the world and to let it go unpunished would be to risk Their anger.

"We have religious freedom here; you are being punished for your crime against Debbie Meijer, not against the Powers who make and shape the world, whatever else we mean by it. However, insulting our morals is blasphemy and will be met with severe penalties. And you . . . well, you *are* a rapist."

She nodded to Alex, who unstrapped the gag device. Billy Bob spit out the tongue depressor and drew in a breath . . . and froze as his eyes met hers. She held them until he let go of the breath and slumped slightly.

"Better," she approved. "Did you rape Debbie Meijer?"

Once again he drew in a breath and met her eyes . . . and hesitated.

"You can't prove it!" he challenged.

"Why not? Are you sure nobody saw you?"

"Of course . . . nobody saw me. I wasn't there!" Juniper grimaced wryly.

Good recovery, she thought. *Not going to get him on a* Perry Mason.

Juniper nodded. "We do not depend on people seeing you. Proof, as you call it, is a matter of belief. Everybody in the Dun's Óenach believes you did what you are accused of, based on observations and tracking of movements and knowledge of who and what you are. Your guilt has been established to the satisfaction of the Dun, and I have accepted it.

"Debbie's unsupported word and the state of her

body are enough to prove to us she has been raped. Her struggle with your continual harassment is enough to condemn you in the eyes of the community. The mark of your ring on her body in three places is also very telling. Keep in mind that I was not asked to come and decide if you were guilty. That was established yesterday afternoon when you were locked up and Judy Barstow Mackenzie made her examination of Debbie. You are the man who raped her. My task is to determine what to do with you.

"In Clan Mackenzie our guiding principle is the weregeld principal, of compensation. For injury to property or failure to do your share you may be fined labor or goods for the waste you caused. For repeated offenses, expulsion by the vote of the community.

"For injury—which can cover malicious gossip, physical assault, and damage to a persons' property or animals—the only question is how dangerous the perpetrator is. We have a responsibility. We cannot turn a dangerous person out to the world if we reasonably believe that he or she will injure another person.

"For murder. The circumstances of the cause of death must be reviewed by a coroner appointed by the Dun's Ollam and the decision will rest upon those findings and the conclusion with the Ollam and the Óenach."

She could see that Billy Bob was relaxing. He shrugged. After a few seconds' thought, she nodded at him. "I have reached my decision. Do you have any final words to say?"

"Sure!" he said, sitting up again. "Gimme my bike,

load the saddlebags with enough food, and I'll be
gone north before the door hits the back wheel!"

The members of Dun Carson stirred, anger on
many faces; a few shouted wordlessly in rage or de-
nial. Juniper let them settle down; Billy Bob started
to twist, but Sam was still holding his shoulder and
he could no more break that hold than he could the
steel grip of a vise.

"As far as the Dun is concerned, you have not
managed to work enough to justify your keep in the
four months you have been here. You came with nothing but an old bike, which has been, since, broken up
for repair parts."

"Fuck!" yelled Billy Bob. "That was *my* bike and
you owe *me*!"

"No," said Juniper. "You owe the Clan four months'
room and board. Room is assessed at a pint of wheat
a day and board at three pints of wheat a day. For one
hundred and twenty-six days, total. This is a little
more than five bushels of wheat."

"You're crazy!" he said, staring at her. "Where'm
I going to get wheat?"

"From the sweat of your brow!" said Brian, anger
clotting his voice.

Billy Bob swung around but Juniper spoke; her
voice diamond edged. "Stop. That is moot; infliction
of injury trumps all else."

There was silence before she went on: "Does anybody from the Óenach have anything to say about
the potential of Billy Bob raping another woman if
he is expelled?"

One of the older children—*eòghann,* she reminded
herself—raised a hand. "May I speak?" he asked.

Juniper frowned as the boy's mother reached out a hand and then drew it back.

"Yes. You have a voice, but not a vote."

"He . . . yesterday—early; and before, he used to work next to me. I tried to get changed around, but Brian said that it would hurt morale and I should be able to ignore him. But he always talked; he'd say really ugly things about Debbie. He was always talking about her. Sometimes he talked about other women, not from here, and not all from Hood River. He'd laugh and chuckle . . . like it was as much . . . fun . . . to talk about it to me, yelling at him to shut up, as it was to do the gross things he told me about."

Juniper didn't put her head down on the table, or scream, or dance with rage. But the impulse was surely there.

"Does anybody else have a similar story?"

She winced, and so did the Óenach. All the raised hands were of the *eòghann* and a sprinkling went up in the children's section.

Brian's red face went white and his arm went around Rebekah. Their thirteen-year-old daughter's hand was waving in the air. Juniper counted.

"Failure to properly address the issue has left your children vulnerable to a rapist. And he took advantage of your carelessness. Nine *eòghann* and three children have been molested, physically or verbally.

"Before I proceed, Dun Carson Óenach, your Ollam have failed you. Do you wish to vote in a new Ollam?"

The Óenach seethed as people turned and spoke with each other. Cynthia and Ray stood close to their mother, all three crying. Rebekah and Brian had opened their arms for Sara, who came running to them, tears flying off her cheeks.

"You told Debbie to not make too many waves or provoke him . . ."

Eilir turned with her pen poised and her face grim.

What a can of worms, oh mother-mine. Juniper nodded. *I keep thinking we've understood the Change and all the little Changes. But it keeps biting us in the butt.*

A man stood up, looking around at the rest of the Óenach and twisting his cap in his hands. Nods and encouraging hand waves pushed him forward:

"I'm Josh Heathrow. I kind'a called myself a pagan before the Change. Accepting the Goddess was easy for me; but I haven't really wanted to go for the full priesthood. Still, the Óenach asked me to speak for all of them. And the bottom line is, we don't think any of us could have done better. And it sucks to kick somebody out to starve . . . or get taken by Eaters . . . and that's what it would be. But . . . things have changed. We've got to work with that, and it isn't easy getting our heads around it.

"Once something physical actually happened, Brian did something about it; quick too. I guess we all feel that this is one of those lessons and we need to make real sure we don't do it again. But, nobody seems to want the Carsons booted out. They're all good folk and pretty conscientious, and this *was* their land, for generations. Uh, maybe the fields, you know, wouldn't like it if we changed that."

He looked around and abruptly sat again. Juniper had been scanning the faces as he spoke.

"There is consensus, then?" she asked.

"*Aye!*"

"Very well. Brian, you and Rebekah will have to come to the Hall. I expect that I will come here, as well. We'll take time to examine different situations and possible strategies. Sharon, Cynthia, and Ray will spend extra hours with Judy, reviewing their soon-to-be responsibilities.

"Having done that, I pronounce the sentence."

"Hey! Wait! I ain't been found guilty yet . . . or convicted!"

Peer's eyes bulged with the sudden terror of illusions pierced at last.

"Didn't you hear me tell you I was not brought to judge your guilt? I am here to pronounce your doom."

Billy Bob started up, screaming obscenities and denials, and Sam forced the gag back in his mouth. A swift kick to the back of the leg put him on his knees, whooping air in and out through his nose, and the armsman gripped him by a handful of hair.

Juniper stood and raised her staff again: "Hear the word of the Ollam Brithem of Clan Mackenzie!"

Silence fell, except for the slobbering panting of the gagged man and the far-off nicker of a horse:

"Dun Carson will accept two trained priestesses and a priest into the Dun to help those wounded in their hearts by this man's deeds. These will not be members of the Dun, but will work, as we all do.

"Debbie has six months to decide if she wishes to stay with Dun Carson, join another Dun, or lead a group north to reclaim her land near Lebanon, becoming an Ollam chief in her turn. Should she leave Dun Carson, Dun Carson shall dower her with goods equivalent to her hard work as set forward by Brian Carson in this sheet. Dun Juniper will give her support against the amount her surrender of the title to the acres in Silverton has given the Clan. Dun Carson will add a weregeld of an extra one-fifth for allowing her to suffer sexual harassment for four months, and will make formal apology."

Juniper stood and took the spear from Chuck. She pointed it at the prone body of Billy Bob, and the light flashed off it, flickering in the graven Ogham characters.

"This man is a mad dog. He attacks the young, and destroys the reputation of his victims as well as their honor and integrity. Expelling him will not protect us from him. He could return at any moment, hide and attack us and ours by stealth, knowing our defenses. Or he would find and prey on others. We must re-move him from the circle of the world, for we are responsible. We found him in our nest, on our land, despoiling our people. Last night I and my advisors discussed the possible permutations. We have estab-lished a ritual and will deliver death through it. Let the Guardians of the Northern Gate judge him; let him make amends and come to know himself in the Land of Summer.

"Death is a dread thing and all of us have found ourselves over the past year confronted by death and the fear of death. I killed a man scant hours after the Change, saving another. But we must not let ourselves become calloused by it, nor shut it away and out of our minds. And so Dun Carson will carry out the sentence. We will not hide from ourselves what we have decided to do, nor let another bear the burden."

Billy kicked and tried to spasm himself upright. His scream was blurred, but he struggled until the hair began to tear out by the roots.

Sam thoughtfully backheeled him in the stomach. "Oi'd give it a rest, if Oi was you, mate. It'll hurt more, else."

Chuck lifted up a pot.

"There are fifty-three marbles in this urn. Six green ones, four red ones, a black one, and forty-two blue ones. Each adult will take a marble. The six people who pick a green marble will dig the grave, six feet down, by six feet long by three feet wide."

He pointed to the unoccupied northeastern corner of the crossroads, where three shovels stood driven into the sod.

"The four red marbles are for the four people who will escort him to his place of execution and hold him there. The black marble is for the executioner. Everybody over sixteen will witness. Parents may allow children from fourteen to sixteen to be present.

"The youngsters are to return to the Dun, out of the sight and sound of the execution."

Billy Bob's body bucked, thrashing. A stink suddenly filled the air as his bowels loosed and he fainted. Judy gestured forward some of the witnesses from the other Duns. They stripped the unconscious man, wiped him down with rags, and put an old polyester bathrobe on him, grimacing in distaste.

Sam Aylward snorted. "Oi'd have made 'im dig it 'isself," he observed mildly.

The pot passed around the Óenach; some snatched at the marbles, some hesitated, some held theirs up, and others looked at it in their palm before opening their fingers. One or two sobbed with relief when their marble was blue. Gradually six people walked over to the shovels and began to lay out the grave and dig, using tarps to heap up the soil. Four people, three men and a woman, came to stand over the prone man. Then a sound burst across the pavilion and a woman Juniper did not know walked up to the man and opened her hand. The black marble fell on his shirt.

"Fitting," said Brian. "She's been trying to make us do something about the man. And threatening to do it herself."

Juniper grimaced. "Well, unless she's a stone-cold killer, she's going to learn precisely the lesson I want to teach the entire Dun and the moiety of Clan Mackenzie, about paying and punishment."

"Lady," said Brian. "Sara's only thirteen, but she wants to stay . . . and Rebekah and I think she should."

Juniper was reaching for Rudy, shifting her blouse and plaid so that she could nurse the cranky baby. She hesitated, focused on getting Rudy latched on; not that that generally took much, but she usually didn't nurse him under a shawl.

What are we going to do when nursing bras fall apart? Stays . . . ugh!

As Rudy began to feed she met Sara's eyes. "Why?" she asked simply.

The girl looked ready to cry and angry at the same time. "He . . . he threatened to kill me. Said . . . well, said he'd killed Bunny FooFoo and he'd do me just like that."

The girl looked sick and Juniper had to force herself to lift a brow at Brian. The heavyset man shook his head gloomily.

"You know, Lady. I wasn't one for your religion. But it seems like I've got an almighty clout upside the head for being careless.

"Yeah, the rabbit was killed. I tried to tell her it was a coyote, but even I didn't believe it and for sure she didn't; but she didn't fight me on it. And we really needed the rabbit; it was a French Angora and we were hoping to start a specialty wool stock with it. Sara's trying to breed back the traits from the kits, but it'd be a lot easier if the male was still here.

"I'm babbling. Sara needs to see he really does die. And I do too. I just wish he could die ten times."

Juniper shook her head, rocking the baby. "It's easy and normal for you to feel you are punishing him. And warning others about it. But it doesn't work that way. Think of it as culling the herd. This is a protective measure and we're going to make it pretty much as quick as possible."

She shifted the baby to the other breast and looked at Sara. "I don't want you to watch. I understand why you do, but I don't think it is healthy."

She looked at Brian and then Rebekah.

"Do you have a better reason for her watching? There's going to be no doubt that he's dead."

Brian shook his head and hesitated. "You know, Lady. It says in the Bible, *the wages of sin is death*. But it's been a long, long time since we really meant those words. We all focus on the living gift of God. How many people are going to try to live by sacred works, like you Mackenzies do . . . and what's it going to mean to justice?"

Chuck was standing by them and he shook his head. "If you think we had true, pure, unadulterated justice in the old world . . ."

"No," said Rebekah. "It was flawed, and people got off scot-free . . . and we nearly let this man get off scot-free. But that doesn't mean that the old ways were any better. The law was cruel and harsh. Did it really need to be?"

She shook her head and then looked at her daughter. "Is that it? You're afraid we'll let him get off, like they let that teacher go free after Melly complained about him?"

Sara nodded, tears in her eyes. The four adults shook their heads. Rebekah turned her daughter to the group of children.

"Go. He is going to die. And if he escapes, in that ratty tatty bathrobe of your uncle's, I promise to tell you."

Sara resisted and then moved back towards the group of younger people. Rebekah was frowning and started when Brian placed a hand on her shoulder.

"What is it, love?" he asked.

She shook her head. "A thought. One we need to talk over, later."

The grave-diggers climbed out of the pit and pulled the ladder after themselves, wiping brows; one stopped and looked at the sweat on his palm, as if shocked that it was the same as any other work. The rest crowded together around the hole, far enough back that they didn't break down the fragile walls. The escorts slapped Billy Bob awake and heaved him up. He struggled, but the four held him tightly.

He was struggling too hard for them to get him down into the cool, loamy recess. Juniper walked forward to stand at the north end of the grave. When the escorts looked to her for ideas on what to do, she spread her hands.

"This is the burden the Powers have chosen for you, my friends," she said quietly, her voice cutting through the strangled grunts. "And it is yours."

They held him in the center and looked at each other. One gestured the ladder to be placed at the far end. The woman and one of the men let go and climbed down. With shocking suddenness the two men grabbed Peers by the arms and legs, swung him over the grave, and let his feet go. He dropped and the two down below grabbed him and shoved him down onto the ground; it was moist and brown-gray, with an earthworm crawling from a clod. The scent rose from the dark earth, loamy and rich. There was a sense of *rightness* to it.

Ropes and stakes bound his feet and arms and shoulders to the ground.

"Lady? Do we take off the gag?" asked one of them, just as Judy came bustling up with the soiled ground cloth, clothes, and rags.

"Ask him. And ask yourselves. Do you care if he goes silenced to his death, or would you rather hear his last screams? What are you willing to live with?"

They climbed out, all but one. "Well?" he asked. Juniper stood, her arms aching from holding the hefty weight of the nine-month-old . . . and refusing to give him back to Melissa. The Óenach murmured and shifted, whispered and rustled.

Josh Heathrow stepped forward again, carefully on the verge. He looked down and asked.

"What do you want? Gag out before you are killed or shall we leave it in?"

Juniper heard a thump. The man on the ladder gave an impatient exclamation and jumped down. "He wants it out, but it's clear he's going to be ugly about it," he called up.

"No class," said Chuck in a regretful sotto voice. "Nothing like the grand old tradition of English highwaymen proudly declaiming their prowess on the gibbets."

Juniper sighed and gently kicked him on the shin. Josh was consulting with the Óenach and Ollam again.

Finally he leaned over. "We don't need his curses, and we don't need to give him any further opportunity to work harm. And we don't need more fuel for nightmares. Leave the gag in."

Judy neatly dropped the bundle of dirty cloth in at the foot of the grave.

Brian stepped forward with Ray by his side, white, and shuddering, but gulping in a big breath of air as his uncle spoke.

"Óenach and Ollam have agreed that this man did"—he looked over at Juniper for a second— "profane the Great Rite and the precious mysteries of love by raping a woman of the Dun, yesterday. His offense against the Powers is his, but it is our right to judge him for his offense against our sister. We have since learned that he also attempted to corrupt some of our children. Mad dogs must die. There is no cure that is worth the price we'd pay.

"Mairead, are you ready?"

The woman who'd taken the black marble stepped forward. Like many, her face was white as she realized just what she was going to do.

This is not the heat of battle, when you strike out blindly in fury and in fear, Juniper thought. *This is not the hot blood of a quarrel. This we do with deliberation and with ceremony. We have our doubts, but we hide them. We call upon the Powers; we say, the Law; we say, we the People; we say, the State. But what we do, we still do as human souls.*

The Chief stepped forward; Chuck and she grasped the spear to hand it to the chosen one. Juniper gasped, and felt the High Priest's hand stiffen on the rowan wood beside hers. Eilir's head came around too, and more than one among the onlookers. The jolt she felt was still hot and angry, but it was the wound tension before the lightning strikes, and there was something else in it, a calling—

"This man was a child once," she said, as if the words welled up from the innermost part of her mind. "The Mother gave him being, and his mother loved him. He was given great gifts—a strong healthy body, a cunning mind, a nimble tongue, a great will to live, or he would not have survived this long. He was given a *life*, and such a sorry botch he has made of it for himself and for others."

All of them were looking at her, wire-tense and focused. Her voice rose:

"Can you not *feel* the anger of the Powers at what he has done, and what he has profaned? The slighting of the Mystery that They give us, for our joy and that we might join Them in bringing forth life?"

A sound like wind through trees as the people nodded.

"Yet now we help him make atonement; and so also we appease Them with this sacrifice. But even in the anger of the Dark Mother, there is love. The Keeper of Laws is stern, but just. Beyond the Gate in the Land of Summer, Truth stands naked and he will know himself. He himself will choose how to make himself whole, and be reborn through the cauldron of Her who is Mother-of-All into the life he chooses. So mote it be!"

"So mote it be!"

Mairead shook as the High Priestess and High Priest solemnly handed her the spear.

"This spear was made for this purpose alone," Juniper said. "It is blessed and consecrated for it."

The shaft wobbled dangerously and Sam jumped to the rescue.

" 'Ere," said Sam. "Hold on, lass. Let me reverse it. Now, poke it over the edge. You, Danny, put it where Oi told you to. There. Now, both 'ands on the shaft . . . see, where I wrapped deer-hide around it so it won't slip. One hard shove. Don't let 'im suffer. It's at the right angle now. It'll go into his heart, neat and quick. *Now.*"

Juniper kept her face calm by main force of effort. *Have I asked too much? Should I start a tradition of black-masked executioners? No! This is* our *justice and we need to own it.*

Mairead trembled and Brian stepped to her left

and Josh to her right. They set their hands on the shaft, above and below hers.

"Come," said Josh. "You must do it. But we'll add our strength to yours. It'll be quick."

Even as Mairead gulped and tightened her hands, Sharon and Rebekah stepped forward and put hands on her shoulders. Juniper watched her close her eyes . . . not to block out the sight, but to feel the position of the shaft, and then she pushed, sudden and hard.

The razor-sharp head sliced into Billy Bob's chest cavity and through his heart and the body bucked once more and was still. The man down in the grave, Sam, and Brian all thrust a little harder, getting the head fixed into the soil beneath.

And something *snapped*. The hot anger that had risen up from her feet was gone, with only a brief cool wind of sorrow. Then the day was merely a day once more, and there was work to be done.

Juniper thrust Rudy into Eilir's arms and turned, took up a shovel and filled it with the grave dirt.

"I cast you out," she said clearly, and carefully threw the dirt into the grave.

The last man climbed out, pulled by his friends. Willing hands grabbed the shovels and began to rain the dirt back into the grave.

"I cast you out."

"I protect the children."

"I reject your blasphemy."

"I protect myself."

Juniper stood back. Mairead was still trembling. People came to hug her, but the mood remained somber. Juniper nodded to herself as she took back Rudy. Her hands moved in sign, small ones, restrained by the child.

Yes. This is how we own our lives.

The grave filled quickly, the long shaft poking out above the ground. Red and black ribbons were tied around it and Juniper turned north again, the hot afternoon sunshine on her left, now. Eilir reached for Rudy and she let him go.

Sharon moved to stand at her left hand, and to her surprise, not Cynthia, but Rebekah, moved over to her right.

She lifted her arms:

"*Manawyddan—Restless Sea,* cleanse and purify us! We have taken our actions in defense of our people. They are not actions to take lightly. Restless Sea, cleanse us!

"*Rhiannon—White Mare,* hold him deep in the earth, that he may have time to learn and be reborn to try again."

"*Arianrhod—Star-tressed Lady;* bring Your light to us, light of reason. Protect us from the night fears; give us eyes that we may see protect those we love before harm befalls them."

"*This gathering of the Dun for justice is done. We have met in sorrow, debated in pain, and leave with resolution. So mote it be!*"

"So mote it be!" called the Óenach as they picked up their boxes and baskets, pulled down the tarps, and offered hospitality to the neighbors.

Juniper nodded in approval when the witnesses all made *namaste,* and refused quiet words of support and offers of help shared forth before they left to seek their own homes and the labor that would not, could not, wait.

"Lady, what should we do now?" asked Cynthia Carson.

"Keep a wake, I think," said Juniper. "You'll have to play this by ear. But I think the next day or two should be focusing on doing all the small tasks. You are all upset, and it's easier for you to make mistakes."

Brian and Ray and Sharon nodded. They picked up the bundles of tarps the others had left behind and trudged back to the Dun.

Juniper sighed. "And it's home for us, too, now. We may reach there before the sunset, we may indeed."

She rubbed her forehead fretfully. "I wish we hadn't needed to deal with something this grotesque for our first foray into a capital crime."

Sam shrugged, holding Melissa close. "If not this, then something else, Lady. Whatever it was, it would have felt loik the worst thing to us."

Juniper sighed and shrugged. *I want to be home and with my loved ones. I think we'll be waking the night too.*

Caroline Spector

Caroline Spector has been an editor and writer in the science fiction, fantasy, and gaming fields for the last twenty-five years. She is the author of three novels, *Scars, Little Treasures,* and *Worlds Without End,* and her short fiction has appeared in the Wild Cards collections *Inside Straight* and *Busted Flush*. In the gaming world, she has written and edited several adventure modules and sourcebooks for several TSR game lines, notably Top Secret/S.I. and the Marvel Superheroes advanced role-playing game, both on her own and coauthored with her husband, gaming legend Warren Spector.

Here she gives us a deadly cat-and-mouse game between a woman with superhuman abilities and a faceless, enigmatic adversary who may be able to use her own powers against her, a game that she can't afford to lose, where the highest stakes of all are on the table, waiting for the next turn of a card.

LIES MY MOTHER TOLD ME

Zombie brains flew through the air, leaving a trail of blood and ichor on the throne riser of Michelle's parade float. She smiled as another bubble formed in her hand. This one was larger and heavier—the size of a baseball. She let it fly, and it caught the zombie full in the chest and exploded. The zombie fell backwards off the float and was trampled by the panicking crowd.

Michelle saw more zombies moving toward her. They clambered over the floats in front of hers, pushing people aside as they flowed up the street. Another zombie crawled up onto her float, using the papier-mâché arbor for purchase. The arbor came loose, and Michelle watched in dismay as the sign reading "The Amazing Bubbles, Savior of New Orleans" broke off and fell into the street. Her daughter, Adesina, who'd been hiding under Michelle's throne, let out a frightened shriek. Michelle released the bubble, knowing it would fly unerringly where she wished. When it hit, it would explode and leave a big, gooey zombie smear all over the decorations. Her beautiful float was getting ruined, and it really pissed her off.

There were three things Michelle hated about Mardi Gras: the smell, the noise, and the people. Add in a zombie attack, and it was going to put her off appearing in parades altogether.

To make sure she could bubble as much as needed during the parade, she spent the morning throwing herself off the balcony of her hotel room . . . until the hotel manager came up and made her stop.

"But I'm doing the Bacchus parade," she explained. "I won't be able to bubble through the whole parade if I don't get fat on me. And the only way to do that is to take damage. A lot of damage. A fall from a fourth story is good, but not great."

At this point, the manager turned an interesting shade of green.

"Look, Miss Pond," he said. "We're all grateful that you saved us from that nuclear explosion three years ago, but you're starting to scare the other guests. It just isn't normal."

Michelle stared at him, nonplussed. *Of course it isn't normal,* she thought. *If I were normal, New Orleans would be a radioactive hole in the ground and you'd be a black shadow against some wall. I didn't ask for this. None of us wild carders did.*

"Well," she said, thinking if she just explained it to him, he'd be less freaked out. "It isn't as if when I get hit, or slam into the ground, or even when I absorbed that explosion that it hurts me. I just turn that energy into fat. Actually, it feels pretty good." *Too good sometimes,* she thought. "So you don't have to worry that I'm in pain or anything like that."

But his expression said he really didn't want to hear about her wild card power. He just wanted her knock it off. So she stopped trying to explain and said, "I'm sorry I frightened the other guests. It won't happen again." It meant she didn't have as much fat on her as she wanted, but she'd make it work.

Adesina was still watching TV when Michelle closed the door after talking to the manager. She was perched on the foot of the bed, her iridescent wings folded against her back and her chin propped on her front feet. Just seeing Adesina made Michelle smile. Michelle had loved the child from the moment she'd pulled her from a charnel pit in the People's Paradise of Africa a year and a half ago.

Michelle still couldn't believe that Adesina had survived being injected with the wild card virus, much less being thrown into a pit of dead and dying children when her wild card had turned her into a joker instead of an ace. She shook her head to clear it. The memory of rescuing the children who were being experimented on in that camp in the African jungle was too fresh and raw. And her own failure to save all of them haunted her.

And Michelle wasn't certain how Adesina might develop. Right now she was small—medium-dog size. Her beautiful little girl's face was perched atop an insect body. But there was no telling if she would stay in this shape forever. She'd gone into chrysalis form after her card had turned and come out of that in her current state. It was possible she might change again—it all depended on how the virus had affected her.

"What on earth are you watching?" Michelle asked.

"Sexiest and Ugliest Wild Cards," Adesina replied. "You're on both lists. One for when you're fat and one for when you're thin."

Christ, Michelle thought. *I saved an entire city, and they're really judging me on how "hot" I am? Seriously?*

"You know, these lists are really stupid," Michelle began. "Everybody likes something different."

Adesina shrugged. "I guess," she replied. "But you *are* prettier when you're thin. They always want you to do pictures when you're thin."

Shit, Michelle thought. *That didn't take long. We've been in the States a year, and already she's thinking about who's prettier. And who's fat and thin.*

"Do you think a boy will ever like me?" Adesina asked. She turned her head and looked at Michelle. Her expression was serious. *Oh God,* Michelle thought. *It's too soon for this conversation. I'm not ready for this conversation.*

"Well," she began as she sat down next to Adesina. The bedsprings gave an unhappy groan under her weight. "I . . . I . . . I don't know." *Oh, great.* This was going well. "I don't see why not. You're beautiful."

"You have to say that," Adesina said. "You're my mother." She rubbed her back pair of legs together and made a chirping noise.

"Well, no one falls in love with you just because of how you look," Michelle said.

Adesina turned back to the TV. "Don't be dumb, Momma," she said. "Everyone loves the pretty girls."

A lump formed in Michelle's throat. She swallowed hard, refusing to cry. There was no way to ignore it. Every TV show, magazine, billboard, and website had some pretty, young, skinny, half-naked girl selling something. And up until a couple of years ago, a lot of the time that girl had been Michelle— but that was before her card had turned. And now Adesina was worrying about this crap. Michelle was at a loss.

She stared at the TV. The bumper coming in from the commercial break flashed a rapid succession of images. There was footage from the various seasons of *American Hero*. There were some still black-and-white photos from the forties when the Wild Card virus had first hit. And then there were pictures of Golden Boy testifying before the House Un-American Activities Committee. Shots of Peregrine at the height of her modeling days, looking like the ultimate disco chick—with wings. *Of course they have pictures of her,* Michelle thought. *She's gorgeous.*

"Since 1946, when the alien bomb carrying the wild card virus exploded over Manhattan, they've walked among us," the voice-over began. "The lucky few Aces and the hideously maimed Jokers. But who cares about that? We're here to determine the hottest of the hot and grossest of the gross—Wild Card style!"

Michelle grabbed the remote. "Okay, that's it," she said, snapping off the TV. "Look, honey, America is a stupid place sometimes. We get all caught up in unimportant junk like that show, and we forget the stuff that really means something. And I am really sucking at this mom thing right now. The truth is that the world is going to be unkind sometimes because you're different. But that doesn't have anything to do with you, honey. It's just that the world is full of idiots."

Adesina crawled into Michelle's lap—such as it was when she was in bubbling mode—and put her front two feet on either side of Michelle's face, pushing away Michelle's long, silvery hair. "Oh Momma," she said. "I already *knew* that. I just get scared sometimes."

Michelle kissed Adesina on top of her head. "I know, sweetie. I do, too."

It wasn't so bad up on the float. *Lots of sight lines,* Michelle thought. *That's good and bad.* Good because she could see anything coming, bad because it put Adesina at risk. But being Michelle's daughter was going to put Adesina at risk no matter what.

The crowd was especially boisterous in this section of the parade route. Maybe it was because they'd had longer to drink. The parade had been going on for a couple of hours, and now it was heading into the French Quarter.

Michelle's float was decorated in silver and green. A riser with a throne was at the rear, and a beautiful arbor of papier-mâché flowers arched over the throne. Adesina had commandeered the throne for herself while Michelle stayed out on the lower platform to toss beads, wave, and bubble. Michelle thought Adesina looked adorable in her pale lavender dress—even if it did have six cutouts for her legs and another pair for her wings. Michelle's dress was the same color, but made of a spandex blend. As she bubbled off fat, the dress would shrink along with her.

A couple of drunken blondes yelled at her, "Bubbles! Hey, Bubbles! Throw me some beads!" They pulled up their tops, revealing perky breasts. Michelle was unimpressed, but she threw them beads anyway.

"Momma," Adesina said. "Why do they keep doing that?"

"Got me," Michelle replied. "I guess they think they'll get more beads."

"That's dumb."

Michelle tossed more beads, then started bubbling soft, squishy bubbles that she let drift into the crowd. "You said it. Sadly, I think it works. I just tossed them some myself."

There was a commotion up ahead on the parade route. Michelle stopped bubbling and tried to see what was happening. The crowd was panicking—people were shoving, and others were caught in between, unable to move.

The frenzy moved toward Michelle's float like a tidal wave. Some of the crowd spilled off the sidewalks into the street, knocking down the containment barricades, and then they began clambering onto the floats in front of hers. Cops tried to calm the crowd and started pulling people off the floats, but they were soon overwhelmed.

And that's when she saw them: zombies coming up the street.

Joey, she thought. *What the hell are you doing?*

Then she saw a zombie grab a guy in an LSU T-shirt and snap his neck. Michelle was horrified.

But she immediately slammed that feeling down. She couldn't help him—she had a job to do.

As she scanned the crowd, she saw the zombies brutalizing anyone in their way. A couple of cops tried to stop one of the zombies, and they each got a broken arm for their trouble before Michelle blasted the thing. And then she realized that the zombies were heading for her float.

"Momma!" Adesina's frightened voice came from behind Michelle. She spun around and saw a red-faced, pudgy man and a skinnier man in a striped polo shirt climbing onto the float.

"Hey!" Michelle shouted at them. "It isn't safe here. They're coming for me."

"Behind you is the safest place to be right now," the pudgy one said. "We're not going."

Michelle sighed. "You're leaving me no choice here, guys." The bubbles were already forming in her hands, and she let them fly. The bubbles—big as a medicine ball and just as heavy—bowled the men off the float. Michelle heard them cursing. "Hey," she yelled. "Language! There's a child here!" She picked up Adesina, tucking her under her left arm.

"Momma," Adesina complained, "you're embarrassing me."

"Sorry, sweetie," Michelle replied. "Now behave while I take Aunt Joey's zombies out."

Michelle let a tiny, bullet-size bubble fly at the closest zombie. Its head exploded, sending bits of brain, skull, and decaying flesh into the air. It was immensely satisfying. Unfortunately, this only made some of the people in the crowd even more panicked. And now Michelle could feel her dress getting looser. *Dammit,* she thought. *I knew I needed more fat.*

Michelle spotted another zombie and let a bubble go. There were more shrieks as its brains and pieces of its skull splattered everywhere. The float rocked as the crowd pressed against it, and she struggled to keep her balance.

"Momma, please, put me down."

"Not on your life," Michelle replied, yelling to be heard over the commotion. "Zombies and panicking nats are not a good combination. It would be too dangerous, so, yeah, that is not going to happen."

Adesina let out an exasperated sigh. "You're mean," she said.

Michelle destroyed another zombie. She felt her dress get a little looser. The zombies were coming faster, and one-handed bubbling wasn't getting the job done fast enough. "Oh darnit," she said, putting Adesina down. "Go stay under the throne. And let me know if anyone—anything—tries to get up here."

If there was anything Dan Turnbull liked better than blowing shit up in a first-person shooter, it was making a mess that someone else would have to clean up. His mother had left his father six months ago, and since she'd been gone, neither of them had cleaned up much of anything. Stacks of dirty laundry were piled like Indian burial mounds in different parts of the house. A variety of molds were growing on plates in the kitchen—and in the fridge, heads of lettuce were now the size of limes. Rancid, greasy water filled the sink, and Dan wasn't sure if the sink had stopped draining or if the stopper at the bottom needed to be pulled. What he knew was that he wasn't putting his hand down there to find out.

But lying up here on the roof of the St. Louis Hotel looking down on the mess he'd made just now, well, *that* made him seriously happy. Zombies were breaking up the Bacchus parade, and that Bubbles chick was trying to stop it.

He watched her pick up the freak she called her daughter while at the same time she methodically blasted the shit out of the zombies. And he had a grudging admiration for how cool she was, given the situation. She didn't get hysterical or spaz out the way most women would. No, she just mowed those zombies right down without ever hitting a single civilian. And he wondered what it would be like when he grabbed her power.

It had been a rush when he'd grabbed Hoodoo Mama's power. Of course, he'd only taken one other ace's power before, and that had been an accident.

He'd been walking down the street and had bumped into a teenage girl. Reflexively, he grabbed her bare arm to steady himself. The expression on her face when Dan's touch had taken her power was high-larious. He'd been so surprised that she had a power, he'd used it without thinking and teleported himself across the street, slamming into a wall as he materialized.

When Dan realized that he'd almost teleported into the wall, he started shaking. In a few moments, after the adrenaline rush of fear had passed, he looked around to find the girl. But she'd vanished.

Of course she had, he thought. *What else would she do?*

Unlike the teleporting girl, Hoodoo Mama's power about blew his skull off. But he was only going to get one chance at using it before it reverted back to Hoodoo Mama, and he had orders to make a mess. What was happening out on the street was megaplus cool. He'd done his job well.

There were all kinds of local news video filming the parade, but this was the view he wanted. A nice long shot of the whole scene. He'd brought a video camera to get it, but he knew that there would be plenty of civilians making recordings, too. Those would be on YouTube before the end of the day. What mattered was having a lot of videos of all hell breaking loose. And the one that showed it all in perfect detail would be the icing on the cake.

It didn't matter to Dan why his employers wanted a mess. For 5K and an hour's work, it was a no-brainer. He didn't even care how they knew about his power. His father had started demanding rent, and Dan had no job. And he had no intention of giving up his status as top shooter on his server. It had taken way too long for him to get there, and his team needed him. A job would just get in the way of that.

With his video camera tucked into the pocket of his baggy jeans, he climbed down the fire escape and slipped down the back alley. A couple of stragglers from the parade came toward him. As they got closer, he saw that they were girls. They were trying to run, but drunk as they were, it was more like fast staggering.

"Oh my God," one of them said to him. She was

wearing what looked like a pound of beads. Long dark hair framed her face, and he wondered if she was drunk enough to fuck him. "Did you see what happened back there?"

He shrugged. "Looked like a bunch of drunk assholes. Like every Mardi Gras."

They gave him a baffled look. "No," the other one said. She wasn't as pretty as her companion. *There's always a dog and a pretty one,* he thought. "I mean Bubbles. She was so incredible, like, she just demolished those zombies. Oh shit, I think I have some zombie on me." She wiped at her shirt.

"Looked like she just made a mess of things to me," Dan replied. Neither girl had looked at him with anything like interest, and it annoyed him. He'd been the one who'd made everything go crazy, not Bubbles. He'd made her look bad, too. It was his job to make her look bad. These chicks were drunk and stupid. He started past them, then impulsively grabbed the one with dark hair by the arm.

"Asshole!" she yelped, yanking away from him. But he hadn't wanted to cop a feel—he was checking whether she had a power. But there was nothing. She was an empty battery. It made him sad—and he hated that feeling more than anything.

"Jerk!" The uglier one snarled at him and looked like she might actually do something.

But then he put his hand up, using the universal gesture for a gun. He sighted down his finger at the girls.

"Bang," he said.

———

The zombies were nothing more than piles of dead flesh now. Zombie goo was splattered everywhere, but that couldn't be helped. *You kill zombies, it's gonna make a mess,* Michelle thought.

The parade had stopped, and some of the crowd who had climbed up onto the floats to get away from the zombies were making no effort to get down now. The rest of the crowd had poured into the street and surrounded the floats as well. It was a compete log-jam. People were sitting on the ground crying. Some of them were wounded.

Adesina crawled out from under the throne, and Michelle picked her up. "You okay?" Michelle asked, kissing her on the top of her head. Adesina nodded. "Will you be okay sitting on the throne?"

"Yes," Adesina replied. "But there are some men trying to get up here." Michelle put Adesina on the throne, then spun around. A couple of different men were pulling themselves up.

"Guys, other people are going to be needing this space," she said, growing a bubble her hand. She'd lost most of her fat during the parade and zombie fight, but there was still enough on her to deal with a couple of drunken douches.

"Hey, it's really crowded down here," complained one of them.

Michelle shrugged. "I don't care," she said. "Right now, this isn't a democracy. I'm queen of this float, and I refuse."

"Bitch."

"That's Queen Bitch, and there's a child here. Watch your language. Besides, the people who are in-jured need to be up here more than you do." The men grumbled, but dropped down and began pushing their way back through the crowd.

The cops were trying to restore order. Michelle called out to them, and they began bringing the wounded to her float. One of them stayed and started triage. Then Michelle heard sirens and a surge of relief went through her. Blowing things up and taking damage was the sort of thing she excelled at. But the aftermath was always more complicated and messy than she liked.

Now that things were starting to calm down, one of the krewe running the parade got on the loudspeaker for the float in front of hers and encouraged people to get out of the street and back up on the sidewalks. A couple of teenage boys helped the police reset the barricades.

Michelle pulled her phone out of her dress pocket as she moved away from the wounded. Michelle hated purses, and because her clothes were specially made, she always had pockets added. Though why women's clothes never had pockets was a mystery to her. She scrolled through her favorites and then hit dial when she found Joey's number.

"What the hell is wrong with you," Michelle hissed as Joey answered. "Do you have any idea what a fu . . . freaking mess you made here today?"

There was a long pause on the other end of the line. "What are you talking about?"

A fine red curtain of rage descended on Michelle. "I'm talking about zombies attacking a parade," she whispered. "Killing people in the crowd—and they were coming for me and Adesina."

"You fucking think I'd do something like that,

Bubbles?" Joey's voice was tremulous. It sounded worse than when they'd been in the People's Paradise of Africa and Joey had been running a hundred-and-four-degree fever. The hairs on Michelle's arms rose.

"Are you saying there's another wild carder who can raise the dead? Am I going to have to deal with two of you?" The red veil lifted, just long enough that another horrible thought slipped in. What if this had been just the first wave? *Honestly,* she thought. *Enough with the goddamn zombies already.*

The laugh that came over the line was hollow and mirthless. "For a smart bitch, you're awful fucking stupid. Obviously, we need to fucking talk. When can you get to my house?"

"I'm stuck here," Michelle replied. She looked around at the wounded on the float and the cops trying to get the crowd cleared out. There was zombie ick all over the sidewalks, and Michelle really wanted to smack Joey hard. "I'm kinda busy."

"Just get here quick as you can."

The connection went dead. Michelle stared at the blank screen.

"Are we going to Aunt Joey's now?" Adesina asked, tugging on Michelle's dress.

"Soon," Michelle replied, surveying the ruins of the parade. "Soon."

If there was one thing Joey hated, it was nosey cocksuckers sniffing about her business. Not that Bubbles was usually a nosey cocksucker. Given what she said had happened at the parade, Joey could even understand her being fucking pissed. But now she had to explain what was going on with her children.

The problem was that she had no idea.

One minute she'd been making her way back from the bakery up the street—early, because it was Mardi Gras, and there would be tons of tourist dickweeds otherwise—and the next thing she knew, it was as if a light had just shut off inside her head. Usually, she knew where every dead body lay for miles around, and she often had zombie bugs and birds moving about keeping an eye on things. And today had been no different, until the lights went out.

She'd been "blind" for a few hours, and then, just as abruptly, her power was back. Truth be told, she'd been out of her mind while her power was gone. And she'd been scared. Really scared. She couldn't remember the last time she'd been this frightened. *Yes, you can remember that time,* whispered a voice in the back of her mind. But Joey shut that thought down hard and fast—or tried to. *What did your mother say about lying?* the voice persisted. *Well, she'd lied, too,* Joey reminded herself. Her mother had lied, and left Joey alone, and what had happened after that . . .

Then Bubbles had shown up on her caller ID, and Joey had been relieved. Bubbles was the most powerful person she knew. Bubbles would keep her safe.

But when Joey picked up the phone, Bubbles started giving her shit. But Joey didn't know what had happened. And if she was being honest with herself, she was scared. What if she was losing her power?

Without her children, she wasn't safe. Without

them, she was just Joey Hebert, not Hoodoo Mama. Without Hoodoo Mama, no one, not even Bubbles, could protect her.

And when she thought about what not being Hoodoo Mama anymore would mean, she began to shake.

There wasn't much that Adesina didn't like. She liked American ice cream, American TV, and American beds. Ever since Momma had brought her to America, Adesina had been making a list of all the things she liked.

She liked Hello Kitty, the Cartoon Network, and taking classes from a tutor (even though sometimes she missed being in school with other kids). She even liked the way the cities looked. They were so big and shiny, and everyone talked so fast and moved around like they were all in a big rush to get somewhere important. Even if it was just to go to the grocery store.

And she liked Momma's friends. Aunt Joey (even though when they'd lived together in the PPA, Momma had kept yelling at Aunt Joey about her language), Aunt Juliette, Drake (even though he was a god now and they never saw him anymore), and Niobe. Sometimes they were invited to *American Hero* events, and she got to meet even more wild carders. But she liked Joker Town the best of all because no one there ever turned around and stared at her.

And she had liked being in the Joker Town Halloween parade with Momma, but she didn't like this parade now at all. Aunt Joey's zombies had attacked, and people were hurt. So they were going to Aunt

Joey's, and Adesina knew Momma was mad. She didn't need to go into Momma's mind to know that. It was pretty obvious.

Once, she and Momma had had a conversation about her ability to enter Momma's mind. Momma had made her promise she wouldn't do it anymore, but it was difficult to control. Once she'd gone into someone's mind, it became easier. She couldn't go into nats' minds—only people whose card had turned. She'd discovered that while they were still in the PPA.

And she wasn't going to tell Momma that she had already been in more people's minds than Momma knew. Sometimes it just happened when she was dreaming, but mostly it happened if she liked someone. The next thing she knew, she was sliding into their thoughts.

The police and ambulances came. The ambulance took the wounded away, and the police cleared out the crowd so the parade could head back to the storage facility. There was no more music, no more beads thrown, and no more bubbles.

Adesina didn't mean to, but she found herself in Momma's mind. Momma was worried. Worried about Aunt Joey and what she might have to do to her if Aunt Joey really had made her zombies attack. She was worried about Adesina and how much violence she was around. And she was worried about the people who'd been hurt at the parade.

Adesina wanted to tell her that zombies weren't as bad as being in the charnel pit. And that that wasn't as bad as what had happened to her after she'd been injected with the virus and her card had turned. Even though Adesina's mind wanted to skitter away from that memory, it rose up. She couldn't—wouldn't—forget what had happened.

The doctors had grabbed her and strapped her down to the table with brown leather straps that were stained almost black in places. Then they slid a needle full of the wild card virus into her arm. She'd looked away and stared up at the sweet, fairy-tale pictures they'd put on the stark white walls. But the girls in the pictures were all pale, not at all like Adesina.

The virus burned as it rocketed through her veins. She looked away from the smiling children in the pictures and stared at the ceiling. There were reddish-brown splatter marks there. Then blinding pain swallowed her and she was wracked with convulsions. Her body bowed up from the table. She tried not to, but she screamed and screamed and screamed. And then there was darkness and relief when she'd gone into chrysalis form.

The doctors didn't want Jokers, they wanted only Aces, and so they threw her body into the pit with the other dead and dying children. But she wasn't dying. She was changing. And while she was cradled in her cocoon, she found that she could slip into the minds of other people infected with the virus.

That was how she'd found Momma. Both of them were floating in a sea of darkness. But Adesina wasn't lonely anymore, not now that she had Momma.

But if she said anything about that time, Momma would know she'd been in her mind. So she grabbed Momma and made her sit on the throne and cuddled in her lap until the parade came to its final stop.

———

Bullets flew across the smoking landscape, past the charred and burned wreckage of tanks and jeeps. A grenade exploded next to Dan, and he took a massive amount of damage. His health bar was blinking red, and he was out of bandages.

"Jesus, RocketPac, you were supposed to take that bitch with the grenade launcher out," Dan snarled into his mic. He'd logged on as soon as he'd gotten home from the parade. "You fucking faggot."

"Suck my dick, CF," Rocket replied. Feedback screamed into Dan's headset. "If you'd given me the suppressing fire, I could have gotten close enough to get a shot off. Go blow a goat, you asshole."

"Turn down your fucking outbound mic, bitch," Teninchrecord said to Rocket. "And your goddamn speakers, you big homo. CF, tell me again why the fuck we let this useless scrub onto the team."

Dan fell back. He's been using a bombed-out building for cover, but it was clear it wasn't doing any good. And he needed to find some bandages. If they made it out of this without losing, he was going to kick that useless POS RocketPac off the team. He couldn't figure out how this team he'd never heard of was pwning them. Especially since they had the utterly fag team name We Know What Boys Like.

A shadow passed in front of the TV. Dan jumped and dropped his controller. "What the fuck!"

"Mr. Turnbull, we need to talk," Mr. Jones said as he picked up the controller and handed it to Dan. He wore a sleek dark grey suit, a white shirt, and a black tie. No one Dan knew ever wore anything like that. Dan was certain Jones wasn't his real name, but he could identify with not wanting everyone to know who you were. And Dan didn't want any more information than necessary about Mr. Jones.

He was afraid of Mr. Jones because Mr. Jones looked like he could snap Dan's neck without blinking an eye. Mr. Jones reminded Dan of a coiled rattlesnake.

Dan ripped off his headphones and yanked the headphone jack out of his computer. "That's a voice-activated mic," he snapped, but his hands were trembling. "I don't want those dipshits knowing who I am in real life. And I told my dad no one was supposed to come down here when the sign was up."

Mr. Jones shrugged. "Your father isn't home and I don't care about your little game," he said.

"I did what you asked," Dan said more defensively than he wanted. "I've got the video here on this USB drive." He stood up and dug around in his pocket until he came up with the lint-speckled drive.

Mr. Jones plucked it from Dan's fingers, then delicately blew off the lint. "I doubt we'll need it," Mr. Jones said, slipping the drive into the breast pocket of his suit. "There are already more than fifty YouTube videos up. More going up by the minute. And the local news interrupted programming to report on it. CNN and Fox are running breaking-news tickers, and we know they're working up their own spin on things. You did well."

Dan didn't know what to say. He was both flattered and scared. "Uh, thanks," he replied, and jammed his hands into his pockets. Out of the corner of his eye, he saw that his CntrlFreak avatar was down. *Shit.*

"We may need you to do another small task for

us," Mr. Jones said. He held out a thick manila envelope. "The payment. And a little extra."

A tingle slid up Dan's spine as he took the envelope. He thought about touching Mr. Jones's fingers to see if he was an Ace but, for the first time, it occurred to him that he might be out of his depth. "Sure, dude, whatever," he said. "But coming to my house, uh, maybe we could meet somewhere else?"

Mr. Jones's smile was shockingly white against his dark skin. "Looks like your team lost," he said, nodding at the monitor. "Combat Over" flashed on the screen. "I'll see myself out."

Dan took a long, shuddering breath when he heard the front door close. Then he opened the envelope and started counting.

The cab pulled to a stop in front of Joey's house. Michelle paid the driver, and she and Adesina got out. The house was a dilapidated Victorian with peeling paint and an overgrown garden surrounded by a wrought-iron fence. Dead birds nested in the trees and perched on the utility lines. In unison, they all cocked their heads to the left.

"Knock it off, Joey," Michelle said as she opened the gate. It gave a screeching complaint. *Has she never heard of WD-40? Even I know about that.* "Save it for the tourists."

"Caw," said one of the birds.

"Jerk," Michelle muttered.

A relatively fresh female zombie answered the door. She wore a cheerful floral print dress and was less filthy than most of Joey's corpses. *The dead don't groom,* Michelle thought. *They are so nasty.*

"Follow me," the zombie said. But it was Joey's voice Michelle heard. All the zombies had Joey's voice, and that was okay when the zombie was a woman. But it was weird as hell coming from a six-foot-tall former linebacker, as it sometimes happened.

"For crying out loud, Joey," Michelle said. "I know every inch of this house. You in the living room?"

The zombie nodded and Michelle pushed past it. Adesina flew up to Michelle's shoulder. "Momma, don't be too mad," she whispered.

"I'm just the right amount of mad," Michelle replied. Then she sighed, paused, and tried to get her mood under control. Adesina was right. Joey never responded well to an angry confrontation. Angry was Joey's stock-in-trade.

The living room was mostly bare. There were tatty curtains on the windows and a sagging couch against one wall. The new addition to the room was a large flat-screen TV. Across from the TV was Joey's Hoodoo Mama throne with Joey perched on it. She was slightly built and was wearing a shapeless Joker Plague T-shirt and skinny jeans. There was a shock of red in her dark brown hair and her skin was a beautiful caramel color. A zombie dog lay at her feet, and two huge male zombies flanked her chair.

Michelle and Adesina flopped on the couch. Joey frowned, but Michelle ignored it. "So, you want to explain what happened?"

The zombies growled, and then Joey said, "I had fuck-all to do with it." Her hands were gripping the arms of her throne, and her knuckles had turned white. "I can't believe you think I'd do something like that."

"Are you saying there's another person whose card has turned, who lives in New Orleans, and who can raise the dead just like you?" Michelle gave Joey her very best "Seriously, what the hell?" look. "That's a lot of coincidences, Joey."

"No, there's not a new fucking wild card who can control zombies," Joey said leaning forward on her throne. "There's one who can fucking well snatch powers."

"Jesus, Joey, language." Michelle glanced at Adesina, but she was already engrossed in a game on her iPad.

"Oh, fuck you, Bubbles," Joey said. "Adesina has heard it all and more. Haven't you, Pumpkin?"

Adesina glanced up and shrugged. "Yep. You cuss. A lot. But I'm not going to."

For a moment, Joey looked hurt. "Michelle, are you planting weird fucking ideas in my girl there?"

"No, just normal ones."

"That's a goddamn fool's errand for a Joker."

Michelle glared at Joey. "Back to your mystery wild card," she said. "What makes you think your powers were snatched? Maybe you just lost control."

The two big male zombies started across the room towards Michelle. Calmly, she dispatched them with a couple of tiny, explosive bubbles to the head. It took her last reserves of fat, but she wasn't putting up with any more of Joey's aggressive zombie shit.

"Motherfucker! Goddamnit, Bubbles, look at this

dick-licking mess! Christ!" The female zombie came in and began cleaning up the remains. "I'm fucking fine," Joey continued. "What happened wasn't my cocksucking fault. I went out to get some pastries at the bakery. On my way home, I bumped into some-one, then bang, my power just went away and I couldn't see any of my children anymore."

Her voice trailed off, and she looked so sad and scared that Michelle believed her. Michelle knew that Joey's card had turned because she'd been raped. But she didn't know any details and really didn't want to know them. She imagined that Joey must have felt as helpless now as she had then.

"Do you remember anything specific about how your powers were stolen?" Michelle asked. A wild card who could grab powers was frightening to con-template. They needed to figure out who it was. But even more, she needed to protect Joey from having her powers stolen again. Joey had never been espe-cially emotionally stable—Michelle reminded her-self that a lot of the wild carders she knew were just shy of permanent residence in Crazytown—but see-ing Joey's reaction now worried Michelle. Whatever having her power grabbed was triggering in Joey was bad. And Michelle was beginning to think it might be more important to help Joey deal than to get the person yanking her power.

Joey shook her head. "Fuck me, I've tried. I just remember being jostled, then . . . nothing."

Adesina tugged on Michelle's arm. "Momma, look," she said, pointing at the TV.

There was a long shot of the Bacchus parade as the zombies were attacking. The image zoomed in on Michelle as she began killing zombies. Joey turned up the volume on the TV.

"—ack on today's Bacchus parade. Michelle Pond, the Amazing Bubbles, was on one float and was the apparent target of the zombie attack. More horrifying is that Miss Pond had her seven-year-old daughter with her. Though Miss Pond managed to stop the attack, it is troubling that she had her daughter at an event where she would be exposed to such adult sights as women showing their naked breasts for beads. This isn't the first time that a public event featuring Miss Pond has turned violent. It does make one wonder about her choices."

Michelle jumped up from the couch. "What the fuck!" she yelled.

"Language," Joey said.

Adesina was worried. Momma was looking at videos of the parade on her laptop. Aunt Joey had switched off the TV after the news report, but Momma had pulled her laptop out of her bag and started looking for more reports online.

She'd found a lot of them. And even though Adesina tried not to, she couldn't help slipping into Momma's mind. And what she saw there was fear and anger and worry.

So she slipped out and started playing *Ocelot Nine* on her iPad again. Getting Organza Sweetie Ocelot out of the clutches of the Cherry Witch was easier than understanding the workings of the adult world.

———

Michelle's cell was buzzing. It had been buzzing since the attack on the parade. But she'd been ignoring the calls—she already knew things were screwed. The old adage "There's no such thing as bad publicity" was complete crap in her experience.

But she hadn't realized just how bad it was until she saw the news reports at Joey's house. And then she'd gone on YouTube and saw all the amateur videos.

It made her sick. *Of course there is going to be video everywhere, you idiot. It was Mardi Gras. Hell, it's just the way things are now. Not a moment unobserved.*

And there was still the issue of how Joey had lost her powers. More to the point, Joey's reaction to losing her powers was preying on Michelle's mind. She couldn't leave Joey alone in that state. Michelle decided she and Adesina would stay with Joey tonight and try to figure out what had happened. Much as she hated even considering it, Michelle thought she might have to ask Adesina for help. But God, she didn't want to do that. She didn't want to send her baby into Joey's mind. There were things Adesina did *not* need to see at her age—or any other age, as far as Michelle was concerned.

Since Michelle had decided that Joey shouldn't be alone for even an hour, the three of them cabbed it back to Michelle's hotel. Both Joey and Adesina were hungry, so Michelle left them in the hotel coffee shop while she went up to the room to pack a bag.

She slipped out of her dress and tossed it onto the bed. Then she pulled on a pair of baggy drawstring pants and a T-shirt. She needed to get fatter—throwing herself off Joey's roof hadn't done much—and her clothes needed to cooperate with a variety of sizes.

As she was packing an overnight bag, her cell began to ring again. She grabbed it off the bed and glanced at the number. It looked familiar, so she answered it saying, "Michelle here." She threw underwear, baggy pants, and T-shirts for herself into the bag, and then tossed in Adesina's favorite dress and nightgown.

There was a pause on the other end of the line. "Hey, Michelle. It's me." For a moment, Michelle's stomach lurched. It was Juliette. They hadn't spoken much since Juliette had left the PPA. And when they had, it was awkward. Sleeping with Joey had ruined Michelle's relationship with Juliette. And no matter how she tried, Michelle knew that there were some mistakes that couldn't be forgiven. "I saw some of the footage from the parade online," Juliette said.

Michelle's hands started shaking. *Crap, crap, crap.* She thought. *This is not the time to get emotional.*

"Yeah, it, uh, was intense."

"Was it really Joey?"

Michelle went into the bathroom and started grabbing toiletries. "She says no and I believe her," Michelle said. "This just isn't her style. She says someone stole her power, and right after the attack, her power came back."

There was another long pause. "So, you've been seeing her while you're there?"

Crap, Michelle thought again as she dumped the toiletries into a travel case. Then she released a stream of rubbery bubbles into the bathtub. A couple bounced out and rolled around the bathroom floor. Michelle kicked them, and they ricocheted off the wall. One hit her hard in the thigh.

"Yes, I went to see her," Michelle replied, reflexively rubbing her leg. *Stupid bubbles*. "Hello? Zombie attack. Who else am I going to see?" She went to the mirror and looked into it. *Stupid girl*. "We're not screwing, if that's what you're asking. And we haven't since that one time. And you broke up with me and I'm pretty sure that means I'm allowed to see anyone I like. And I'm really sorry."

Shit.

"You done?" Juliette asked.

"Yes," Michelle said meekly.

"I'm glad you went to see her. This thing is a PR disaster for both of you."

This flummoxed Michelle. "I thought, well, I mean . . ."

"Look, Michelle, this isn't about you and Joey and me. This is about Adesina. You suck as a girlfriend, but you've been a good mother to her. And I really hate the idea that someone's playing a political game that'll impact on Adesina's life."

Michelle slid down the bathroom wall and sat on the floor. The tiles were cold against her butt.

"I'm not sure what you mean. Why would this affect Adesina?"

An exasperated sigh, not unlike the one Adesina often gave, escaped Juliette. "How can you still be this naive? You're too damn powerful and too damn popular. They can't do much about the powerful, but they will happily destroy people's fondness for you. They need to marginalize you."

Michelle opened her left palm and let a light bubble form in it. She let it go and it floated around the bathroom. "Well, who would do that? And why use Joey?"

"Oh, it could be a lot of people: the NSA, CIA, and the PPA, for starters. Also, the Committee might be involved, though that's less likely. It could even be an entirely new group with their own agenda. And it's tough to come at you directly, but going through people you love . . ."

"I don't love Joey," Michelle said emphatically. What she wanted to say was "I love you. Please come back." Instead she said, "I've been off the radar for almost a year. It doesn't make any sense." Michelle rubbed her middle finger between her eyebrows.

"But you're back and already you're doing parades that remind people how you saved New Orleans. Not to mention that you adopted Adesina, who is just about the most adorable Joker in the world."

Michelle smiled. "Yeah, she is filled with adorableness, isn't she? I think she has a creamy chocolate center, too."

Juliette laughed, and Michelle thought her heart might break. "I'm gonna e-mail you a link to something," Juliette said. "This is what's at stake and how far they're willing to go to marginalize you."

Will this bullshit never stop? Michelle thought. *I'm just trying to have a life.* "Thanks for the help, Juliette. And . . . I'm sorry. I know it's not enough, but I'm really sorry."

There was another long pause. "Yeah, I know," Juliette said. Then the line went dead. *Great,* Michelle thought, rubbing away tears. *Just great. You're never*

going to make the Joey thing up to her, so stop trying.
You're lucky she even called.

But Michelle knew Juliette hadn't called for her
sake. She got up and ran cold water over a washcloth
and held it against her face for a few minutes. The
last thing she needed was Adesina seeing that she'd
been crying. Her daughter saw too much anyway.

Even though her power was back, Joey was still
grateful that Michelle was spending the night. She
had her children, of course. But now there was the
nagging fear that at any moment someone could grab
her power.

Adesina was sitting on the coach playing that
goofy game. *What the fuck are ocelots, anyway?* Joey
thought as she sat down next to her. "So, you really
like this game?" Joey asked. She wasn't a fan of video
games, but she'd played a few here and there.

Adesina nodded. "The ocelots are really cute, and
Organza Sweetie Ocelot is amazing. She has these
cool powers and she just goes right after the Cherry
Witch who wants to take all the ocelots' food and
land . . ."

Joey tuned Adesina out. It was something she did
on occasion. She just stopped listening and let herself
slide into her children. There were dead dogs and
cats. Dead people. Dead insects. She moved into
them all, seeing through their dead eyes. Her children
were the reason she was safe. No one could escape
the dead. They were all around. So no one could get
the drop on her.

But losing her powers for a few hours had been

horrible. She tried to push away the memory of losing control—but that made another, darker, memory come to the surface. Bile rose in her throat, and sweat broke out across her back. No, she wouldn't let it come back. She was Hoodoo Mama. She'd already killed that motherfucker. That was over and done—he couldn't touch her anymore.

"Aunt Joey! Aunt Joey!"

Joey opened her eyes. It took a moment for her to snap out of the memory. Adesina was sitting on her lap, and her front feet were on Joey's face. Tears were streaming down Adesina's cheeks. "Aunt Joey, please stop!" she cried.

"What the fuck?" Joey said. "What are you doing, Pumpkin?"

"You were stuck," Adesina replied. She slid off Joey's lap and wiped at her tears and runny nose with her feet the way a praying mantis might groom itself.

Joey got up. "I'll get you a Kleenex," she said, running for the bathroom. She grabbed the box off the back of the commode and headed to the living room. She saw Michelle running into the room from the other side.

"What the heck is going on here?" Michelle asked. "I could hear Adesina crying from upstairs." *What the ever-fucking hell?* Joey thought. *Am I really losing it? Fuck me!*

Michelle went to console Adesina. Awkwardly, Joey held out the box of tissues. A withering glance was all Joey got from Michelle as she pulled tissues out and started dabbing Adesina's face.

"You want to tell me what happened?" Michelle

asked Adesina. But Adesina wouldn't answer. She just curled up in Michelle's lap and closed her eyes.

When Michelle looked up, Joey wished she weren't on the receiving end of that look—and despite herself, Joey took a step back. *What happened?* Michelle mouthed silently. Joey shrugged and shook her head. And then Joey was pissed. Michelle *knew* she'd never do anything to hurt Adesina.

"Adesina," Michelle said softly. "Look at me."

For a moment, Adesina just lay there, but then she slowly opened her eyes. There was a stern expression on Michelle's face, and it struck Joey as mean. "Adesina," Michelle continued. "Did you go into Aunt Joey's mind without permission?"

"What the fuck are you talking about, Bubbles?" Joey asked. There were too many things she didn't want anyone to know about, much less have the Pumpkin see.

"Adesina can go into the minds of people who have the virus," Michelle said. "And I know she's been in yours before. Adesina, I told you about doing that, didn't I?"

Adesina nodded, and a tear slipped down her cheek. "I'm sorry, Momma," she said in a quavering voice.

"There are grown-up things you shouldn't be seeing, and it's an invasion of the other person's privacy. Like when you don't want me going into your room without asking."

That made Adesina burst into tears. Michelle hugged her. "It's okay, you just have to be more careful, honey." She looked up at Joey. "I think I'm putting Adesina to bed. It's been a long day."

"Yeah," Joey said. "Yeah, it really has."

After Michelle got Adesina settled for the evening, she
went back downstairs to talk to Joey. She found her in
the kitchen, pulling bottles of beer out of the fridge.

"You wanna tell me why the ever-lovin' fuck you
never mentioned that Adesina can get into my cocksucking mind?" Joey demanded, handing Michelle
a beer.

Michelle twisted off the bottle cap, flipped the cap
in the trash, and then took a long swig. "She's knows
she's not supposed to. And the one time before when
she ended up in your head, it upset her so much she
swore to me it would never happen again." What
Michelle wanted to tell Joey was that being in her
mind had made Adesina violently ill. That the garbage Joey was dragging around was toxic to Adesina
and most likely to Joey, too. But Michelle knew that
telling Joey anything was a losing proposition.

Another hard pull of the beer made Michelle's head
swim a little. Aside from jumping off Joey's roof before they went back to the hotel, she hadn't done anything to bulk up again even though she'd meant to.
She was thinner now, even more so than when she'd
been a model. It meant she got buzzed much more
quickly. And that wasn't feeling like a bad thing at all
at the moment.

"Did she tell you what she saw?" Joey asked.

Michelle shook her head. "I didn't really ask her
much about it. She's only seven. But really, how
much of what's in your head does she need to see?"
It was a cruel thing to say, but Michelle didn't much
care. No, that wasn't true. She was just worn out.

"I don't want the Pumpkin seeing . . . things." Joey chugged her beer, plunked the empty bottle on the counter, then went to one of the cabinets and pulled out a bottle of Jack Daniel's. "Best fucking way I can think of to forget. You want a shot?"

Michelle shook her head, then killed the rest of her beer. Golden warmth encased her. Her lips went a little numb. "That's not going to help us figure out what happened to you. And I actually thought about having Adesina go into your mind to try to find out what happened. But that's obviously a terrible idea." Michelle took another beer out of the fridge. *Screw it,* she thought. *So I get hammered. My life is rapidly going into the toilet.* "Oh, and I talked to Juliette when we were at the hotel. And then she sent me some links. The new meme out there is that I'm a terrible mother who routinely endangers the life of her child."

"What the fuck is a meme?" Joey asked after she took a swig of the JD.

Dan jammed dirty laundry into the washer, then dumped laundry soap on top. Laundry pissed him off. If his mother hadn't left, the house would be clean, there would be food in the fridge, dinner on the table, and he would have clean clothes when he needed them. Instead, he was going commando in some ratty jeans (and he hated that commando shit), and his T-shirt was so smelly it grossed him out.

But the day wouldn't be a complete loss. He and Teninchrecord had booted RocketPac from the team, and they were interviewing replacements in an hour. He knew that they needed someone good, but weeding out the noobs and scrubs was going to be hilarious. After starting the washer, he headed back down to the basement. He'd replaced his old sofa with a tricked-out gaming chair using some of the money he'd gotten for grabbing Hoodoo Mama's power. The chair had built-in speakers and an ergonomic design in black leather that perfectly cradled his ass. His dad was at work, and Dan was looking forward to settling in for a nice long gaming session.

Except when he got to the bottom of the stairs, he saw that Mr. Jones was ensconced in his chair. *Son of a bitch,* Don thought. "Most people might start by knocking on the front door."

Mr. Jones smiled, and Dan didn't like it at all. "Dan, you might remember I told you the other day we might have need of you again. It appears we need you sooner than we expected."

For a moment, Dan thought about trying to get more money this time. But Mr. Jones's persistent smile made him leery. "What are you looking for? More of the same? There's all kinds of Mardi Gras stuff happening."

Mr. Jones had Dan's controller in his hands. He hit the start button, and Dan wished he could just kill him. The password page came up, and Mr. Jones punched in Dan's password.

"What the fuck?" Dan said.

"Do you seriously think we don't know everything there is to know about you, Dan? Your password is nothing. The location of your mother? That was simple, too. In fact, Dan, with the exception of your power, you're just not that complicated."

Mr. Jones was putting Dan's CntrlFreak avatar through his paces. And he was kicking major amounts of ass. It made Dan feel sick.

"Then why not just have me take Bubbles's power and then kill her?" Dan asked.

"Because we may have need of her in the future," Mr. Jones replied. "In your scenario, you could use her power once—and then, if she were dead, it would be gone and you couldn't take it again. A matchless resource would be lost."

Mr. Jones executed a perfect jump and roll with CntrlFreak, then single-head-shotted two combatants. "Perfect!" flashed on the screen.

"Not everyone is as uncomplicated as you are, Dan," Mr. Jones continued. "Take the lovely Miss Pond, for instance. She's ridiculously powerful, and yet, she cares little for that. But her friends, well, they're what matter to her.

"I could have had you steal her power, but that wouldn't have mattered to her. And we're not in the business of destroying people. We're in the business of managing them."

Watching Mr. Jones play the game made Dan want to jump straight out of his skin. And he didn't really give a shit about why Mr. Jones was doing anything he was doing—or why he was asking Dan to do anything. Just so long as they paid him. But he itched for Mr. Jones to put down the controller, get out of Dan's new chair, and tell him what the hell he wanted this time. The rest was just jacking off as far as Dan was concerned.

"But tormenting her friend," Mr. Jones said smiling beatifically, "well, that's another matter. That will teach her the lesson I mean for her to learn. That no one she loves is safe. That she can't protect them. There are a lot of people in the world now who are extremely powerful, Dan. Controlling them isn't always about their personal peril. It's about explaining to them the limits of their power. The world may be changed because of the virus, but people, well, they're still the same."

Mr. Jones made CntrlFreak do a diving jump over several dead bodies, then he rolled up into a perfect kneeling position, gun extended, and squeezed off a single-bullet killing shot.

"We'll need you tomorrow morning," Mr. Jones said as he put another bullet into the head of another player's avatar. "I'll send a van to get you at six a.m."

"Winner!" flashed on the screen. Mr. Jones got out of Dan's chair and tossed him the controller. "Have fun playing," he said.

Michelle woke up feeling muzzy-headed. She'd only had two beers, but at her current weight, it had hit her like a Mack truck. Actually, it wasn't that bad. She'd been hit by a couple of Mack trucks. And even a bus once. It was frustrating that there wasn't a large vehicle handy at the moment. She'd have to make do with having Joey's zombies pound on her for a while to get fat.

She rolled over and saw Adesina curled up in the center of the extra pillow. Michelle smiled. She reached out and touched Adesina's new braids. They'd been experimenting with different hairstyles, trying to find one Adesina liked. But Michelle suspected Adesina just enjoyed having her hair done.

"Stop playing with my braids, Momma," Adesina said.

Michelle pulled her close, saying, "But they're so awesome! I'm jealous!"

Adesina giggled, opening her eyes. "We could braid your hair. It's long enough."

"Yes, but it would look like crap the next day, and yours looks amazing. Let's go downstairs and see if Aunt Joey has anything for breakfast in the fridge besides beer."

But when they got downstairs, Joey was gone. There were no zombies in the parlor and none in the kitchen. And when Michelle went outside, there wasn't a single dead pigeon in sight.

Dammit, Michelle thought as she pushed open the gate, left the yard, and began looking up and down the street. *I told her not to go off alone. And now I've got to do something I really don't want to do. I am so going to kick her ass when we find her.*

"Adesina," Michelle said, "I know I told you not to go into Aunt Joey's mind, but we need to find her fast."

"It's okay, Momma," Adesina replied, flying into Michelle's arms. As Michelle cradled her, Adesina closed her eyes.

A minute later, her eyes snapped open. She squirmed out of Michelle's arms and floated down to the ground. Then she began running. Adesina could only fly short distances, but she ran fast. Michelle followed, wishing again that she'd piled on some fat.

Adesina ran down the street, turned right, then left. Then she ducked into an alleyway. The stink of puke and rotting garbage hit Michelle in a wave. A large Dumpster squatted at the end of the alley. Adesina slowed as she reached it, and Michelle heard sobbing. She stopped running and hesitantly approached the far side of the Dumpster.

Joey was sitting on ground with her back against the building's brick wall. Her arms were clasped around her legs, hugging them tight against her body.

"Joey," Michelle said softly as she crept forward. *Oh God,* she thought. *I should have been there for her.* "Joey, honey, it's me. It's Michelle."

Joey's shoulders shuddered, and then she looked up at Michelle. "Jesus, Bubbles," she said, her voice jerky from crying. "I shouldn't have come out here alone. They took my power again. I can't see any of my children."

Adesina flew to Joey's shoulder and gave her a quick kiss on the cheek, then hopped to the ground. "It's okay, Aunt Joey, we're here now," she said.

"I just wanted to get some pastries for breakfast," Joey said, wiping her nose on her sleeve. "Croissants, maybe a few turnovers. I know the Pumpkin likes turnovers. I just wanted to get something for breakfast. And then everything went dark."

Michelle reached out and took Joey's hands. They were shaking and cold. "C'mon," she said, pulling Joey to her feet. "Let's go home."

"But I didn't get the goddamn pastries," Joey said stubbornly. "There's nothing for breakfast. The Pumpkin needs breakfast."

"We can get breakfast later, Joey," Michelle said as she slowly pulled Joey down the alley. "Adesina will be fine without breakfast for a little while longer, won't you, sweetie?"

Adesina flew back up and into Joey's arms. Joey reflexively caught her. "I'm not hungry at all, Aunt Joey."

"But you need something to eat," Joey said stubbornly. "I was going to get pastries." Joey toyed with Adesina's braids. "My mother used to braid my hair."

Holy hell, Michelle thought. *She's unspooling. We've got to find whoever is stealing her powers. And, barring that, figure out a way for her to cope with losing them. And why steal Joey's power? Why not mine?* She'd rarely felt this helpless. She couldn't figure out a way to help Joey and she couldn't stop the person stealing Joey's power. It was infuriating. *When I find the person who's doing this to Joey, I will end them.* But she knew that was a lie. She'd give up ever finding them if she could only keep Joey safe.

"We could stop and get some turnovers on the way home," Joey said. She hugged Adesina tight. "You want something for breakfast, Pumpkin?" Adesina glanced at Michelle.

"We should get you home," Michelle said. "I'll go out after and get something."

Joey shifted Adesina into one arm, then grabbed Michelle's wrist. "No," she said. "You can't fucking leave me alone. Please. Not while my children are gone."

"It's okay," Michelle said, gently pulling Joey's hand away. "I won't go anywhere if you don't want me to. We'll figure it out." Michelle put her arm around Joey and led her home.

"So, where do you want me to use the zombies?" Dan asked. He was sitting in the paneled van with Mr. Jones and some other dude who was driving. It felt like his head was about to come off. Hoodoo Mama's power was kicking around in his skull and rattling his bones. It sang in his blood. It wanted to *move*.

"Dan," Mr. Jones said in a bored voice. "Don't be impatient."

Dan scratched at his arms. The power felt different this time. Angrier. This was the first time he'd grabbed a big Ace power more than once. He'd assumed it would be the same, but it wasn't. It felt like its own entity. As if he'd swallowed a bowl of bees.

"Mr. Jones," he said. "I'm not feeling so good."

Jones turned and looked at Dan. "Would you care to be more specific?" he asked in a flat voice.

"I . . . I . . . I'm not sure," Dan stuttered out. "Hoodoo Mama's power feels different this time. I'm having a hard time keeping it in. I've never grabbed a power like hers more than once." He didn't want Mr. Jones to know how strange the power felt this time.

Mr. Jones's cold, dark eyes appraised Dan. Normally, this would have scared Dan, but the power felt bad and was getting worse by the second.

"How annoying," Mr. Jones said. "We didn't anticipate your power would be so . . . inconsistent. He turned back around, and then said to the driver, "It's early, but let's do the drop."

The van jerked forward. Dan's head hit the side window. "Ow," he said, but neither Mr. Jones nor the driver said anything.

A few minutes later, the van stopped. Dan looked around. Victorian houses lined the street. Most were shabby looking and run-down.

"Bring me a zombie," Mr. Jones said as he pulled an envelope out of his breast pocket. Gratefully, Dan reached out and found a wealth of dead all around. "What do you want?" he asked. "Rats, dogs, cats?"

Mr. Jones glanced over his shoulder with an expression of contempt on his face. "Bring me a dead person, Dan."

Dan got the closest one he could find. It was a relief to be using the power. He could feel it starting to drain away from him. The buzzing died down to a dull hum. "Where do you want it?" Dan asked.

"Bring it here, have it take this note, and send it to that house two doors down across the street. Have it ring the bell and give the note to whomever answers the door."

"The one with the wrought-iron fence?" Dan asked to be sure. He didn't want to make Mr. Jones mad.

"Yes."

Dan did as he had been instructed.

The doorbell rang. Joey jumped, and Michelle reached out and patted her on the arm. It didn't help. She felt Joey trembling.

There was a zombie standing on the porch when Michelle answered the door. It held out an envelope. Michelle took the envelope, and then the zombie fell over in a heap.

The envelope was addressed to Michelle. *Okay,* she thought warily. *This isn't weird at all.*

There was a single sheet of paper inside the envelope.

Miss Pond,

   We haven't been introduced, but my employers are big fans of yours. They've admired your many good works for years now. That said, they think you've had quite a nice run, but it might be time for you to retire and take a long vacation from the public eye.

   The incidents with Joey Hebert are just a small sample of what we can do to people you care about. Persist in having such a public profile, and we will take more drastic measures. Perhaps something having to do with your child.

   I look forward to meeting you soon.

                                          Sincerely Yours,
                                               Mr. Jones

Michelle stared at the letter, trying to figure out who sent it. "Mr. Jones" was a transparent pseudonym.

Was Juliette right? Was this whole thing designed to marginalize her? And why target Joey? Joey helped the people who needed it who lived on the fringes of New Orleans society—why would anyone want to shut that down? Sure, some of them were grifters and other shady types, but some were home-less people who just needed looking after.

And me, Michelle thought. *What the hell? I'm not affiliated with any agency anymore. I don't try any of that vigilante bullshit. Why would anyone even care?*

"Michelle!" Joey said as she came running down the hall. "My children! I can fucking see them again!" She danced gleefully around Michelle, then glanced outside. "Why is that body on the porch?" The body sat up as Joey possessed it.

Michelle held the letter out to Joey, who took it and read it quickly.

"Is this Mr. Jones the motherfucker who's been taking my power?" Joey was jumping from one leg to another as if she'd been hitting the Red Bull hard all day.

"I'm not sure," Michelle said. "He could just be an errand boy. There's no way of knowing. My guess is that they're going to do something again—I just don't know why they're going after you." She looked at Joey and didn't like what she saw.

Joey's eyes were wide, and she was jittery as hell. Losing her power wasn't just making her ner-vous—it was making her angry, too.

"Joey," Michelle said. "I know losing your power is horrible, but you told me when we were in the PPA that knowing where all the nearby dead bodies were all the time made you kinda crazy. Wasn't it a little bit of a relief when it went away?"

Hands shaking, Joey gave the letter back to Mi-chelle. "No, yes, no," she said. "In the PPA there were so many bodies. And so many of them were dead children. You remember, Bubbles. And at first, when my powers vanished, I was just me. And that was nice. But then I started remembering how it was before I turned into Hoodoo Mama . . ." Her voice trailed off.

Michelle frowned as she closed the door. "I don't know what to do. It's clear they want me to stay the hell out of the public eye, and they're willing to fu . . . mess with you to get me to do it. Maybe I should reach out to someone from the Committee."

"No!" Joey exclaimed. "No! I don't want anyone to know this is happening. What if they take my powers away forever? Jesus, Bubbles, what the fuck would I do then?" Her face began to crumple as if she was about to cry, and then a furious expression replaced it. "And, Bubbles, *I* want the fucker who's been yanking my power. This Mr. Jones mother-fucking turd prick-ass bastard is going to pay."

"I'd like nothing more than to see him pay, too," Michelle said. She needed Joey to remember what had happened when her powers were taken. That was the most important thing right now. "This time was like the last time, right?"

Joey nodded, but she was still shaking.

"So," Michelle said. "They grab your power, use it, and then you get it back?"

"Yeah."

"Then my guess is they *can't* keep it. Otherwise, they'd just grab both our powers and be done with it. That's what I'd do. And you were out both times they took your powers, so maybe there needs to be line of sight, or proximity?"

Joey nodded and looked relieved. "I'm glad you're here, Bubbles," she said, with just a hint of a smile. "I mean, you know I still think you're a cocksucking bitch, right?"

"Well," Michelle replied. "You got that half right."

"Let's see what the Pumpkin wants for breakfast," Joey said as they went into the living room.

"Unless it's beer and bourbon," Michelle replied, "we've got to make a grocery run."

"You go make the run," Joey said. "I'll be okay here for that long. But I'm pretty sure I heard her saying she looooves bourbon for breakfast. Girl after my own heart."

Momma and Aunt Joey were laughing. Adesina felt the knot in her stomach loosen a little—until they came into the room. Then it was clear to her that they were putting a nice face on things. She didn't need to slip into their minds to know that.

There was a smile on Momma's face, but it wasn't one of her real smiles. And Aunt Joey was smiling, too, but Adesina could see the ghosts in her eyes.

"You up for some breakfast?" Momma asked as she sat on the couch next to Adesina.

"Your mom says you're not down with bourbon for breakfast," Aunt Joey put in. "I keep telling her you're my homegirl, but she doesn't believe me."

Adesina made her sincere face. "I'd love bourbon for breakfast, Momma."

"Okay," Momma replied. "But I'm going to pour it over your cereal. Yum."

"Gah," Adesina said. Once she'd been very bad

and snuck a taste of Aunt Joey's bourbon. It was disgusting. "I want French toast."

"I'll go to the market," Michelle said as she leaned over and kissed the top of Adesina's head.

"Be careful, Bubbles. They could grab your power," Joey said. She bent down to tie the laces of her ratty Converse sneakers. Her hands shook as she did so. "It was bad when they took my power. It'd be much fucking worse if they got yours."

Momma shrugged. "I've been out in public and they could've already gotten my powers. So I don't think they're interested in it, Joey." She leaned over and kissed Adesina. "Don't let Aunt Joey do anything stupid like go out of the house, sweetie."

"I won't, Momma," Adesina replied.

Dan rubbed his face. He'd been about to explode when he'd had Hoodoo Momma's power. Even after using it, he was still jittery as hell. But maybe that was because he was stuck in a van with Mr. Jones and the creepily silent driver.

"Uhm, can you drop me back at my house?" he asked as he fidgeted in his seat.

"Yes, Dan, we will drop you off at your house," Mr. Jones said with barely concealed distaste. "I'm very disappointed in you, Dan. These things need to be timed properly and you didn't do your part."

A cold, slippery feeling slid into Dan's gut. "Uh, I know," he replied. "It's like I told you. I've never grabbed a big Ace power twice. And I didn't know it would be so weird the second time. I just don't know what happened. I'm sure it was nothing."

Mr. Jones didn't reply. Dan rubbed his palms on his pants. A silent Mr. Jones was worse than a talking one.

He decided that the next time Mr. Jones wanted him for anything, he'd just say no. It'd never occurred to him that there might be limitations on what he could do, or that yanking a big power more than once might have blowback. He needed to figure out what the real parameters of his ability were. And there was no way Mr. Jones was interested in helping him with that. Mr. Jones was interested in whatever weird-ass mind-fuck shit he was up to. And nothing else.

The van slowed in front of Dan's house. Dan was reaching for the door handle before it came to a stop. But before he could open the door, Mr. Jones's hand was clasped hard around his wrist.

"Just a moment, Dan," he said. "I forgot to give you your pay." He held out a fat manila envelope.

For a fleeting moment, Dan thought about turning it down. But then he took it.

"I'll be in touch," Mr. Jones said.

Dan nodded. What he wanted to say was "Fuck no, you crazy prick. I'd rather eat ground glass than deal with you again."

And it wasn't until he got to the front door that he realized Mr. Jones had no wild card abilities in him at all.

I'm not afraid, Michelle thought. *Well, not much anyway.* The streets were still pretty empty despite the fact that it was Mardi Gras. She went into the local corner store and began grabbing what she needed to make French toast.

"Hey, you're the Amazing Bubbles, aren't you?"

Michelle looked up and saw a young girl. She was maybe sixteen with hair dyed black, black clothes, black Doc Martens, and a wealth of silver studded and spiked jewelry. A pale face with heavy black eyeliner and crimson lips completed the look. Michelle wondered how she hadn't sweated through everything, including the heavy Pan-Cake makeup.

"Yeah," she replied. "I am." She dropped a loaf of bread into her basket and started to the dairy section. The girl followed.

"I thought what you did at the parade was awesome," the girl said. "I mean, you were really great."

Eggs, half-and-half, and butter went into Michelle's basket. "Thanks," she said as she walked to the produce section. "Just doing what I can."

What if this is the wild card who can grab powers? Michelle thought. *What kind of sick asshole would send a girl after me?* But then she realized that if this was the wild card who'd grabbed Joey's power, she would be just as helpless as Joey had been.

"Well," the girl said, "I just wanted you to know I really admire you. You've been my favorite wild card since *American Hero.*"

Michelle smiled at the girl. If they were going to grab her power, they would be doing it soon. "Would you like an autograph?" she asked.

"Oh, I couldn't ask for that," the girl said. "But would you mind a picture of us together?" She held up her phone.

"Sure," Michelle replied. Michelle put her arm around the girl and smiled as the picture was snapped. "And what's your name?"

"Dorothy," the girl said as she looked at the image. "Hey, this came out amazing."

Michelle laughed. "Well, I am a professional. Or I was."

"Hey, thanks," Dorothy said. "Uhm, I just want you to know I don't think you're a lousy mother. I don't care what anyone is saying."

Michelle tried to keep her expression neutral, but she was irritated. And then she reminded herself that this was the way it was. You become famous, and you give up part of yourself. And Michelle knew she was lucky. Even with all the weird crap in her life, she could pay the bills and give herself and Adesina a decent life. So she made herself smile brightly and say, "I really appreciate that, Dorothy. It was nice to meet you."

"Mr. Jones would like to see you and Joey Hebert in two days, nine in the morning, at Jackson Square," Dorothy said. "He thinks it's time for you to meet in person." She gave Michelle a bright smile, then vanished.

For a moment, Michelle just stared at the spot where Dorothy had been. *Yeah, I was not expecting that,* she thought. Then she went and grabbed a bottle of vanilla extract. It was going to be one of those lives.

Joey was washing the breakfast dishes while Michelle dried. It was nice. Nice and normal, and that made Joey mad. She didn't know why. But she knew it wasn't the way she should be feeling.

After they'd finished eating, Michelle had asked for a couple of Joey's zombies to knock her around and fatten her up. It took a while, but eventually Michelle stopped looking like a horrific thinspiration photo and was pleasantly plump. Joey thought Michelle looked especially pretty when she was plump. Joey liked her girls curvy.

Then they'd come back inside and started cleaning up the kitchen. Adesina was flopped on the couch, playing her game, so Joey didn't bother to have her help. Sure, her mother might have said they were spoiling the child, but Joey didn't see it that way.

"I had another message from Mr. Jones," Michelle said softly while wiping a dish.

Joey looked over her shoulder to see if Adesina had heard. But she was still engrossed in her game. "What the fuck did he want?"

"He wants us to meet him in Jackson Square day after tomorrow morning at nine," Michelle replied. "Oh, and the messenger was a sixteen-year-old girl who can teleport."

"We're not going to go, right?" Joey asked. "That would be fucking insane." Joey wanted to hit something. Hard.

"I'm going," Michelle whispered. She kept drying dishes as if it were the most normal thing in the world to do while talking about some thug who wanted to steal your powers. "It's the only real choice we have. Unless you want to go underground, leave your home, and assume a new identity. Avoiding these people—whoever they are—just gives them power over you."

"But they've already got power over us, Michelle," Joey hissed, soapy water splashing on the floor as she angrily dumped the frying pan into it. "In case you've forgotten, they've yanked my power twice. Maybe they'll yank yours next."

Michelle nodded, then opened the silverware drawer and began putting utensils away. "They might," she said. "But if that happened, it wouldn't be the end of my life. I'd go back to what I was before. It wouldn't change what I've done and it wouldn't change who I am." Michelle slid the drawer shut.

"Well, it's fucking easy for you to say, Bubbles," Joey replied. "You had a life before your card turned. I had jack shit. Except for my mother." The thought of her mother made a hideous lump form in the back of Joey's throat. She swallowed and tried not to cry. "I was just a kid when my card turned."

And even though Joey had banished almost every moment of that day, flashes of what had happened would still swim to the surface. And she knew if she hadn't turned into Hoodoo Mama, she would have died then.

"I know it's easy for me," Michelle replied gently. She dropped the towel on the counter and turned to face Joey. "And that's why I need to do something to help you. If you'll let me."

Joey threw her sponge into the sink. "And what the fuck do you think you can do?"

Michelle grabbed Joey's hands. "I can have Adesina

go into your mind—into your memories—and she
can . . . help you."

Joey grew very still. "What do you mean?" she
asked.

"You know that Adesina can go into your mind?
Well, when we were in the PPA, after all the fighting
had stopped and we stayed to help the children
we'd found there, Adesina went into some of their
minds and she . . . she took their pain away. She
made them forget what had happened to them."
Michelle paused and then she dropped Joey's hands.
She picked up the dishtowel, folded it, and then
hung it on the rack. "I stopped her from doing it
because I didn't like how depressed she got afterward."

"Well, why would you fucking let her into my
mind knowing that she's already been in there once
before and it wasn't a fucking fun time?" Joey's
hands were shaking and she jammed them into the
pockets of her jeans. "I don't want her in my head.
And I don't want to remember. I *won't* remember.
Why should I?"

"I've been giving this a lot of thought," Michelle
said. "And I talked to Adesina about it—to see if my
plan would even work. She'll be in your mind, but
not in the way she usually goes into someone's
mind. I'm going in for her. Well, more like with her."
Michelle rubbed her forehead and sighed. "I'm not
describing this well. Adesina has linked two sepa-
rate minds together before—by accident. So it'll be
difficult. But she wants to help. And given our time
frame, I don't see that there are any other solutions.

So, yeah, I'm not going to be winning Mother of the Year anytime soon."

"Fuck," Joey said rocking back on her heels. She shook her head. "I don't think I can let Adesina do that. What if she sees . . . something a kid shouldn't see? What if *you* see?"

"Joey," Michelle said, exasperation hard in her voice. "We can't go on the run from these people. Christ, I can't even figure out who they work for. You freak when your power is lifted. I think I have a way to fix that—or at least a way to make the memory this is triggering go away. You have to be okay with not having your power. Otherwise, they can get to you. And I can't be here all the time. You need to deal with this. Yeah, it's a suck solution, but it's the only one we have. Do you really think I'd do this to my daughter if I could think of any other option? And may I remind you that Adesina is in danger from these assholes, too?"

"Honestly, Bubbles," Joey replied as she rocked back and forth on the balls of her feet. "I've seen you do some pretty bad shit."

"Yeah?" Michelle replied as she turned away from Joey and began putting dishes in the cupboard. "Welcome to the working world."

It took another two hours of arguing before Joey finally agreed to let Michelle and Adesina into her mind—and then only with the understanding that if Joey gave the word, the experiment ended.

"Where do you want to do this?" Joey asked.

They were in the living room, and Joey had cleared out the usual zombie guard because Adesina mentioned that they were stinky.

"It easiest when the other person is asleep," Adesina said. "That's how I found Momma. When she was in the coma."

"Well, I'm not tired," Joey said.

"We could go upstairs and use the guest bedroom," Michelle suggested. "You could lie down and just try to relax."

"Fuck," Joey muttered as she turned and stomped out of the room. Michelle and Adesina followed her. And Joey couldn't help noticing that Michelle didn't say anything about her bad language in front of the child.

Adesina had a fluttery feeling in her tummy. She was pretty sure she could bring Momma into Aunt Joey's mind. But once they were there, could Momma really protect her? Adesina loved Aunt Joey, but there were things lurking in the dark corridors and rooms there that scared her.

Aunt Joey lay down on the bed, and Momma lay down beside her. Adesina hopped up and snuggled between them. Aunt Joey's body was rigid, her arms stiff and tight against her side. Momma rolled onto her side, reached out, and took Aunt Joey's left hand. Aunt Joey sighed, then relaxed a little. And then Adesina slid into Momma's mind.

It was a comfortable place for Adesina. Momma's mind was like a big, open house. There were pretty views out the windows and lots of bright, airy rooms.

There were a couple of rooms Momma wouldn't let her go into, but Adesina didn't mind. Momma had explained that some of it was grown-up stuff, and some of it was private.

And there were bunnies in Momma's mind, too. Adesina liked the bunnies, but never could figure out why Momma had so many of them.

"Hey there, kiddo," Momma said. She was standing next to the windows looking out at the view holding a fat rabbit. "You ready to do this?" She turned toward Adesina, put the bunny down, and Adesina ran and jumped into her arms.

"I'm ready, Momma," Adesina said. And then she reached out for Aunt Joey.

One moment Michelle was in her own mind, or at least Adesina's interpretation of her mind—and the next, she and Adesina were in the front entryway of a version of Joey's house. But it was bigger than Joey's actual house. There were corridors that spawned from the main hallway. Michelle saw that they were lined with closed doors.

"Joey?" Michelle yelled. She tried not to shout in Adesina's ear, even though she knew she wasn't really carrying the child in the crook of her arm. "Where are you, Joey?"

"Here," Joey replied from behind her. Startled, Michelle spun around. There, in the multicolored light from the stained-glass windows in the front door, was Joey. She looked frailer and younger than she did in real life.

"You scared the crap out of me," Michelle said.

She reached out and touched the intricately carved chair rail that ran the length of the hall. "Your house looks different in here."

"Yeah, I don't know if that's me doing it or the Pumpkin," Joey replied as she slowly turned around and took in the front entrance and hallway. "I guess if I ever got around to sprucing the place up, it might look like this. And that front door is really fucking cool."

Michelle kissed Adesina on the head and then put her down. "End of the line for you, kiddo," she said. "I want you to stay here, okay? Aunt Joey and I need to go the rest of the way alone."

"Wait," Joey said. She brushed by Michelle and opened the first door on the left. "I did something for the Pumpkin."

Adesina and Michelle turned and peered through the doorway. Inside the room were overstuffed couches upholstered in a faded chrysanthemum print. The couches were positioned in front of a large flat-screen TV. A couple of burly zombies played checkers on a table under the bay window. Several otters sat on the couches eating popcorn and watching cartoons on the TV. Adesina gave a squeal of delight, then ran into the room and hopped up on the couch next to the smallest otter.

Michelle looked at Joey and then cocked her head. "Really? Do otters even eat popcorn?"

"My head, my rules," Joey replied with a grin that surprised Michelle. "Besides, Adesina really loves those otters."

"I know," Michelle said. "Weird, huh? I guess we should get going."

Joey's smile faded. "Yeah, I guess we should."

"You're going to have to lead," Michelle said. "I have no idea where to start."

"I do," Joey replied. Her voice was sad. "It's this way." Then, much to Michelle's surprise, Joey took her hand.

They went to the second to the last corridor leading off the main hallway and turned into it. There were sconces lining the walls here, but several of the bulbs had burned out. The walls were painted a dull grey, and the hall runners sported an undulating pattern in chartreuse, smoke, and brown. There were three doors along each wall in this hallway, and there was a door at the far end as well. Joey slowed, and Michelle had to tug her hand to get her to move forward again.

"I know you don't want to do this," Michelle said. "But it's the only choice."

Joey stopped in front of the first door on the right. "I know," she said as she reached out and threw open the door.

Sunlight spilled into the hallway. They stepped through the doorway. The light was so bright that, for a moment, Michelle was blinded. She blinked, and blurry images turned into people.

Michelle and Joey stood at the top of a hill. Below them, a tall, willowy woman in a blue sundress was laughing at something a bandy-legged man standing beside her had said. She took a long drink from the tallboy in her hand. Around them ran a short, skinny, young girl.

"Mommy," Joey whispered. Then she pointed at the little girl. "And that's me down there, too."

"How old were you?" Michelle asked. She couldn't take her eyes away from the scene. Everything about it was golden and warm.

"Eleven," Joey replied, her voice wavering. Michelle glanced at her.

"Why are you crying?" Michelle asked, perplexed. "You look so happy here."

"It's the last fucking happy memory I have."

Michelle looked back to the scene. Joey's hair was done up in braids, and she wore a pink T-shirt and overalls. She threw head back and laughed and laughed, the perfect image of her mother.

"Screw this," Joey said. She yanked them out of the room, then slammed the door shut. The golden light was gone, and they were back in the gloomy hall-way.

Joey dropped Michelle's hand, then ran to another door and yanked it open. Michelle sprinted to catch up with her. Inside, Joey's mother was sitting on a bed with Joey. Joey's mother wore a tatty floral housedress and her hair hadn't been combed. Joey was wearing a blue T-shirt with faded but clean jeans.

"I'm never gonna leave you, baby girl," Joey's mother said, her words slurring. She patted Joey's head and toyed with her braids. "I don't know where you get these crazy ideas."

There was a sick look on Joey's face. "You've been spending a lot of time in bed, Mommy," Joey said, touching her mother's cheek. "And you forget stuff. And you never want to eat anymore . . ." Joey's voice trailed off.

"Oh, baby girl, you know your mother has a bad memory," her mother said as she lay back against the pillows. Michelle saw now that Joey's mother's belly was distended and her skin was ashy. Even the whites of her eyes were yellow. Joey's mother was ill—very ill. "Always have had a poor memory," Joey's mother continued. "There's nothing to that. Your uncle Earl John is here to help me remember things."

"Mommy," Joey said, inching closer to her mother. "I don't like Uncle Earl John. I don't understand why you're with him."

"Baby girl," her mother said as she pushed herself up again. It looked like it took an effort. "When you get older you'll understand that it's hard to make a living. Your uncle Earl John takes care of us. He buys us what we need."

"I don't fucking want what he buys," Joey said in a surly voice.

Her mother slapped her across the face.

"Don't you take that tone with me," Joey's mother said. Her tone was angry, but her eyes were scared. "And don't you use that nasty language."

Young Joey rubbed her cheek, and adult Joey mimicked her. Michelle wanted to say something to help, but she was at a loss. Her parents had been horrible, but at least they had never hit her.

Then Joey's mother began to cry.

"Oh God," she said, pulling young Joey into her arms. "I'm so sorry, baby girl. I love you and I just want you to be safe after . . . I just want you to be safe. Uncle Earl John will keep you safe. He promised."

"It was the only time she ever hit me," adult Joey said, her voice hitching with tears. "She never let *anyone* touch me. Not ever. None of those cocksuckers she married. None of the ones she just fucked. They could beat the hell out of her, but never once did she let them hit me." She pulled Michelle out into the hall again and slammed the door shut.

"Where to now?" Michelle asked. At the dead end of the hall was a door flanked by flickering sconces. She pointed at it. "What about that one?"

"No," Joey said, taking a step backward while wiping the tears from her cheeks.

"Maybe it's what we're looking for," Michelle said, grabbing Joey's hand and pulling her toward the door.

"Michelle, don't!" Joey cried.

But it was too late. Michelle was already opening the door. She stepped through the doorway, dragging Joey along, and found herself on a rise overlooking a cemetery. A small knot of mourners was gathered around one of the small crypts.

Michelle saw young Joey. She as wearing a dark blue dress and was sobbing. Next to her was the man from the first room. He was rubbing Joey's back, and the sight of that action made the hairs on Michelle's neck stand up.

Abruptly, Michelle found herself in the living room of a shotgun house. There were casserole dishes laid out on card tables, and a group of women were fussing over the dishes and Joey. Michelle could see into the kitchen where a group of men were talking and drinking. The women in the living room clucked over the men's boozing between attempts to get Joey to eat. But Joey just sat curled up on the ratty sofa and cried.

The scene shifted again. It was dark outside, and

in the back of the house Michelle heard someone banging around. Joey was still on the sofa, her legs pulled up under her chin. Her face was vacant. The guests had left, and someone had cleaned up the living room.

"Hey, baby girl," came a loud, slurred voice. Joey didn't respond, but Michelle turned. The short man with bandy legs leaned against the doorjamb. There were sweat stains on his shirt, and he'd pulled his tie loose. It was the man from the funeral. Joey's uncle Earl John.

"Baby girl!" he said louder. Michelle could smell the liquor on his breath. "You hear me?"

For a moment Joey didn't answer, but then she turned toward him. "Don't call me that," she said in a flat voice. "No one but my mother calls me that."

"Well, your drunk-ass, junkie momma is dead as a doornail," he said, pushing himself from the doorjamb. He staggered into the living room. "All the money I spent on that lush, down the drain. But you, well, you're going to fix it. Goin' to clean my house, goin' to fix my dinner, and goin' to get in my bed."

He grabbed her. Joey shrieked and tried to yank her arm away. But he held on tight and jerked her off the sofa.

Michelle instinctively tried to bubble—but nothing happened.

Of course not. This was Joey's memory, and Michelle was just a spectator. And then Michelle realized that her Joey—grown-up Joey—was gone.

"Let me go!" Joey screamed, but her voice and face switched back and forth from child to adult

Joey. "Let me go!" She kicked, but it didn't do any good. Joey was just a skinny slip of a thing.

No. No. No. No. I don't want to see this, Michelle thought. *God, I don't want to.*

The memory began to fragment. Michelle found herself in a bedroom. A slice of light fell across the bed from the open bathroom door. The heavy smell of bourbon was everywhere.

The ceiling had a stain on it, a brown water stain from a roof leak. Joey remembered exactly how it looked. The edges were darker than the center. And then he was grabbing her legs and forcing them open. Joey screamed, and he released one of her legs and fumbled with his pants. The stain looked like Illinois.

There was a heavy weight on Joey's chest. She couldn't move. The world spun, and she thought she was going to be sick. She rolled over and started gagging. Earl John pushed her off the bed.

"You puke in the bathroom," he said.

Joey crawled to the bathroom. The floor tiles were blue, and until today Joey had always loved the color of them. She lifted the seat on the toilet and dry heaved. Nothing came up because she hadn't eaten in two days.

Something ran down her leg. She wiped at it. Her hand came away sticky and smelled like the river.

The memory jumped again. Earl John was holding Joey facedown on the bed. Joey pushed her face into the pillow and breathed in her mother's smell that still lingered there. It was Mommy's favorite rose perfume. Joey heard her own pathetic cries and Earl John's grunting, but it sounded as if it were coming from somewhere else. Somewhere far away.

Then he was done and he rolled off Joey and went into the kitchen. There was the sound of the refrigerator opening, and a glass being filled with ice cubes.

Joey wanted to die. She could die here with Mommy's smell in her nose. They'd be together, and she wouldn't have to feel the disgusting stickiness between her legs anymore.

"You just stay like you are, baby girl," Earl John said. "I'm going to break all your cherries tonight."

Joey didn't know what he meant. But she knew Mommy wouldn't want him to touch her. Mommy never let any of them touch her. Ever!

Earl John threw back his drink and set the glass on the dresser. He started toward Joey and there was another jump in time.

Someone was banging on the front door. Then there was the sound of wood smashing. Earl John jumped up, went to the side table, and pulled a gun out of the drawer.

"What the hell?" he said as he turned around. Then he gave a high-pitched shriek. Joey rolled over and saw Mommy in the doorway.

"You hurt my baby," Mommy said. But it was Joey's voice that came out of her mouth. "I told you to take care of her."

Earl John shot Mommy twice in the chest.

But Mommy just smiled.

"Can't hurt us no more, Earl John," she said. Joey

mouthed the words, too. "Can't hurt us no more, you fucker."

And then Mommy ripped Earl John's head off.

Joey sat in the middle of the bed, her knees pulled up under her chin. She hurt all over. Mommy came and sat on the bed, too.

"I'm sorry, baby girl, I shouldn't have left you alone," she said. Her voice was still Joey's.

"It's okay, Mommy," Joey said. She crawled to Mommy and put her arms around her. Then she laid her head on Mommy's shoulder. "You're here now." Then Joey looked around the room. Earl John was scattered everywhere. The sheets were gross and streaked with blood. Then she looked at herself. There were bruises on her legs and arms and blood on her thighs. She started to shake. "What do I do?" she asked. "I gotta do something."

Mommy laughed. "Well, baby girl, you need to get dressed. But before you do that, you should wash up. Use my shower."

Joey slid off the bed, but her legs were weak and barely held her. Mommy grabbed her and helped her get to the bathroom. Mommy ran the water in the shower until it was warm—almost hot. She helped Joey into the shower, and then Joey lathered herself over and over until all she could smell was Mommy's soap.

Then Mommy helped her get dressed and braided her hair again. And together they went into Joey's room and packed a suitcase. Then Mommy went back into her own bedroom and rifled through all of Earl John's things until she came up with all the cash he had. Joey waited for Mommy to finish.

"Where are we going, Mommy?" Joey asked when Mommy returned.

"Wherever you want, baby girl," Mommy said in Joey's voice. "Wherever you want."

After Joey's mother saved her, the memories fragmented.

But the one constant from that terrible night onward were the zombies. After reanimating her mother, Joey began to raise more and more of the dead. They were often in different stages of decomposition, but the smell didn't bother Joey at all. And the more zombies Joey raised, the stronger she felt. And Mommy was proud of her.

But, like all zombies, Mommy began to fall apart. It was then that Joey realized her mother was really gone.

Joey put her mother back into her crypt and left her there. Then she plunged into the underworld of New Orleans and turned herself into Hoodoo Mama. As Hoodoo Mama she ruled the grifters, the street hustlers, and the people who were lost and stuck on the fringes. Joey was a queen in this world, and her justice against men who hurt women was swift and terrible.

And Hoodoo Mama never let anyone hurt Joey again.

———

And as she watched all of this, Michelle realized she'd
been wrong. Even though Michelle wanted nothing
more than to erase the horror of what had happened that night from Joey's mind, it wouldn't be
right to do it. What had happened was part of Joey
now. It had made her who and what she was. There
were ways for Joey to deal with her pain, but having
Adesina just cut that part out was wrong. To do so
would banish Hoodoo Mama forever.

They'd have to deal with Mr. Jones and his power-
stealing Ace some other way.

As soon as she realized that, Michelle found herself back in the hall with Joey and Adesina. Joey was
sitting on the floor.

"Sweetie, how did you get here?" Michelle asked
Adesina. "I thought we said you were going to stay
back in the otter room."

"I know, Momma," Adesina replied. She was sitting on her back legs with her front legs in Joey's
hands. Tears were running down Joey's cheeks. "But
Aunt Joey needed me, and you were stuck."

"Did you see anything?" Michelle asked ner-
vously.

Adesina shook her head. "No, just some zombies.
But they're everywhere in here."

Michelle plopped down on the floor next to Joey.
"You okay?" she asked.

Joey shook her head. "I don't know," she said. She
looked at Michelle. Tears stained her cheeks, and
her eyes were red and puffy. "My mother came back
for me and she made him pay. She told me she'd
keep me safe." Tears ran down her cheeks. "Fuck, I

hate crying," she said. "And I never, ever, wanted to think about that again. Hoodoo Mama shut it away."

"Look," Michelle began as she reached out and wiped the tears from Joey's face. "What happened to you was unspeakable. And you were just a child. You did what you needed to in order to survive."

"Fucker asked for it," Joey said with a hiss.

"Oh, I think that barely begins to cover it," Michelle said. She sat down in front of Joey and took her hands. "But you were just a little girl then. Even if they steal your power, you're a grown woman now. They can't control you."

"But if I'm not Hoodoo Mama, who am I?" Joey asked with a plaintive cry. "You saw what happened to me. If I'm not Hoodoo Mama, how can I stop those fuckers?"

"You're Joey fucking Hebert," Michelle replied. "And Joey fucking Hebert *is* Hoodoo Mama whether she has a wild card power or not. That's who the hell you are. And day after tomorrow we're going to tell this Mr. Jones he's gonna stop fucking with *both* of us."

"Momma," Adesina said. "Language."

It was muggy and hot the morning they were to meet Mr. Jones. Joey's eyes were gritty from lack of sleep, and she rubbed them. She'd heard Michelle get up in the middle of the night and go downstairs. Then she'd come back up to bed around four. Joey had assumed she couldn't sleep, either.

At 8 a.m. there was a knock on the front door. Joey went to the door flanked by two linebacker-sized zombies. She found a blond woman wearing a neat navy blue suit on the porch. Then she saw a black SUV with tinted windows parked in front of the house.

"Good morning. I'm Clarice Cummings, and I'm here to pick up Miss Pond's daughter," the blond woman said politely. "Will you tell her I'm here?"

Another one of Mr. Jones's scams, Joey immediately thought. Her zombies stepped toward the Cummings woman. "Yeah, I call bullshit, lady. You can tell Mr. Jones to fuck all the hell off. Or I could just send you back to him in pieces."

"Joey, it's okay," Michelle said as she ran to the front door. "I called in a favor. Thank you for the help, Miss Cummings. Adesina will be right here."

Miss Cummings smiled, and Joey decided she liked her just a little. "I'm happy to help. Adesina is one of my favorite pupils."

"Miss Cummings!" Adesina exclaimed, pushing herself between Joey and Michelle's legs. "Momma, you didn't tell me Miss Cummings was going to be here!"

Michelle grinned. "I wanted it to be a surprise. Besides, you've missed too much school this week. Now you're going to go with her, and I'll come to get you later this afternoon."

"I don't have my school bag," Adesina fretted.

"That won't be a problem," Miss Cummings said. "Everything today is on the computer."

Adesina jumped up and down excitedly. Miss

Cummings laughed, then turned and started down the steps. Adesina followed her.

"Don't I get a kiss?" Michelle asked, her voice mock sad.

Adesina spun around, and then flew up into Michelle's arms. "Sorry, Momma," she said, planting a big kiss on Michelle's cheek.

Michelle kissed Adesina's forehead. "I'll see you soon," she said, and then she put Adesina down.

Adesina ran back to Miss Cummings and began chattering excitedly about lessons.

Joey shook her head. "I don't fucking get it," she said. "I hated school."

"Well, Adesina loves it," Michelle said. "And I needed someplace safe for her today. Before we came back to the States, I talked to Juliette about how to approach Adesina's education. I didn't want to send her to regular school, and it would have been dumb for me to homeschool her. I even thought about moving to Joker Town and having her go to school there, but I was worried everything there would be about being a Joker. And I wanted her to have as normal an education as possible."

Joey laughed. "You mean as normal as possible for a Joker who can go into other wild cards' minds? With a mother who's one of the most powerful Aces on earth?" She turned and went inside. "You coming?"

"I guess," Michelle replied. She followed Joey inside and then shut the front door. "Anyway, Juliette found out about this program for kids with wild cards. They monitor their development, they get

classes, and they give them a place where they're not
the only wild card. And it's a mix of Deuces, Aces,
and Jokers. They also allow a really flexible schedule. Adesina started there when we got back from
Africa."

Michelle and Joey went down the hall into the
kitchen. Joey pulled out her coffeepot and Michelle
got the coffee from the cupboard. She toyed with
the edge of the bag.

"There's one more thing," Michelle began. "Miss
Cummings knows that Juliette gets Adesina if anything happens to me."

"But nothing is going to happen to you," Joey
said. "I mean, what can they do to you?"

Michelle shrugged. "Who knows?"

But they both knew. If Michelle's power could be
stolen, she could be killed.

Michelle hadn't been back to Jackson Square since
she'd absorbed Little Fat Boy's nuclear blast. There
was a shrine to her in one corner of the park. Flowers and handmade signs decorated a small official
placard.

She knew Mr. Jones had chosen Jackson Square
to screw with her. Absorbing that blast had done
something terrible to Michelle. It had driven her
half-mad and had caused her to fall into a coma
where she'd wandered alone for over a year. That is,
until Adesina had found her and pulled her out of
that dark, insane place.

The Square and surrounding area were oddly
vacant, and Michelle didn't like that at all. She and

Joey were the only people there. Even Café Du Monde was bizarrely vacant. And there were usually a least a couple of homeless people camped out on the benches. But not this morning. No doubt part of Mr. Jones's preparations.

She scanned the area. Mr. Jones hadn't arrived yet, but she and Joey were a little early. Joey was keeping watch on the whole square using zombie birds and insects. They'd agreed that Joey wouldn't make a big display of zombie power. Not only because they wanted Mr. Jones to see they were cooperating, but in case Joey's power got taken again, there would be fewer dead things for the other wild card to use.

"How the hell did they clear everyone out of here?" Joey asked. She jammed her hands into her jeans pockets and rocked back on her heels.

Michelle shrugged. "I have no idea," she replied. "But they must have clout to clear it during Mardi Gras."

"You're early," Mr. Jones said.

Michelle jumped, and then turned. Dorothy and a young man in a hooded sweatshirt were standing next to him. A bubble formed in her hand. She made it heavy. When it released, it would be fast as hell. When it hit, there would be carnage. They might nab her power, but she was going to get one last bubble off. And make it count.

"Hello, Michelle," Dorothy called out brightly. Today she was wearing a pale blue dress with a striped apron, and her hair was done up in pigtails.

"You're running with a bad crowd," Michelle replied. The bubble quavered in her hand. "But cute outfit."

Dorothy grinned and smoothed her skirt. "Thanks! My mother always said I'd end up in trouble."

It was an odd group: the girl, the boy in the hoodie, and the man who was so obviously a kill-first-ask-questions-later type. Michelle knew Dorothy's power was teleportation, so she wasn't the power thief. That just left Mr. Jones and the kid with the unfortunate complexion.

"I'm just here for a little conversation," Mr. Jones said with a toothy smile. Despite the mugginess and rapidly rising heat, he looked cool. Michelle wondered how that was possible. Even his suit was crisp and impeccable.

"Dorothy you already know. This is Dan. He's the one who's been lifting Miss Hebert's power."

"Fucker!" Joey yelled.

"Oh, most likely not," Mr. Jones said. "If you were downwind of him, you'd know why."

"Hey!" Hoodie Boy said.

"Why are you telling us this?" Michelle asked. "I mean, can you not see this bubble? Can your boy yank both our powers before I get this bubble off?"

Mr. Jones smiled, and Michelle really wished she hadn't seen it. She'd battled crazy people before. She'd even fought people she was convinced were evil. But Mr. Jones was worse. His eyes were cold and dead. And the suit and all of his smiles couldn't disguise that he was devoid of humanity.

"I thought I was clear, Miss Pond," he said. "Killing me—or even all three of us—won't stop my organization. Consider me an errand boy. I make deliveries, send messages, take out the trash. In the great scheme of things, I am unimportant."

He smiled again. It didn't improve upon repetition.

"For instance," he said. "I could kill young Dan here." Then, in one swift motion, he reached into his jacket, pulled out a Glock, and held it to Hoodie Boy's head.

"Fuck!" Joey said.

"Shit!" Hoodie Boy said.

Michelle let her bubble fly—but Dorothy touched Mr. Jones and Hoodie Boy, and they teleported ten feet to the left. The bubble hit the wrought-iron fence surrounding the park and blew an enormous hole in it.

"Settle down, Miss Pond," Mr. Jones said. "I'm just trying to explain that even useful people reach an end to their usefulness. Dan's been handy, but his power, unlike yours, now appears to be unpredictable. But we adapt."

"Jesus, dude," Hoodie Boy said his voice quavering. "I'll do whatever you want, just don't shoot me."

"Miss Hebert has a very nice power, but her psychological profile is . . . subpar," Mr. Jones continued with a slight smile, ignoring Dan. "She's too unstable to be of any real use to us other than to manipulate you."

Michelle wanted to blow a hole in him but knew that Dorothy would just teleport them again.

That's when Michelle heard it. A faint rustling noise above her.

She looked up and there—spiraling down towards them—were hundreds of zombie birds. Dan, Mr. Jones, and Dorothy followed her gaze.

"How irritating," Mr. Jones said. "Dorothy . . ."

The girl grabbed the back of Dan's hoodie, and they ported. They reappeared next to Joey, and Dan grabbed her hand. Joey shrieked.

The zombie birds suddenly started flying erratically, crashing into one another.

Then Dan screamed, and his face turned red. Veins bulged out from his neck.

"Dan," Mr. Jones said calmly. "You're such a disappointment." He grimaced and leveled his Glock at Dan again. One moldy pigeon flew into Mr. Jones's face, and then Dan and Joey gasped at the same time.

The flock of zombie birds coalesced again and began to lower onto Mr. Jones and Dan.

"You played with my pain, fucker," Joey said. "That wasn't nice."

Dan scrambled to his knees and lunged at Michelle. He touched her bare arm, and there was a terrible wrenching inside her. The world tilted and went grey for a moment. Then the contact was broken, and Michelle staggered backwards. She was empty inside, as if someone had scooped out part of her. It was awful.

Dan made a whimpering noise and fell to his knees as bubbles filled his hands and rose into the zombie birds coming for him. But instead of exploding, the bubbles just kept floating upward as if made from soapy water.

Then Michelle's power flowed back into her like a tidal wave. It filled her up and made her whole. Relief surged into her. She was Bubbles again.

Dan was still on the ground. It was clear to Michelle that his power-snatching ability was spent. So that just left Dorothy and her teleportation, and Mr. Jones and his Glock.

"Little girl," Joey said, her voice cold, "Dorothy's your name? I suggest you bounce back to the fuckers who sent you and you tell them that we're off-limits. Or there will be more of *this*."

And then, in an eyeblink, the zombie flock descended on Mr. Jones and Dan.

Dan just lay there, twitching and crying, as the birds blanketed him. Michelle had a momentary twinge of guilt at seeing him buried under the birds, but then she remembered how she felt when he lifted her power and a cold anger filled her.

Mr. Jones pulled his Glock and began firing, but his bullets were useless against the zombie flock. Then he lowered his gun and aimed at Joey, but it was too late.

The birds engulfed him, and he shrieked as they ripped his flesh. He dropped his gun and began yanking the birds away from his face, tearing them to pieces as he did. But there were too many. And still they rained down on him.

"I'm Hoodoo Mama, fuckers," Joey said. Her tone was icy and imperious. "And this is *my* parish."

Dorothy squeaked, then vanished.

It grew dark, and Michelle looked up again. The sky was filled now with thousands of dead birds blotting out the sun. Crows, pigeons, waterfowl, sparrows, and more that she didn't recognize. She'd never seen Joey resurrect so many dead things at once before.

And when Michelle looked back at Joey, she was filled with awe. The scared and nervous girl Michelle had been trying to protect was gone. Joey's eyes had turned solid black, and her face was filled with rage. It seemed as if she were growing larger and larger. As if she had become a force of nature.

No. She had become a force *beyond* nature.

A force stronger than death.

She had become Hoodoo Mama.

And God help anyone who messed with her.

In the next instant Mr. Jones vanished, enveloped by the zombie flock. He screamed and screamed and screamed. Blood pooled under the mass of birds.

"Oh Jesus!" he shrieked. "Help me! Jesus, help me!"

"Jesus can't save you, fucker," Joey said in a cold voice. "No one can."

Then the mass of birds collapsed as Mr. Jones crumpled to the ground. Even then he kept kicking and screaming.

"Mommy," he cried. "Mommy!" His voice rose up into a high-pitched keen.

Then he fell silent. For almost a minute, one of his feet would pop out of the mass of birds as he kicked and flailed.

But after a while, Mr. Jones stopped doing even that.

And Dan was already still and silent.

Joey turned then and looked at Michelle with a beatific smile on her face.

"I think you were right, Bubbles," she said. "I think I *am* going to be okay."

With that, Joey threw her arms wide open and spun around. Ten thousand zombie birds swirled around her and rose back up to the sky.

Samuel Sykes

Sometimes you'd better *listen,* as hard as you can, if you want to survive . . .

Samuel Sykes is a relatively new author. His novels to date include *Tome of the Undergates, Black Halo,* and *The Skybound Sea,* which together make up the Aeons' Gate series. Born in Phoenix, Arizona, he now lives in Flagstaff, Arizona.

NAME THE BEAST

When the fires of the camp had died and the crows settled in the boughs of the forest, she could hear everything her husband said.

"And the child?" Rokuda had asked her. He spoke in the moment the water struck the flame. His words were in the steam: as airy, as empty.

They only spoke at night. They only spoke when the fires were doused.

"She's asleep," Kalindris had replied. Her words were heavier in the darkness.

"Good. She will need her rest." There had never been a darkness deep enough to smother the glimmer of his green eyes. *"You should, too. I want you bright and attentive."*

She had not looked up from sharpening her knife. Just as she had decided not to stab him with it for talking to her in such a way. Fair trade, she had reasoned. She ran her finger along the edge, felt it bite cleanly. She slid it into a scabbard before reaching for her boots, just where she had always left them.

"She can rest. She can stay resting. I'll leave before

dawn. I'll be back before dusk. She never has to know."

"No."

For want of hackles, her ears rose up, sharp and pointed like her knife. They folded flat against her head. Rokuda had not seen it. Even if he had, she had reasoned, he wouldn't care. He was like that.

"I asked no question," she had replied.

"What am I to tell her, then?" Rokuda had asked.

"Whatever you wish. I left without her. The beast was too close. The tribe was in danger. I could not to wait for her." She had pulled on her boots. *"I don't need your words. You can give them to her."*

"No."

"Do not say that word to me."

"She has to learn. She has to learn to hunt the beast, to hate the beast, to kill it."

"Why?"

"Because we are shicts. Our tribes came to this world from the Dark Forest. Before humans, before tulwars, before any monkey learned to walk on two legs, we were here. And we will be here long after them. Because to protect this land, they all must die."

His speeches no longer inflamed her. She felt only chill in his words now.

"She has to learn to be like a shict," Rokuda had said. *"She has to learn our legacy."*

"Yours."

Kalindris felt him in the darkness as he settled beside her. She felt his hand even before he had touched her. In the prickle of gooseflesh upon her skin, in the cold weight in the pit of her belly. Her body froze, tensing for a tender blow. She felt each knucklebone of each finger as he pressed his hand against the skin of her flank.

Like it belonged there.

"Be reasonable about this . . ." Honey sliding down bark, his voice had come.

"Don't touch me."

"The other tribesmen won't look at her. They won't listen to her. They look at her and wonder what kind of creatures she came from. What her parents were to raise . . . her. You must take her to the forest. You will show her how it's done."

"I must do nothing. And you can't change everything you don't like."

"Yes I can."

Bark peeling off in strips, his voice came. He tightened his fingers. She felt every hair of every trace of skin rising up. She felt the knife at her belt. She heard it in its sheath. She heard her own voice.

Steam in darkness. Airy. Empty.

"Don't touch me."

Between the sunlight seeping through the branches overhead, she could hear the forest.

A deer's hoof scratching at the moss of a fallen log. A tree branch shaking as a bird took off into the sky. A line of ants so thick as to forget they were ever individuals marching across a dead root.

Sounds of life. Too far. Her ears rose. Kalindris listened closer.

A moth trying hard to remain motionless as a badger snuffed around the fallen branch it sat upon. A tree groaning as it waited for the rot creeping down its trunk to reach its roots. The crunch of dead leaves beneath a body as a boar, snout thick with disease and phlegm, settled down to die.

Closer. She drew in a breath, let it fill her, exhaled.

Air leaving dry mouths. Drops of salt falling on hard earth. A whining, noisy plea without words.

And she heard it.

The Howling told Kalindris who needed to die.

"This is taking forever."

Her ears lowered. Her brows furrowed. Her frown deepened.

The child.

Talking.

Again.

"You already *found* the tracks," the child complained. "Two *hours* ago. We could have found the beast by now. Instead I've spent half an hour waiting, half an hour searching for more tracks, half an hour shooting arrows through the gap between those branches over there and half an hour wondering how best to shoot myself with my own bow so I can deny boredom the pleasure of killing me."

The Howling left her, swift and easy as it had come. The shicts asked for nothing for their goddess, Riffid. To invite her attention was to invite her ire. She had given them nothing but life and the Howling and then left to the Dark Forest. They had spent generations honing it, the sense above all others, the voice of life and of death.

And somehow, the child's whining could send it away in an instant.

"When do we get to the *hunt*?"

It didn't matter. The Howling had shown Kalindris enough. The other noises of life and death weren't important. She held on only to that final one, that which teetered between the two. The sound of uncertainty. The sound that waited for her to tip the balance toward darkness.

Kalindris rose. The leaves fell from her hunting leathers as she slung the bow and quiver over her shoulder. The leather settled into a familiar furrow upon the bare skin of her neck's crook, the only other presence she had ever allowed that close to her throat. And the only one she ever would again, she thought as she rubbed a scar across her collarbone. She could still feel as she ran her hands across the scarred flesh. Every knucklebone of every finger, sinking into her skin.

Without a glance behind her, Kalindris hopped off the rock and set off after the noise. The forest rose up around her in aloof pillars, not like the familial closeness of the inner woods that left no room for sunlight. Too much light here on the border of the sea of trees; too much seeing, not enough listening. The Howling didn't speak clearly here. She had to keep her ears up and open.

They rose up like spears and she listened. Leaves crunching, an offended cry, hurried breath.

The child.

Following.

Still.

"*Hey!* Don't treat me like I'm an idiot!" the child protested, hurrying after her. "If you're going to try to abandon me, at least be a little less obvious about it. It might give me the opportunity to track you and get *something* done today."

Abandonment needed more than she had to give.

That needed malice, anger, and she could spare none for the child. That was for someone else, along with her arrows, her knife and this day.

"Why won't you talk to me?" the child asked. "I did everything right. I followed the tracks like you showed me. I've done everything you told me to. What did I do wrong?"

The child spoke too much. That was why Kalindris didn't speak; the child used all the words. That was what she did wrong. She shouldn't need nearly as much as she used. She shouldn't need *any*. The Howling was the shict language, that which came with breath and wailing as they were born.

And the child couldn't hear it. The child couldn't use it. She could only breathe. She could only wail.

It hurt Kalindris' ears.

"Are we at least going the right way?" the child asked. "I can't come back until the beast is dead. If I do, I don't get my feathers. I won't be accepted." The child's voice dropped. "Father said."

She stopped and cringed.

Rokuda said. Rokuda said lots of things. Rokuda said things like they were fact, like his word was all that mattered. Anyone that disagreed saw those bright green eyes and wide, sharp smile and heard his honey when he told them they were wrong.

Before Kalindris knew it, her back hurt. Her spine was rigid like a spear and visible beneath her skin. She turned around, ears flat against the side of her head, teeth bared.

The child stood there. Her hair was too bright, cut like some golden shrubbery and the feathers in her locks stuck out at all strange angles. The bow around skinny shoulders was strung and strung wrong, the skinny arms were too small to pull back the arrow. And her ears stuck out awkwardly, one up and one down, long and smooth and without notches in them. They were always trying to listen for something they couldn't hear.

Her eyes were far too green.

"Your father," she said, "is not always right."

"If that were true, everyone wouldn't listen to him when he speaks," the child protested. She swelled with a rehearsed kind of pride, the kind she clearly felt she should have, rather than actually possessed. "When Father speaks, people listen. When he tells them to do something, they *do it*."

Words. Heavy words coming from the child. Like she believed them.

An agonizing moment of concentration was needed for Kalindris to unclench every knucklebone of every finger from her fist. She had to turn away and tear her eyes and shut her ears to the child. She hefted her quiver, continued to follow the noise through the trees.

"We shouldn't have come here. We should have listened to it."

"We had no choice. Just keep moving. *Keep* moving."

Mother and Father were fighting again.

"It got Eadne. That *thing* got my Eadne. And we left her. And we ran. From our own land!"

"Gods, will you just *shut up* and let me think?"

Mother and Father were not scared because they were fighting. And so neither was Senny.

Whenever she would get scared, she would look to Mother and Father. Mother would look at Father and get mad. Father would look at Mother and start yelling. And they would fight too much to be scared. So she would hold onto the little knife tucked away in her belt and she would be ready to fight and she wouldn't be scared, either.

No matter how fast they were running. No matter how hard Mother was pulling on her arm.

"It *killed* her. It left her in a tree and painted the bark red with her. We should have stayed. We should have buried her. We shouldn't have run."

"We didn't have a choice, you *idiot*. It was going to come for us next. It's coming for us *now*. Think of her."

Senny knew who they were talking about. Father called them monsters. They had come to their little house and told him to leave. They said it was their forest. He told them he wouldn't. So they took Eadne.

Their name sounded like an angry word.

Father reached down and took Senny's other hand. He pulled on it, too. Maybe to show Mother he could pull harder, so he wasn't as scared. She pulled her hand back so she could grab the little knife and show Father she wasn't scared, either.

But he didn't notice.

He was looking forward. Mother was looking back. They said Eadne was back there, but Eadne wasn't coming with them. They weren't talking about

Eadne. Maybe they didn't want her to feel scared. She already knew, though. She had seen Eadne up in the tree with the branches and the leaves and her legs all blowing the same way in the wind.

Mother wanted to go back, but she kept moving forward with Father. Through the trees, back to their little house by the brook.

It was a good house. She knew that even if Father hadn't said so when he told Mother they were going to live there. Bushes full of berries that were good to eat grew by the brook. And there were snares to set and rabbits to catch and Mother had showed her how to make stew. The forest was scary, but Father had given her the little knife. They told her never to go in there.

She looked past Mother's arm at the trees. When they had come here, they looked dark and scary. But she had gone in there with the little knife. She knew there were places there they could hide from the beast, from that *thing* that got Eadne.

"Father," she said.

"Keep moving," Father said.

"But, Father, the forest—"

"I know, I know, I know."

Senny held up the little knife. "There are places, and there are berries and we could go there and I'm not—"

"Gods damn it, not *now,* you little shit!"

He didn't say that word around her a lot. Because he thought she didn't know what it meant. But he said it before, when he told them they were coming to the forest, when he built the house, when the people

with the feathers in their hair came and told him to
go away. His name for them was that word. She
knew what it meant.

And he used it a lot more when he was scared. It
was what the monsters were named. What their name
sounded like.

"I don't care if the shit's upset because we're in a
lot more shit than we need to be because you won't
shut the shit up about all the *shit*!"

Mother wasn't talking anymore.

Maybe Mother was scared, too.

She held on to her little knife. And she held on to
Mother's hand.

When the moon began to sink over the sea of trees
and the starving owls went to their holes hungry,
she tried not to hear him.

"*One more thing.*"

Only in darkness did Rokuda speak to her. Only
when he could not see her trying to ignore him,
when she could not go busy herself with some other
task and pretend, for a while, he wasn't hers. Only
when he couldn't see her run her fingers along the
scar on her collarbone.

"*I want you to bring back proof,*" he had said.

"*Proof,*" Kalindris had echoed.

"*A trophy. Something to show the tribe she has
done it. I want you to make sure she had blood on
her hands.*"

"*You want me to bring it back to you.*"

"*Yes. Take it and shove it in her hands, if you*

must. Tell her that it will make me proud. She will do it then."

"She can't shoot," Kalindris had said. *"She can't draw the bow back far enough and she can't stalk prey. She's loud. Like you."* Kalindris continued lacing up her boots. *"She can't do it."*

"She has to."

Kalindris froze as Rokuda sat on the furs next to her. The furs that had remained cold for years. She never slept in them unless the winter was too cold. But when she lay beside him, she didn't feel the biting chill of winter. She felt sweaty, cold, clammy. Sick.

As she did now.

"They look at her like she's not one of them. I can't have that. And so she has to know what it is to be shict."

He spoke that name too easily. Like it was a word. Shict was more than that. It should not have been uttered in the darkness, Kalindris had thought.

"She should know that already," Kalindris had replied, securing the laces tightly.

"No one taught her." Rokuda had edged closer.

"No one should have to. We are born knowing who we are. The Howling tells us."

"She wasn't. You have to teach her."

Kalindris had said nothing as she rose up and moved to her bow. It was never far from her, save those times when he moved it. In the darkness, she preferred to keep it close.

But when she rose, he reached out. He took her by her wrist and she felt herself freeze. It grew cold again, cold as their bed.

"*You have to show her,*" Rokuda had insisted.

"*I don't have to do anything,*" she had tried to speak. But her words were smothered in the darkness.

He tightened his fingers around her wrist and she felt cold all over. She felt every point he had ever touched her, a bead of cold sweat forming everywhere his fingerprint lingered on her skin. She grew silent, rigid. And when he spoke, his voice was an icicle snapping on a winter's day.

"*You will.*"

She stared across the clearing and spoke softly, as to not stir the leaves before her.

"Do you know why?"

Kalindris' own voice.

Strange and uncomfortable in her own mouth.

But the child was looking up at her. The child had her bow in her hands, an arrow in the string.

Kalindris pointed out to the log. The deer scratched at the moss with a hoof, pulled green scraps from the wood, and slurped them up from the ground. It wasted many sounds as it ate: grinding its teeth, grunting in satisfaction, slurping the greenery down noisily. It couldn't hear her whispering to the child from the underbrush.

"Why it has to die?" Kalindris reiterated.

The child stared at the deer, squinting hard. She could almost hear the child's thoughts, imagined them as noisy, jumbled things. The Howling was not there to give them clarity and focus.

"Food?" the child asked.

"No."

"I don't know. Competition? We kill it or we are killed?"

"By a deer?"

"It has horns!" the child protested.

The deer looked up at the sudden noise. Kalindris and the child were still and quiet. The deer was too hungry to leave. It continued to gnaw and to make noise.

"Why does it have to die?" Kalindris asked.

The child thought carefully. She winced with the realization.

"Because we can only know who we are by who everyone else is. We can only know what it means to be us if we know that we are not the others. And so we kill them, to know that, to know who we are and why we are here and why Riffid gave us life and nothing else. We kill. And because we are the killers, we are who we are."

She felt her ears flatten against the side of her head. Her father's words. Her father's words repeated to a thousand people who would never speak against him, never tell him no. She hadn't told him no, either. Not when she first heard it. Not until it was too late.

"No," she said.

"But Father said—"

"No." She spoke more forcefully. "Look at it. Why does it have to die?"

And the child looked at the deer. And then the child looked at her.

"Does it have to?" she asked.

The sound of ears rising. The sound of eyelids opening wide. The sound of a breath going short. Realization. Acknowledgment. Resignation. Sorrow.

The child.

Listening.

Wordless.

"Why does it have to die?" she asked again.

"Because," the child said, "I have to kill it."

Kalindris nodded. No smiles. No approval. No sounds.

The child raised her bow, drew the arrow back and held it. She trusted only her eyes. She checked her aim once, then twice, then a third time. On the fourth, when her hands had started to quiver from the strain, she shot.

The arrow struck the deer in the tender part between the leg and the nethers. It quivered there, severing something that the deer needed. The beast let out a groan, its breath mist. It staggered on its hooves, turned to flee. But its legs didn't remember anything before the arrow. It shambled, bleeding, toward the forest.

The child drew an arrow and shot again. She trusted only her heart now. The arrow flew too wide. She shrieked, her voice panicked, and shot again. Words befouled the air and the arrow sank into the earth, heavy with her fear.

The deer took another step before it fell. The arrow stood quivering in the deer's neck and the beast lay on its side, breathing heavily, spilling breath and blood onto the earth.

Kalindris approached it, the child behind her. She reached behind and grabbed the child, shoving her forward. The child stared at the deer's eyes, at herself reflected in the great brown mirror of its gaze.

The child looked to her.

Kalindris reached into her belt and pulled the knife free. She held it out to the child. The child looked at it like it was something that shouldn't be there, something that she would only ever see hung upon the wall of her father's tent.

She thrust the handle toward the child.

"Why?" Kalindris asked the child.

The child looked up at her. The sight of eyes wide and pleading. The sight of resentment. The sight of fear and hate and betrayal for making the child do this.

But no words.

The child took the knife and knelt beside the deer. She pressed it to its throat. She winced and she cut through the fur and the hide and the sinew to the root of the beast's neck.

She opened it up and it spilled upon her. It spilled over her hands and onto her arms. And the child kept cutting silently.

As the brook babbled alongside them, she tried to keep up with her parents.

"Are you scared, darling?"

Senny wasn't. She was trying hard not to be, anyway. She shook her head and held up the little knife. Father didn't seem to notice.

"You don't need to be scared," he said. "Not when I'm here. We're going to get through this, all right?"

She nodded. She wasn't scared.

"I'm sorry for what I said earlier, darling. I was just irritated. Your mother was screaming so loud."

Mother didn't seem to notice that they were talking about her. Mother held on to her hand and kept pulling her toward the cottage. The brook was nearby, churning away. Vines of berries grew nearby, ripe and bright in the sunlight.

They could go to the forest to avoid the beast, maybe. They could run there and live together there. The cottage was nice and she would miss it and she would miss Eadne and she tried very hard not to think about Eadne because whenever she did she felt like she was going to throw up and then Mother would cry.

"Darling, everything's going to be all right," Father said. He wasn't looking at her, though. "Everything will be fine, don't worry."

"I'm not worried, Father," she said. "I'm not scared. I still have the knife you gave me. Look."

"It'll be all right, darling."

"Father, we could go deeper into the forest. We could escape the beast there and come back when it's gone. I've been there, Father. It's not as dark as it looks. There are berries and food and we could go there instead of the cottage."

"Yes, darling. The forest."

"Father, Mother is scared. She's holding on to my hand so hard that it hurts. Father?"

Father said the same thing again. Over and over. All "darling" and "mm-hm" and "fine, fine, all right." She soon stopped talking. Father wasn't listening. Because if Father listened, he would hear her voice starting to sound like it always did whenever her throat felt funny and she wanted to cry.

And then he'd be scared. And then Mother would be more scared.

He needed to say his words so he couldn't hear her. And she needed to stay quiet. And Mother needed to hold her hand until it hurt. And she needed not to throw up or cry or do any of those things that a scared little child would do.

Maybe when Eadne was around, she could do that.

Eadne was dead.

When the sun began to scowl over their tent and the first wolves rose to the hunt, she hated herself like she hated him.

"I want to ask you something," Rokuda had said.

"No." Kalindris had replied.

It was a noise Rokuda only heard from her. He had no idea what it meant. *"Why aren't you bothered by this?"* he had asked, undeterred.

"By what?"

"By how they see her, by the fact that they think she's not one of us. Not a shict." He forced difficult words through a snarl. *"Not mine."*

"I don't pay attention to what she does."

"Why not? Haven't you seen what they think of her? How they look at her?"

"No."

"They look at her like . . . like she's . . . like she isn't . . ."

His words had failed him and he had begun to snarl. He hated it when words would not work for him, because when his words would not work, neither would the Howling speak for him. And when he couldn't speak, he started snarling, because people couldn't agree with him. People could tell him "no."

And that was when he started making scars.

"She reaches out to try to hold on to your hand when she's scared. She . . . she asks them things, instead of knowing *what the Howling tells her."* She heard his nails rake the fur and find that insufficient for his rage. She heard strands of his hair snap from his scalp as he pulled it. *"She cries when she gets hurt. She snarls when she gets angry."*

"Children do that."

"Not my heir."

"Your heir is a child."

"Not one of our children. *Not one of our people. We don't . . . do that."*

"She does."

"And you don't even care! *You don't even look at her. Don't you know what they're saying about us? How they look at us?"*

"Don't care."

"You used to."

"Don't anymore."

And she had heard it. Silence before a crack of thunder. Grains of earth falling after a drop of rain kicks them up. Moan of wind over hillsides. The moment before he drew a breath, before he spoke with the intent of being heard.

"You used to stand with me in front of them, remember? You and your bow, the proud huntress next to me, so strong and brave. They looked up to

*us as I spoke. They listened to me and I cared only if
you heard me."*

Honey fermenting in a skein. Dandelions flying
on the breeze. Steam after the fire had been doused.
The words he spoke that had made her listen, the
words he spoke that made him powerful, the words
he spoke when he had been Rokuda and she had
been Kalindris and they had no need for words.

*"You used to listen to my words, you used to nod
when they nodded and cheer when they cheered. And
when I was done and I looked out over all of them
smiling, I looked beside me and yours was always the
biggest smile and the best."*

The words he spoke when she thought those were
all she ever needed.

"You had a lot of words," Kalindris had said.

*"I still do. I still have everything. Everything ex-
cept that proud huntress that stood beside me. Where
did she go?"*

Kalindris had waited at the flap of the tent. When
she opened it to the cold dawn light, the world was
silent. She looked briefly over her shoulder and saw
his eyes, so vast and green. And out the corner of her
eye, she saw only a glimpse of it. But the scar on her
collarbone, the one he had given her, was still there.

*"She fell in love with someone silent and gentle.
They ran away and died somewhere far in the woods
and left you and I behind."*

She had spoken briefly. And then she had left.

"You're not doing it right. You're not *doing* it right."
Teeth coming in through a cub's mouth. "You're

supposed to talk to me. You're supposed to be able to do this." Claws digging for something in the earth that wasn't there. "Stop it. *Stop it.* Stop it and do it already." A leg in a snare, being gnawed off.

The child.

Talking to the earth.

Still.

She watched, arms folded, impassive as the child crawled through the riverbank, following a flayed line through the mud. The child followed it over the bank, through the ebb, around the trees, back to where it began. The child cursed at it, made demands of it, whined at it and now simply spewed words, to the tracks, to the earth, to herself.

The child's hands were thick with mud, belly smeared with it, face painted brown where she had clutched her head in frustration. And she crawled with her hands upon the ground, as though she could strangle answers out of the earth.

The earth wouldn't talk to her.

The child wanted everything. The child wanted the tracks to tell her without listening to them. The child wanted the land to yield to her because she wanted it to that badly. The child wanted. The child spoke. The child whined and demanded and she never listened.

Like her father.

Kalindris was surprised to find her hands clenched into fists at her side.

"He said it was supposed to be easy," the child whined. "It's supposed to be easy. Why didn't he—" She slammed the heel of her palm against her forehead. A muddy bruise was left behind. "*No, no.* It's you, not him. You're doing something wrong. It's you, *you're* the failure, *that's* why they hate you."

His legacy. In the mud. Striking herself in the head.

In some wordless part of herself, Kalindris tried to convince herself that the child deserved this. The child who couldn't listen, the child who always spoke, his child belonged in the mud.

Kalindris was surprised to hear her own voice.

"It's metaphor. The earth doesn't actually talk to you." The child continued to paw at it and plead to it. "Look. You've ruined the tracks. We can start—"

"Shut up!"

The child.

Baring teeth.

Snarling.

"I don't want to hear it or you or anything, I just want to find the beast and kill it and bring it back and show it to him and then he'll talk to me and I don't *need* you or anyone else to talk to me if Father will so I never have to see you again!"

The child was liquid. White flecks of spittle gathered at her mouth. Tears brimmed in the corners of her eyes. Viscous mucus dripped from her nostrils. The child was melting, trembling herself to death. The child turned away, looked back into the silent earth.

"I wasn't asleep."

And Kalindris had no words for the child. The child who had just spoken to her like it was *her* fault the child's ears couldn't hear. The child who presumed to dismiss *her*. The child who acted like it was *her* fault, *her* problem, *her* flaw that made this moment of mud and tears and spit.

Like her father. Every bit.

She was surprised to find tears in her eyes.

And she, too, turned. The earth spoke to her, though. Told her where the beast had gone. Told her how to deny the child and how that made sense that she should be angry and vengeful against a child.

The child.

Weeping.

And she shut her ears and walked away.

Mother was scared. And Father was scared.

Senny knew this because no one was yelling anymore.

Mother wrapped her hands tightly around her and held her close in the corner of their cottage. Father stood with his hatchet in his hand, peering through the windows. Mother had her. Father had his hatchet. And they were both still scared.

She wasn't, though. She had her little knife. Father had given it to her so she wouldn't be scared. She couldn't be scared with the little knife, even if Father was.

She thought about giving it to Father, to see if it would help. But she pulled it back when she heard a voice, even if it was Father's.

"I'm going out there."

"What? Why would you do that?"

"To look for that thing. It might not even be around. We didn't see it when we found—"

"No. Don't go out there," Mother said. "It already got Eadne. You can't let it get your daughter and me, you have to stay here, you have to, you *have* to."

"I have to protect you," Father said. "I have to

keep you safe. We can't live like this. We can't let that beast chase us away. We have to . . ."

To not be scared, Senny wanted to say. We have to be brave.

"I'm going," Father said. "Not far. Not long. Just stay here. I'll be back."

Senny nodded. She held her little knife tightly. Mother held her tightly. So tightly it hurt. She leaned into it, though, let Mother hold on to her because Mother didn't have a little knife.

Father pushed the door open. Birds were singing outside. The sun was shining that orange way it got when it started going beneath the trees. The brook was babbling outside, talking loud and wondering where the little girl was that talked back to it. Father walked out two steps from the doorway and looked around with his hatchet in his hand.

The birds kept singing. The brook kept talking. The sun kept shining.

And Father was dead.

She knew it. She saw the arrow in his shoulder, pinning him to the cottage door. She saw another fly out and hit him in the wrist. He dropped his hatchet. Mother screamed. Father screamed. Father bled all over the door. And Senny held on to the little knife.

The beast came up. The beast was a lady. Her hair was long and wild and she wore dirty clothes and her ears were huge and she had big teeth and a scar on her neck. Her knife was big. Her knife was shiny. And she brought it up and against Father's neck and opened him up and his blood spilled all over her.

And the birds just kept on singing, even though Father was dead.

When the birds kept singing and the woman would not stop weeping, she looked at the Beast.

There were many names for them: intruder, human, monkey, *kou'ru*. It was Rokuda that had began calling them Beasts, to make them a threat instead of a people, a word instead of a thing that had children. It had made the tribe nod in approval and mutter how they were Beasts, these creatures that came and threatened the shict lands.

She had killed one already, left the body swinging in a tree as warning to these two. But she had known, even then, that she would have to kill them, too. She had killed many.

Even before Rokuda gave them a new name, she had killed them. They were the enemy, they were the disease. Killing defined a shict. And these kills were meant for the child. The blood that poured down Kalindris' hands should have been on the child's. She was supposed to have come back to the tribe with her hands red and her eyes shut and the tribe would know she was one of them and her father would be proud of his heir.

The child's kill. Rokuda's glory. Kalindris denied one through the other.

The little human girl stood in front of her cowering mother, holding up a little knife like it was a match for the broad red blade in Kalindris' hands. She looked up at Kalindris, trying her hardest not to show fear. Kalindris looked down at her, trying to decide how best to end this quickly. A clean blow through one, then the other, she thought, in the heart to end it quickly.

Clean and quick.

Just as soon as the child stopped staring at her.

Like she owed her an explanation.

"Do you know why?" Heavy, choked, weak. Kalindris' words.

The human child did not say a thing. Her mother wrapped her arms around the child's tiny form, tried to hold her back. The child would not lower her knife.

"Why I have to kill you?" she asked again.

The child said nothing. Kalindris opened her mouth to tell her. No words came.

"Your knife is too small," Kalindris said. She held up her own blade, thick and choked with red. "You can't do anything with it. You aren't meant to hold it. Put it down."

The child did not put it down. Kalindris raised her weapon, took a step forward, as if to step around the child. The child moved in front of her, thrust her little knife at Kalindris like it would do something. Like she could use it. Like she wasn't scared.

Kalindris hesitated. She looked over her shoulder, as though she expected the child—her child—to be there.

"You don't have to die here," she said, without looking at the child—the human child. "Your . . . your father isn't you. Your mother isn't you. I'll take them. You can run."

She looked at the child and her little knife.

"Go. Run away."

The child did not run. The child did not move.

"Why aren't you running?"

"I can't." The child spoke in a terrified voice.

"Why not?"

"Because she's my mother."

The pages of a book fallen from a shelf, turning. Ashes in a long-dead fireplace settling beneath charred logs. A mother weeping. Birds singing. Blood pattering onto the floor from a hole in a soft throat, drop by drop.

Slow sounds.

Quiet sounds.

Full of nothing.

Kalindris could hear the whisper of leather as she slid the blade back into its sheath. Kalindris could hear the sound of her boots on the floor as she turned around and walked out of the cabin. Kalindris could hear the sound of the human child drop to the floor and weep.

She could hear it all the way back to the forest.

And her child.

A river running. Wind blowing through the leaves. A wolf howling.

And birds singing.

No matter how hard she tried, how she angled her ears, how she strained to hear something else, something full of meaning, this was all she could hear. These sounds, common and pointless, the sort of thing any ugly creature could hear.

The Howling wasn't talking to her.

"Where were you?"

The child.

Asking.

Concerned.

She walked into the clearing with her bow on her back and her knife in her belt. The child was sitting down on her heels, looking up at her as she walked past.

"You washed," the child noted, looking at her clean, bloodless hands. "When? What did you do?"

She did not look back at the child as she sat down beside her. She let her legs hang over a small ledge, dangling over a dying brook whose babble had turned to poetic muttering as it sputtered into a thin stream. She looked to her right and saw the child's feet in their little boots, covered in mud, flecked with blood from the dead deer.

Only a few droplets of red. The rest mixed with the mud. It seemed like so much to look at it.

"Why do we kill, child?" she asked absently.

"You already asked me this."

"I know. Tell me again."

The child kicked her feet a little. A few flecks of mud came off. Not the blood.

"I guess I don't know," the child said.

She said nothing.

They stared, together, into the forest. Their ears pricked up, listening to the sounds. Birds kept singing, one more day they marked by noisy chatter. The wind kept blowing, same as it always had. Somewhere far away, one more deer loosed a long, guttural bugle into the sky.

"Did you kill the beast?" the child asked.

She said nothing.

"I was supposed to do it."

"I didn't."

The child looked at her. "I'm not an idiot."

"No."

She reached over, wrapped an arm around the child and drew her close. A heart beating; excited. A breath drawn in sharply; quivering. A shudder through the body; terrified. She drew the child closer.

"But let me pretend you are for a little while."

No more noises. No more sounds. No more distant cries and close Howling. Only words. Only the child's voice.

"I was supposed to kill it. Father said."

"Your father isn't always right."

"You are?"

"No."

"Then why should I believe you?"

"Because."

"That's not a good reason."

She looked down at the child and smiled. "I'll think of one later, all right?"

The child looked back at her. Her smile came more slowly, more nervous, like she was afraid it would be slapped out of her mouth at any moment. Kalindris blamed herself for that look, for these words that came heavy and slowly. She would learn how to use them better.

There would be time for that. Without so much blood and cold nights. Without so many thoughts of Rokuda and his words. She would learn them on her own. She would tell them to the child.

Her child.

Her daughter.

Smiling.

There would be time enough to look into her daughter's eyes, long from now, and know what it meant to need no words. There would be a time when she would look into her daughter's eyes and simply know.

For now, she had only the sound of her daughter's smile. And forever.

Nancy Kress

Nancy Kress began selling her elegant and incisive stories in the mid-seventies, and has since become a frequent contributor to *Asimov's Science Fiction, The Magazine of Fantasy & Science Fiction, Omni, Sci Fiction,* and elsewhere. Her books include the novel version of her Hugo- and Nebula-winning story, *Beggars in Spain,* and a sequel, *Beggars and Choosers,* as well as *The Prince of Morning Bells, The Golden Grove, The White Pipes, An Alien Light, Brainrose, Oaths and Miracles, Stinger, Maximum Light, Crossfire, Nothing Human, Crucible, Dogs, Steal Across the Sky,* and the Probability Trilogy, comprised of *Probability Moon, Probability Sun, and Probability Space.* Her short work has been collected in *Trinity and Other Stories, The Aliens of Earth, Beaker's Dozen,* and *Nano Comes to Clifford Falls and Other Stories.* Her most recent books are a new novel, *After the Fall, Before the Fall, During the Fall,* and two new collections, *Fountain of Age* and *Five Stories.* In addition to the awards for "Beggars in Spain," she has also won Nebula Awards for her stories "Out of All Them Bright Stars" and

"The Flowers of Aulit Prison," the John W. Campbell Memorial Award in 2003 for her novel *Probability Space*, and another Hugo in 2009 for "The Erdmann Nexus." She lives in Seattle, Washington, with her husband, writer Jack Skillingstead.

Here she takes us to a ruined future America to ask the question, in a world where only basic brute survival counts, is there any room left for beauty? And would you be willing to kill for it if you found it?

SECOND ARABESQUE, VERY SLOWLY

When we came to the new place it was already night and I couldn't see anything. It wasn't like Mike to move us after dark. But our pack had taken longer than he'd expected, or longer than the scouts had said, to travel south. That was partly my fault. I can't walk as fast or long as I once could. And neither could Pretty, because that day turned out to be her Beginning.

"My belly hurts, it does," the girl moaned.

"Just a little farther," I said, hoping that was true. Hoping, too, that I wouldn't have to threaten her. Pretty turned ugly when she felt bad and whined when she didn't, although never in Mike's presence. "A little farther, and tomorrow you'll have your ceremony."

"With candy?"

"With candy."

So Pretty trudged through the dark, broken, rubble-choked streets with me and the other six girls, behind a swinging lantern. The night was cold for July. The men closest to us—although I don't call fifteen-year-olds men, even if Mike does—walked bent over with the weight of our belongings. The men on the perimeter carried weapons. The danger was partly from other packs wanting foraging territory, although there are fewer territorial firefights than when I was young. Still, we have desirable assets: seven young women, at least two of them fertile, plus three children and me. And then there are the dogs. Cities are full of wild dogs.

I could hear them, howling in the distance. As that distance grew smaller and Mike still had us stumbling along by patchy moonlight and one lantern, I left the girls in Bonnie's charge and walked double time to find Mike.

"What be you doing here?" he demanded, gaze and rifle both focused outward. "Get back to them girls!"

"It's the girls I'm concerned about. How much farther?"

"Get back there, Nurse!"

"I'm asking because Pretty is in some pain. She's at her Beginning."

That took his attention from any dangers in the darkness. "Yeah? You sure?"

"Yes," I said, although I wasn't.

Mike gave his slow, rare smile. He wasn't a bad pack leader. Huge, strong, illiterate—well, they all were, and I needed them to be—he cared about his people, and wasn't any more brutal to us than discipline required. A big improvement on Lew, our previous leader. Sometimes Mike could even lurch into moments of grace, as he did now. "She be okay?"

"Yes." Nothing that the start of her monthlies and a little candy wouldn't cure.

And then, even more surprising, "You be okay, Nurse?"

"Yes."

"How old you be now?"

"Sixty," I said, shaving off four years. I was under no illusions what Mike would do once I could no longer keep up with the pack. Already Bonnie had learned half of what I had to teach her. Not even a Nurse would be allowed to slow down the nomadic moving that meant food.

We had kept walking as we talked. Mike said, "I be first, with Pretty."

"She knows that."

He grunted, not asking her thoughts about it. If Pretty were fertile, she must be mated with a fertile male, and no one knew which of the pack men that might be. Nor did we have any idea how to find out. So Pretty, like Junie and Lula before her, would be mated with all of them in turn. Already Pretty, a natural flirt when she wasn't a natural whiner, tossed her long blond hair and flashed her shapely legs at all of them.

The dogs were closer now, and I had lost Mike's attention. I stood still, waiting for the center of the pack to reach me, and rejoined my charges.

By the time we reached our new building, the moon had vanished behind the clouds, a drizzle had started, and I could see nothing. The men led us past some large structures—the city was full of large structures, most ruined but mostly on the insides—and through a metal door. Steps downward. Cold, damp. A featureless corridor. Still, this place would

be easy to defend, since it was underground and
nearly windowless. The scouts had prepared the
women's room, which did have a small window, to
which they'd vented our propane stove. The room
was warm and blanketed. Junie and Lula bedded
down their children, who were already half-asleep.
So were the girls. I stayed awake long enough to prepare Pretty a hot tisane—only herbs, not drugs—to
ease her cramps, and then fell into sleep.

In the morning I woke first and made my way
outside to pee. The guard, a gentle sixteen-year-old
named Guy, nodded at me. "Morning, Nurse."

"Good morrow to you, sir," I said, and Guy
grinned. He was one of the few that was interested in
the learning—history, literature—I sometimes tossed
out. He could even read; I was teaching him. "Where
is the piss pit?"

He told me. I continued outside, blinking a little
in the bright sunshine, along the side of the building
and around a corner, where I stopped dead.

I knew this place. I had never been here before,
but I knew it.

Three large buildings set around a vast square of
now broken and weedy stone, with steps at the far
end leading down to a deserted street. On the tallest building, five wide, immensely tall arches looked
down on a sea of smashed glass. The other two buildings, glass fronts also smashed, bristled with balco-
nies, with marble, with stone sculptures too large to
break or carry away. Inside, still visible, were remnants
of ancient, tattered carpet.

I said aloud, "This is Lincoln Center." But the perimeter guard, sitting with his rifle on the edge of

what had once been a fountain, was too far away to hear. I wasn't talking to him, anyway. I was talking to my grandmother.

"My best job, Susan," she'd said to me, "was when I was on the cleaning crew at Lincoln Center."

"Tell me," I said, although I'd heard all this so many times before that I could recite it. I never tired of it.

"I was young, before I went to nursing school. We deep-cleaned the Metropolitan Opera House the last two weeks in August and the first two weeks in September, when there were no performances," she always began. "It was way before the Infertility Plague, you know."

I knew. My grandmother was very old then, older than I am now, and dying. I was twelve. Grandmother was frantically teaching me to Nurse, in case I should prove infertile, which the following year, I did. Packs not desperate for bedmates have no use for infertile women unless a girl can prove herself as a fighter. I was no fighter.

"We lowered all twenty-one electric chandeliers at the Met—think of that, Susan, *twenty-one*—and cleaned each crystal drop individually. Every other year all the red carpet was completely replaced, at a cost of $700,000. In 1990s dollars! Every five years the seats were replaced in the New York State Theater—that's what it was called then, although later they changed the name, I forget to what. Five window washers worked every day of the year, constantly keeping the windows bright. At night, when all the buildings were lit up, they shone out on the

plaza like liquid gold. People laughed and talked
and lined up by the hundreds to hear opera and see
ballet and watch plays and listen to concerts. And
such rich performances as I saw . . . you can't imagine!"

No liquid gold now. No performances, no electricity, no opera nor ballet nor plays nor concerts.
Grandmother had been talking about a time gone
when I was born, and I am old.

I went back inside. Pretty was awake, her huge blue
eyes filled with awe at herself. "Nurse! It started—my
blood! I'm at my Beginning!"

"Congratulations," I said. "We'll have your ceremony today."

"I am a woman now," she said, with pride. I looked
at her round, childish, simple face; at her skinny arms
and legs; at her concave belly, not even distended with
fluid retention. She was thirteen, early for our girls to
Begin. Kara was a year older, with no sign of her
monthlies. I said gently, "Yes, Pretty. You're a woman
now. You can bear the pack a child."

"You other childless," Pretty said importantly,
"you have to obey me now!"

The younger girls, Seela and Tiny, scowled fero-
ciously.

My grandmother taught me a great deal more than
nursing. And I read. Books might have survived the
destruction and stupid rioting when the world realized that 99 percent of its women had contracted a
virus that destroyed their eggs. Most books had not,

however, survived time and damp and rats and insects. But some did.

How many other people are left in the world? There is no way to tell. Census organizations, radio and TV stations, central governments—all that vanished decades ago. Too few people left to sustain them. The world now—or at least this part of it—consists of the communities and the packs. The communities live outside the city, and they farm. I have never seen one. I was born to a pack—although not this one—my mother and grandmother captive to it. The packs prefer to be hunter-gatherers in urban environments. We hunt meat—rabbits, deer, dogs—and gather canned goods. Not exactly what happened during the Stone Age, but we manage. Every once in a while rumors come of places that have preserved more of civilization, usually small cities north and west—"Endicott," "Bath," "Ithaca"—but I have no knowledge of them.

However, it turned out that among the others that *were* left in the world was a pack based just blocks away, in an old hotel on a street called "Central Park South," and Mike was furious with his scouts. "You don't *find this out?*"

The men hung their heads.

"You put us in danger 'cause you don't find this out? I deal with you later. Now we gotta parley."

I was startled. Parley, not move? But later Guy, off duty and cleaning his guns, explained it to me. "There be a big forest here, Nurse, with lotsa game. Mike wants to stay."

So Mike left with half his pack, all heavily armed,

to parley for hunt-gather rights with the other pack. Meanwhile, guarded by Guy and his friend Jemmy, Bonnie and I looked for a good place to hold Pretty's ceremony.

Bonnie, my apprentice, might or might not make a good Nurse when I can no longer keep up with the pack. Smart and strong, she already knew more than I let Mike realize. She could use our dwindling supplies of pre-plague medicines, those miracles whose making is lost to us. More important, she could find, prepare, and administer the plant drugs we relied on: bilberry for diarrhea, horsetail to stop bleeding, elderberry for fever, primrose for rashes. She could set a bone, dig out a bullet, use maggots to clean a wound.

But Bonnie had neither warmth nor that brisk reassurance that, as much as drugs, brings men to healing. Bonnie was like stone. I'd never seen her smile, seldom heard her speak except in answer to a question, never surprised interest or delight on her face. Big, ungainly, painfully homely, she had colorless hair and almost no chin. I think she had a bad time when she Began, which was before I was taken into this pack. Her thighs and breasts bore permanent scars. Lew might have had her shot when she was declared infertile except it was about that time he was killed in a pack war. I persuaded Mike to let Bonnie become my apprentice. That also rescued her from the sex list, since Nurses—even apprentice Nurses—were the only women who got to invite men to bed. Bonnie never did.

She said nothing as she and I, Guy and Jemmy, went into all the ruined buildings of what had been Lincoln Center. From Grandmother's descriptions I

recognized them all. Above us, in the New York
State Theater, broken seats once supported the asses
of people watching dancers. Our housing below had
probably been practice rooms. In the Metropolitan
Opera House, the building with five tall arches, the
caved-in stage had once held opera singers. Here, in
Somebody Hall (my memory wasn't what it had
been), orchestras had played music. All the musicians
wore black, with the women in long and sparkly
dresses. Grandmother told me. In the Vivian Beaumont Theater, off to the side of the Met, the collapsed
roof sheltered actors performing plays. The small library beside the Met had been burned and was now
overgrown with weeds, wildflowers, and saplings.

But it was underneath the Vivian Beaumont, below
street level and behind two locked doors that Guy
shot open with his rifle, that we found it. I had brought
a lantern, and now I lit it, although we'd left both
doors open for light. The first door led to a downward-
sloping ramp of concrete, the second to another small
theater, eight rows of seats in a half circle, windowless
and untouched except for time and rats. No looters
had taken or destroyed the seats; no rain had rotted
the wooden, uncurtained stage; no wild dogs nested
in the tiny rooms beyond.

Jemmy let out a whoop and swung himself up to
a booth on the back wall. Probably he hoped for
undestroyed machinery, and his second whoop said
he'd found it. A faint glow appeared in the booth.

"Jemmy!" I shouted up. "If you waste candles like
that, Mike will flog you himself!"

No answer, and the light did not go off. Guy
shrugged and laughed. "You know Jemmy."

"Help me up onto that stage," I said.

He did, leaping up gracefully to stand beside me, the lantern at our feet. I looked out over the darkened seats. What must it have been like, to stand here as an actor, a musician, a dancer? To perform in front of people who watched you with delight? To control an audience?

"Such rich performances as I saw . . . you can't imagine."

Boots on the corridor, and then a voice in the darkness: "Nurse? Get your ass back to them girls! Pretty waiting!"

"Is that you, Karl?"

"Yeah."

"Don't you ever again talk to me in that tone of voice, young man, or I will tell Mike that you're disrespecting a Nurse and you will go to the bottom of the sex list, if you even stay on it at all!"

Silence, then a sullen, "Yes'm."

"In fact, you bring all the girls here. This is where we'll have Pretty's ceremony, and we'll have it now."

"Here? Now?"

"You heard me."

"Yes'm." And then: "You tell Mike I disrespected you?"

"Not if you get those girls here right away."

Karl galloped off, his boots loud on the concrete ramp. Guy grinned at me. Then he gazed out into the darkness and I saw that he had been doing just what I had: imagining himself a performer in a vanished time. All at once he grabbed me around the waist and swung me into a dance.

I was never a dancer, and I am old. I stumbled,

and Guy let me go. He danced alone, as he never would have done had anybody been present except me and his trusted friend Jemmy, who probably wasn't even looking away from his precious machinery. I watched Guy move gracefully through the two-step that packs danced at the rare gatherings, and sadness washed over me that Guy could never be anything but a low-level pack soldier. He was too kind and too dreamy to ever become a leader like Mike, too male to ever be as important as a fertile girl.

Bonnie watched, wooden-faced, before she turned away.

Pretty's ceremony was lit by thirteen candles, one for each year of her age, as was customary. No men present, of course, not even the two male children, year-old Davey and eight-year-old Rick, whose mother, Emma, died last year giving birth to a stillborn girl. Nothing I did saved either one of them, and if Lew had still been pack chief, I think I would have been shot then and there.

The two mothers, Junie and Lula, sat on chairs, with Lula's baby, Jaden, on her lap. Jaden started to fuss and Lula gave her the breast. Bonnie, as my apprentice but also as an infertile female, stood behind the mothers. The girls who had not yet had their Beginnings sat to one side on the floor, their hands full of wildflowers. Seela and Tiny, ten and nine, looked interested. Kara, her own Beginning only a few months off, judging from her buds of breasts, wore an expression I could not interpret.

Pretty, now neither child nor mother, sat in the

center of the circle, on a sort of throne made of a chair covered with a blanket, which in turn was spread with towels. Old, as faded as everything else we take from abandoned buildings, the towels had once been sun-yellow. Pretty's legs were spread wide, the thighs smeared with the new blood she was so proud of. One by one, the unBegun girls laid flowers between Pretty's legs.

"May you be blessed with children," said Tiny, looking excited.

"May you be blessed with children." Seela, jealousy on her thin little face.

"May you be . . . blessed with . . . children." Kara could barely get the words out. Her face creased with anguish. Her fingers trembled.

Pretty looked at her in astonishment. "What be wrong with *you*?"

Bonnie pushed forward. "Be you sick, Kara? What be your symptoms?"

"I'm not sick! Leave me alone!"

"Come here, Kara," I said in the tone that all of the girls, and most of the younger men, obeyed instantly. I had been in charge of these girls since the pack acquired them, of Kara since she was four. Kara came to me. She had always been complicated, sweet-natured and hardworking (unlike lazy Pretty), but too excitable. Death distressed her too much, happiness elated her too much, beauty transported her too much. I have seen her in tears over a sunset.

"Do not spoil Pretty's ceremony," I said to her in a low voice, and she subsided.

Afterward, however, while the two mothers took Pretty aside for the traditional sex instruction that was hardly ever needed and the unBegun girls played with Jaden, I led Kara off the stage, to the back of the theater. "Sit."

"Yes, Nurse. What is this place?"

"It was a theater. Kara, what troubles you?"

She looked away, looked down, looked everywhere but at me until I took her chin in my hand and made her face me. Then she blurted, "I don't want to!"

"Don't want to what?"

"Any of it! Begin, have a ceremony, bed with Mike and all them. Have a baby—I don't want to!"

"Many girls are frightened at first." I remembered my own first bedding, with a pack leader much less gentle than I suspected Mike would be. So long ago. Yet I had come to like sex, and right up until a few years ago, I had sometimes gone with Buddy off-list, until he was killed by that wild dog.

"I be frightened, yes. But I also don't want to!"

"Is there something you want to do instead?" I was afraid she would say "nurse." I already had Bonnie, and anyway, even if she proved infertile, Kara would not make a Nurse. No amount of hard work would make up for her lack of stability and brains.

"No."

"What, then?" For girls there was only mother, nurse, or infertile bedmate, and the last became camp drudges with little respect, when packs kept infertile women at all. Our last such, Daisy, had run away. I didn't like to imagine what had happened to her. Kara knew all this.

"I don't know!" It was a wail of pure anguish. I had no time for this: a self-indulgent girl with no aim, merely obstruction of what was necessary. A

woman did what she had to do, just as men did. I
left her sitting in the tattered velvet chair and went
back to Pretty. It was her day, not Kara's.

Bonnie still stood, stony, beside Pretty's flower-
strewn chair.

Mike returned from the parley looking pleased, a
rare look for him. The other pack, smaller than
ours, was not only unwilling to go to war over the
urban forest but was interested in trading, even in
possible joint hunting and foraging trips. I knew
without being told that Mike hoped to eventually
unite the two packs and become chief of both. The
men brought back gifts from the other pack. Evidently their base had heaps of things so sealed in
plastic—blankets, pillows, even clothing—that no
rats had gotten into them and they looked almost
new. Each of the girls got a fluffy white robe stitched
with "St. Regis Hotel."

"Can't we move to a hotel?" Lula cried, twirling
around in hers.

"Too hard to defend," Karl said. He reached up to
catch Lula and pull her onto his lap. She giggled.
Lula has always liked Karl; she maintained that she
"knows" he fathered Jaden. Jaden did have his
bright blue eyes.

We were all at Pretty's ceremony feast in the common room, an underground room in what Grandmother remembered as the New York State Theater.
The common room had a wooden floor, a curious
wooden rail on three sides, and a smashed, unusable

piano in one corner. The boys had swept up the huge amount of mirror glass that yesterday lay all around. Junie had spread blankets on the floor for the feast, which tasted wonderful. Rabbit shot that morning and roasted with wild onions over open fires built on the stone terrace in front of the Vivian Beaumont. Cans of beans that Eric had brought back from foraging. A salad of dandelion greens and the candy that Pretty so loved and I had been hoarding since winter: maple sap mixed with nuts. Every lantern we owned was lit, giving the room a romantic glow.

Mike eyed Pretty, who blushed and cast eyes at him. The younger men watched enviously. I didn't have much sympathy for them. They were at the bottom of the sex list, of course, and, they didn't get much. Too bad—they should have treated Bonnie better when they had her.

Besides Bonnie, two of the young men seemed unaware of the heavy scent of sex filling the common room. Guy and Jemmy kept giving me significant looks, and eventually I got up from my dinner and went to them. "Do you need me?"

"I have a pain," Jemmy said, loud enough for Mike to hear. Jemmy was a terrible actor. His eyes shone, and every muscle in his body tensed with excitement. I had never seen anybody less in pain.

I went to Mike. "Jemmy is ill. I'm taking him to the sickroom to examine, in case it's contagious."

Mike nodded, too absorbed by Pretty to pay much attention.

Jemmy and I slipped out. Guy followed with a lantern. As soon as we were beyond earshot of the sullen guard—he was missing the feast—I said to Jemmy, "Well?"

"We want to show you something. Please come, Nurse!"

The pack had raised Jemmy since he was six and his mother died. He had a lively curiosity but, unlike Guy, Jemmy had never learned to read, although not because he shared the men's usual scorn for reading as useless and feminine. Jemmy said that the letters jumped places in front of his eyes, which made no sense but seemed to be true, since otherwise he was intelligent. Too delicately built to ever be of much use to Mike, he could make any mechanical equipment function again. It was Jemmy who figured out how to get the generators we sometimes found to run on the fuel we also sometimes found. The generators never lasted long, and most of the machinery they were supposed to power had decayed or rusted beyond use, but every once in a while we got lucky. Until the fuel ran out.

"Is it another generator?" I asked.

"Half be that!" Jemmy said.

Guy added mysteriously, "No, one-third."

But this arithmetic was too much for Jemmy, whose instincts about machinery were just that: instincts. He ignored Guy and pulled me along.

We went outside the building, across the square to the Vivian Beaumont, and to the rear of the building. It was dark out and there was a light drizzle, but the boys ignored it. I didn't get much choice. In the little underground theater our single lantern cast a forlorn glow.

"You climb up there," Jemmy said, pointing to

the booth halfway up the wall. "The steps be gone, but I found a ladder."

"I'm not going up a ladder," I said, but of course I did. Their excitement was contagious. Also worrying: This was not the way Mike wanted his pack men to behave. In Mike's mind, fighters spoke little and showed less.

I was no longer young nor agile, and the ladder was a trial. But, lit from above by the lantern Guy carried, I heaved myself into the small space. The first thing I saw was a pile of books. "Oh!"

"That's not first," Guy said gleefully, preventing me from snatching at one. "The other things first!"

I said, "Let go of those books!"

Jemmy, scampering up the ladder like a skinny squirrel, echoed, "The other things first!"

I demanded of Guy, "Where did you find the books?"

"Here."

A noise filled the small space: another of Jemmy's generators. I was far more interested in the books.

Jemmy said, "I can't believe this still works! It be already connected or I don't know how to do. Look!"

A flat window standing on a table flickered and glowed. A moment of surprise, and then the word came to me: *teevee*. Grandmother had told me about them. I never saw one work before, and when I was a child I confused *teevee* and *teepee*, so that I thought tiny people must live in the window, as we sometimes lived in teepees on summer forages.

They did.

She started out alone on the stage, except for words that appeared briefly below her:

Pas De Deux from The Four Temperaments
Music by Paul Hindemith
Choreography by George Balanchine

The girl wore tight, clinging clothes that Mike would never have permitted on his women: too inflaming for men far down the sex list. On her feet were flimsy pink shoes with pink ribbons and square toes. The girl raised one arm in a curve above her head and then raised her body up onto the ends of those pink shoes—how could she do that? Music started. She began to dance.

I heard myself gasp.

A man came onto the screen and they moved toward each other. She turned away from him, turned back, moved toward him. He lifted her then, waist-high, and carried her so that she seemed to float, legs stretched in a beautiful arch, across the stage. They danced together, all their movements light and precise and swift—so swift! It was achingly beautiful. Coiling around each other, the girl lifting her leg as high as her head, standing on her other on the ends of her toes. They flowed from one graceful pose to another, defying gravity. I had never seen anything so fragile, so moving. Never.

It lasted only a short time. Then the teevee went black.

"I can't believe the cube still works!" Jemmy said gleefully. "Want to see the other one?"

But Guy said nothing. In the shadows cast upward from the lantern, his face looked much older, and almost in pain. He said, "What is it? What is it called?"

"Ballet," I said.

Silently he handed me the pile of books. Three, four, five of them. The top one read in large gold letters: *The Story of Giselle*. The others were *A Ballet Companion: The Joy of Classical Dance, Basic Ballet Positions, Dancing for Mr. B.*, and a very small *2016 Tour Schedule*.

Guy shivered. Jemmy, oblivious to all but his mechanical miracle, said, "The other one be longer. See, these cubes fit into this slot. Only two cubes still work, though."

White words on a black screen: TAKING CLASS ON VIDEO. Then a whole roomful of women and men standing—oh! at wooden railings before mirrors; the place might be our common room, long ago. Music from a piano and then a woman's voice said, "Plié . . . and *one* two three four. Martine, less tense in your hand. Carolyn, breathe with the movement. . . ."

They were not on the ends of their toes, not until partway through "class." Before that came strange commands from the unseen woman: *battement tendu, rondes de jambs a terre, porte de bras*. After they rose on the ends of their toes—but only the women, I noticed—came more commands: "Jorge, your hand looks like a dead chicken—hold the fingers loosely!" "No, no, Terry—you are doing *this*, and you should be doing *this*." Then the woman herself appeared, and she looked as old or older than I, although much slimmer.

"Now center work. . . . No, that is too slow, John, and one and one and one . . . good. Now an *arabesque penchée*. . . . Breathe with it, softly, softly . . ."

On the teevee, dancers doing impossible, bewitching things with their bodies.

"Again. . . . Timon, please start just before the arabesque. . . ."

A roomful of dancers, each with one leg rising slowly behind, arms curved forward, to balance on one foot and make a body line so exquisite that my eyes blurred.

The teevee again went black. Jemmy said, "Let's not play it again—I want to save fuel." Guy, to my astonishment, knelt before me, as if he were doing atonement to Mike.

"Nurse, I need your help," he said.

"Get up, you young idiot!"

"I need your help," he repeated. "I want to bring Kara here, and I can't without you."

Kara. All at once, certain speculative looks he has given her sprang into my mind. I pushed him away, scandalized. "Guy! You can't bed Kara! Why, she hasn't Begun, and even if she had, Mike would kill you!"

"I don't want to bed her!" He rose, looking no less desperate but much more determined. "I want to dance with her."

"Dance with her!"

"Like that." He gestured toward the blank teevee and tried out his new word, with reverence. "Ballet."

Even Jemmy looked shocked. "Guy—you can't do that!"

"I can learn. So can Kara."

I said the first thing that came into my mind, which, like most first things, was idiotic. "The Nurse on the teevee said it takes years of work to become a dancer!"

"I know," Guy said, "years to be like them be. But we could learn *some,* Kara and me, and maybe dance for the pack. Mike might like that."

"Mike like a girl who has not yet Begun to be handled by you? You're crazy, Guy!"

"I have to dance," he said doggedly. "Ballet. With Kara. She be the only one possible!"

He was right about that. Pretty, spoiled and conventional, would never learn the hard things which that dance Nurse had demanded. Tiny and Seela were too young, Lula and Junie busy with children, Bonnie big and ungainly—what was I thinking? The whole thing was not only ridiculous, but dangerous.

"Put ballet out of your mind," I said severely. "If you don't, I will tell Mike."

I climbed ponderously down the ladder and made my way alone through the dark little theater to the door. But I carried the five books, and in my bare room in the underground of the David H. Koch Theater (I had finally found a faded sign with the correct name), I used an entire precious candle, reading them for most of the night.

Two days later, the chief of the St. Regis pack returned Mike's visit. This was a risk for him, since he arrived with only two lieutenants. It was a clear gesture of cooperation, not war, and it put everyone in a good mood. We ate at noon under a bright summer sky on a not-too-cracked terrace, beside a long shallow pool filled with both debris and two huge jutting pieces of stone that, looked at from certain directions, might be a person lying down. A sentence from my grandmother floated into my troubled mind: "Every autumn they had trouble with leaves in the Vivian Beaumont reflecting pool."

My girls built fires at first light and cooked all morning. None of the girls were present at the meal, of course; Mike would not let anyone but sworn pack men see how many women the pack possessed, nor which ones might be fertile. But I was there, serving the dishes, and the only one not cheerful.

Mike had made a bad mistake.

I knew it as soon as the chief of the other pack, Keither, began to talk. No, before—when I watched him as he studied Mike, studied our pack, studied the way the guards were set, studied everything he could see. Keither had a long, intelligent face and continuously darting eyes. He spoke well; I would bet my medicine box that this man could, and did, read. More, he had the ability to say whatever would be well received, without slipping into outright flattery. Mike, of much simpler mind, saw none of this. He had a leader's nose for treachery but not for subtlety. He could not see that Keither, with a smaller and more lightly armed pack than Mike's, aspired to the leadership of ours. There would be trouble. Not yet, maybe not even soon, but eventually.

It would do no good to tell Mike this, of course. He would not listen. I was Nurse, but I was a woman.

"I brought you a gift," Keither said, when the food had been consumed and praised. From his sack he pulled out a bottle of Jack Daniel's. Mike already knew it was there, of course—no sack could be brought unexamined beyond our perimeter. But if the men were not surprised, they were enormously pleased. Cups were passed around, toasts made, jokes exchanged. The younger men drank too much. Neither Mike nor Keither took more than a courtesy sip.

Still, the liquor prolonged the meeting. Talk grew louder. The men agreed to a joint hunting expedition, to leave the next morning. Both chiefs would go—a much greater risk on their part than on ours, since their pack was so much smaller. We would also send twice as many men as they did, further lessening our risk. Keither had been based in Manhattan for months and offered to show Mike good and bad foraging areas, boundaries of other packs' territories, and other useful information.

"We have no Nurse," Keither said. "Is yours up for trade? Or does she have an apprentice who is?"

"No," Mike said, with courtesy but without explanation. Keither didn't mention it again.

I was tired. Serving sixteen men, sitting cross-legged for hours on the concrete terrace, is hard on a body of my age. When the first tinges of sunset touched the sky, I caught Mike's eye. He nodded and let me go.

In the women's room, the girls crowded around me. "What be they like?" "Did they bring any more gifts?" "Did you find out how many women they have?" The girls sounded too insistent, crowded too close; they were hiding something. And: "Be you tired, Nurse? Maybe you go to your room and rest?"

I pushed off the wave of white robes. "Where's Kara?"

She sat alone in a corner. But the minute she raised her face, shining with exaltation, I knew. Or maybe I had known all along. After all, I could have left the feast hours earlier, and had not.

This way, I was innocent. So far.

My false innocence did not last past the next afternoon. Mike and nine other men departed on the hunting trip, leaving his first lieutenant, Joe, in command. Joe sent me with a guard of three men to the ruins of a nearby drugstore to see if there were any medicines I could use. There weren't; the place had been picked over long ago. Most of my medicines came from homes, left in ruined bathrooms, stored in drawers beside beds crawling with vermin. The expiration dates on the drugs have long since passed. However, a surprising number of them were still effective, and scalpels, scissors, gauze, and alcohol swabs don't decay.

By the time we got back, it was mid-afternoon of a gorgeous July day. Men sat in the sunshine, weapons on their knees, talking and laughing. Lula and Junie had the babies on blankets to kick their fat little legs. Pretty sat combing her hair in full view of the lounging men. She had taken to sex like a squirrel to trees, and with Mike gone her list was due for variety.

I didn't ask anyone where the other girls were. Tiny and Seela would be playing together, under guard. Bonnie would be preparing medicinal plants,

pounding leaves and boiling bark and drying berries. I slipped around the back of the Vivian Beaumont, pushed open the door to the underground
corridor, and made my way in the dark to the theater. That door was locked. I pounded on it, and
eventually Jemmy opened it.

"Nurse—"

I slapped him across the face and strode down the
aisle.

They were onstage and had not even heard me
over the music. Over their intense concentration.
Over their wonder, visible on both faces.

Guy noticed me first. "Nurse!"

Kara turned ashen and clutched what I now knew
was called a barre. The boys must have brought it
from the base building: a heavy-looking length of
wood fastened not to a wall, as in the common room,
but to heavy metal poles on either end. They had
lugged the generator and the teevee down from the
booth—I couldn't imagine how—and installed both
onstage. On the teevee the music abruptly stopped
and the older woman said, "No, no—drop your right
shoulder, Alicia!"

Kara dropped her right shoulder.

Guy's face turned stony, such a good imitation of
Mike that I was startled. I said, "What are you doing?"

"We're taking class."

Taking class. Following the movements of the
dancers on the screen. All at once my anger was
swamped by pity. They were so young. Growing up
in such a barren world (my grandmother saying,
"*Such rich performances as I saw!*"), but they hadn't

known how barren it was. Now they did, and they thought things could be changed.

"Children, you *can't*. If Mike ever finds out that you put your hands on a girl who hasn't Begun—"

"I didn't touch her!" Guy said.

"—you know you'd be shot. Instantly. Guy, *think*!"

He came to the edge of the stage and knelt, looking down at me. "Nurse, I have to do this. I *have* to. And I can't dance alone. 'Ballet is woman.'"

I had read that just last night. Some famous ballet maker whose name I had never heard. I said, "You stole my books."

"I borrowed one. It has pictures that— Nurse, I have to."

"So do I," Kara said.

"Kara, come with me this minute."

"No," she said. Her defiance shocked me even more than their stupid notion that they could teach themselves to dance. I turned on Jemmy.

"And what about *you*? Is this insane love of machinery worth getting yourself shot?"

I saw from his face that Jemmy hadn't even considered this. He looked from me to Guy, back again, then at the ground. I had him.

"Go, Jemmy. Now. None of us will ever tell anyone you were here."

He scuttled down the aisle like a rabbit pursued by dogs. One misguided idiot down.

"If Mike ever finds out you were alone with her—"

"We're not alone!" Kara said. "We have a chaperone!"

"Who? If you mean Jemmy—"

"Me," Bonnie said, stepping from the shadows at the side of the stage.

If Kara had been a shock, Bonnie was an earthquake. Bonnie, who did not break rules and who had always treated Kara with faint disdain: for her high-strung emotion, for her fragile beauty. Bonnie had no command over Guy, but she had a borrowed—from me—authority over Kara.

"Bonnie? You *allowed* this?"

Bonnie said nothing. In the dimness onstage I couldn't see her face.

"Nurse," Guy said again, "we *have* to."

"No, you don't. Kara, come with me."

"No." And then, in a rush, "I won't be like Pretty! I won't let men touch me and sex with me and stick themselves up me until I get swollen and pregnant and maybe die like Emma did! I won't, I won't, *I won't*!" Her voice rose to a shriek, surprising Guy. Kara had just broken the strongest rule among the pack: loyalty. You followed the chief, you obeyed those above you, you did not cause trouble. And you kept your fear to yourself.

I made my voice soothing. "Kara, you heard what the woman on the teevee said. It takes years to become a real dancer. *Years*. This isn't possible, dear heart."

"We know that," Guy said. "We don't be stupid enough to think we can do everything they do. But we can do *some*."

"And that's worth dying for?"

"Nobody will die if you tell Joe that you give us reading lessons here. Everybody knows Kara and me are learning to read off you!"

"No," I repeated. "It's too great a risk, for nothing."

And then Bonnie—Bonnie!—spoke up. "Not for nothing. Nurse, first watch the dancing."

Guy seized on this. "Yes! Watch just once! It's so beautiful!"

It wasn't beautiful. Kara and Guy took their places beside the railing, and he turned on Jemmy's teevee. The woman said, *"Battement tendu,"* and Guy and Kara swung their legs forward, down, to the side, down, to the back down. Their legs reached neither the height nor the purity of line of the dancers on-screen, but they were not without grace. Guy showed a flexibility and power I had not expected, and Kara a flowing delicacy. None of it made any difference.

They went through a few more steps and Guy turned off the screen. "We have to learn all we can before the generator fuel runs out. But we have the books, too. And later on in class there be combinations of steps!"

Five window washers worked every day of the year, constantly keeping the windows bright. At night, when all the buildings were lit up, they shone out on the plaza like liquid gold. So little in this hard life was bright, and nothing was liquid gold. But not at risk of our lives.

"No," I said.

Two days later, I fell in the forest—which I had learned from an old map was called "Central Park"—and tore my knee open on a pointed rock.

"Oh!" The pain was immediate and sharp, but not as sharp as my fear. I was old; if I couldn't walk when the pack moved on, I would be finished.

Bonnie was instantly beside me. "Nurse?"

I tried to rise, could not, was caught in her strong arms. I blinked back tears as we both stared at the white bone below my leathery flesh.

Then I fainted.

The sickroom under the New York State Theater, bare and dark, was no larger than a big closet. Lula sat beside me nursing Jaden, Madonna and child by a single smoky candle. "Grandmother . . ." I whispered, or maybe it was another word, I couldn't be sure. Everything felt blurry, as if I'd opened my eyes underwater.

"Nurse?" Lula said. She put down the baby, who immediately began to scream, and picked up a cup. "Here, drink this now, you be needing to sleep—"

A smell of mint, a bitter taste beneath the sweetness of honey. I slept.

The sickroom still, and I lay alone. Complete darkness. I groped for my leg and felt the hump of bandages, the wooden splint over the knee. Pain, muted. How long had I lain here?

Hours went by until Bonnie came with breakfast, with hot tea, with her wooden, unrevealing face.

"How bad is it, Bonnie? Will I walk again?"

"Can't say until you can stand."

"Is Mike back?"

"Not yet. Drink this."

"What is—"

"Just tea."

I needed more than just tea. I needed to be able to walk.

"Nurse? Nurse, you hear me?"

I did, dragging myself back from far away, or maybe it was Pretty who was far away. Only she was not. She crouched beside me, except that now there were two of her, and then three. How could that be? One Pretty was enough. Unless she was fertile and had given birth to herself again and yet again. . . .

"I be pregnant!" one of the Prettys shouted triumphantly. And then: "Can she hear me?"

"I don't know," Bonnie said.

"It be Mike's! I know! Bonnie, can she hear me?"

"I don't know."

And then, all of a sudden, I couldn't.

I was Grandmother, walking through Lincoln Center, watching the light spill from high arched windows, liquid gold. I took down twenty-one chandeliers and polished each crystal so bright that it burned my hand. The burning spread to the Library for the Performing Arts and charred it to the ground. Windows shattered and pieces of glass pierced me. "Lincoln Kirstein won't like that!" my grandmother cried. "He spent a fortune to build this place!" I laughed and kept on tacking down red carpet.

Finally, clarity returned. I knew who I was and where I was, and it was not Bonnie standing beside my bedroll but Joe, Mike's lieutenant, who'd been left in charge for—how long now?

"How be you, Nurse?" Joe said awkwardly.

I had known Joe since he was ten. A ferocious fighter, loyal, careful about guarding our camps but easygoing about what happened within the perimeter. However, he didn't look easy now.

I said, "My head is clear."

It wasn't my head he was interested in. "Can you walk?"

"I don't know."

"Find out." He left, abrupt and unsmiling. Cold slid down my spine.

Junie arrived a few minutes later, breathless with running, carrying Davey. "Oh, Nurse, be you better?"

"Yes. Send Bonnie to me."

"I don't know where she be! I wanted her a while ago to give Jaden something for that teething, she fusses so, Lula said maybe Bonnie give her something to calm her down but—"

Junie prattled on while I put one palm flat against the wall and tried to stand. I could do so, but only barely.

"Junie, how long have I been here?"

"Be . . . let me think . . . be a month? More?"

More than a month. Drugged for more than a month for the pain of a torn kneecap.

I said, "Find Bonnie and send her to me."

"I will. But, Nurse, Joe says—no, Tony, he be back and he—"

"Tony?" Tony had gone on the joint hunting trip with Mike and Keither's pack. I looked more closely at Junie, and now I saw the fear on her face. Davey felt it, too; his fat little hands clutched her body. I said, "Is Mike dead?"

"Tony says not when he ran off. Tony, he escaped. They got ambushed two days out—Nurse, Keither's pack be big, he lied, most of them not at the hotel when our men went there. They going to trade Mike for somebody, I forget who or why, and Tony escaped and Joe says we move out tomorrow morning! It ain't safe here no more. Oh, Nurse, can you walk?"

"Find Jemmy. Tell him to cut me a stick—*this* long—to lean on. Tell him I want it this minute."

"But you told me to find Bonnie and—"

"Not Bonnie. Jemmy. Now."

By the time Jemmy arrived with the stick, I'd eased my weight onto my leg, fallen, discovered the splint would hold, and gotten up again. Bonnie's splint was heavy; the cane balanced it. Leaning on Jemmy's shoulder, I got myself into the corridor without injuring anything further. In the women's room, the girls worked frantically even though the pack would not move until dawn and there was little enough to gather up. Anything taken must be carried. Each girl had her backpack, and the mothers had baby slings. The pockets of winter coats were stuffed with food. The coats themselves must be worn, no matter how hot the day, because we couldn't afford to lose them. In the morning, blankets would be rolled up with cooking utensils and strapped to Rick, eight years old and not ready to fight, and to whichever of the other men Joe chose.

Outside the building, the first stars shone faintly in a deep blue sky, although on the western horizon clouds mounted high. The air smelled of rain to come and the trees swayed. The Met loomed dark against the cobalt sky. *At night, when all the buildings were lit up, they shone out on the plaza like liquid gold. People laughed and talked and lined up by the hundreds to hear opera and see ballet and watch plays and listen to concerts.*

Somewhere a dog bayed, then another. A pack, hunting.

I said to Jemmy, "Take me to them."

Shadows beside the Vivian Beaumont, shadows in the sloping underground corridor. Jemmy wedged open the door with a rock so that I could hear if the guards started shooting. Inside the theater, more shadows.

They didn't see me. The barre had been pushed to the back of the stage, out of the way. Guy, barefoot, was stripped to the waist. Kara, also barefoot, wore white tights and something filmy and clinging and dotted with holes, unearthed from who knows what ancient storage area. Music played. It wasn't the thin, slightly tinny music of the piano that played for "class." This was the full, glorious sound of the music from the other recording, *The Four Temperaments*. And I realized what Guy had done.

While he arranged steps and combinations for him and Kara, he had held Paul Hindemith's music in his mind. Their dancing perfectly matched the music, blended with it, *was* it. In that blending, Guy's and Kara's inexperience became less important, in part because he had chosen so well movements that they could perform with grace. From studying the ballet books, I could even name some of them: *bourrées, pas de chat, battements.*

The names were unimportant. What mattered was the dancing. They never touched, but Kara's young body, on demi-pointe, bent toward his with sorrow, with loss, with longing, without ever reaching him. He yearned toward her but I knew it was not her he yearned for, nor she for him. The sorrow was for the dancing itself, so briefly embraced, lost tomorrow. The loss was of all the beauty they once might have had, were the world different. Guy raised his leg, extended his arm, and balanced in a perfect arabesque. In the soft glow of lantern light, the dancing figures were liquid gold, and they lit up the bare stage with heartbreaking regret for vanished beauty.

But it was Bonnie who stunned me.

She stood to one side of the stage: chaperone, guard, and something more. Never had I imagined that her homely face could look like that. She was not just alive; she shone with the ferocity of the angel guarding the gate to Eden. I had not known, not even suspected.

"Bonnie," I said. It came out a whisper, heard only by Jemmy. Before I could find a louder voice, the door behind me jerked open and a man roared, "What the fuck!"

Mike.

I turned. Blood caked the left side of his face, matted his beard. His left arm was in a crude sling. Behind him crowded three or four men. Mike pushed past me and ran toward the stage.

I lurched after him as fast as I could, pushing through the pain in my knee. "Wait! Wait! Don't—"

The men rammed past me. Mike stood below the stage, on which Kara and Guy had frozen.

"—do anything!" I yelled. "Bonnie was here the whole time, they were never alone!"

One of the other men—his back to me, I couldn't see who—raised a second lantern high in the air beside Mike, and I saw what Mike saw: the blood on Kara's thighs, brilliant red on the white tights. She had Begun.

I grabbed Mike's good arm. "Never alone! Do you understand, they were never alone! He never touched her!"

If it had been Joe, he might have shot Guy right there on the stage. If it had been Lew, he might have shot them both. Mike gave Guy a look of profound disgust: at his bare chest, at the arabesque Mike had interrupted, at everything about Guy that Mike would never understand. To me, apparently not even noticing my leg, Mike growled, "Take them girls to where they belong."

Someone fired a rifle at the teevee screen, and the music stopped.

Bonnie would answer none of my questions. She sat, silent and wooden, in the sickroom until Mike had time to send for her. "What did you give me?" I demanded. "In what dosage? And, Bonnie—*why*?"

She said nothing.

Lincoln Kirstein, Grandmother once told me, *got this place built. He used his own money and made others donate money and founded a great ballet company. He wasn't a dancer or a choreographer or a musician. He didn't make ballets, but he made ballet happen.*

Kara was not with us. She had been sent to the women's room. In a week or so, when she stopped bleeding, she would be sent to Mike's bed, to Joe's, to Karl's, to every man who might prove her fertile. Even shrieking, she would be sent.

A few hours later, Mike sent for me. Two men carried me between them to a room at the end of the corridor. Small, with concrete walls, it still held the twisted and rusted remains of those big machines that once gave out food and drink in exchange for coins. There was an ancient sofa nested by rats, a sagging table, a few chairs. I could picture dancers coming here from the practice rooms, throwing themselves across the sofa, resting for a moment with a candy bar or soda.

Mike's men sat me in a mostly intact chair and he said, "Why, Nurse?"

The same question I had asked Bonnie. My concern now was to shield her as much as I could. "They wanted to dance, Mike, that's all. They were never alone and he never—"

"You don't know that. You be unconscious the whole time." He eyed my leg. Someone had cleaned up the blood from his eye and beard.

"Yes, that's true, but if Bonnie says she was always with them, then she was. She obeys orders, Mike. I told her that I'd given Kara and Guy permission to dance and that she must stay with them."

"You? *You* gave permission?"

"Yes, me. I mean, you know Bonnie—does she seem the type of person interested in dancing?"

Mike frowned; he was not used to considering what "type of person" a woman might be. "You did this, Nurse? Not Bonnie?"

"Not Bonnie. And she's a good Nurse, Mike. She can make medicines just as well as I did. And do everything else, too."

Finally his gaze lifted from my bandaged knee to my face. He said simply, "Do you want to be shot or left behind?"

Shooting would be kinder. But I said, "Left behind."

He shrugged, losing interest. He still had a Nurse; Kara had not been touched; there were fighting tactics to occupy his mind. Into that indifference I dared to ask, "Guy?"

Mike scowled. To his men he said, "Take her wherever she wants to be left, and bring me the new Nurse." He strode from the room, having already forgotten me.

Mike's men left me under the Vivian Beaumont, just inside the first door, at the top of the sloping corridor. In the dark I groped in my pocket for the candle and matches. It wasn't easy to keep one hand on the wall, hold the candle and my cane in the other, and hobble my painful way down the corridor and through the second door. By the time I reached the shallow steps at the far side of the stage, I was crawling.

My five ballet books lay neatly stacked in a corner, where Guy had studied them who knew how many nights while I lay drugged and Kara, locked in the women's room, flexed and pointed her toes and dreamed of pointe shoes. I opened *The Story of Giselle* and turned the pages by candlelight until I found a photograph of a dancer in a long, filmy skirt held impossibly high by her partner, soaring in an exquisite arc above him. There are worse ways to die than gazing at beauty. From my pocket, I drew my packet of distilled monkshood leaves. Fairly quick, and not as painful as most.

Something moaned somewhere behind me.

They had beaten him bloody and chained him to a concrete column in one of the tiny dressing rooms behind the stage. Guy breathed as if in pain, but I could find no broken bones. Mike had not wanted him to die too quickly. He would either starve or be found by Keither's pack when they came looking for revenge, or for our women, or just for war.

"Guy?"

He moaned again. I searched the room but found no key to his chains. Sitting beside him, I held in one hand that packet of monkshood that did not contain enough for both of us, and in the other *The Story of Giselle*. And then, because I am old and had broken my knee and had lain inactive for over a month while Guy and Kara reinvented the dangers of ballet, I fell asleep.

"Nurse? Nurse?" And then: "Susan!"

The candle had gone out. But the dressing room was lit by a lantern—two lanterns. Bonnie and Kara stood there, dressed in men's clothing and backpacks, and both carried semiautomatic machine guns. On Kara, it looked like a butterfly equipped with a machete. In the sudden light, Guy's eyelids fluttered open.

"Oh!" Kara said, one hand flying to her mouth. The gun wobbled.

Bonnie snapped, "Don't you dare fuss!" and I was startled at her tone, which was my own. Had been my own. "Nurse, can you—"

"No," I said.

Bonnie didn't argue. She dropped to her knees and ran her hands impersonally over Guy.

"I already did that," I said. "Nothing broken."

"Then he can walk. Kara, pull Nurse out of here, back to the stage. Guy, pull yourself as far from the post as you can."

He did, closing his swollen and blood-crusted eyes. Kara tugged me away. Even from the stage, the sound of Bonnie's gun—not the semiautomatic—was loud as she shot at the chain. Even the ricochets—surely dangerous!—made my ears ring. After a few moments Guy and Bonnie emerged, he leaning on her and dragging lengths of chain on both ankles. But he was able to bend and scoop them off the floor. I caught at Bonnie's knee.

"Bonnie—how—"

"In their stew. Kara and I were serving."

"Dead?"

"I don't know. Some, maybe."

"What did you use? Pokeweed? Cowbane? Snakeroot?"

"Skyweed. The seeds."

Kara said suddenly, "Not the other girls, though. We wouldn't do that." And then: "But I won't bed anybody!"

Bonnie said, "And you have to dance."

I gaped at her. Kara wanted to dance, Guy wanted to dance, but it was *Bonnie* who was determined that they would dance. Slowly I said, "Where will you go?"

"North. Away from the city. It's going to rain hard, and that will cover our tracks before the pack revives."

"Try to find a farm community. Or, if you can, places called 'Ithaca' or 'Endicott' or 'Bath.' I'm not sure they exist, but they might. Have you got that map I found? And my medicine sack?"

"Yes. Do you have—"

"Yes."

"We have to go now, Nurse. Jemmy is with us, too."

Jemmy. Perhaps they would find a generator. Bonnie extracted the two recording cubes, *The Four Temperaments* and *Taking Class on Video*, from the blasted teevee. Kara was helping Guy dress in warm coat, boots, a rain poncho. He swayed on his feet but remained upright. She handed him her rifle, which actually seemed to steady him. Kara turned to me and her lips trembled.

"Don't," I said in my harshest tone. Kara, not understanding, looked hurt. But Bonnie knew.

"Good-bye, Nurse," she said, without painful sentiment, and grasped the other two to lead them away.

I waited until the sound of their boots crossed the stage, until the door to the theater closed, until they had had enough time to leave camp. Then I crawled out of the Vivian Beaumont. The rain had just started, sweet on the summer night air. The cook-fires on the plaza sputtered and hissed. Beside them lay the men. Farther out would be the perimeter, and then the guards who had gone from their hearty dinner to the outposts on nearby streets or rooftops.

Two of the men by the fire were already dead. I thought most of the others, including Mike, might recover, but skyweed seeds are tricky. So much depends on how they are dried, pounded, leached, and stored. Bonnie knew a lot, but not as much as I did. I gathered up the men's guns, made a pile of them under a rain poncho, and sat beside it under another poncho, a loaded semiautomatic beside me.

This could happen several ways. If Keither's pack showed up soon, the kindest thing would be to shoot Mike and the others before they revived. Keither's pack would claim the girls, who would be no better nor worse off than they were now. Fertile women were precious.

If Mike and the others revived after I judged Bonnie to be far enough away, I would swallow my packet of monkshood and let Mike take on Keither.

But . . . with skyweed, more of these men should have vomited before their paralysis. If Bonnie had misjudged her preparation or dosages, and the pack regained their senses and strength soon enough to follow her, I would do what was necessary.

We lowered all twenty-one electric chandeliers at the Met—think of that, Susan, twenty-one—and cleaned each crystal drop individually. Every other year all the red carpet was completely replaced, at a cost of $700,000. Every five years the seats were replaced. Five window washers worked every day of *the year, constantly keeping the windows bright. At night, when all the buildings were lit up, they shone out on the plaza like liquid gold. People laughed and talked and lined up by the hundreds to hear opera and see ballet and watch plays and listen to concerts. And such rich performances as I saw . . . you can't imagine!*

No, I can't. No more than I can imagine what will happen to Guy, and Kara, and ballet. No more than I could have imagined Bonnie caught in an enchantment she had never expected: the enchantment of the lost past, rising from ruin like a dancer rising into arabesque. Had that storm lain in her all along, needing only something to passionately love?

There are all kinds of storms, and all kinds of performances. Under the poncho, I hold my gun, and listen to the rain falling on Lincoln Center, and wait.

Diana Gabaldon

New York Times bestselling author Diana Gabaldon is a winner of the Quill Award and of the RITA Award given by the Romance Writers of America. She's the author of the hugely popular Outlander series of time-travel romances, international bestsellers that include *Cross Stitch, Dragonfly in Amber, Voyager, Drums of Autumn, The Fiery Cross, A Breath of Snow and Ashes,* and *An Echo in the Bone.* Her historical series about the strange adventures of Lord John include the novels *Lord John and the Private Matter; Lord John and the Brotherhood of the Blade;* a chapbook novella, *Lord John and the Hell-Fire Club;* and a collection of Lord John stories, *Lord John and the Hand of Devils.* Her most recent novels are two new Lord John books, *The Scottish Prisoner* and *Red Ant's Head,* and a novel omnibus, *A Trail of Fire.* She's also written a contemporary mystery, *White Knight.* A guidebook to and appreciation of her work is *The Outlandish Companion.*

In the fast-paced story that follows, the young Jamie Fraser, one day to be one of the protagonists of the Outlander books, is forced out of his Scottish home and set to wandering in the world, with many new experiences waiting ahead of him, some pleasant, some decidedly not—and some dangerous and dark.

VIRGINS

Ian Murray knew from the moment he saw his best friend's face that something terrible had happened. The fact that he was seeing Jamie Fraser's face at all was evidence enough of that, never mind the look of the man.

Jamie was standing by the armorer's wagon, his arms full of the bits and pieces Armand had just given him, white as milk and swaying back and forth like a reed on Loch Awe. Ian reached him in three paces and took him by the arm before he could fall over.

"Ian." Jamie looked so relieved at seeing him that Ian thought he might break into tears. "God, Ian."

Ian seized Jamie in embrace, and felt him stiffen and draw in his breath at the same instant he felt the bandages beneath Jamie's shirt.

"Jesus!" he began, startled, but then coughed and said, "Jesus, man, it's good to see ye." He patted Jamie's back gently and let go. "Ye'll need a bit to eat, aye? Come on, then."

Plainly they couldn't talk now, but he gave Jamie a quick private nod, took half the equipment from him, and then led him to the fire, to be introduced to the others.

Jamie'd picked a good time of day to turn up, Ian thought. Everyone was tired, but happy to sit down, looking forward to their supper and the daily ration of whatever was going in the way of drink. Ready for the possibilities a new fish offered for entertainment, but without the energy to include the more physical sorts of entertainment.

"That's Big Georges over there," Ian said, dropping Jamie's gear and gesturing toward the far side of the fire. "Next to him, the wee fellow wi' the warts is Juanito; doesna speak much French and nay English at all."

"Do any of them speak English?" Jamie likewise dropped his gear, and sat heavily on his bedroll, tucking his kilt absently down between his knees. His eyes flicked round the circle, and he nodded, half-smiling in a shy sort of way.

"I do." The captain leaned past the man next to him, extending a hand to Jamie. "I'm *le capitaine*—Richard D'Eglise. You'll call me Captain. You look big enough to be useful—your friend says your name is Fraser?"

"Jamie Fraser, aye." Ian was pleased to see that Jamie knew to meet the Captain's eye square, and had summoned the strength to return the handshake with due force.

"Know what to do with a sword?"

"I do. And a bow, forbye." Jamie glanced at the unstrung bow by his feet, and the short-handled ax beside it. "Havena had much to do wi' an ax before, save chopping wood."

"That's good," one of the other men put in, in French. "That's what you'll use it for." Several of the others laughed, indicating that they at least understood English, whether they chose to speak it or not.

"Did I join a troop of soldiers, then, or charcoal-burners?" Jamie asked, raising one brow. He said that in French—very good French, with a faint Parisian accent—and a number of eyes widened. Ian bent his head to hide a smile, in spite of his anxiety. The wean might be about to fall face-first into the fire, but nobody—save maybe Ian—was going to know it, if it killed him.

Ian *did* know it, though, and kept a covert eye on Jamie, pushing bread into his hand so the others wouldn't see it shake, sitting close enough to catch him if he should in fact pass out. The light was fading into gray now, and the clouds hung low and soft, pink-bellied. Going to rain, likely, by the morning. He saw Jamie close his eyes just for an instant, saw his throat move as he swallowed, and felt the trembling of Jamie's thigh near his own.

What the devil's happened? he thought in anguish. *Why are ye here?*

It wasn't until everyone had settled for the night that Ian got an answer.

"I'll lay out your gear," he whispered to Jamie, rising. "You stay by the fire that wee bit longer—rest a bit, aye?" The firelight cast a ruddy glow on Jamie's face, but he thought his friend was likely still white as a sheet; he hadn't eaten much.

Coming back, he saw the dark spots on the back of Jamie's shirt, blotches where fresh blood had seeped through the bandages. The sight filled him with fury as well as fear. He'd seen such things; the wean had been flogged. Badly, and recently. *Who? How?*

"Come on, then," he said roughly, and, bending, got an arm under Jamie's and got him to his feet and away from the fire and the other men. He was alarmed to feel the clamminess of Jamie's hand and hear his shallow breath.

"What?" he demanded, the moment they were out of earshot. "What happened?"

Jamie sat down abruptly.

"I thought one joined a band of mercenaries because they didna ask ye questions."

Ian gave him the snort this statement deserved, and was relieved to hear a breath of laughter in return.

"Eejit," he said. "D'ye need a dram? I've got a bottle in my sack."

"Wouldna come amiss," Jamie murmured. They were camped at the edge of a wee village, and D'Eglise had arranged for the use of a byre or two, but it wasn't cold out, and most of the men had chosen to sleep by the fire or in the field. Ian had put their gear down a little distance away, and with the possibility of rain in mind, under the shelter of a plane tree that stood at the side of a field.

Ian uncorked the bottle of whisky—it wasn't good, but it *was* whisky—and held it under his friend's nose. When Jamie reached for it, though, he pulled it away.

"Not a sip do ye get until ye tell me," he said. "And ye tell me *now, a charaid*."

Jamie sat hunched, a pale blur on the ground, silent. When the words came at last, they were spoken so softly that Ian thought for an instant he hadn't really heard them.

"My faither's dead."

He tried to believe he *hadn't* heard, but his heart had; it froze in his chest.

"Oh, Jesus," he whispered. "Oh, God, Jamie." He was on his knees then, holding Jamie's head fierce against his shoulder, trying not to touch his hurt back. His thoughts were in confusion, but one thing was clear to him—Brian Fraser's death hadn't been a natural one. If it had, Jamie would be at Lallybroch. Not here, and not in this state.

"Who?" he said hoarsely, relaxing his grip a little. "Who killed him?"

More silence, then Jamie gulped air with a sound like fabric being ripped.

"I did," he said, and began to cry, shaking with silent, tearing sobs.

It took some time to winkle the details out of Jamie—and no wonder, Ian thought. He wouldn't want to talk about such things, either, or to remember them. The English dragoons who'd come to Lallybroch to loot and plunder, who'd taken Jamie away with them when he'd fought them. And what they'd done to him then, at Fort William.

"A hundred lashes?" he said in disbelief and horror. "For protecting your *home*?"

"Only sixty, the first time." Jamie wiped his nose on his sleeve. "For escaping."

"The *first* ti—Jesus, God, man! What . . . how . . ."

"Would ye let go my arm, Ian? I've got enough bruises, I dinna need any more." Jamie gave a small, shaky laugh, and Ian hastily let go, but wasn't about to let himself be distracted.

"Why?" he said, low and angry. Jamie wiped his nose again, sniffing, but his voice was steadier.

"It was my fault," he said. "It—what I said before. About my . . ." He had to stop and swallow, but went on, hurrying to get the words out before they could bite him in a tender place. "I spoke chough to the commander. At the garrison, ken. He—well, it's nay matter. It was what I said to him made him flog me again, and Da—he—he'd come. To Fort William, to try to get me released, but he couldn't, and he—he was there, when they . . . did it."

Ian could tell from the thicker sound of his voice that Jamie was weeping again but trying not to, and he put a hand on the wean's knee and gripped it, not too hard, just so as Jamie would ken he was there, listening.

Jamie took a deep, deep breath and got the rest out.

"It was . . . hard. I didna call out, or let them see I was scairt, but I couldna keep my feet. Halfway through it, I fell into the post, just—just hangin' from the ropes, ken, wi' the blood . . runnin' down my legs. They thought for a bit that I'd died—and Da must ha' thought so, too. They told me he put his hand to his head just then, and made a wee noise and then . . . he fell down. An apoplexy, they said."

"Mary, Mother o' God, have mercy on us," Ian said. "He—died right there?"

"I dinna ken was he dead when they picked him up or if he lived a bit after that." Jamie's voice was desolate. "I didna ken a thing about it; no one told me until days later, when Uncle Dougal got me away." He coughed, and wiped the sleeve across his face again. "Ian . . . would ye let go my knee?"

"No," Ian said softly, though he did indeed take his hand away. Only so he could gather Jamie gently into his arms, though. "No. I willna let go, Jamie. Bide. Just . . . bide."

Jamie woke dry-mouthed, thickheaded, and with his eyes half swollen shut by midgie bites. It was also raining, a fine, wet mist coming down through the leaves above him. For all that, he felt better than he had in the last two weeks, though he didn't at once recall why that was—or where he was.

"Here." A piece of half-charred bread rubbed with garlic was shoved under his nose. He sat up and grabbed it.

Ian. The sight of his friend gave him an anchor, and the food in his belly another. He chewed slower now, looking about. Men were rising, stumbling off for a piss, making low rumbling noises, rubbing their heads and yawning.

"Where are we?" he asked. Ian gave him a look.

"How the devil did ye find us if ye dinna ken where ye are?"

"Murtagh brought me," he muttered. The bread turned to glue in his mouth as memory came back;

he couldn't swallow, and spat out the half-chewed bit. Now he remembered it all, and wished he didn't. "He found the band, but then left; said it would look better if I came in on my own."

His godfather had said, in fact, *The Murray lad will take care of ye now. Stay wi' him, mind—dinna come back to Scotland. Dinna come back, d'ye hear me?* He'd heard. Didn't mean he meant to listen.

"Oh, aye. I wondered how ye'd managed to walk this far." Ian cast a worried look at the far side of the camp, where a pair of sturdy horses was being brought to the traces of a canvas-covered wagon. "*Can* ye walk, d'ye think?"

"Of course. I'm fine." Jamie spoke crossly, and Ian gave him the look again, even more slit-eyed than the last.

"Aye, right," he said, in tones of rank disbelief. "Well. We're maybe twenty miles from Bordeaux; that's where we're going. We're takin' the wagon yon to a Jewish moneylender there."

"Is it full of money, then?" Jamie glanced at the heavy wagon, interested.

"No," Ian said. "There's a wee chest, verra heavy so it's maybe gold, and there are a few bags that clink and might be silver, but most of it's rugs."

"Rugs?" He looked at Ian in amazement. "What sort of rugs?"

Ian shrugged.

"Couldna say. Juanito says they're Turkey rugs and verra valuable, but I dinna ken that he knows. He's Jewish, too," Ian added, as an afterthought. "Jews are—" He made an equivocal gesture, palm flattened. "But they dinna really hunt them in France, or exile them anymore, and the Captain says they dinna even arrest them, so long as they keep quiet."

"And go on lending money to men in the government," Jamie said cynically. Ian looked at him, surprised, and Jamie gave him the *I went to the Université in Paris and ken more than you do* smart-arse look, fairly sure that Ian wouldn't thump him, seeing he was hurt.

Ian looked tempted, but had learned enough merely to give Jamie back the *I'm older than you and ye ken well ye havena sense enough to come in out of the rain, so dinna be trying it on* look instead. Jamie laughed, feeling better.

"Aye, right," he said, bending forward. "Is my shirt verra bloody?"

Ian nodded, buckling his sword belt. Jamie sighed and picked up the leather jerkin the armorer had given him. It would rub, but he wasn't wanting to attract attention.

He managed. The troop kept up a decent pace, but it wasn't anything to trouble a Highlander accustomed to hill-walking and running down the odd deer. True, he grew a bit light-headed now and then, and sometimes his heart raced and waves of heat ran over him—but he didn't stagger any more than a few of the men who'd drunk too much for breakfast.

He barely noticed the countryside, but was conscious of Ian striding along beside him, and took pains now and then to glance at his friend and nod, in order to relieve Ian's worried expression. The two of them were close to the wagon, mostly because he didn't want to draw attention by lagging at the back of the troop, but also because he and Ian were taller than the rest by a head or more, with a stride that eclipsed the others, and he felt a small bit of pride in that. It didn't occur to him that possibly the others didn't *want* to be near the wagon.

The first inkling of trouble was a shout from the driver. Jamie had been trudging along, eyes half-closed, concentrating on putting one foot ahead of the other, but a bellow of alarm and a sudden loud *bang!* jerked him to attention. A horseman charged out of the trees near the road, slewed to a halt and fired his second pistol at the driver.

"What—" Jamie reached for the sword at his belt, half-fuddled but starting forward; the horses were neighing and flinging themselves against the traces, the driver cursing and on his feet, hauling on the reins. Several of the mercenaries ran toward the horseman, who drew his own sword and rode through them, slashing recklessly from side to side. Ian seized Jamie's arm, though, and jerked him round.

"Not there! The back!" He followed Ian at a run, and sure enough, there was the Captain on his horse at the back of the troop, in the middle of a melee, a dozen strangers laying about with clubs and blades, all shouting.

"*Caisteal DHOON!*" Ian bellowed, and swung his sword over his head and flat down on the head of an attacker. It hit the man a glancing blow, but he staggered and fell to his knees, where Big Georges seized him by the hair and kneed him viciously in the face.

"*Caisteal DHOON!*" Jamie shouted as loud as

he could, and Ian turned his head for an instant, a big grin flashing.

It was a bit like a cattle raid, but lasting longer. Not a matter of hit hard and get away; he'd never been a defender before and found it heavy going. Still, the attackers were outnumbered, and began to give way, some glancing over their shoulders, plainly thinking of running back into the wood.

They began to do just that, and Jamie stood panting, dripping sweat, his sword a hundredweight in his hand. He straightened, though, and caught the flash of movement from the corner of his eye.

"Dhooon!" he shouted, and broke into a lumbering, gasping run. Another group of men had appeared near the wagon and were pulling the driver's body quietly down from its seat, while one of their number grabbed at the lunging horses' bridles, pulling their heads down. Two more had got the canvas loose and were dragging out a long rolled cylinder, one of the rugs, he supposed.

He reached them in time to grab another man trying to mount the wagon, yanking him clumsily back onto the road. The man twisted, falling, and came to his feet like a cat, knife in hand. The blade flashed, bounced off the leather of his jerkin and cut upward, an inch from his face. Jamie squirmed back, off balance, narrowly keeping his feet, and two more of the bastards charged him.

"On your right, man!" Ian's voice came sudden at his shoulder, and without a moment's hesitation he turned to take care of the man to his left, hearing Ian's grunt of effort as he laid about himself.

Then something changed; he couldn't tell what, but the fight was suddenly over. The attackers melted away, leaving one or two of their number lying in the road.

The driver wasn't dead; Jamie saw him roll half over, an arm across his face. Then he himself was sitting in the dust, black spots dancing before his eyes. Ian bent over him, panting, hands braced on his knees. Sweat dripped from his chin, making dark spots in the dust that mingled with the buzzing spots that darkened Jamie's vision.

"All . . . right?" Ian asked.

He opened his mouth to say yes, but the roaring in his ears drowned it out, and the spots merged suddenly into a solid sheet of black.

He woke to find a priest kneeling over him, intoning the Lord's Prayer in Latin. Not stopping, the priest took up a little bottle and poured oil into the palm of one hand, then dipped his thumb into the puddle and made a swift sign of the Cross on Jamie's forehead.

"I'm no dead, aye?" Jamie said, then repeated this information in French. The priest leaned closer, squinting nearsightedly.

"Dying?" he asked.

"Not that, either." The priest made a small disgusted sound, but went ahead and made crosses on the palms of Jamie's hands, his eyelids and his lips.

"*Ego te absolvo,*" he said, making a final quick sign of the Cross over Jamie's supine form. "Just in case you've killed anyone." Then he rose swiftly to

his feet and disappeared behind the wagon in a flurry
of dark robes.

"All right, are ye?" Ian reached down a hand and
hauled him into a sitting position.

"Aye, more or less. Who was that?" He nodded in
the direction of the recent priest.

"Père Renault. This is a verra well-equipped outfit," Ian said, boosting him to his feet. "We've got
our own priest, to shrive us before battle and give us
extreme unction after."

"I noticed. A bit overeager, is he no?"

"He's blind as a bat," Ian said, glancing over his
shoulder to be sure the priest wasn't close enough to
hear. "Likely thinks better safe than sorry, aye?"

"D'ye have a surgeon, too?" Jamie asked, glancing
at the two attackers who had fallen. The bodies had
been pulled to the side of the road; one was clearly
dead, but the other was beginning to stir and moan.

"Ah," Ian said thoughtfully. "That would be the
priest, as well."

"So if I'm wounded in battle, I'd best try to die of
it, is that what ye're sayin'?"

"I am. Come on, let's find some water."

They found a rock-lined irrigation ditch running between two fields, a little way off the road. Ian pulled
Jamie into the shade of a tree and, rummaging in his
rucksack, found a spare shirt, which he shoved into
his friend's hands.

"Put it on," he said, low voiced. "Ye can wash
yours out; they'll think the blood on it's from the

fightin'." Jamie looked surprised but grateful and, with a nod, skimmed out of the leather jerkin and peeled the sweaty, stained shirt gingerly off his back. Ian grimaced; the bandages were filthy and coming loose, save where they stuck to Jamie's skin, crusted black with old blood and dried pus.

"Shall I pull them off?" he muttered in Jamie's ear. "I'll do it fast."

Jamie arched his back in refusal, shaking his head.

"Nay, it'll bleed more if ye do." There wasn't time to argue; several more of the men were coming. Jamie ducked hurriedly into the clean shirt and knelt to splash water on his face.

"Hey, Scotsman!" Alexandre called to Jamie. "What's that you two were shouting at each other?" He put his hands to his mouth and hooted, "Goooooon!" in a deep, echoing voice that made the others laugh.

"Have ye never heard a war cry before?" Jamie asked, shaking his head at such ignorance. "Ye shout it in battle, to call your kin and your clan to your side."

"Does it mean anything?" Petit Phillipe asked, interested.

"Aye, more or less," Ian said. "Castle Dhuni's the dwelling place of the chieftain of the Frasers of Lovat. *Caisteal Dhuin* is what ye call it in the *Gàidhlig*—that's our own tongue."

"And that's our clan," Jamie clarified. "Clan Fraser, but there's more than one branch, and each one will have its own war cry, and its own motto." He pulled his shirt out of the cold water and wrang it out; the bloodstains were still visible, but faint brown marks now, Ian saw with approval. Then he saw Jamie's mouth opening to say more.

Don't say it! he thought, but as usual, Jamie wasn't reading his mind, and Ian closed his eyes in resignation, knowing what was coming.

"Our clan motto's in French, though," Jamie said, with a small air of pride. *"Je suis prest."*

It meant "I am ready," and was, as Ian had foreseen, greeted with gales of laughter, and a number of crude speculations as to just what the young Scots might be ready for. The men were in good humor from the fight, and it went on for a bit. Ian shrugged and smiled, but he could see Jamie's ears turning red.

"Where's the rest of your queue, Georges?" Petit Phillipe demanded, seeing Big Georges shaking off after a piss. "Someone trim it for you?"

"Your wife bit it off," Georges replied, in a tranquil tone indicating that this was common badinage. "Mouth like a sucking pig, that one. And a *cramouille* like a—"

This resulted in a further scatter of abuse, but it was clear from the sidelong glances that it was mostly performance for the benefit of the two Scots. Ian ignored it. Jamie had gone squiggle-eyed; Ian wasn't sure his friend had ever heard the word *cramouille* before, but he likely figured what it meant.

Before he could get them in more trouble, though, the conversation by the stream was stopped dead by a strangled scream beyond the scrim of trees that hid them from the roadside.

"The prisoner," Alexandre murmured, after a moment.

Ian knelt by Jamie, water dripping from his cupped

hands. He knew what was happening; it curdled his wame. He let the water fall and wiped his hands on his thighs.

"The Captain," he said softly to Jamie. "He'll . . . need to know who they were. Where they came from."

"Aye." Jamie's lips pressed tight at the sound of muted voices, the sudden meaty smack of flesh and a loud grunt. "I know." He splashed water fiercely onto his face.

The jokes had stopped. There was little conversation now, though Alexandre and Josef-from-Alsace began a random argument, speaking loudly, trying to drown out the noises from the road. Most of the men finished their washing and drinking in silence and sat hunched in the shade, shoulders pulled in.

"Père Renault!" The Captain's voice rose, calling for the priest. Père Renault had been performing his own ablutions a discreet distance from the men, but rose at this summons, wiping his face on the hem of his robe. He crossed himself and headed for the road but, on the way, paused by Ian and motioned toward his drinking cup.

"May I borrow this from you, my son? Only for a moment."

"Aye, of course, Father," Ian said, baffled. The priest nodded, bent to scoop up a cup of water, and went on his way. Jamie looked after him, then at Ian, brows raised.

"They saw he's a Jew," Juanito said nearby, very quietly. "They want to baptize him first." He knelt by the water, fists curled tight against his thighs.

Hot as the air was, Ian felt a spear of ice run right

through his chest. He stood up fast, and made as though to follow the priest, but Big Georges snaked out a hand and caught him by the shoulder.

"Leave it," he said. He spoke quietly, too, but his fingers dug hard into Ian's flesh. He didn't pull away, but stayed standing, holding Georges's eyes. He felt Jamie make a brief, convulsive movement, but said, "No!" under his breath, and Jamie stopped.

They could hear French cursing from the road, mingled with Père Renault's voice. *"In nomine Patris, et Filii . . ."* Then struggling, spluttering and shouting, the prisoner, the Captain and Mathieu, and even the priest all using such language as made Jamie blink. Ian might have laughed, if not for the sense of dread that froze every man by the water.

"No!" shouted the prisoner, his voice rising above the others, anger lost in terror. "No, please! I told you all I—" There was a small sound, a hollow noise like a melon being kicked in, and the voice stopped.

"Thrifty, our Captain," Big Georges said, under his breath. "Why waste a bullet?" He took his hand off Ian's shoulder, shook his head, and knelt down to wash his hands.

There was a ghastly silence under the trees. From the road, they could hear low voices—the Captain and big Mathieu speaking to each other and, over that, Père Renault repeating *"In nomine Patris, et Filii . . ."* but in a very different tone. Ian saw the hairs on Jamie's arms rise and he rubbed the palms of his hands against his kilt, maybe feeling a slick from the chrism oil still there.

Jamie plainly couldn't stand to listen, and turned to Big Georges at random.

"Queue?" he said with a raised brow. "That what ye call it in these parts, is it?"

Big Georges managed a crooked smile.

"And what do you call it? In your tongue?"

"*Bot,*" Ian said, shrugging. There were other words, but he wasn't about to try one like *clipeachd* on them.

"Mostly just cock," Jamie said, shrugging, too.

"Or 'penis,' if ye want to be all English about it," Ian chimed in.

Several of the men were listening now, willing to join in any sort of conversation to get away from the echo of the last scream, still hanging in the air like fog.

"Ha," Jamie said. "Penis isna even an English word, ye wee ignoramus. It's Latin. And even in Latin, it doesna mean a man's closest companion—it means 'tail.' "

Ian gave him a long, slow look.

"Tail, is it? So ye canna even tell the difference between your cock and your arse, and ye're preachin' to me about *Latin*?"

The men roared. Jamie's face flamed up instantly, and Ian laughed and gave him a good nudge with his shoulder. Jamie snorted, but elbowed Ian back, and laughed, too, reluctantly.

"Aye, all right, then." He looked abashed; he didn't usually throw his education in Ian's face. Ian didn't hold it against him; he'd floundered for a bit, too, his first days with the company, and that was the sort of thing you did, trying to get your feet under you by making a point of what you were good at. But if Jamie tried rubbing Mathieu's or Big

Georges's face in his Latin and Greek, he'd be prov-
ing himself with his fists, and fast, too. Right this
minute, he didn't look as though he could fight a
rabbit and win.

The renewed murmur of conversation, subdued
as it was, dried up at once with the appearance of
Mathieu through the trees. Mathieu was a big man,
though broad rather than tall, with a face like a mad
boar and a character to match. Nobody called him
"Pig-face" *to* his face.

"You, cheese-rind—go bury that turd," he said to
Jamie, adding with a narrowing of red-rimmed eyes,
"Far back in the wood. And go before I put a boot in
your arse. Move!"

Jamie got up—slowly—eyes fixed on Mathieu with
a look Ian didn't care for. He came up quick beside
Jamie and gripped him by the arm.

"I'll help," he said. "Come on."

"Why do they want this one buried?" Jamie muttered to Ian. "Giving him a *Christian* burial?" He
drove one of the trenching spades Armand had lent
them into the soft leaf mold with a violence that
would have told Ian just how churned up his friend
was, if he hadn't known already.

"Ye kent it's no a verra civilized life, *a charaid*,"
Ian said. He didn't feel any better about it himself,
after all, and spoke sharp. "Not like the *Université*."

The blood flamed up Jamie's neck like tinder taking fire, and Ian held out a palm in hopes of quelling
him. He didn't want a fight, and Jamie couldn't stand
one.

"We're burying him because D'Eglise thinks his friends might come back to look for him, and it's better they don't see what was done to him, aye? Ye can see by looking that the other fellow was just killed fightin'. Business is one thing; revenge is another."

Jamie's jaw worked for a bit, but gradually the hot flush faded and his clench on the shovel loosened.

"Aye," he muttered, and resumed digging. The sweat was running down his neck in minutes, and he was breathing hard. Ian nudged him out of the way with an elbow and finished the digging. Silent, they took the dead man by the oxters and ankles and dragged him into the shallow pit.

"D'ye think D'Eglise found out anything?" Jamie asked as they scattered matted chunks of old leaves over the raw earth.

"I hope so," Ian replied, eyes on his work. "I wouldna like to think they did that for nothing."

He straightened up and they stood awkwardly for a moment, not quite looking at each other. It seemed wrong to leave a grave, even that of a stranger and a Jew, without a word of prayer. But it seemed worse to say a Christian prayer over the man—more insult than blessing, in the circumstances.

At last Jamie grimaced and bending, dug about under the leaves, coming out with two small stones. He gave one to Ian, and one after the other, they squatted and placed the stones together atop the grave. It wasn't much of a cairn, but it was something.

It wasn't the Captain's way to make explanations, or to give more than brief, explicit orders to his

men. He had come back into camp at evening, his face
dark and his lips pressed tight. But three other men
had heard the interrogation of the Jewish stranger,
and by the usual metaphysical processes that happen
around campfires, everyone in the troop knew by the
next morning what he had said.

"Ephraim bar-Sefer," Ian said to Jamie, who had
come back late to the fire after going off quietly to
wash his shirt out again. "That was his name." Ian
was a bit worrit about the wean. His wounds weren't
healing as they should, and the way he'd passed
out . . . He'd a fever now; Ian could feel the heat
coming off his skin, but he shivered now and then,
though the night wasn't bitter.

"Is it better to know that?" Jamie asked bleakly.

"We can pray for him by name," Ian pointed out.
"That's better, is it not?"

Jamie wrinkled up his brow, but after a moment
nodded.

"Aye, it is. What else did he say, then?"

Ian rolled his eyes. Ephraim bar-Sefer had confessed that the band of attackers were professional
thieves, mostly Jews, who—

"Jews?" Jamie interrupted. "Jewish *bandits*?" For
some reason, the thought struck him as funny, but
Ian didn't laugh.

"Why not?" he asked briefly, and went on without waiting for an answer. The men gained advance
knowledge of valuable shipments and made a practice of lying in wait, to ambush and rob.

"It's mostly other Jews they rob, so there's nay
much danger of being pursued by the French army
or a local judge."

"Oh. And the advance knowledge—that's easier come by, too, I suppose, if the folk they rob are Jews. Jews live close by each other in groups," he explained, seeing the look of surprise on Ian's face. "They all read and write, though, and they write letters all the time; there's a good bit of information passed to and fro between the groups. Wouldna be that hard to learn who the moneylenders and merchants are and intercept their correspondence, would it?"

"Maybe not," Ian said, giving Jamie a look of respect. "Bar-Sefer said they got notice from someone—he didna ken who it was, himself—who kent a great deal about valuables comin' and goin'. The person who knew wasna one of their group, though; it was someone outside, who got a percentage o' the proceeds."

That, however, was the total of the information bar-Sefer had divulged. He wouldn't give up the names of any of his associates—D'Eglise didn't care so much about that—and had died stubbornly insisting that he knew nothing of future robberies planned.

"D'ye think it might ha' been one of ours?" Jamie asked, low voiced.

"One of—oh, our Jews, ye mean?" Ian frowned at the thought. There were three Spanish Jews in D'Eglise's band: Juanito, Big Georges, and Raoul, but all three were good men, and fairly popular with their fellows. "I doubt it. All three o' them fought like fiends. When I noticed," he added fairly.

"What I want to know is how the thieves got away wi' that rug," Jamie said reflectively. "Must have weighed, what, ten stone?"

"At least that," Ian assured him, flexing his shoulders at the memory. "I helped load the wretched things. I supposed they must have had a wagon somewhere nearby, for their booty. Why?"

"Well, but . . . *rugs*? Who steals rugs? Even valuable ones. And if they kent ahead of time that we were comin', presumably they kent what we carried."

"Ye're forgettin' the gold and silver," Ian reminded him. "It was in the front of the wagon, under the rugs. They had to pull the rugs out to get at it."

"Mmphm." Jamie looked vaguely dissatisfied—and it was true that the bandits had gone to the trouble to carry the rug away with them. But there was nothing to be gained by more discussion and when Ian said he was for bed, he came along without argument.

They settled down in a nest of long yellow grass, wrapped in their plaids, but Ian didn't sleep at once. He was bruised and tired, but the excitements of the day were still with him, and he lay looking up at the stars for some time, remembering some things and trying hard to forget others—like the look of Ephraim bar-Sefer's head. Maybe Jamie was right and it was better not to have kent his right name.

He forced his mind into other paths, succeeding to the extent that he was surprised when Jamie moved suddenly, cursing under his breath as the movement hurt him.

"Have ye ever done it?" Ian asked suddenly.

There was a small rustle as Jamie hitched himself into a more comfortable position.

"Have I ever done what?" he asked. His voice sounded that wee bit hoarse, but none so bad. "Killed anyone? No."

"Nay, lain wi' a lass."

"Oh, that."

"Aye, *that*. Gowk." Ian rolled toward Jamie and aimed a feint toward his middle. Despite the darkness, Jamie caught his wrist before the blow landed.

"Have you?"

"Oh, ye haven't, then." Ian detached the grip without difficulty. "I thought ye'd be up to your ears in whores and poetesses in Paris."

"Poetesses?" Jamie was beginning to sound amused. "What makes ye think women write poetry? Or that a woman that writes poetry would be wanton?"

"Well, o' course they are. Everybody kens that. The words get into their heads and drive them mad, and they go looking for the first man who—"

"Ye've bedded a poetess?" Jamie's fist struck him lightly in the middle of the chest. "Does your mam ken that?"

"Dinna be telling my mam anything about poetesses," Ian said firmly. "No, but Big Georges did, and he told everyone about her. A woman he met in Marseilles. He has a book of her poetry, and read some out."

"Any good?"

"How would I ken? There was a good bit o' swoonin' and swellin' and burstin' goin' on, but it seemed to be to do wi' flowers, mostly. There was a good wee bit about a bumblebee, though, doin' the business wi' a sunflower. Pokin' it, I mean. With its snout."

There was a momentary silence as Jamie absorbed the mental picture.

"Maybe it sounds better in French," he said.

"I'll help ye," Ian said suddenly, in a tone that was serious to the bone.

"Help me . . . ?"

"Help ye kill this Captain Randall."

He lay silent for a moment, feeling his chest go tight.

"Jesus, Ian," he said, very softly. He lay for several minutes, eyes fixed on the shadowy tree roots that lay near his face.

"No," he said at last. "Ye can't. I need ye to do something else for me, Ian. I need ye to go home."

"Home? What—"

"I need ye to go home and take care of Lallybroch— and my sister. I—I canna go. Not yet." He bit his lower lip hard.

"Ye've got tenants and friends enough there," Ian protested. "Ye need me here, man. I'm no leavin' ye alone, aye? When ye go back, we'll go together." And he turned over in his plaid with an air of finality.

Jamie lay with his eyes tight closed, ignoring the singing and conversation near the fire, the beauty of the night sky over him, and the nagging pain in his back. He should perhaps be praying for the soul of the dead Jew, but he had no time for that just now. He was trying to find his father.

Brian Fraser's soul must still exist, and he was positive that his father was in heaven. But surely there must be some way to reach him, to sense him. When first Jamie had left home, to foster with Dougal at Beannachd, he'd been lonely and homesick, but Da

had told him he would be, and not to trouble over-
much about it.

"Ye think of me, Jamie, and Jenny and Lallybroch.
Ye'll not see us, but we'll be here nonetheless, and
thinking of you. Look up at night, and see the stars,
and ken we see them, too."

He opened his eyes a slit, but the stars swam, their
brightness blurred. He squeezed his eyes shut again
and felt the warm glide of a single tear down his
temple. He couldn't think about Jenny. Or Lallybroch.
The homesickness at Dougal's had stopped. The
strangeness when he went to Paris had eased. This
wouldn't stop, but he'd have to go on living anyway.

Where are ye, Da? he thought in anguish. *Da, I'm
sorry!*

He prayed as he walked next day, making his way
doggedly from one Hail Mary to the next, using his
fingers to count the Rosary. For a time, it kept him
from thinking and gave him a little peace. But eventually the slippery thoughts came stealing back, memories in small flashes, quick as sun on water. Some he
fought off—Captain Randall's voice, playful as he
took the cat in hand—the fearful prickle of the hairs
on his body in the cold wind when he took his shirt
off—the surgeon's *"I see he's made a mess of you,
boy. . . ."*

But some memories he seized, no matter how
painful they were. The feel of his da's hands, hard
on his arms, holding him steady. The guards had
been taking him somewhere, he didn't recall and it
didn't matter, just suddenly his da was there before

him, in the yard of the prison, and he'd stepped forward fast when he saw Jamie, a look of joy and eagerness on his face, this blasted into shock the next moment, when he saw what they'd done to him.

"Are ye bad hurt, Jamie?"

"No, Da, I'll be all right."

For a minute, he had been. So heartened by seeing his father, sure it would all come right—and then he'd remembered Jenny, taking that bastard into the house, sacrificing herself for—

He cut that one off short, too, saying, "Hail Mary, full of grace, the Lord is with thee!" savagely out loud, to the startlement of Petit Phillipe, who was scuttling along beside him on his short bandy legs. "Blessed art thou amongst women," Phillipe chimed in obligingly. "Pray for us sinners, now and at the hour of our death, amen!"

"Hail Mary," said Père Renault's deep voice behind him, taking it up, and within seconds seven or eight of them were saying it, marching solemnly to the rhythm, and then a few more. . . . Jamie himself fell silent, unnoticed. But he felt the wall of prayer a barricade between himself and the wicked sly thoughts and, closing his eyes briefly, felt his father walk beside him, and Brian Fraser's last kiss soft as the wind on his cheek.

They reached Bordeaux just before sunset, and D'Eglise took the wagon off with a small guard, leaving the other men free to explore the delights of the city—though such exploration was somewhat constrained by the fact that they hadn't yet been paid. They'd get their money after the goods were delivered next day.

Ian, who'd been in Bordeaux before, led the way to a large, noisy tavern with drinkable wine and large portions.

"The barmaids are pretty, too," he observed, watching one of these creatures wend her way deftly through a crowd of groping hands.

"Is it a brothel upstairs?" Jamie asked, out of curiosity, having heard a few stories.

"I dinna ken," Ian said, with a certain regret, though in fact he'd never been to a brothel, out of a mixture of penury and fear of catching the pox. His heart beat a little faster at the thought, though. "D'ye want to go and find out, later?"

Jamie hesitated.

"I—well. No, I dinna think so." He turned his face toward Ian and spoke very quietly. "I promised Da I wouldna go wi' whores, when I went to Paris. And now . . . I couldna do it without . . . thinkin' of him, ken?"

Ian nodded, feeling as much relief as disappointment.

"Time enough another day," he said philosophically, and signaled for another jug. The barmaid didn't see him, though, and Jamie snaked out a long arm and tugged at her apron. She whirled, scowling, but seeing Jamie's face, wearing its best blue-eyed smile, chose to smile back and take the order.

Several other men from D'Eglise's band were in the tavern, and this byplay didn't pass unnoticed.

Juanito, at a nearby table, glanced at Jamie, raised a derisive eyebrow, then said something to Raoul in the Jewish sort of Spanish they called Ladino; both men laughed.

"You know what causes warts, friend?" Jamie said pleasantly—in Biblical Hebrew. "Demons inside a man, trying to emerge through the skin." He spoke slowly enough that Ian could follow this, and Ian in turn broke out laughing—as much at the looks on the two Jews' faces as at Jamie's remark.

Juanito's lumpy face darkened, but Raoul looked sharply at Ian, first at his face, then, deliberately, at his crotch. Ian shook his head, still grinning, and Raoul shrugged but returned the smile, then took Juanito by the arm, tugging him off in the direction of the back room, where dicing was to be found.

"What did you say to him?" the barmaid asked, glancing after the departing pair, then looking back wide-eyed at Jamie. "And what tongue did you say it in?"

Jamie was glad to have the wide brown eyes to gaze into; it was causing his neck considerable strain to keep his head from tilting farther down in order to gaze into her décolletage. The charming hollow between her breasts drew the eye . . .

"Oh, nothing but a little bonhomie," he said, grinning down at her. "I said it in Hebrew." He wanted to impress her, and he did, but not the way he'd meant to. Her half-smile vanished, and she edged back a little.

"Oh," she said. "Your pardon, sir, I'm needed . . ." and with a vaguely apologetic flip of the hand, she vanished into the throng of customers, pitcher in hand.

"Eejit," Ian said, coming up beside him. "What did ye tell her that for? Now she thinks ye're a Jew."

Jamie's mouth fell open in shock. "What, me? How, then?" he demanded, looking down at himself. He'd meant his Highland dress, but Ian looked critically at him and shook his head.

"Ye've got the lang neb and the red hair," he pointed out. "Half the Spanish Jews I've seen look like that, and some of them are a good size, too. For all yon lass kens, ye stole the plaid off somebody ye killed."

Jamie felt more nonplussed than affronted. Rather hurt, too.

"Well, what if I was a Jew?" he demanded. "Why should it matter? I wasna askin' for her hand in marriage, was I? I was only talkin' to her, for God's sake!"

Ian gave him that annoyingly tolerant look. He shouldn't mind, he knew; he'd lorded it over Ian often enough about things he kent and Ian didn't. He did mind, though; the borrowed shirt was too small and chafed him under the arms and his wrists stuck out, bony and raw-looking. He didn't look like a Jew, but he looked like a gowk and he knew it. It made him cross-grained.

"Most o' the Frenchwomen—the Christian ones, I mean—dinna like to go wi' Jews. Not because they're Christ-killers, but because of their . . . um . . ." He glanced down, with a discreet gesture at Jamie's crotch. "They think it looks funny."

"It doesna look *that* different."

"It does."

"Well, aye, when it's . . . but when it's—I mean, if it's in a state that a lassie would be lookin' at it, it isna . . ." He saw Ian opening his mouth to ask just how he happened to know what an erect, circumcised cock looked like. "Forget it," he said brusquely, and pushed past his friend. "Let's be goin' down the street."

At dawn, the band gathered at the inn where D'Eglise and the wagon waited, ready to escort it through the streets to its destination—a warehouse on the banks of the Garonne. Jamie saw that the Captain had changed into his finest clothes, plumed hat and all, and so had the four men—among the biggest in the band—who had guarded the wagon during the night. They were all armed to the teeth, and Jamie wondered whether this was only to make a good show, or whether D'Eglise intended to have them stand behind him while he explained why the shipment was one rug short, to discourage complaint from the merchant receiving the shipment.

He was enjoying the walk through the city, though keeping a sharp eye out as he'd been instructed, against the possibility of ambush from alleys, or thieves dropping from a roof or balcony onto the wagon. He thought the latter possibility remote, but dutifully looked up now and then. Upon lowering his eyes from one of these inspections, he found that the Captain had dropped back, and was now pacing beside him on his big gray gelding.

"Juanito says you speak Hebrew," D'Eglise said, looking down at him as though he'd suddenly sprouted horns. "Is this true?"

"Aye," he said cautiously. "Though it's more I can read the Bible in Hebrew—a bit—there not bein' so

many Jews in the Highlands to converse with." There
had been a few in Paris, but he knew better than to
talk about the *Université* and the study of philoso-
phers like Maimonides. They'd scrag him before
supper.

The Captain grunted, but didn't look displeased.
He rode for a time in silence, but kept his horse to a
walk, pacing at Jamie's side. This made Jamie ner-
vous, and after a few moments, impulse made him
jerk his head to the rear and say, "Ian can, too. Read
Hebrew, I mean."

D'Eglise looked down at him, startled, and glanced
back. Ian was clearly visible, as he stood a head taller
than the three men with whom he was conversing as
he walked.

"Will wonders never cease?" the Captain said, as
though to himself. But he nudged his horse into a
trot and left Jamie in the dust.

It wasn't until the next afternoon that this conversation returned to bite Jamie in the arse. They'd delivered the rugs and the gold and silver to the warehouse
on the river, D'Eglise had received his payment, and
consequently the men were scattered down the length
of an *alle* that boasted cheap eating and drinking es-
tablishments, many of these with a room above or
behind where a man could spend his money in other
ways.

Neither Jamie nor Ian said anything further regarding the subject of brothels, but Jamie found his
mind returning to the pretty barmaid. He had his

own shirt on now, and had half a mind to find his way back and tell her he wasn't a Jew.

He had no idea what she might do with that information, though, and the tavern was clear on the other side of the city.

"Think we'll have another job soon?" he asked idly, as much to break Ian's silence as to escape from his own thoughts. There had been talk around the fire about the prospects; evidently there were no good wars at the moment, though it was rumored that the King of Prussia was beginning to gather men in Silesia.

"I hope so," Ian muttered. "Canna bear hangin' about." He drummed long fingers on the tabletop. "I need to be movin'."

"That why ye left Scotland, is it?" He was only making conversation, and was surprised to see Ian dart him a wary glance.

"Didna want to farm, wasna much else to do. I make good money here. *And* I mostly send it home."

"Still, I dinna imagine your da was pleased." Ian was the only son; Auld John was probably still livid, though he hadn't said much in Jamie's hearing during the brief time he'd been home, before the redcoats—

"My sister's marrit. Her husband can manage, if . . ." Ian lapsed into a moody silence.

Before Jamie could decide whether to prod Ian or not, the Captain appeared beside their table, surprising them both.

D'Eglise stood for a moment, considering them. Finally he sighed and said, "All right. The two of you, come with me."

Ian shoved the rest of his bread and cheese into his mouth and rose, chewing. Jamie was about to do likewise when the Captain frowned at him.

"Is your shirt clean?"

He felt the blood rise in his cheeks. It was the closest anyone had come to mentioning his back, and it was too close. Most of the wounds had crusted over long since, but the worst ones were still infected; they broke open with the chafing of the bandages or if he bent too suddenly. He'd had to rinse his shirt almost every night—it was constantly damp and that didn't help—and he knew fine that the whole band knew, but nobody'd spoken of it.

"It is," he replied shortly, and drew himself up to his full height, staring down at D'Eglise, who merely said, "Good, then. Come on."

The new potential client was a physician named Dr. Hasdi, reputed to be a person of great influence among the Jews of Bordeaux. The last client had made the introduction, so apparently D'Eglise had managed to smooth over the matter of the missing rug.

Dr. Hasdi's house was discreetly tucked away in a decent but modest side street, behind a stuccoed wall and locked gates. Ian rang the bell, and a man dressed like a gardener promptly appeared to let them in, gesturing them up the walk to the front door. Evidently, they were expected.

"They don't flaunt their wealth, the Jews," D'Eglise murmured out of the side of his mouth to Jamie. "But they have it."

Well, these did, Jamie thought. A manservant greeted them in a plain tiled foyer, but then opened the door into a room that made the senses swim. It was lined with books in dark wood cases, carpeted thickly underfoot, and what little of the walls was not covered with books was adorned with small tapestries and framed tiles that he thought might be Moorish. But above all, the scent! He breathed it in to the bottom of his lungs, feeling slightly intoxicated, and looking for the source of it, finally spotted the owner of this earthly paradise, sitting behind a desk and staring . . . at him. Or maybe him and Ian both; the man's eyes flicked back and forth between them, round as sucked toffees.

He straightened up instinctively, and bowed.

"We greet thee, Lord," he said, in carefully rehearsed Hebrew. "Peace be on your house." The man's mouth fell open. Noticeably so; he had a large, bushy dark beard, going white near the mouth. An indefinable expression—surely it wasn't amusement?—ran over what could be seen of his face.

A small sound that certainly *was* amusement drew his attention to one side. A small brass bowl sat on a round, tile-topped table, with smoke wandering lazily up from it through a bar of late afternoon sun. Between the sun and the smoke, he could just make out the form of a woman standing in the shadows. She stepped forward, materializing out of the gloom, and his heart jumped.

She inclined her head gravely to the soldiers, addressing them impartially.

"I am Rebekah bat-Leah Hauberger. My grandfather bids me make you welcome to our home, gentlemen," she said, in perfect French, though the old gentleman hadn't spoken. Jamie drew in a great breath of relief; he wouldn't have to try to explain their business in Hebrew, after all. The breath was so deep, though, that it made him cough, the perfumed smoke tickling his chest.

He could feel his face going red as he tried to strangle the cough, and Ian glanced at him out of the sides of his eyes. The girl—yes, she was young, maybe his own age—swiftly took up a cover and clapped it on the bowl, then rang a bell and told the servant something in what sounded like Spanish. *Ladino?* he thought.

"Do please sit, sirs," she said, waving gracefully toward a chair in front of the desk, then turning to fetch another standing by the wall.

"Allow me, Mademoiselle!" Ian leapt forward to assist her. Jamie, still choking as quietly as possible, followed suit.

She had dark hair, very wavy, bound back from her brow with a rose-colored ribbon, but falling loose down her back, nearly to her waist. He had actually raised a hand to stroke it before catching hold of himself. Then she turned round. Pale skin, big, dark eyes, and an oddly knowing look in those eyes when she met his own—which she did, very directly, when he set the third chair down before her.

Annalise. He swallowed, hard, and cleared his throat. A wave of dizzy heat washed over him, and he wished suddenly that they'd open a window.

D'Eglise, too, was visibly relieved at having a more reliable interpreter than Jamie, and launched into a gallant speech of introduction, much decorated with

French flowers, bowing repeatedly to the girl and her grandfather in turn.

Jamie wasn't paying attention to the talk; he was still watching Rebekah. It was her passing resemblance to Annalise de Marillac, the girl he'd loved in Paris, that had drawn his attention—but now he came to look, she was quite different.

Quite different. Annalise had been tiny and fluffy as a kitten. This girl was small—he'd seen that she came no higher than his elbow; her soft hair had brushed his wrist when she sat down—but there was nothing either fluffy or helpless about her. She'd noticed him watching her, and was now watching *him,* with a faint curve to her red mouth that made the blood rise in his cheeks. He coughed and looked down.

"What's amiss?" Ian muttered out of the side of his mouth. "Ye look like ye've got a cocklebur stuck betwixt your hurdies."

Jamie gave an irritable twitch, then stiffened as he felt one of the rawer wounds on his back break open. He could feel the fast-cooling spot, the slow seep of pus or blood, and sat very straight, trying not to breathe deep, in hopes that the bandages would absorb the liquid before it got onto his shirt.

This niggling concern had at least distracted his mind from Rebekah bat-Leah Hauberger, and to distract himself from the aggravation of his back, he returned to the three-way conversation between D'Eglise and the Jews.

The Captain was sweating freely, whether from the hot tea or the strain of persuasion, but he talked easily, gesturing now and then toward his matched pair of tall, Hebrew-speaking Scots, now and then toward the window and the outer world, where vast legions of similar warriors awaited, ready and eager to do Dr. Hasdi's bidding.

The Doctor watched D'Eglise intently, occasionally addressing a soft rumble of incomprehensible words to his granddaughter. It did sound like the Ladino Juanito spoke, more than anything else; certainly it sounded nothing like the Hebrew Jamie had been taught in Paris.

Finally the old Jew glanced among the three mercenaries, pursed his lips thoughtfully, and nodded. He rose and went to a large blanket chest that stood under the window, where he knelt and carefully gathered up a long, heavy cylinder wrapped in oiled cloth. Jamie could see that it was remarkably heavy for its size from the slow way the old man rose with it, and his first thought was that it must be a gold statue of some sort. His second thought was that Rebekah smelled like rose petals and vanilla pods. He breathed in, very gently, feeling his shirt stick to his back.

The thing, whatever it was, jingled and chimed softly as it moved. Some sort of Jewish clock? Dr. Hasdi carried the cylinder to the desk and set it down, then curled a finger to invite the soldiers to step near.

Unwrapped with a slow and solemn sense of ceremony, the object emerged from its layers of linen, canvas, and oilcloth. It *was* gold, in part, and not unlike statuary, but made of wood and shaped like a prism, with a sort of crown at one end. While Jamie was still wondering what the devil it might be, the Doctor's arthritic fingers touched a small clasp and the box opened, revealing yet more layers of cloth, from which yet another delicate, spicy scent emerged. All three soldiers breathed deep, in unison, and Rebekah made that small sound of amusement again.

"The case is cedarwood," she said. "From Lebanon."

"Oh," D'Eglise said respectfully. "Of course!"

The bundle inside was dressed—there was no other word for it; it was wearing a sort of caped mantle and a belt—with a miniature buckle—in velvet and embroidered silk. From one end, two massive golden finials protruded like twin heads. They were pierced work, and looked like towers, adorned in the windows and along their lower edges with a number of tiny bells.

"This is a *very* old Torah scroll," Rebekah said, keeping a respectful distance. "From Spain."

"A priceless object, to be sure," D'Eglise said, bending to peer closer.

Dr. Hasdi grunted and said something to Rebekah, who translated:

"Only to those whose Book it is. To anyone else, it has a very obvious and attractive price. If this were not so, I would not stand in need of your services." The Doctor looked pointedly at Jamie and Ian. "A respectable man—a Jew—will carry the Torah. It may not be touched. But you will safeguard it—and my granddaughter."

"Quite so, Your Honor." D'Eglise flushed slightly, but was too pleased to look abashed. "I am deeply honored by your trust, sir, and I assure you . . ." But Rebekah had rung her bell again, and the manservant came in with wine.

The job offered was simple. Rebekah was to be married to the son of the chief rabbi of the Paris synagogue. The ancient Torah was part of her dowry, as was a sum of money that made D'Eglise's eyes glisten. The Doctor wished to engage D'Eglise to deliver all three items—the girl, the scroll, and the money—safely to Paris; the Doctor himself would travel there for the wedding, but later in the month, as his business in Bordeaux detained him. The only things to be decided were the price for D'Eglise's services, the time in which they were to be accomplished, and the guarantees D'Eglise was prepared to offer.

The Doctor's lips pursed over this last; his friend Ackerman, who had referred D'Eglise to him, had not been entirely pleased at having one of his valuable rugs stolen en route, and the Doctor wished to be assured that none of *his* valuable property— Jamie saw Rebekah's soft mouth twitch as she translated this—would go missing between Bordeaux and Paris. The Captain gave Ian and Jamie a stern look, then altered this to earnest sincerity as he assured the Doctor that there would be no difficulty; his best men would take on the job, and he would offer whatever assurances the Doctor required. Small drops of sweat stood out on his upper lip.

Between the warmth of the fire and the hot tea, Jamie was sweating, too, and could have used a glass of wine. But the old gentleman stood up abruptly and, with a courteous bow to D'Eglise, came out from behind his desk and took Jamie by the arm, pulling him up and tugging him gently toward a doorway.

He ducked, just in time to avoid braining himself on a low archway, and found himself in a small, plain room with bunches of drying herbs hung from its beams. What—

But before he could formulate any sort of question, the old man had got hold of his shirt and was pulling it free of his plaid. He tried to step back, but there was no room, and willy-nilly, he found himself set down on a stool, the old man's horny fingers pulling loose the bandages. The Doctor made a deep sound of disapproval, then shouted something in which the words *agua caliente* were clearly discernible, back through the archway.

He daren't stand up and flee—not and risk D'Eglises's new arrangement. And so he sat, burning with embarrassment, while the physician probed, prodded, and—a bowl of hot water having appeared— scrubbed at his back with something painfully rough. None of this bothered Jamie nearly as much as the appearance of Rebekah in the doorway, her dark eyebrows raised.

"My grandfather says your back is a mess," she told him, translating a remark from the old man.

"Thank ye. I didna ken that," he muttered in English, but then repeated the remark more politely in French. His cheeks burned with mortification, but a small, cold echo sounded in his heart. *"He's made a mess of you, boy."*

The surgeon at Fort William had said it, when the soldiers had dragged Jamie to him after the flogging, legs too wabbly to stand by himself. The surgeon had been right, and so was Dr. Hasdi, but it didn't mean Jamie wanted to hear it again.

Rebekah, evidently interested to see what her grandfather meant, came round behind Jamie. He stiffened, and the Doctor poked him sharply in the back of the neck, making him bend forward again. The two Jews were discussing the spectacle in tones of detachment; he felt the girl's small, soft fingers trace a line between his ribs and nearly shot off the stool, his flesh erupting in goose bumps.

"Jamie?" Ian's voice came from the hallway, sounding worried. "Are ye all right?"

"Aye!" he managed, half-strangled. "Don't—ye needn't come in."

"Your name is Jamie?" Rebekah was now in front of him, leaning down to look into his face. Her own was alive with interest and concern. "James?"

"Aye. James." He clenched his teeth as the Doctor dug a little harder, clicking his tongue.

"Diego," she said, smiling at him. "That's what it would be in Spanish—or Ladino. And your friend?"

"He's called Ian. That's—" He groped for a moment and found the English equivalent. "John. That would be . . ."

"Juan. Diego and Juan." She touched him gently on the bare shoulder. "You're friends? Brothers? I can see you come from the same place—where is that?"

"Friends. From . . . Scotland. The—the—Highlands. A place called Lallybroch." He'd spoken unwarily, and a pang shot through him at the name, sharper than whatever the Doctor was scraping his back with. He looked away; the girl's face was too close; he didn't want her to see.

She didn't move away. Instead, she crouched gracefully beside him and took his hand. Hers was very warm, and the hairs on his wrist rose in response, in spite of what the Doctor was doing to his back.

"It will be done soon," she promised. "He's cleaning the infected parts; he says they will scab over cleanly now and stop draining." A gruff question from the Doctor. "He asks, do you have fever at night? Bad dreams?"

Startled, he looked back at her, but her face showed only compassion. Her hand tightened on his in reassurance.

"I . . . yes. Sometimes."

A grunt from the Doctor, more words, and Rebekah let go his hand with a little pat, and went out, skirts a-rustle. He closed his eyes and tried to keep the scent of her in his mind—he couldn't keep it in his nose, as the Doctor was now anointing him with something vile smelling. He could smell himself, too, and his jaw prickled with embarrassment; he reeked of stale sweat, campfire smoke, and fresh blood.

He could hear D'Eglise and Ian talking in the parlor, low voiced, discussing whether to come and rescue him. He would have called out to them, save that he couldn't bear the Captain to see . . . He pressed his lips together tight. Aye, well, it was nearly done; he could tell from the Doctor's slower movements, almost gentle now.

"Rebekah!" the Doctor called, impatient, and the girl appeared an instant later, a small cloth bundle in one hand. The Doctor let off a short burst of words, then pressed a thin cloth of some sort over Jamie's back; it stuck to the nasty ointment.

"Grandfather says the cloth will protect your shirt until the ointment is absorbed," she told him.

"By the time it falls off—don't peel it off, let it come off by itself—the wounds will be scabbed, but the scabs should be soft and not crack."

The Doctor took his hand off Jamie's shoulder, and Jamie shot to his feet, looking round for his shirt. Rebekah handed it to him. Her eyes were fastened on his naked chest, and he was—for the first time in his life—embarrassed by the fact that he possessed nipples. An extraordinary but not unpleasant tingle made the curly hairs on his body stand up.

"Thank you—ah, I mean . . . *gracias, Señor*." His face was flaming, but he bowed to the Doctor with as much grace as he could muster. "*Muchas gracias*."

"*De nada,*" the old man said gruffly, with a dismissive wave of one hand. He pointed at the small bundle in his granddaughter's hand. "Drink. No fever. No dream." And then, surprisingly, he smiled.

"Shalom," he said, and made a shooing gesture.

D'Eglise, looking pleased with the new job, left Ian and Jamie at a large tavern called Le Poulet Gai, where some of the other mercenaries were enjoying themselves—in various ways. The Cheerful Chicken most assuredly did boast a brothel on the upper floor, and slatternly women in various degrees of undress wandered freely through the lower rooms, picking up new customers with whom they vanished upstairs.

The two tall young Scots provoked a certain amount of interest from the women, but when Ian solemnly turned his empty purse inside out in front of them—having put his money inside his shirt for safety—they left the lads alone.

"Couldna look at one of those," Ian said, turning his back on the whores and devoting himself to his ale. "Not after seein' the wee Jewess up close. Did ye ever seen anything like?"

Jamie shook his head, deep in his own drink. It was sour and fresh and went down a treat, parched as he was from the ordeal in Dr. Hasdi's surgery. He could still smell the ghost of Rebekah's scent, vanilla and roses, a fugitive fragrance among the reeks of the tavern. He fumbled in his sporran, bringing out the little cloth bundle Rebekah had given him.

"She said—well, the Doctor said—I was to drink this. How, d'ye think?" The bundle held a mixture of broken leaves, small sticks, and a coarse powder, and smelled strongly of something he'd never smelled before. Not bad; just odd. Ian frowned at it.

"Well . . . ye'd brew a tea of it, I suppose," he said. "How else?"

"I havena got anything to brew it in," Jamie said. "I was thinkin' . . . maybe put it in the ale?"

"Why not?"

Ian wasn't paying much attention; he was watching Mathieu Pig-face, who was standing against a wall, summoning whores as they passed by, looking them up and down and occasionally fingering the merchandise before sending each one on with a smack on the rear.

He wasn't really tempted—the women scairt him, to be honest—but he was curious. If he ever *should* . . . how did ye start? Just grab, like Mathieu was doing, or did ye need to ask about the price first, to be sure you could afford it? And was it proper to bargain, like ye did for a loaf of bread or a flitch of bacon, or would the woman kick ye in the privates and find someone less mean?

He shot a glance at Jamie, who, after a bit of choking, had got his herbed ale down all right and was looking a little glazed. He didn't think Jamie knew, either, but he didn't want to ask, just in case he did.

"I'm goin' to the privy," Jamie said abruptly and stood up. He looked pale.

"Have ye got the shits?"

"Not yet." With this ominous remark, he was off, bumping into tables in his haste, and Ian followed, pausing long enough to thriftily drain the last of Jamie's ale as well as his own.

Mathieu had found one he liked; he leered at Ian and said something obnoxious as he ushered his choice toward the stairs. Ian smiled cordially and said something much worse in *Gàidhlig*.

By the time he got to the yard at the back of the tavern, Jamie had disappeared. Figuring he'd be back as soon as he rid himself of his trouble, Ian leaned tranquilly against the back wall of the building, enjoying the cool night air and watching the folk in the yard.

There were a couple of torches burning, stuck in the ground, and it looked a bit like a painting he'd seen of the Last Judgement, with angels on the one side blowing trumpets and sinners on the other, going down to Hell in a tangle of naked limbs and bad behavior. It was mostly sinners out here, though now and then he thought he saw an angel floating past the corner of his eye. He licked his lips thoughtfully, wondering what was in the stuff Dr. Hasdi had given Jamie.

Jamie himself emerged from the privy at the far side of the yard, looking a little more settled in himself, and, spotting Ian, made his way through the little knots of drinkers sitting on the ground singing, and the others wandering to and fro, smiling vaguely as they looked for something, not knowing what they were looking for.

Ian was seized by a sudden sense of revulsion, almost terror; a fear that he would never see Scotland again, would die here, among strangers.

"We should go home," he said abruptly, as soon as Jamie was in earshot. "As soon as we've finished this job."

"Home?" Jamie looked strangely at Ian, as though he were speaking some incomprehensible language.

"Ye've business there, and so have I. We—"

A skelloch and the thud and clatter of a falling table with its burden of dishes interrupted them. The back door of the tavern burst open and a woman ran out, yelling in a sort of French that Ian didn't understand but knew fine was bad words from the tone of it. Similar words in a loud male voice, and big Mathieu charged out after her.

He caught her by the shoulder, spun her round, and cracked her across the face with the back of one meaty hand. Ian flinched at the sound, and Jamie's hand tightened on his wrist.

"What—" Jamie began, but then stopped dead.

"Putain de . . . merde . . . tu fais . . . chier," Mathieu panted, slapping her with each word. She shrieked

some more, trying to get away, but he had her by the arm, and now jerked her round and pushed her hard in the back, knocking her to her knees.

Jamie's hand loosened, and Ian grabbed his arm, tight.

"Don't," he said tersely, and yanked Jamie back into the shadow.

"I wasn't," Jamie said, but under his breath and not noticing much what he was saying, because his eyes were fixed on what was happening, as much as Ian's were.

The light from the door spilled over the woman, glowing off her hanging breasts, bared in the ripped neck of her shift. Glowing off her wide round buttocks, too; Mathieu had shoved her skirts up to her waist and was behind her, jerking at his flies one-handed, the other hand twisted in her hair so her head pulled back, throat straining and her face white-eyed as a panicked horse.

"*Pute!*" he said, and gave her arse a loud smack, open-handed. "Nobody says no to me!" He'd got his cock out now, in his hand, and shoved it into the woman with a violence that made her hurdies wobble and knotted Ian from knees to neck.

"*Merde,*" Jamie said, still under his breath. Other men and a couple of women had come out into the yard and were gathered round with the others, enjoying the spectacle as Mathieu set to work in a businesslike manner. He let go of the woman's hair in order to grasp her by the hips and her head hung down, hair hiding her face. She grunted with each thrust, panting bad words that made the onlookers laugh.

Ian was shocked—and shocked as much at his own arousal as at what Mathieu was doing. He'd not seen open coupling before, only the heaving and giggling of things happening under a blanket, now and then a wee flash of pale flesh. This . . . He ought to look away, he knew that fine. But he didn't.

Jamie took in a breath, but no telling whether he meant to say something. Mathieu threw back his big head and howled like a wolf and the watchers all cheered. Then his face convulsed, gapped teeth showing in a grin like a skull's, and he made a noise like a pig gives out when you knock it clean on the head, and collapsed on top of the whore.

The whore squirmed out from under his bulk, abusing him roundly. Ian understood what she was saying now, and would have been shocked anew if he'd had any capacity for being shocked left. She hopped up, evidently not hurt, and kicked Mathieu in the ribs once, then twice, but having no shoes on, didn't hurt him. She reached for the purse still tied at his waist, stuck her hand in and grabbed a handful of coins, then kicked him once more for luck and stomped off into the house, holding up the neck of her shift. Mathieu lay sprawled on the ground, his breeks around his thighs, laughing and wheezing.

Ian heard Jamie swallow and realized he was still gripping Jamie's arm. Jamie didn't seem to have noticed. Ian let go. His face was burning all the way down to the middle of his chest, and he didn't think it was just torchlight on Jamie's face, either.

"Let's . . . go someplace else," he said.

———

"I wish we'd . . . done something," Jamie blurted. They hadn't spoken at all after leaving Le Poulet Gai. They'd walked clear to the other end of the street and down a side alley, eventually coming to rest in a small tavern, fairly quiet. Juanito and Raoul were there, dicing with some locals, but gave Ian and Jamie no more than a glance.

"I dinna see what we *could* have done," Ian said reasonably. "I mean, we could maybe have taken on Mathieu together and got off with only bein' maimed. But ye ken it would ha' started a kebbie-lebbie, wi' all the others there." He hesitated, and gave Jamie a quick glance before returning his gaze to his cup. "And . . . she *was* a whore. I mean, she wasna a—"

"I ken what ye mean." Jamie cut him off. "Aye, ye're right. And she did go with the man, to start. God knows what he did to make her take against him, but there's likely plenty to choose from. I wish—ah, feckit. D'ye want something to eat?"

Ian shook his head. The barmaid brought them a jug of wine, glanced at them, and dismissed them as negligible. It was rough wine that took the skin off the insides of your mouth, but it had a decent taste to it, under the resin fumes, and wasn't too much watered. Jamie drank deep, and faster than he generally did; he was uneasy in his skin, prickling and ir-ritable, and wanted the feeling to go away.

There were a few women in the place, not many. Jamie had to think that whoring maybe wasn't a profitable business, wretched as most of the poor

creatures looked, raddled and half-toothless. Maybe
it wore them down, having to . . . He turned away
from the thought and finding the jug empty, waved
to the barmaid for another.

Juanito gave a joyful whoop and said something in
Ladino. Looking in that direction, Jamie saw one of
the whores who'd been lurking in the shadows come
gliding purposefully in, bending down to give Juanito
a congratulatory kiss as he scooped in his winnings.
Jamie snorted a little, trying to blow the smell of her
out of his neb—she'd passed by close enough that
he'd got a good whiff of her: a stink of rancid sweat
and dead fish. Alexandre had told him that was from
unclean privates, and he believed it.

He went back to the wine. Ian was matching him,
cup for cup, and likely for the same reason. His
friend wasn't usually irritable or crankit, but if he
was well put out, he'd often stay that way until the
next dawn—a good sleep erased his bad temper, but
'til then you didn't want to rile him.

He shot a sidelong glance at Ian. He couldn't tell
Ian about Jenny. He just . . . couldn't. But neither
could he think about her, left alone at Lallybroch . . .
maybe with ch—

"Oh, God," he said, under his breath. "No. Please.
No."

"*Dinna come back,*" Murtagh had said, and plainly
meant it. Well, he *would* go back—but not yet awhile.
It wouldn't help his sister, him going back just now
and bringing Randall and the redcoats straight to
her like flies to a fresh-killed deer. . . . He shoved
that analogy hastily out of sight, horrified. The truth
was, it made him sick with shame to think about

Jenny, and he tried not to—and was the more ashamed because he mostly succeeded.

Ian's gaze was fixed on another of the harlots. She was old, in her thirties at least, but had most of her teeth and was cleaner than most. She was flirting with Juanito and Raoul, too, and Jamie wondered whether she'd mind if she found out they were Jews. Maybe a whore couldn't afford to be choosy.

His treacherous mind at once presented him with a picture of his sister, obliged to follow that walk of life to feed herself, made to take any man who . . . Blessed Mother, what would the folk, the tenants, the servants, do to her if they found out what had happened? The talk . . . He shut his eyes tight, hoping to block the vision.

"That one's none sae bad," Ian said meditatively, and Jamie opened his eyes. The better-looking whore had bent over Juanito, deliberately rubbing her breast against his warty ear. "If she doesna mislike a Jew, maybe she'd . . ."

The blood flamed up in Jamie's face.

"If ye've got any thought to my sister, ye're no going to—to—pollute yourself wi' a French whore!"

Ian's face went blank, but then flooded with color in turn.

"Oh, aye? And if I said your sister wasna worth it?"

Jamie's fist caught him in the eye and he flew backward, overturning the bench and crashing into the next table. Jamie scarcely noticed, the agony in his hand shooting fire and brimstone from his crushed knuckles up his forearm. He rocked to and fro, injured hand clutched between his thighs, cursing freely in three languages.

Ian sat on the floor, bent over, holding his eye and breathing through his mouth in short gasps. After a minute, he straightened up. His eye was puffing already, leaking tears down his lean cheek. He got up, shaking his head slowly, and put the bench back in place. Then he sat down, picked up his cup and took a deep gulp, put it down and blew out his breath. He took the snot-rag Jamie was holding out to him and dabbed at his eye.

"Sorry," Jamie managed. The agony in his hand was beginning to subside, but the anguish in his heart wasn't.

"Aye," Ian said quietly, not meeting his eye. "I wish we'd done something, too. Ye want to share a bowl o' stew?"

Two days later, they set off for Paris. After some thought, D'Eglise had decided that Rebekah and her maid would travel by coach, escorted by Jamie and Ian. D'Eglise and the rest of the troop would take the money, with some men sent ahead in small groups to wait, both to check the road ahead, and so that they could ride in shifts, not stopping anywhere along the way. The women obviously would have to stop, but if they had nothing valuable with them, they'd be in no danger.

It was only when they went to collect the women at Dr. Hasdi's residence that they learned the Torah scroll and its custodian, a sober-looking man of middle age introduced to them as Monsieur Peretz, would be traveling with Rebekah. "I trust my greatest treasures to you, gentlemen," the Doctor told them, through his granddaughter, and gave them a formal little bow

"May you find us worthy of trust, Lord," Jamie managed in halting Hebrew, and Ian bowed with great solemnity, hand on his heart. Dr. Hasdi looked from one to the other, gave a small nod, and then stepped forward to kiss Rebekah on the forehead.

"Go with God, child," he whispered, in something close enough to Spanish that Jamie understood it.

All went well for the first day, and the first night. The autumn weather held fine, with no more than a pleasant tang of chill in the air, and the horses were sound. Dr. Hasdi had provided Jamie with a purse to cover the expenses of the journey, and they all ate decently and slept at a very respectable inn— Ian being sent in first to inspect the premises and insure against any nasty surprises.

The next day dawned cloudy, but the wind came up and blew the clouds away before noon, leaving the sky clean and brilliant as a sapphire overhead. Jamie was riding in the van, Ian post, and the coach was making good time, in spite of a rutted, winding road. As they reached the top of a small rise, though, Jamie saw that a small stream had run through the roadbed in the dip below, making a bog some ten feet across. He brought his horse to a sudden stop, raising a hand to halt the coach, and Ian reined up alongside him.

"What—" he began, but was interrupted. The driver had pulled his team up for an instant but, at a peremptory shout from inside the coach, now snapped the reins over the horses' backs and the coach lunged forward, narrowly missing Jamie's horse, which shied violently, flinging its rider off into the bushes.

"Jamie! Are ye all right?" Torn between concern for his friend and for his duty, Ian held his horse, glancing to and fro.

"Stop them! Get them! *Ifrinn!*" Jamie scuttled crabwise out of the weeds, face scratched and bright red with fury. Ian didn't wait, but kicked his horse and lit out in pursuit of the heavy coach, this now lurching from side to side as it ran down into the boggy bottom. Shrill feminine cries of protest from inside were drowned by the driver's exclamation of *"Ladrones!"*

That was one word he kent in Spanish—"thieves." One of the *ladrones* was already skittering up the side of the coach like an eight-legged cob, and the driver promptly dived off the box, hit the ground and ran for it.

"Coward!" Ian bellowed, and gave out with a Hieland screech that set the coach-horses dancing, flinging their heads to and fro, and giving the would-be kidnapper fits with the reins. He forced his own horse—who hadn't liked the screeching any better than the coach-horses—through the narrow gap between the brush and the coach, and as he came even with the driver, had his pistol out. He drew down on the fellow—a young chap with long yellow hair—and shouted at him to pull up.

The man glanced at him, crouched low, and slapped the reins on the horses' backs, shouting at them in a voice like iron. Ian fired, and missed—but the delay had let Jamie catch them up; he saw Jamie's red head poke up as he climbed the back of the coach, and there were more screams from inside as Jamie pounded across the roof and launched himself at the yellow-haired driver.

Leaving that bit of trouble to Jamie to deal with, Ian kicked his horse forward, meaning to get ahead and seize the reins, but another of the thieves had beat him to it and was hauling down on one horse's head. Aye, well, it worked once. Ian inflated his lungs as far as they'd go and let rip.

The coach-horses bolted in a spray of mud. Jamie and the yellow-haired driver fell off the box, and the whoreson in the road disappeared, possibly trampled into the mire. Ian hoped so. Blood in his eye, he reined up his own agitated mount, drew his broadsword, and charged across the road, shrieking like a *ban-sidhe* and slashing wildly. Two thieves stared up at him openmouthed, then broke and ran for it.

He chased them a wee bit into the brush, but the going was too thick for his horse, and he turned back to find Jamie rolling about in the road, earnestly hammering the yellow-haired laddie. Ian hesitated—help him, or see to the coach? A loud crash and horrible screams decided him at once and he charged down the road.

The coach, driverless, had run off the road, hit the bog, and fallen sideways into a ditch. From the clishmaclaver coming from inside, he thought the women were likely all right, and, swinging off his horse, wrapped the reins hastily round a tree and went to take care of the coach-horses before they killed themselves.

It took no little while to disentangle the mess

single-handed—luckily the horses had not managed
to damage themselves significantly—and his efforts
were not aided by the emergence from the coach of
two agitated and very disheveled women carrying on
in an incomprehensible mix of French and Ladino.

Just as well, he thought, giving them a vague
wave of a hand he could ill-spare at the moment. *It
wouldna help to hear what they're saying.* Then he
picked up the word "dead," and changed his mind.
Monsieur Peretz was normally so silent that Ian had
in fact forgotten his presence in the confusion of the
moment. He was even more silent now, Ian learned,
having broken his neck when the coach overturned.

"Oh, Jesus," he said, running to look. But the man
was undeniably dead, and the horses were still creat-
ing a ruckus, slipping and stamping in the mud of
the ditch. He was too busy for a bit to worry about
how Jamie was faring, but as he got the second horse
detached from the coach and safely tethered to a
tree, he did begin to wonder where the wean was.

He didn't think it safe to leave the women; the
banditti might come back, and a right numpty he'd
look if they did. There was no sign of their driver,
who had evidently abandoned them out of fright.
He told the ladies to sit down under a sycamore tree
and gave them his canteen to drink from, and after
a bit, they stopped talking quite so fast.

"Where is Diego?" Rebekah said, quite intelligibly.

"Och, he'll be along presently," Ian said, hoping it
was true. He was beginning to be worrit himself.

"Perhaps he's been killed, too," said the maidser-
vant, who shot an ill-tempered glare at her mistress.
"How would you feel then?"

"I'm sure he wouldn't—I mean, he's not. I'm sure," Rebekah repeated, not sounding all that sure.

She was right, though; no sooner had Ian decided to march the women back along the road to have a keek, when Jamie came shambling around the bend himself, and sank down in the dry grass, closing his eyes.

"Are you all right?" Rebekah asked, bending down anxiously to look at him from under the brim of her straw traveling hat. He didn't look very peart, Ian thought.

"Aye, fine." He touched the back of his head, wincing slightly. "Just a wee dunt on the heid. The fellow who fell down in the road," he explained to Ian, closing his eyes again. "He got up again, and hit me from behind. Didna knock me clean out, but it distracted me for a wee bit, and when I got my wits back, they'd both gone—the fellow that hit me, and the one I was hittin'."

"Mmphm," said Ian, and, squatting in front of his friend, thumbed up one of Jamie's eyelids and peered intently into the bloodshot blue eye behind it. He had no idea what to look for, but he'd seen Père Renault do that, after which he usually applied leeches somewhere. As it was, both that eye and the other one looked fine to him; just as well, as he hadn't any leeches. He handed Jamie the canteen and went to look the horses over.

"Two of them are sound enough," he reported, coming back. "The light bay's lame. Did the bandits take your horse? And what about the driver?"

Jamie looked surprised.

"I forgot I had a horse," he confessed. "I dinna

ken about the driver—didna see him lyin' in the
road, at least." He glanced vaguely round. "Where's
Monsieur Pickle?"

"Dead. Stay there, aye?"

Ian sighed, got up, and loped back down the road,
where he found no sign of the driver, though he
walked to and fro calling for a while. Fortunately
he did find Jamie's horse, peaceably cropping grass
by the verge. He rode it back and found the women
on their feet, discussing something in low voices,
now and then looking down the road, or standing on
their toes in a vain attempt to see through the trees.

Jamie was still sitting on the ground, eyes closed—
but at least upright.

"Can ye ride, man?" Ian asked softly, squatting
down by his friend. To his relief, Jamie opened his
eyes at once.

"Oh, aye. Ye're thinkin' we should ride into Saint-
Aubaye, and send someone back to do something
about the coach and Peretz?"

"What else is there to do?"

"Nothing I can think of. I dinna suppose we can
take him with us." Jamie got to his feet, swaying a
little, but without needing to hold on to the tree. "Can
the women ride, d'ye think?"

Marie could, it turned out—at least a little. Rebekah had never been on a horse. After more discussion than Ian would have believed possible on the
subject, he got the late M. Peretz decently laid out on
the coach's seat with a handkerchief over his face
against the flies, and the rest of them finally mounted:
Jamie on his horse with the Torah scroll in its canvas
wrappings bound behind his saddle—between the

profanation of its being touched by a Gentile and the prospect of its being left in the coach for anyone happening by to find, the women had reluctantly allowed the former—the maid on one of the coach horses, with a makeshift pair of saddlebags made from the covers of the coach's seats, these filled with as much of the women's luggage as they could cram into them, and Ian with Rebekah on the saddle before him.

Rebekah looked like a wee dolly, but she was surprisingly solid, as he found when she put her foot in his hands and he tossed her up into the saddle. She didn't manage to swing her leg over, and instead lay across the saddle like a dead deer, waving her arms and legs in agitation. Wrestling her into an upright position, and getting himself set behind her, left him red-faced and sweating far more than dealing with the horses had.

Jamie gave him a raised eyebrow, as much jealousy as amusement in it, and he gave Jamie a squinted eye in return and put his arm round Rebekah's waist to settle her against him, hoping that he didn't stink too badly.

It was dark by the time they made it into Saint-Aubaye and found an inn that could provide them with two rooms. Ian talked to the landlord, and arranged that someone should go in the morning to retrieve M. Peretz's body and bury it; the women weren't happy about the lack of proper preparation of the body, but as they insisted he must be buried before the next sundown, there wasn't much else to be done. Then he inspected the women's room, looked under the beds, rattled the shutters in a confident manner, and bade them good night. They looked that wee bit frazzled.

Going back to the other room, he heard a sweet chiming sound, and found Jamie on his knees, pushing the bundle that contained the Torah scroll under the single bed.

"That'll do," he said, sitting back on his heels with a sigh. He looked nearly as done up as the women, Ian thought, but didn't say so.

"I'll go and have some supper sent up," he said. "I smelled a joint roasting. Some of that, and maybe—"

"Whatever they've got," Jamie said fervently. "Bring it all."

They ate heartily, and separately, in their rooms. Jamie was beginning to feel that the second helping of tarte tatin with clotted cream had been a mistake when Rebekah came into the men's room, followed by her maid carrying a small tray with a jug on it, wisping aromatic steam. Jamie sat up straight, restraining a small cry as pain flashed through his head. Rebekah frowned at him, gull-winged brows lowering in concern.

"Your head hurts very much, Diego?"

"No, it's fine. No but a wee bang on the heid." He was sweating and his wame was wobbly, but he pressed his hands flat on the wee table and was sure he looked steady. She appeared not to think so, and came close, bending down to look searchingly into his eyes.

"I don't think so," she said. "You look . . . clammy."

"Oh. Aye?" he said, rather feebly.

"If she means ye look like a fresh-shucked clam, then aye, ye do," Ian informed him. "Shocked, ken? All pale and wet and—"

"I ken what 'clammy' means, aye?" He glowered at Ian, who gave him half a grin—damn, he must look awful; Ian was actually worried. He swallowed, looking for something witty to say in reassurance, but his gorge rose suddenly and he was obliged to shut both mouth and eyes tightly, concentrating fiercely to make it go back down.

"Tea," Rebekah was saying firmly. She took the jug from her maid and poured a cup, then folded Jamie's hands about it and, holding his hands with her own, guided the cup to his mouth. "Drink. It will help."

He drank, and it did. At least he felt less queasy at once. He recognized the taste of the tea, though he thought this cup had a few other things in it, too.

"Again." Another cup was presented; he managed to drink this one alone and, by the time it was down, felt a good bit better. His head still throbbed with his heartbeat, but the pain seemed be standing a little apart from him, somehow.

"You shouldn't be left alone for a little while," Rebekah informed him, and sat down, sweeping her skirts elegantly around her ankles. He opened his mouth to say that he wasn't alone, Ian was there— but caught Ian's eye in time and stopped.

"The bandits," she was saying to Ian, her pretty brow creased, "who do you think that they were?"

"Ah . . . well, depends. If they kent who ye were, and wanted to abduct ye, that's one thing. But could be they were no but random thieves, and saw the coach and thought they'd chance it for what they might get. Ye didna recognize any of them, did ye?"

Her eyes sprang wide. They weren't quite the color of Annalise's, Jamie thought hazily. A softer brown . . . like the breast feathers on a grouse.

"Know who I was?" she whispered. "Wanted to abduct me?" She swallowed. "You . . . think that's possible?" She gave a little shudder.

"Well, I dinna ken, of course. Here, *a nighean,* ye ought to have a wee nip of that tea, I'm thinkin'." Ian stretched out a long arm for the jug, but she moved it back, shaking her head.

"No, it's medicine—and Diego needs it. Don't you?" she said, leaning a little forward to peer earnestly into Jamie's eyes. She'd taken off the hat, but had her hair tucked up—mostly—in a lacy white cap with pink ribbon. He nodded obediently.

"Marie—bring some brandy, please. The shock . . ." She swallowed again, and wrapped her arms briefly around herself. Jamie noticed the way it pushed her breasts up, so they swelled just a little above her stays. There was a little tea left in his cup; he drank it automatically.

Marie came with the brandy, and poured a glass for Rebekah—then one for Ian, at Rebekah's gesture, and when Jamie made a small polite noise in his throat, half-filled his cup, pouring in more tea on top of it. The taste was peculiar, but he didn't really mind. The pain had gone off to the far side of the room; he could see it sitting over there, a wee glowering sort of purple thing with a bad-tempered expression on its face. He laughed at it, and Ian frowned at him.

"What are ye giggling at?"

Jamie couldn't think how to describe the pain-beastie, so just shook his head, which proved a mistake—the pain looked suddenly gleeful and shot back into his head with a noise like tearing cloth. The room spun and he clutched the table with both hands.

"Diego!" Chairs scraped and there was a good bit of clishmaclaver that he paid no attention to. Next thing he knew, he was lying on the bed looking at the ceiling beams. One of them seemed to be twining slowly, like a vine growing.

". . . and he told the Captain that there was someone among the Jews who kent about . . ." Ian's voice was soothing, earnest and slow so Rebekah would understand him—though Jamie thought she maybe understood more than she said. The twining beam was slowly sprouting small green leaves, and he had the faint thought that this was unusual, but a great sense of tranquility had come over him and he didn't mind it a bit.

Rebekah was saying something now, her voice soft and worried, and with some effort, he turned his head to look. She was leaning over the table toward Ian, and he had both big hands wrapped round hers, reassuring her that he and Jamie would let no harm come to her.

A different face came suddenly into his view; the maid, Marie, frowning down at him. She rudely pulled back his eyelid and peered into his eye, so close he could smell the garlic on her breath. He blinked hard, and she let go with a small "Hmph!" then turned to say something to Rebekah, who re-

plied in quick Ladino. The maid shook her head du-
biously, but left the room.

Her face didn't leave with her, though. He could
still see it, frowning down at him from above. It had
become attached to the leafy beam, and he now realized that there was a snake up there, a serpent
with a woman's head, and an apple in its mouth—
that couldn't be right, surely it should be a pig?—
and it came slithering down the wall and right over
his chest, pressing the apple close to his face. It smelled
wonderful, and he wanted to bite it, but before he
could, he felt the weight of the snake change, going
soft and heavy, and he arched his back a little, feeling the distinct imprint of big round breasts squash-
ing against him. The snake's tail—she was mostly a
woman now, but her backend seemed still to be
snakeish—was delicately stroking the inside of his
thigh.

He made a very high-pitched noise, and Ian came
hurriedly to the bed.

"Are ye all right, man?"

"I—oh. Oh! Oh, Jesus, do that again."

"Do *what*—" Ian was beginning, when Rebekah
appeared, putting a hand on Ian's arm.

"Don't worry," she said, looking intently at Jamie.
"He's all right. The medicine—it gives men strange
dreams."

"He doesna look like he's asleep," Ian said dubi-
ously. In fact, Jamie was squirming—or thought he
was squirming—on the bed, trying to persuade the
lower half of the snake-woman to change, too.
He *was* panting; he could hear himself.

"It's a waking dream," Rebekah said reassuringly. "Come, leave him. He'll fall quite asleep in a bit, you'll see."

Jamie didn't think he'd fallen asleep, but it was evidently some time later that he emerged from a remarkable tryst with the snake-demon—he didn't know how he knew she was a demon, but clearly she was—who had not changed her lower half, but had a very womanly mouth about her—and a number of her friends, these being small female demons who licked his ears—and other things—with great enthusiasm.

He turned his head on the pillow to allow one of these better access and saw, with no sense of surprise, Ian kissing Rebekah. The brandy bottle had fallen over, empty, and he seemed to see the wraith of its perfume rise swirling through the air like smoke, wrapping the two of them in a mist shot with rainbows.

He closed his eyes again, the better to attend to the snake-lady, who now had a number of new and interesting acquaintances. When he opened them sometime later, Ian and Rebekah were gone.

At some point, he heard Ian give a sort of strangled cry and wondered dimly what had happened, but it didn't seem important, and the thought drifted away. He slept.

He woke sometime later, feeling limp as a frostbitten cabbage leaf, but the pain in his head was gone. He just lay there for a bit, enjoying the feeling. It was dark in the room, and it was some time before he realized from the smell of brandy that Ian was lying beside him.

Memory came back to him. It took a little time to disentangle the real memories from the memory of dreams, but he was quite sure he'd seen Ian embracing Rebekah—and her, him. What the devil had happened *then*?

Ian wasn't asleep; he could tell. His friend lay rigid as one of the tomb-figures in the crypt at St. Denis, and his breathing was rapid and shaky, as though he'd just run a mile uphill. Jamie cleared his throat, and Ian jerked as though stabbed with a brooch-pin.

"Aye, so?" he whispered, and Ian's breathing stopped abruptly. He swallowed, audibly.

"If ye breathe a word of this to your sister," he said in an impassioned whisper, "I'll stab ye in your sleep, cut off your heid, and kick it to Arles and back."

Jamie didn't want to think about his sister, and he did want to hear about Rebekah, so he merely said, "Aye. So?"

Ian made a small grunting noise, indicative of thinking how best to begin, and turned over in his plaid, facing Jamie.

"Aye, well. Ye raved a bit about the naked she-devils ye were havin' it away with, and I didna think the lass should have to be hearing that manner o' thing, so I said we should go into the other room, and—"

"Was this before or after ye started kissing her?" Jamie asked. Ian inhaled strongly through his nose.

"After," he said tersely. "And she was kissin' me back, aye?"

"Aye, I noticed that. So then . . . ?" He could feel Ian squirming slowly, like a worm on a hook, but waited. It often took Ian a moment to find words, but it was usually worth waiting for. Certainly in this instance.

He was a little shocked—and frankly envious— and he did wonder what might happen when the lass's affianced discovered she wasn't a virgin, but he supposed the man might not find out; she seemed a clever lass. It might be wise to leave D'Eglise's troop, though, and head south, just in case. . . .

"D'ye think it hurts a lot to be circumcised?" Ian asked suddenly.

"I do. How could it not?" His hand sought out his own member, protectively rubbing a thumb over the bit in question. True, it wasn't a very big bit, but . . .

"Well, they do it to wee bairns," Ian pointed out. "Canna be that bad, can it?"

"Mmphm," Jamie said, unconvinced, though fairness made him add, "Aye, well, and they did it to Christ, too."

"Aye?" Ian sounded startled. "Aye, I suppose so—I hadna thought o' that."

"Well, ye dinna think of Him bein' a Jew, do ye? But He was, to start."

There was a momentary, meditative silence before Ian spoke again.

"D'ye think Jesus ever did it? Wi' a lass, I mean, before he went to preachin'?"

"I think Père Renault's goin' to have ye for blasphemy, next thing."

Ian twitched, as though worried that the priest might be lurking in the shadows.

"Père Renault's nowhere near here, thank God."

"Aye, but ye'll need to confess yourself to him, won't ye?"

Ian shot upright, clutching his plaid around him.

"What?"

"Ye'll go to hell, else, if ye get killed," Jamie pointed out, feeling rather smug. There was moonlight through the window and he could see Ian's face, drawn in anxious thought, his deep-set eyes darting right and left from Scylla to Charybdis. Suddenly Ian turned his head toward Jamie, having spotted the possibility of an open channel between the threats of hell and Père Renault.

"I'd only go to hell if it was a mortal sin," he said. "If it's no but venial, I'd only have to spend a thousand years or so in Purgatory. That wouldna be so bad."

"Of course it's a mortal sin," Jamie said, cross. "Anybody kens fornication's a mortal sin, ye numpty."

"Aye, but . . ." Ian made a "wait a bit" gesture with one hand, deep in thought. "To be a *mortal* sin, though, ye've got the three things. Requirements, like." He put up an index finger. "It's got to be seriously wrong." Middle finger. "Ye've got to *know* it's seriously wrong." Ring finger. "And ye've got to give full consent to it. That's the way of it, aye?" He put his hand down and looked at Jamie, brows raised.

"Aye, and which part of that did ye not do? The full consent? Did she rape ye?" He was chaffing, but Ian turned his face away in a manner that gave him a sudden doubt. "Ian?"

"Noo . . ." his friend said, but it sounded doubtful, too. "It wasna like that—exactly. I meant more the seriously wrong part. I dinna think it was . . ." his voice trailed off.

Jamie flung himself over, raised on one elbow.

"Ian," he said, steel in his voice. "What did ye *do* to the lass? If ye took her maidenheid, it's seriously wrong. Especially with her betrothed. Oh—" a thought occurred to him, and he leaned a little closer, lowering his voice. "Was she no a virgin? Maybe that's different." If the lass was an out-and-out wanton, perhaps . . . She probably *did* write poetry, come to think . . .

Ian had now folded his arms on his knees and was resting his forehead on them, his voice muffled in the folds of his plaid. ". . . dinna ken . . ." emerged in a strangled croak.

Jamie reached out and dug his fingers hard into Ian's calf, making his friend unfold with a startled cry that made someone in a distant chamber shift and grunt in their sleep.

"What d'ye mean ye dinna ken? How could ye not notice?" he hissed.

"Ah . . . well . . . she . . . erm . . . she did me wi' her hand," Ian blurted. "Before I could . . . well."

"Oh." Jamie rolled onto his back, somewhat deflated in spirit, if not in flesh. His cock seemed still to want to hear the details.

"Is that seriously wrong?" Ian asked, turning his face toward Jamie again. "Or—well, I canna say I really gave full *consent* to it, because that wasna what I had in mind doing at all, but . . ."

"I think ye're headed for the Bad Place," Jamie assured him. "Ye meant to do it, whether ye managed or not. And how did it happen, come to that? Did she just . . . take hold?"

Ian let out a long, long sigh, and sank his head in his hands. He looked as though it hurt.

"Well, we kissed for a bit, and there was more brandy—lots more. She . . . er . . . she'd take a mouthful and kiss me and, er . . . put it into my mouth, and . . ."

"*Ifrinn!*"

"Will ye not say 'Hell!' like that, please? I dinna want to think about it."

"Sorry. Go on. Did she let ye feel her breasts?"

"Just a bit. She wouldna take her stays off, but I could feel her nipples through her shift—did ye say something?"

"No," Jamie said with an effort. "What then?"

"Well, she put her hand under my kilt and then pulled it out again like she'd touched a snake."

"And had she?"

"She had, aye. She was shocked. Will ye no snort like that?" he said, annoyed. "Ye'll wake the whole house. It was because it wasna circumcised."

"Oh. Is that why she wouldna . . . er . . . the regular way?"

"She didna say so, but maybe. After a bit, though, she wanted to look at it, and that's when . . . well."

"Mmphm." Naked demons versus the chance of damnation or not, Jamie thought Ian had had well the best of it this evening. A thought occurred to him. "Why did ye ask if being circumcised hurts? Ye werena thinking of doing it, were ye? For her, I mean?"

"I wouldna say the thought hadna occurred to me,"

Ian admitted. "I mean . . . I thought I should maybe marry her, under the circumstances. But I suppose I couldna become a Jew, even if I got up the nerve to be circumcised—my mam would tear my heid off if I did."

"No, ye're right," Jamie agreed. "She would. *And* ye'd go to Hell." The thought of the rare and delicate Rebekah churning butter in the yard of a Highland croft or waulking urine-soaked wool with her bare feet was slightly more ludicrous than the vision of Ian in a skullcap and whiskers—but not by much. "Besides, ye havena got any money, have ye?"

"A bit," Ian said thoughtfully. "Not enough to go and live in Timbuktoo, though, and I'd have to go at least that far."

Jamie sighed and stretched, easing himself. A meditative silence fell, Ian no doubt contemplating perdition, Jamie reliving the better bits of his opium dreams, but with Rebekah's face on the snake-lady. Finally he broke the silence, turning to his friend.

"So . . . was it worth the chance of goin' to Hell?"

Ian sighed long and deep once more, but it was the sigh of a man at peace with himself.

"Oh, aye."

Jamie woke at dawn, feeling altogether well, and in a much better frame of mind. Some kindly soul had brought a jug of sour ale and some bread and cheese. He refreshed himself with these as he dressed, pondering the day's work.

He'd have to collect a few men to go back and deal with the coach. He supposed the best thing to do with M. Peretz was to fetch him here *in* the coach, and then see if there were any Jews in the vicinity who might be prevailed upon to bury him— the women insisted that he ought to be buried before sundown. If not . . . well, he'd cross that road when he came to it.

He thought the coach wasn't badly damaged; they might get it back upon the road again by noon. . . . How far might it be to Bonnes? That was the next town with an inn. If it was too far, or the coach too badly hurt, or he couldn't dispose decently of M. Peretz, they'd need to stay the night here again. He fingered his purse, but thought he had enough for another night and the hire of men; the Doctor had been generous.

He was beginning to wonder what was keeping Ian and the women. Though he kent women took more time to do anything than a man would, let alone getting dressed—well, they had stays and the like to fret with, after all. . . . He sipped ale, contemplating a vision of Rebekah's stays, and the very vivid images his mind had been conjuring ever since Ian's description of his encounter with the lass. He could all but see her nipples through the thin fabric of her shift, smooth and round as pebbles. . . .

Ian burst through the door, wild-eyed, his hair standing on end.

"They're gone!"

Jamie choked on his ale.

"What? How?"

Ian understood what he meant, and was already heading for the bed.

"No one took them. There's nay sign of a struggle,

and their things are gone. The window's open, and the shutters aren't broken."

Jamie was on his knees alongside Ian, thrusting first his hands and then his head and shoulders under the bed. There was a canvas-wrapped bundle there, and he was flooded with a momentary relief— which disappeared the instant Ian dragged it into the light. It made a noise, but not the gentle chime of golden bells. It rattled, and when Jamie seized the corner of the canvas and unrolled it, the contents were shown to be nought but sticks and stones, these hastily wrapped in a woman's petticoat to give the bundle the appropriate bulk.

"Cramouille!" he said, this being the worst word he could think of on short notice. And very appropriate, too, if what he thought had happened really had. He turned on Ian.

"She drugged me and seduced you, and her bloody maid stole in here and took the thing whilst ye had your fat heid buried in her . . . er . . ."

"Charms," Ian said succinctly, and flashed him a brief, evil grin. "Ye're only jealous. Where d'ye think they've gone?"

It was the truth, and Jamie abandoned any further recriminations, rising and strapping on his belt, hastily arranging dirk, sword, and ax in the process.

"Not to Paris, would be my guess. Come on, we'll ask the ostler."

The ostler confessed himself at a loss; he'd been the worse for drink in the hay shed, he said, and if someone had taken two horses from the shelter, he hadn't waked to see it.

"Aye, right," said Jamie, impatient, and, grabbing

the man's shirtfront, lifted him off his feet and slammed him into the inn's stone wall. The man's head bounced once off the stones and he sagged in Jamie's grip, still conscious but dazed. Jamie drew his dirk left-handed and pressed the edge of it against the man's weathered throat.

"Try again," he suggested pleasantly. "I dinna care about the money they gave ye—keep it. I want to know which way they went, and when they left."

The man tried to swallow, and abandoned the attempt when his Adam's apple hit the edge of the dirk.

"About three hours past moonrise," he croaked. "They went toward Bonnes. There's a crossroads no more than three miles from here," he added, now trying urgently to be helpful.

Jamie dropped him with a grunt.

"Aye, fine," he said in disgust. "Ian—oh, ye've got them." For Ian had gone straight for their own horses while he dealt with the ostler, and was already leading one out, bridled, the saddle over his arm. "I'll settle the bill, then."

The women hadn't made off with his purse, that was something. Either Rebekah bat-Leah Hauberger had some vestige of conscience—which he doubted very much—or she just hadn't thought of it.

It was just past dawn; the women had perhaps six hours' lead.

"Do we believe the ostler?" Ian asked, settling himself in the saddle.

Jamie dug in his purse, pulled out a copper penny and flipped it, catching it on the back of his hand.

"Tails we do, heads we don't?" He took his hand away and peered at the coin. "Heads."

"Aye, but the road back is straight all the way through Yvrac," Ian pointed out. "And it's nay more than three miles to the crossroads, he said. Whatever ye want to say about the lass, she's no a fool."

Jamie considered that one for a moment, then nodded. Rebekah couldn't have been sure how much lead she'd have—and unless she'd been lying about her ability to ride (which he wouldn't put past her, but such things weren't easy to fake and she was gey clumsy in the saddle), she'd want to reach a place where the trail could be lost before her pursuers could catch up with her. Besides, the ground was still damp with dew; there might be a chance. . . .

"Aye, come on, then."

Luck was with them. No one had passed the inn during the late night watches, and while the road-bed was trampled with hoof marks, the recent prints of the women's horses showed clear, edges still crumbling in the damp earth. Once sure they'd got upon the track, the men galloped for the crossroads, hoping to reach it before other travelers obscured the marks.

No such luck. Farm wagons were already on the move, loaded with produce headed for Parcoul or La Roche-Chalais, and the crossroads was a maze of ruts and hoofprints. But Jamie had the bright thought of sending Ian down the road that lay toward Parcoul, while he took the one toward La Roche-Chalais, catching up the incoming wagons and questioning the drivers. Within an hour, Ian came pelting back with the news that the women had been seen, riding slowly and cursing volubly at each other, toward Parcoul.

"And *that*," he said, panting for breath, "is not all."

"Aye? Well, tell me while we ride."

Ian did. He'd been hurrying back to find Jamie, when he'd met Josef-from-Alsace just short of the crossroads, come in search of them.

"D'Eglise was held up near Poitiers," Ian reported in a shout. "The same band of men that attacked us at Marmande—Alexandre and Raoul both recognized some of them. Jewish bandits."

Jamie was shocked, and slowed for a moment to let Ian catch him up.

"Did they get the dowry money?"

"No, but they had a hard fight. Three men wounded badly enough to need a surgeon, and Paul Martan lost two fingers of his left hand. D'Eglise pulled them into Poitiers, and sent Josef to see if all was well wi' us."

Jamie's heart bounced into his throat. "Jesus. Did ye tell him what happened?"

"I did not," Ian said tersely. "I told him we'd had an accident wi' the coach, and ye'd gone ahead with the women; I was comin' back to fetch something left behind."

"Aye, good." Jamie's heart dropped back into his chest. The last thing he wanted was to have to tell the Captain that they'd lost the girl and the Torah scroll. And he'd be damned if he would.

They traveled fast, stopping only to ask questions now and then, and by the time they pounded into the village of Aubeterre-sur-Dronne, were sure that their quarry lay no more than an hour ahead of them—if the women had passed on through the village.

"Oh, those two?" said a woman, pausing in the act of scrubbing her steps. She stood up slowly, stretching her back. "I saw them, yes. They rode right by me, and went down the lane there." She pointed.

"I thank you, madame," Jamie said, in his best Parisian French. "What lies down that lane, please?"

She looked surprised that they didn't know, and frowned a little at such ignorance.

"Why, the chateau of the Vicomte Beaumont, to be sure!"

"To be sure," Jamie repeated, smiling at her, and Ian saw a dimple appear in her cheek in reply. *"Merci beaucoup, madame!"*

"What the devil . . . ?" Ian murmured. Jamie reined up beside him, pausing to look at the place. It was a small manor house, somewhat run-down, but pretty in its bones. And the last place anyone would think to look for a runaway Jewess, he'd say that for it.

"What shall we do now, d'ye think?" he asked, and Jamie shrugged and kicked his horse.

"Go knock on the door and ask, I suppose."

Ian followed his friend up to the door, feeling intensely conscious of his grubby clothes, sprouting beard, and general state of uncouthness. Such con-

cerns vanished, though, when Jamie's forceful knock
was answered.

"Good day, gentlemen!" said the yellow-haired
bugger he'd last seen locked in combat in the roadbed
with Jamie the day before. The man smiled broadly
at them, cheerful despite an obvious black eye and a
freshly split lip. He was dressed in the height of fash-
ion, in a plum velvet suit, his hair was curled and
powdered, and his yellow beard was neatly trimmed.
"I hoped we would see you again. Welcome to my
home!" he said, stepping back and raising his hand
in a gesture of invitation.

"I thank you, Monsieur . . . ?" Jamie said slowly,
giving Ian a sidelong glance. Ian lifted one shoulder
in the ghost of a shrug. Did they have a choice?

The yellow-haired bugger bowed. "Pierre Robert
Heriveaux d'Anton, Vicomte Beaumont, by the
grace of the Almighty, for one more day. And you,
gentlemen?"

"James Alexander Malcolm MacKenzie Fraser,"
Jamie said, with a good attempt at matching the
other's grand manner. Only Ian would have noticed
the faint hesitation, or the slight tremor in his voice
when he added, "Laird of Broch Tuarach."

"Ian Alastair Robert MacLeod Murray," Ian said,
with a curt nod, and straightened his shoulders.
"His . . . er . . . the laird's . . . tacksman."

"Come in, please, gentlemen." The yellow-haired
bugger's eyes shifted just a little, and Ian heard the
crunch of gravel behind them, an instant before he
felt the prick of a dagger in the small of his back.
No, they didn't have a choice.

Inside, they were relieved of their weapons, then

escorted down a wide hallway and into a commodious parlor. The wallpaper was faded, and the furniture was good but shabby. By contrast, the big Turkey carpet on the floor glowed like it was woven from jewels. A big roundish thing in the middle was green and gold and red, and concentric circles with wiggly edges surrounded it in waves of blue and red and cream, bordered in a soft, deep red, and the whole of it so ornamented with unusual shapes it would take you a day to look at them all. He'd been so taken with it the first time he saw it he'd spent a quarter of an hour looking at the shapes before Big Georges caught him at it and shouted at him to roll the thing up, they hadn't all day.

"Where did ye get this?" Ian asked abruptly, interrupting something the Vicomte was saying to the two rough-clad men who'd taken their weapons.

"What? Oh, the carpet! Yes, isn't it wonderful?" The Vicomte beamed at him, quite unself-conscious, and gestured the two roughs away toward the wall. "It's part of my wife's dowry."

"Your wife," Jamie repeated carefully. He darted a sideways glance at Ian, who took the cue.

"That would be Mademoiselle Hauberger, would it?" he asked. The Vicomte blushed—actually blushed—and Ian realized that the man was no older than he and Jamie were.

"Well. It—we—we have been betrothed for some time, and in Jewish custom, that is almost like being married."

"Betrothed," Jamie echoed again. "Since . . . when, exactly?"

The Vicomte sucked in his lower lip, contemplating them. But whatever caution he might have had was overwhelmed in what were plainly very high spirits.

"Four years," he said. And unable to contain himself, he beckoned them to a table near the window, and proudly showed them a fancy document, covered with colored scrolly sorts of things and written in some very odd language that was all slashes and tilted lines.

"This is our ketubah," he said, pronouncing the word very carefully. "Our marriage contract."

Jamie bent over to peer closely at it.

"Aye, verra nice," he said politely. "I see it's no been signed yet. The marriage hasna taken place, then?" Ian saw Jamie's eyes flick over the desk, and could see him passing the possibilities through his mind: Grab the letter opener off the desk and take the Vicomte hostage? Then find the sly wee bitch, roll her up in one of the smaller rugs, and carry her to Paris? That would doubtless be Ian's job, he thought.

A slight movement as one of the roughs shifted his weight caught Ian's eye and he thought, *Don't do it, eejit!* at Jamie, as hard as he could. For once, the message seemed to get through; Jamie's shoulders relaxed a little and he straightened up.

"Ye do ken the lass is meant to be marrying someone else?" he asked baldly. "I wouldna put it past her not to tell ye."

The Vicomte's color became higher.

"Certainly I know!" he snapped. "She was promised to me first, by her father!"

"How long have ye been a Jew?" Jamie asked carefully, edging round the table. "I dinna think ye were born to it. I mean—ye *are* a Jew, now, aye? For I kent one or two, in Paris, and it's my understanding that they dinna marry people who aren't Jewish." His eyes flicked round the solid, handsome room. "It's my understanding that they mostly aren't aristocrats, either."

The Vicomte was quite red in the face by now. With a sharp word, he sent the roughs out—though they were disposed to argue. While the brief discussion was going on, Ian edged closer to Jamie and whispered rapidly to him about the rug in *Gàidhlig*.

"Holy God," Jamie muttered in the same language. "I didna see him or either of those two at Marmande, did you?"

Ian had no time to reply and merely shook his head, as the roughs reluctantly acquiesced to Vicomte Pierre's imperious orders and shuffled out with narrowed eyes aimed at Ian and Jamie. One of them had Jamie's dirk in his hand, and drew this slowly across his neck in a meaningful gesture as he left.

Aye, they might manage in a fight, he thought, returning the slit-eyed glare, *but not that wee velvet gomerel.* Captain D'Eglise wouldn't have taken on the Vicomte, and neither would a band of professional highwaymen, Jewish or not.

"All right," the Vicomte said abruptly, leaning his fists on the desk. "I'll tell you."

And he did. Rebekah's mother, the daughter of Dr. Hasdi, had fallen in love with a Christian man, and run away with him. The Doctor had declared his daughter dead, as was the usual way in such a situation, and done formal mourning for her. But she was his only child, and he had not been able to forget her. He had arranged to have information brought to him, and knew about Rebekah's birth.

"Then her mother died. That's when I met her—about that time, I mean. Her father was a judge, and my father knew him. She was fourteen and I sixteen; I fell in love with her. And she with me," he added, giving the Scots a hard eye, as though daring them to disbelieve it. "We were betrothed, with her father's blessing. But then her father caught a flux and died in two days. And—"

"And her grandfather took her back," Jamie finished. "And she became a Jew?"

"By Jewish belief, she was born Jewish; it descends through the mother's line. And . . . her mother had told her, privately, about her lost heritage. She embraced it, once she went to live with her grandfather."

Ian stirred, and cocked a cynical eyebrow. "Aye? Why did ye not convert then, if ye're willing to do it now?"

"I said I would!" The Vicomte had one fist curled round his letter opener as though he would strangle it. "The miserable old wretch said he did not believe me. He thought I would not give up my—my—this life." He waved a hand dismissively around the room, encompassing, presumably, his title and property, both of which would be confiscated by the government the moment his conversion became known.

"He said it would be a sham conversion and the moment I had her, I would become a Christian again, and force Rebekah to be Christian, too. Like her father," he added darkly.

Despite the situation, Ian was beginning to have

some sympathy for the wee popinjay. It was a very romantic tale, and he was partial to those. Jamie, however, was still reserving judgment. He gestured at the rug beneath their feet.

"Her dowry, ye said?"

"Yes," said the Vicomte, but sounded much less certain. "She says it belonged to her mother. She had some men bring it here last week, along with a chest and a few other things. Anyway," he said, resuming his self-confidence and glowering at them, "when the old beast arranged her marriage to that fellow in Paris, I made up my mind to—to—"

"To abduct her. By arrangement, aye? Mmphm," Jamie said, making a noise indicating his opinion of the Vicomte's skills as a highwayman. He raised one red brow at Pierre's black eye, but forbore to make any more remarks, thank God. It hadn't escaped Ian that they were prisoners, though it maybe had Jamie.

"May we speak with Mademoiselle Hauberger?" Ian asked politely. "Just to make sure she's come of her own free will, aye?"

"Rather plainly, she did, since you followed her here." The Vicomte hadn't liked Jamie's noise. "No, you may not. She's busy." He raised his hands and clapped them sharply, and the rough fellows came back in, along with a half dozen or so male servants as reinforcement, led by a tall, severe-looking butler, armed with a stout walking-stick.

"Go with Ecrivisse, gentlemen. He'll see to your comfort."

"Comfort" proved to be the chateau's wine cellar, which was fragrant, but cold. Also dark. The Vicomte's hospitality did not extend so far as a candle.

"If he meant to kill us, he'd have done it already," Ian reasoned.

"Mmphm." Jamie sat on the stairs, the fold of his plaid pulled up around his shoulders against the chill. There was music coming from somewhere outside: the faint sound of a fiddle and the tap of a little hand drum. It started, then stopped, then started again.

Ian wandered restlessly to and fro; it wasn't a very large cellar. If he didn't mean to kill them, what did the Vicomte mean to do with them?

"He's waiting for something to happen," Jamie said suddenly, answering the thought. "Something to do wi' the lass, I expect."

"Aye, reckon." Ian sat down on the stairs, nudging Jamie over. "*A Dhia*, that's cold!"

"Mm," said Jamie absently. "Maybe they mean to run. If so, I hope he leaves someone behind to let us out, and doesna mean to leave us here to starve."

"We wouldna starve," Ian pointed out logically. "We could live on wine for a good long time. Someone would come, before it ran out." He paused a moment, trying to imagine what it would be like to stay drunk for several weeks.

"That's a thought." Jamie got up, a little stiff from the cold, and went off to rummage the racks. There was no light to speak of, save what seeped through the crack at the bottom of the door to the cellar, but Ian could hear Jamie pulling out bottles and sniffing the corks.

He came back in a bit with a bottle and, sitting down again, drew the cork with his teeth and spat it to one side. He took a sip, then another, then tilted back the bottle for a generous swig, and handed it to Ian.

"No bad," he said.

It wasn't, and there wasn't much conversation for the next little while. Eventually, though, Jamie set the empty bottle down, belched gently, and said, "It's her."

"What's her? Rebekah, ye mean. I daresay." Then after a moment, "What's her?"

"It's her," Jamie repeated. "Ken what the Jew said—Ephraim bar-Sefer? About how his gang knew where to strike, because they got information from some outside source? It's her. She told them."

Jamie spoke with such certainty that Ian was staggered for a moment, but then marshaled his wits.

"That wee lass? Granted, she put one over on us—and I suppose she at least kent about Pierre's abduction, but . . ."

Jamie snorted.

"Aye, Pierre. Does the mannie strike ye either as a criminal or a great schemer?"

"No, but—"

"Does she?"

"Well . . ."

"Exactly."

Jamie got up and wandered off into the racks again, this time returning with what smelled to Ian like one of the very good local red wines. It was like drinking his mam's strawberry preserves on toast with a cup of strong tea, he thought approvingly.

"Besides," Jamie went on, as though there'd been

no interruption in his train of thought, "d'ye recall what the maid said to her? When I got my heid half-stove in? 'Perhaps he's been killed. How would you feel then?' Nay, she'd planned the whole thing—to have Pierre and his lads stop the coach and make away with the women and the scroll, and doubtless Monsieur Pickle, too. *But*—" he added, sticking up a finger in front of Ian's face to stop him interrupting, "then Josef-from-Alsace tells ye that thieves—and the *same* thieves as before, or some of them—attacked the band wi' the dowry money. Ye ken well, that canna have been Pierre. It had to be her who told them."

Ian was forced to admit the logic of this. Pierre had enthusiasm, but couldn't possibly be considered a professional highwayman.

"But a lass . . ." he said, helplessly. "How could she—"

Jamie grunted.

"D'Eglise said Doctor Hasdi's a man much respected among the Jews of Bordeaux. And plainly he's kent as far as Paris, or how else did he make the match for his granddaughter? But he doesna speak French. Want to bet me that she didna manage his correspondence?"

"No," Ian said, and took another swallow. "Mmphm."

Some minutes later, he said, "That rug. And the other things Monsieur le Vicomte mentioned—her *dowry*."

Jamie made an approving noise.

"Aye. Her percentage of the take, more like. Ye can see our lad Pierre hasna got much money, and he'd lose all his property when he converted. She was feathering their nest, like—makin' sure they'd have enough to live on. Enough to live *well* on."

"Well, then," Ian said, after a moment's silence. "There ye are."

The afternoon dragged on. After the second bottle, they agreed to drink no more for the time being, in case a clear head should be necessary if or when the door at last opened, and aside from going off now and then to have a pee behind the farthest wine racks, they stayed huddled on the stairs.

Jamie was singing softly along to the fiddle's distant tune when the door finally *did* open. He stopped abruptly, and lunged awkwardly to his feet, nearly falling, his knees stiff with cold.

"Monsieurs?" said the butler, peering down at them. "If you will be so kind as to follow me, please?"

To their surprise, the butler led them straight out of the house, and down a small path, in the direction of the distant music. The air outside was fresh and wonderful after the must of the cellar, and Jamie filled his lungs with it, wondering what the devil . . . ?

Then they rounded a bend in the path and saw a garden court before them, lit by torches driven into the ground. Somewhat overgrown, but with a fountain tinkling away in the center—and just by the fountain, a sort of canopy, its cloth glimmering pale in the dusk. There was a little knot of people standing near it, talking, and as the butler paused, holding them back with one hand, Vicomte Pierre broke away from the group and came toward them, smiling.

"My apologies for the inconvenience, gentlemen," he said, a huge smile splitting his face. He looked drunk, but Jamie thought he wasn't—no smell of spirits. "Rebekah had to prepare herself. And we wanted to wait for nightfall."

"To do what?" Ian asked suspiciously, and the Vicomte giggled. Jamie didn't mean to wrong the man, but it was a giggle. He gave Ian an eye and Ian gave it back. Aye, it was a giggle.

"To be married," Pierre said, and while his voice was still full of joie de vivre, he said the words with a sense of deep reverence that struck Jamie somewhere in the chest. Pierre turned and waved a hand toward the darkening sky, where the stars were beginning to prick and sparkle. "For luck, you know—that our descendants may be as numerous as the stars."

"Mmphm," Jamie said politely.

"But come with me, if you will." Pierre was already striding back to the knot of . . . well, Jamie supposed they must be wedding guests . . . beckoning to the Scots to follow.

Marie the maid was there, along with a few other women; she gave Jamie and Ian a wary look. But it was the men with whom the Vicomte was concerned. He spoke a few words to his guests, and three men came back with him, all dressed formally, if somewhat oddly, with little velvet skullcaps decorated with beads, and enormous beards.

"May I present Monsieur Gershom Ackerman,

and Monsieur Levi Champfleur. Our witnesses. And Reb Cohen, who will officiate."

The men shook hands, murmuring politeness. Jamie and Ian exchanged looks. Why were *they* here?

The Vicomte caught the look and interpreted it correctly.

"I wish you to return to Doctor Hasdi," he said, the effervescence in his voice momentarily supplanted by a note of steel. "And tell him that everything— everything!—was done in accordance with proper custom and according to the Law. This marriage will not be undone. By anyone."

"Mmphm," said Ian, less politely.

And so it was that a few minutes later they found themselves standing among the male wedding guests—the women stood on the other side of the canopy—watching as Rebekah came down the path, jingling faintly. She wore a dress of deep red silk; Jamie could see the torchlight shift and shimmer through its folds as she moved. There were gold bracelets on both wrists, and she had a veil over her head and face, with a little headdress sort of thing made of gold chains that dipped across her forehead, strung with little medallions and bells—it was this that made the jingling sound. It reminded him of the Torah scroll, and he stiffened a little at the thought.

Pierre stood with the rabbi under the canopy; as she approached, he stepped apart, and she came to him. She didn't touch him, though, but proceeded to walk round him. And round him, and round him. Seven times she circled him, and the hairs rose a little on the back of Jamie's neck; it had the faint sense of magic about it—or witchcraft. Something she did, binding the man.

She came face-to-face with Jamie as she made each turn and plainly could see him in the light of the torches, but her eyes were fixed straight ahead; she made no acknowledgment of anyone—not even Pierre.

But then the circling was done and she came to stand by his side. The rabbi said a few words of welcome to the guests, and then, turning to the bride and groom, poured out a cup of wine and said what appeared to be a Hebrew blessing over it. Jamie made out the beginning, "Blessed are you, Adonai our God . . ." but then lost the thread.

Pierre reached into his pocket when Reb Cohen stopped speaking, took out a small object—clearly a ring—and, taking Rebekah's hand in his, put it on the forefinger of her right hand, smiling down into her face with a tenderness that, despite everything, rather caught at Jamie's heart. Then Pierre lifted her veil, and he caught a glimpse of the answering tenderness on Rebekah's face in the instant before her husband kissed her.

The congregation sighed as one.

The rabbi picked up a sheet of parchment from a little table nearby. The thing Pierre had called a ketubah, Jamie saw—the wedding contract.

The rabbi read the thing out, first in a language Jamie didn't recognize, and then again in French. It wasn't so different from the few marriage contracts he'd seen, laying out the disposition of property and what was due to the bride and all . . . though he noted with disapproval that it provided for the possibility of divorce. His attention wandered a bit then; Rebekah's face glowed in the torchlight like pearl and ivory, and the roundness of her bosom showed clearly as she breathed. In spite of everything he thought he now knew about her, he experienced a brief wave of envy toward Pierre.

The contract read and carefully laid aside, the rabbi recited a string of blessings; he kent it was blessings because he caught the words "Blessed are you, Adonai . . ." over and over, though the subject of the blessings seemed to be everything from the congregation to Jerusalem, so far as he could tell. The bride and groom had another sip of wine.

A pause then, and Jamie expected some official word from the rabbi, uniting husband and wife, but it didn't come. Instead, one of the witnesses took the wineglass, wrapped it in a linen napkin, and placed it on the ground in front of Pierre. To the Scots' astonishment, he promptly stamped on the thing—and the crowd burst into applause.

For a few moments, everything seemed quite like a country wedding, with everyone crowding round, wanting to congratulate the happy couple. But within moments, the happy couple was moving off toward the house, while the guests all streamed toward tables that had been set up at the far side of the garden, laden with food and drink.

"Come on," Jamie muttered, and caught Ian by the arm. They hastened after the newly wedded pair, Ian demanding to know what the devil Jamie thought he was doing.

"I want to talk to her—alone. You stop him, keep him talking for as long as ye can."

"I—how?"

"How would I know? Ye'll think of something." They had reached the house and, ducking in close upon Pierre's heels, Jamie saw that, by good luck, the man had stopped to say something to a servant. Rebekah was just vanishing down a long hallway; he saw her put her hand to a door.

"The best of luck to ye, man!" he said, clapping Pierre so heartily on the shoulder that the groom staggered. Before he could recover, Ian, very obviously commending his soul to God, stepped up and seized him by the hand, which he wrang vigorously, meanwhile giving Jamie a private *Hurry the bloody hell* up! sort of look.

Grinning, Jamie ran down the short hallway to the door where he'd seen Rebekah disappear. The grin disappeared as his hand touched the doorknob, though, and the face he presented to her as he entered was as grim as he could make it.

Her eyes widened in shock and indignation at sight of him.

"What are you doing here? No one is supposed to come in here but me and my husband!"

"He's on his way," Jamie assured her. "The question is—will he get here?"

Her little fist curled up in a way that would have been comical, if he didn't know as much about her as he did.

"Is that a threat?" she said, in a tone as incredulous as it was menacing. "Here? You dare threaten me *here*?"

"Aye, I do. I want that scroll."

"Well, you're not getting it," she snapped. He saw her glance flicker over the table, probably in search either of a bell to summon help, or something to bash him on the head with, but the table held nothing but a platter of stuffed rolls and exotic sweeties. There *was* a bottle of wine, and he saw her eyes light on that with calculation, but he stretched out a long arm and got hold of it before she could.

"I dinna want it for myself," he said. "I mean to take it back to your grandfather."

"Him?" Her face hardened. "No. It's worth more to him than *I* am," she added bitterly, "but at least that means I can use it for protection. As long as I have it, he won't try to hurt Pierre or drag me back, for fear I might damage it. I'm keeping it."

"I think he'd be a great deal better off without ye, and doubtless he kens that fine," Jamie informed her, and had to harden himself against the sudden look of hurt in her eyes. He supposed even spiders might have feelings, but that was neither here nor there.

"Where's Pierre?" she demanded, rising to her feet. "If you've harmed a hair on his head, I'll—"

"I wouldna touch the poor gomerel and neither would Ian—Juan, I mean. When I said the question was whether he got to ye or not, I meant whether he thinks better of his bargain."

"What?" He thought she paled a little, but it was hard to tell.

"You give me the scroll to take back to your grandfather—a wee letter of apology to go with it wouldna come amiss, but I willna insist on that—or Ian and I take Pierre out back and have a frank word regarding his new wife."

"Tell him what you like!" she snapped. "He wouldn't believe any of your made-up tales!"

"Oh, aye? And if I tell him exactly what happened to Ephraim bar-Sefer? And why?"

"Who?" she said, but now she really had gone pale to the lips, and put out a hand to the table to steady herself.

"Do ye ken yourself what happened to him? No? Well, I'll tell ye, lass." And he did so, with a terse brutality that made her sit down suddenly, tiny pearls of sweat appearing round the gold medallions that hung across her forehead.

"Pierre already kens at least a bit about your wee gang, I think—but maybe not what a ruthless, grasping wee besom ye really are."

"It wasn't me! I didn't kill him!"

"If not for you, he'd no be dead, and I reckon Pierre would see that. I can tell him where the body is," he added, more delicately. "I buried the man myself."

Her lips were pressed so hard together that nothing showed but a straight white line.

"Ye havena got long," he said, quietly now, but keeping his eyes on hers. "Ian canna hold him off much longer, and if he comes in—then I tell him everything, in front of you, and ye do what ye can then to persuade him I'm a liar."

She stood up abruptly, her chains and bracelets all a-jangle, and stamped to the door of the inner room. She flung it open, and Marie jerked back, shocked.

Rebekah said something to her in Ladino, sharp, and with a small gasp, the maid scurried off.

"All *right*," Rebekah said through gritted teeth, turning back to him. "Take it and be damned, you *dog*."

"Indeed I will, ye bloody wee bitch," he replied with great politeness. Her hand closed round a stuffed roll, but instead of throwing it at him, she merely squeezed it into paste and crumbs, slapping the remains back on the tray with a small exclamation of fury.

The sweet chiming of the Torah scroll presaged Marie's hasty arrival, the precious thing clasped in her arms. She glanced at her mistress and, at Rebekah's curt nod, delivered it with great reluctance into the arms of the Christian dog.

Jamie bowed, first to maid and then mistress, and backed toward the door.

"Shalom," he said, and closed the door an instant before the silver platter hit it with a ringing thud.

"Did it hurt a lot?" Ian was asking Pierre with interest when Jamie came up to them.

"My God, you have no idea," Pierre replied fervently. "But it was worth it." He divided a beaming smile between Ian and Jamie and bowed to them, not even noticing the canvas-wrapped bundle in Jamie's arms. "You must excuse me, gentlemen; my bride awaits me!"

"Did what hurt a lot?" Jamie inquired, leading the way hastily out through a side door. No point in attracting attention, after all.

"Ye ken he was born a Christian, but converted in

order to marry the wee besom," Ian said. "So he had
to be circumcised." He crossed himself at the thought,
and Jamie laughed.

"What is it they call the stick-insect things where
the female one bites off the head of the male one
after he's got the business started?" he asked, nudging the door open with his bum.

Ian's brow creased for an instant.

"Praying mantis, I think. Why?"

"I think our wee friend Pierre may have a more
interesting wedding night than he expects. Come on."

Bordeaux

It wasn't the worst thing he'd ever had to do, but he
wasn't looking forward to it. Jamie paused outside
the gate of Dr. Hasdi's house, the Torah scroll in its
wrappings in his arms. Ian was looking a bit worm-
eaten, and Jamie reckoned he kent why. Having to
tell the Doctor what had happened to his granddaughter was one thing; telling him to his face with
the knowledge of what said granddaughter's nipples
felt like fresh in the mind . . . or the hand . . .

"Ye dinna have to come in, man," he said to Ian.
"I can do it alone."

Ian's mouth twitched, but he shook his head and
stepped up next to Jamie.

"On your right, man," he said, simply. Jamie smiled.
When he'd been five years old, Ian's da, Auld John,
had persuaded his own da to let Jamie handle a sword

cack-handed, as he was wont to do. "And you, lad," he'd said to Ian, very serious, "it's your duty to stand on your laird's right hand, and guard his weak side."

"Aye," Jamie said. "Right, then." And rang the bell.

Afterward, they wandered slowly through the streets of Bordeaux, making their way toward nothing in particular, not speaking much.

Dr. Hasdi had received them courteously, though with a look of mingled horror and apprehension on his face when he saw the scroll. This look had faded to one of relief at hearing—the manservant had had enough French to interpret for them—that his granddaughter was safe, then to shock, and finally to a set expression that Jamie couldn't read. Was it anger, sadness, resignation?

When Jamie had finished the story, they sat uneasily, not sure what to do next. Dr. Hasdi sat at his desk, head bowed, his hands resting gently on the scroll. Finally, he raised his head, and nodded to them both, one and then the other. His face was calm now, giving nothing away.

"Thank you," he said in heavily accented French. "Shalom."

"Are ye hungry?" Ian motioned toward a small *boulangerie* whose trays bore filled rolls and big, fragrant round loaves. He was starving himself, though half an hour ago, his wame had been in knots.

"Aye, maybe." Jamie kept walking, though, and Ian shrugged and followed.

"What d'ye think the Captain will do when we tell him?" Ian wasn't all that bothered. There was always work for a good-sized man who kent what to do with a sword. And he owned his own weapons. They'd have to buy Jamie a sword, though. Everything he was wearing, from pistols to ax, belonged to D'Eglise.

He was busy enough calculating the cost of a decent sword against what remained of their pay that he didn't notice Jamie not answering him. He did notice that his friend was walking faster, though, and, hurrying to catch up, he saw what they were heading for. The tavern where the pretty brown-haired barmaid had taken Jamie for a Jew.

Oh, like that, is it? he thought, and hid a grin. Aye, well, there was one sure way the lad could prove to the lass that he wasn't a Jew.

The place was moiling when they walked in, and not in a good way; Ian sensed it instantly. There were soldiers there, army soldiers and other fighting-men, mercenaries like themselves, and no love wasted between them. You could cut the air with a knife, and judging from a splotch of half-dried blood on the floor, somebody had already tried.

There were women, but fewer than before, and the barmaids kept their eyes on their trays, not flirting tonight.

Jamie wasn't taking heed of the atmosphere; Ian could see him looking round for her; the brown-haired lass wasn't on the floor. They might have asked after her—if they'd known her name.

"Upstairs, maybe?" Ian said, leaning in to half-shout into Jamie's ear over the noise. Jamie nodded and began forging through the crowd, Ian bobbing in his wake, hoping they found the lass quickly so he could eat whilst Jamie got on with it.

The stairs were crowded—with men coming down. Something was amiss up there, and Jamie shoved someone into the wall with a thump, pushing past. Some nameless anxiety shot jolted down his spine, and he was half-prepared before he pushed through a little knot of onlookers at the head of the stairs and saw them.

Big Mathieu, and the brown-haired girl. There was a big open room here, with a hallway lined with tiny cubicles leading back from it; Mathieu had the girl by the arm and was boosting her toward the hallway with a hand on her bum, despite her protests.

"Let go of her!" Jamie said, not shouting, but raising his voice well enough to be heard easily. Mathieu paid not the least attention, though everyone else turned to look at Jamie, startled.

He heard Ian mutter, "Joseph, Mary and Bride preserve us," behind him, but paid no heed. He covered the distance to Mathieu in three strides, and kicked him in the arse.

He ducked, by reflex, but Mathieu merely turned and gave him a hot eye, ignoring the whoops and guffaws from the spectators.

"Later, little boy," he said. "I'm busy now."

He scooped the young woman into one big arm and kissed her sloppily, rubbing his stubbled face hard over hers, so she squealed and pushed at him to get away.

Jamie drew the pistol from his belt.

"I said, let her go." The noise dropped suddenly, but he barely noticed for the roaring of blood in his ears.

Mathieu turned his head, incredulous. Then he snorted with contempt, grinned unpleasantly and shoved the girl into the wall so her head struck with a thump, pinning her there with his bulk.

The pistol was primed.

"*Salop!*" Jamie roared. "Don't touch her! Let her go!" He clenched his teeth and aimed with both hands, rage and fright making his hands tremble.

Mathieu didn't even look at him. The big man half turned away, a casual hand on her breast. She squealed as he twisted it, and Jamie fired. Mathieu whirled, the pistol he'd had concealed in his own belt now in hand, and the air shattered in an explosion of sound and white smoke.

There were shouts of alarm, excitement—and another pistol went off, somewhere behind Jamie. *Ian?* he thought dimly, but no, Ian was running toward Mathieu, leaping for the massive arm rising, the second pistol's barrel making circles as Mathieu struggled to fix it on Jamie. It discharged, and the ball hit one of the lanterns that stood on the tables, which exploded with a *whuff* and a bloom of flame.

Jamie had reversed his pistol and was hammering at Mathieu's head with the butt before he was conscious of having crossed the room. Mathieu's madboar eyes were almost invisible, slitted with the glee of fighting, and the sudden curtain of blood that fell over his face did nothing but enhance his grin, blood running down between his teeth. He shook Ian off with a shove that sent him crashing into the wall, then wrapped one big arm almost casually around Jamie's body and, with a snap of his head, butted him in the face.

Jamie had turned his head reflexively and thus avoided a broken nose, but the impact crushed the flesh of his jaw into his teeth and his mouth filled with blood. His head was spinning with the force of the blow, but he got a hand under Mathieu's jaw and shoved upward with all his strength, trying to break the man's neck. His hand slipped off the sweat-greased flesh, though, and Mathieu let go his grip in order to try to knee Jamie in the stones. A knee like a cannonball struck him a numbing blow in the thigh as he squirmed free, and he staggered, grabbing Mathieu's arm just as Ian came dodging in from the side, seizing the other. Without a moment's hesitation, Mathieu's huge forearms twisted; he seized the Scots by the scruffs of their necks and cracked their heads together.

Jamie couldn't see and could barely move, but kept moving anyway, groping blindly. He was on the floor, could feel boards, wetness . . . His pawing hand struck flesh and he lunged forward and bit Mathieu as hard as he could in the calf of the leg. Fresh blood filled his mouth, hotter than his own, and he gagged but kept his teeth locked in the hairy flesh, clinging stubbornly as the leg he clung to kicked in frenzy. His ears were ringing, he was vaguely aware of screaming and shouting, but it didn't matter.

Something had come upon him and nothing mattered. Some small remnant of his consciousness registered surprise, and then that was gone, too. No

pain, no thought. He was a red thing and while he saw
things, faces, blood, bits of room, they didn't matter.
Blood took him, and when some sense of himself came
back, he was kneeling astride the man, hands locked
around the big man's neck, hands throbbing with a
pounding pulse, his or his victim's, he couldn't tell.

Him. Him. He'd lost the man's name. His eyes
were bulging, the ragged mouth slobbered and gaped,
and there was a small, sweet *crack* as something
broke under Jamie's thumbs. He squeezed with all he
had, squeezed and squeezed and felt the huge body
beneath him go strangely limp.

He went on squeezing, couldn't stop, until a hand
seized him by the arm and shook him, hard.

"Stop," a voice croaked, hot in his ear. "Jamie.
Stop."

He blinked up at the white, bony face, unable to
put a name to it. Then drew breath—the first he
could remember drawing for some time—and with it
came a thick stink, blood and shit and reeking sweat,
and he became suddenly aware of the horrible spongy
feeling of the body he was sitting on. He scrambled
awkwardly off, sprawling on the floor as his muscles
spasmed and trembled.

Then he saw her.

She was lying crumpled against the wall, curled
into herself, her brown hair spilling across the boards.
He got to his knees, crawling to her.

He was making a small whimpering noise, trying
to talk, having no words. Got to the wall and gathered her into his arms, limp, her head lolling, striking
his shoulder, her hair soft against his face, smelling
of smoke and her own sweet musk.

"*A nighean,*" he managed. "Christ, *a nighean.* Are ye . . ."

"Jesus," said a voice by his side, and he felt the vibration as Ian—thank God, the name had come back, of course it was Ian—collapsed next to him. His friend had a bloodstained dirk still clutched in his hand. "Oh, Jesus, Jamie."

He looked up, puzzled, desperate, and then looked down as the girl's body slipped from his grasp and fell back across his knees with impossible boneless grace, the small dark hole in her white breast stained with only a little blood. Not much at all.

He'd made Jamie come with him to the cathedral of St. Andre, and insisted he go to confession. Jamie had balked—no great surprise.

"No. I can't."

"We'll go together." Ian had taken him firmly by the arm and very literally dragged him over the threshold. Once inside, he was counting on the atmosphere of the place to keep Jamie there.

His friend stopped dead, the whites of his eyes showing as he glanced warily around.

The stone vault of the ceiling soared into shadow overhead, but pools of colored light from the stained-glass windows lay soft on the worn slates of the aisle.

"I shouldna be here," Jamie muttered under his breath.

"Where better, eejit? Come on," Ian muttered back, and pulled Jamie down the side aisle to the chapel of Saint Estephe. Most of the side chapels were lavishly furnished, monuments to the importance of wealthy families. This one was a tiny, undecorated stone alcove, containing little more than an altar, a faded tapestry of a faceless saint, and a small stand where candles could be placed.

"Stay here." Ian planted Jamie dead in front of the altar and ducked out, going to buy a candle from the old woman who sold them near the main door. He'd changed his mind about trying to make Jamie go to confession; he knew fine when ye could get a Fraser to do something, and when ye couldn't.

He worried a bit that Jamie would leave, and hurried back to the chapel, but Jamie was still there, standing in the middle of the tiny space, head down, staring at the floor.

"Here, then," Ian said, pulling him toward the altar. He plunked the candle—an expensive one, beeswax and large—on the stand, and pulled the paper spill the old lady had given him out of his sleeve, offering it to Jamie. "Light it. We'll say a prayer for your da. And . . . and for her."

He could see tears trembling on Jamie's lashes, glittering in the red glow of the sanctuary lamp that hung above the altar, but Jamie blinked them back and firmed his jaw.

"All right," he said, low voiced, but he hesitated. Ian sighed, took the spill out of his hand and, standing on tiptoe, lit it from the sanctuary lamp.

"Do it," he whispered, handing it to Jamie, "or I'll gie ye a good one in the kidney, right here."

Jamie made a sound that might have been the breath of a laugh, and lowered the lit spill to the candle's wick. The fire rose up, a pure high flame with blue at its heart, then settled as Jamie pulled the spill away and shook it out in a plume of smoke.

They stood for some time, hands clasped loosely in front of them, watching the candle burn. Ian prayed for his mam and da, his sister and her bairns . . . with some hesitation (was it proper to pray for a Jew?), for Rebekah bat-Leah, and with a sidelong glance at Jamie, to be sure he wasn't looking, for Jenny Fraser. Then the soul of Brian Fraser . . . and then, eyes tight shut, for the friend beside him.

The sounds of the church faded, the whispering stones and echoes of wood, the shuffle of feet and the rolling gabble of the pigeons on the roof. Ian stopped saying words, but was still praying. And then that stopped, too, and there was only peace, and the soft beating of his heart.

He heard Jamie sigh, from somewhere deep inside, and opened his eyes. Without speaking, they went out, leaving the candle to keep watch.

"Did ye not mean to go to confession yourself?" Jamie asked, stopping near the church's main door. There was a priest in the confessional; two or three people stood a discreet distance away from the carved wooden stall, out of earshot, waiting.

"It'll bide," Ian said, with a shrug. "If ye're goin' to Hell, I might as well go, too. God knows, ye'll never manage alone."

Jamie smiled—a wee bit of a smile, but still—and pushed the door open into sunlight.

They strolled aimlessly for a bit, not talking, and found themselves eventually on the river's edge, watching the Garonne's dark waters flow past, carrying debris from a recent storm.